Books by K. Evan Coles &

Single Titles

Wake

Coming Soon

Calm

Wake

ISBN # 978-1-78686-161-0

©Copyright K. Evan Coles, Brigham Vaughn 2017

Cover Art by Posh Gosh ©Copyright 2017

Interior text design by Claire Siemaszkiewicz

Pride Publishing

Published in 2017 by Pride Publishing, Think Tank, Ruston Way, Lincoln, LN6 7FL, United Kingdom.

Pride Publishing is a subsidiary of Totally Entwined Group Limited.

WAKE

K. EVAN COLES
&
BRIGHAM VAUGHN

Dedication

Wake was part of an almost four-year journey. It wouldn't have been possible without the incredibly supportive people in our lives.

For my husband, who is patient (usually) and encouraging (always) of my endless scribbling.

For my son, who makes me laugh every single day.

For the people in and around my life who inspire me, let me be weird and make me feel brave.

And for Brigham Vaughn, who puts up with my thousands of questions, listens to my rants, never complains when I occasionally fall off the face of the planet and is always ready to put pen to paper when our stars align.

— K. Evan Coles

This book is for my friends who were patient when I was too busy writing or editing to spend time with them. For the people who cheered me on and had faith in my writing long before I did. For my parents who are the best patrons of the arts a writer could ask for.

And mostly, for K. Evan Coles, who got me into reading and writing gay romance in the first place. I wouldn't be here without you! It's been a wonderful—and occasionally frustrating—journey. There's no one I would rather have done it with.

—Brigham Vaughn

K. and Brigham would also like to thank their patient beta readers Shell Taylor, Jayme Yesenofski, Rebecca Spence and Kade Boehme. You slogged through two hundred thousand words, multiple times, to help us mold it into the story you see before you today. We could not have done it without you.

Prologue

As the final note of the song resonated in the air, applause rang out, filling the Metropolitan Opera House. Riley clapped robotically, his eyes never leaving the man two boxes over. Even in the relatively dim light, Riley could see Carter's attentive expression as he leaned in to hear something his wife, Kate, said to him. At three inches over six feet, Carter towered over Kate.

Something in Riley's chest clenched at the sight of them together. The feeling had been worsening for months now and it had become increasingly difficult to quell the ache of longing he experienced whenever he saw his friend. At thirty-four, Riley had been friends with Carter Hamilton for sixteen years and his attraction to his friend had grown slowly. Over time it had shifted and deepened, but never dimmed.

Riley dropped his hands to his thighs when the applause faded and the house lights came up. He tried to tear his gaze away from his friend, but he couldn't seem to do so. He watched Carter laugh at something Kate said, his wide grin lighting up his face and causing his eyes to crinkle at the corners. It stung. Riley wanted to be the one making Carter laugh and smile.

A soft hand touched his shoulder and he jolted in his seat, turning abruptly to look at his wife.

Alex frowned down at him. "It's intermission, Riley."

He nodded jerkily and stood, following Alex through the throngs of people on the way to the bar that exclusively served box seat ticket holders. Metropolitan opera patrons had any number of privileges. Alex took full advantage of the perks allowing them to mingle with the rest of the city's elite, but Riley preferred the ones that allowed him to learn more about the opera. A chance to talk with the conductor about the remaining shows for the season thrilled him more than rubbing elbows with other patrons.

Once they had their drinks in hand, Alex went off to socialize and Riley sipped his gin and tonic gratefully. He watched her chat and flirt with other people, her vibrant red hair swept into a neat updo. Against the stark black of her elegant dress, her skin seemed especially pale and smooth tonight. He observed Alex for a long time, trying to understand why he couldn't muster up an ounce of desire for his own wife.

Objectively, Riley could see her beauty. Her body and face were flawless. The shallow, materialistic qualities he disliked about her personality were nothing new. He'd known about them before he'd asked her to marry him. Nothing had changed. But the dim flickers of desire Riley had had for Alex initially had become completely extinguished now.

He watched her flirt with someone whose name and face he couldn't quite identify. The man was on the board of directors for a major company, but for the life of him, Riley couldn't remember which, despite them having interacted at half a dozen cocktail parties and social events in the last few years.

Riley knew he should be angry at the intimate way his wife touched the man's hand, at the way her blue eyes sparkled when he flirted with her. But he felt nothing. Not even a twinge of the jealousy that had rocketed through him when he'd watched Carter and Kate together.

With a sigh, Riley took another gulp of his drink and looked away. He had no idea why he couldn't shake Carter from his thoughts tonight. Riley'd had a busy week and he was tired, but if he was being honest with himself, his strange mood had little to do with stress from work or lack of sleep.

It was more than that. It was the wife he couldn't stand, the life he led and hated and the endless expectations from his family slowly wearing him down, day after day, year after year.

It was the lies Riley told everyone.

The lies he told himself.

Someone stepped close behind Riley and the hair on the back of his neck rose. One whiff of the woodsy cologne Carter always wore and Riley knew it belonged to the man he'd been thinking about all night. Riley turned to his friend, swallowing hard at the sight of him in a tux. How many times had he seen Carter dressed in a tailored black tuxedo, crisp white shirt and neat bow tie? Dozens? Hundreds? It didn't seem to matter. Riley's heart still sped up as if it were the first.

Carter grinned. "Having a good time tonight?"

Riley nodded, mouth parched, so he took a sip of his gin and tonic before speaking. "Very much. I like *Turandot*."

Normally it was one of his favorite operas, but he'd barely paid any attention to it tonight.

"Are you okay?" Carter asked, reaching to grip Riley's biceps.

"Yeah, I'm fine," Riley lied. "Are you enjoying yourself?"

Carter shrugged, letting his hand fall away, and sipped from his glass of bourbon. "Kate's enjoying herself—that's enough for me."

Kate Hamilton and Riley both loved opera, although Carter didn't share their feelings. He attended the performances because it pleased Kate, just as he had gone with Riley when they were in school.

They made small talk for a while, discussing work and mutual friends. Carter told Riley the latest antics of his seven- and four-year-old children, Sadie and Dylan. Riley struggled to focus on anything but the husky cadence of Carter's voice and the shape of his mouth. His breath grew shallow as he stared at the fullness of Carter's upper lip, the soft curve of the lower. He could imagine it against his own, taste the mellow bourbon that would linger on his tongue.

"Jesus, Ri, are you sure you're okay?" Carter asked suddenly, the concern in his voice clear, his hazel eyes worried as he squinted at Riley.

"I'm fine. It's just been a long week. I'll be all right, Car," Riley said, his voice too tight to be believable. He glanced away, unable to tell an untruth while he looked Carter in the eye.

Carter sighed, but, thankfully, his friend didn't push. Instead, Carter gestured to a secluded corner and walked toward it. Wondering why he wanted more privacy, Riley followed him. He gave Carter a questioning glance and rested his shoulder against a pillar. Carter glanced around, leaned in, and spoke in a low voice. "You do know what a week from now is, right?"

It took Riley's muddled brain far too long to piece together his friend's hint. When it finally sank in, he nodded. "It's the third Thursday of the month."

"Our first Thursday without Natalie. I'm going to miss her like hell, but I think we should find her replacement. I don't know about you, but I'd miss those nights."

Riley's cock stirred. He set his almost empty drink on a nearby table and shoved his hands into the pockets of his tuxedo pants. "I'd miss them, too," he said, his tone husky.

The thought of fucking a beautiful woman like Natalie didn't make Riley hard, though. It was sharing her with Carter. Of being able to touch Carter, kiss him. Unfortunately, that thought—and the ones that always went along with it—never failed to leave Riley melancholy. They never failed to make him wonder how he and Carter had ended up married and hiring an escort once a month.

For over six months, Riley and Carter had shared Natalie. When Natalie had retired, they'd been disappointed, though both had been pleased she'd decided to return to her first love, dance. They didn't know a lot about Natalie's past, but she'd told them she'd been a dancer before working as an escort and was now planning to teach.

Now, Carter and Riley had to find someone new and although Carter kept pushing him to do so, Riley wasn't so sure they should. The arrangement they'd had with Natalie was unique. She'd allowed them the freedom to be together in the only way he felt able to. She'd been everything a man could want in a woman—beautiful, skilled in bed, witty and kind. Riley didn't want another woman, though. He didn't even want another man. When it came right down to it, he just wanted Carter. And that was the problem. He couldn't have him. Even if Riley divorced his wife and threw his career and relationship with his family out of the window, he was afraid Carter didn't want him. Or at least not enough for Carter to risk his own career, disrupt his children's lives and divorce his wife. And who could blame him?

Finding a replacement for Natalie wouldn't solve their issues, wouldn't lessen Riley's longing for Carter. It was time Riley came clean about his feelings. He was terrified, but he couldn't live the lie any longer.

"Look, I...I enjoy those nights," Riley said now, his voice softening, trying to tell Carter the truth without saying the actual words. This wasn't the place for this kind of discussion. "You know I do. I'm not sure about finding someone new."

Carter sighed, the brash exterior he sometimes put up as a front to the rest of the world melting away. "I don't want to give up those appointments. I always feel so damned great afterward."

Riley made a noncommittal sound of agreement. He felt good after their appointments, too, up to a point. High from the orgasms with his partners and being near Carter, Riley always felt like he was flying. When they were all naked together in bed, it was bliss. After, when they dressed and went their separate ways, Riley crashed, disappointment tearing him apart. He always hoped he'd feel different the next time but he never had. Riley knew better than to hope, but wasn't that the crux of his addiction to his best friend?

No matter how much he'd tried to stop, tried to believe those evenings wouldn't make the craving worse, they always had.

The feeling of discontent had been building for months. The thought of stopping the monthly appointments with Carter had terrified him. How could he go without touching Carter, without kissing him? The idea of renouncing that was intolerable. But Riley didn't know how much longer he would be content with the status quo, either. He'd been hovering at this point for a while and Natalie's retirement seemed like a sign pushing him to change his life.

The pressure had been building and building and Riley was afraid if he didn't make a change, he'd snap one night, grab Carter and kiss him in the middle of some cocktail party, in front of everyone they knew.

"What's going on with you?" Carter frowned at him in confusion. "You seem off tonight. Have for a while now, starting with whatever was bothering you during our last time with Natalie."

Riley closed his eyes for a moment and took a deep breath. "Yeah, I-I need to talk to you about something."

"You know you can tell me anything."

Riley gave his friend a sad smile, wondering if that was entirely true. He had no idea how Carter would feel once he'd unburdened what had been on his mind lately. "Intermission is nearly up and we can't discuss it here, anyway. I need you to meet me somewhere private tonight. Tell Kate we're going out for drinks or something. I don't care, but I have to talk to you."

Carter gave him a long, searching look, confusion and apprehension mingling in his gaze before he nodded. "Of course. Where do you want to meet?" Carter asked.

Both men paused when the chimes signaling the end of intermission rang out.

"Meet me at the apartment on West 10th."

* * * *

By the time the performance was over, Riley's chest was tight, his pulse raced and he felt flushed and jittery. He wondered if he was having an anxiety attack. He'd paid no more attention to the final act of the opera than he had the first two, although this time he'd rarely glanced at Carter. He'd been too busy trying to muster up the courage to say the words he needed to say to his friend. Riley helped his wife into her coat, trying to think of what to tell her about why he wasn't going home with her.

Once they were outside in the crisp November air, Riley found their car, waving away the driver's help when he moved to open the doors for them. Riley snagged Alex's elbow before she could climb in. "Carter and I are going out for a drink. I'll probably be a few hours."

Alex huffed and pursed her lips. "Fine. I'll call the girls to see what they want to do. Maybe they'll be more fun than my husband."

"I'm sorry, Alex," he said softly. He was sorry he wasn't in love with her, sorry he couldn't be who she wanted him to be. He was sorry he was abandoning her to run off to his secret apartment to spill his heart out to the man he had feelings for. *Jesus, my life is way too fucking complicated,* he thought, rubbing the back of his neck.

"I mean it." He stared down at Alex for a long moment before drawing her close to him. "I'm sorry our relationship isn't better."

"I'm used to it by now," she replied archly and pulled away.

With a sigh, he let go of her, knowing no apologies would excuse the way he'd disrupt her life when he came out.

He watched her drive away, then turned to find Carter. It didn't take him long. Carter stood beside the fountain outside the Met, silhouetted against the brightly lit water. Though Carter's face was shadowed, Riley would know his body anywhere. The broadness of his shoulders, the length of his legs—Riley imagined touching every inch of him.

Slowly he made his way toward Carter, their gazes

locking as Riley drew near. "Ready to head out?"

Carter nodded. "Yeah, Kate's on her way home."

Riley gave the driver of the cab that they eventually found the address — 296 West 10th Street in the West Village — and settled in his seat with a sigh. Neither man spoke much, although Riley was aware of the heat of Carter's thigh against his own, through the layers of their tux pants. Carter's knee seemed to rub against his every so often. Carter's height and long legs made him sprawl when he sat, but somehow Riley suspected the touch wasn't accidental. Or maybe he simply hoped so.

The West Village apartment overlooked the Hudson River. It was where Riley had lived after he'd graduated from Harvard and come to work for Porter-Wright Publishing, his firm.

Carter followed Riley silently out of the cab after paying and neither said a word on the way up to the sixth floor. After months of using this place as their private pied-à-terre with Natalie, Riley couldn't push away a surge of longing, wishing he and Carter were headed to the bedroom alone.

He flicked on the light, automatically hung up his long black wool jacket in the entryway and grabbed Carter's nearly identical one. He crossed into the living room, a fraction of the tension in him easing at the familiar surroundings. The expansive wood floors and neutral furnishings lent a warm sophistication to the place. It was decorated simply, with black and white photographs on the walls, a few sculptural decorations and books on the oblong glass coffee table and wood dining table, and several plants that the cleaning staff tended to.

Riley loved it. It felt familiar in a way the apartment he shared with Alex didn't. Alex had decorated the place on East 77th street without any input from Riley and while stylish and showy, it never seemed like home. Once they'd settled there, Riley had planned to sell the West Village apartment. He'd never gotten around to it, though, and once he and Carter had begun their arrangement with Natalie, it made far more sense to hold on to it and have their encounters in the safety and privacy of a place he owned rather than going the far more risky route of reserving a hotel room every time.

Carter headed straight for the kitchen and fixed himself a drink from the bottle of his favorite brand of bourbon that Riley always kept on hand. "You want a glass?" he asked, and Riley shook his head at the wide expanse of windows overlooking the balcony and the city lights across the river.

A short while later, Carter put his hand on Riley's shoulder and Riley closed his eyes for a brief moment, soaking in his friend's warm touch. He wanted to believe what he was about to tell Carter wouldn't damage the friendship they had, but he had no idea if that was true or not. All he could do was hope.

"I'm sorry to do this, Carter, but there's something I need to tell you." He had to force the words out from between his suddenly frozen lips.

Carter used a firm hand to turn him around and he met Carter's worried gaze.

"What is going on?"

"I don't think I can keep doing what we've been doing. I-I've been struggling with this for a while, trying to figure out how to tell you—if I should tell you. I still don't know if this is the right choice, but I don't think we should find a replacement for Natalie."

"Why? I don't understand," Carter said. "You loved what we did with her. I know you did."

"A part of me did, yes." He wet his lips. "But they hurt, too. Because they made me want things I can't have."

"What are you saying, Riley?"

"I'm… I'm saying I can't go on like this. I can't keep pretending anymore."

"Pretending what?"

Riley closed his eyes tightly while anxiety coursed through him. "I can't keep pretending I don't want you. Just you…without the girls in between us."

The room was silent and Riley took several long, deep breaths before he opened his eyes.

Carter stared at him with a puzzled frown. "I don't understand."

"I want to be with you, Carter." His voice cracked, but he continued. "Not once a month, sharing you with a woman we pay to be with. Every night, every day. I can't...I can't live like this anymore."

Carter's voice shook. "What are you saying?"

"I'm saying I want to end our monthly appointments. I know this seems like it's out of the blue, but I've been thinking about it for a while. I — we — have been living a lie"

"What lie? What...what are you talking about?" Carter sounded numb and dazed.

Riley faced the window again. His voice was soft when he spoke. "I'm in love with you, Carter. Not with my wife, not with anyone else. With you. I have been for years. I suppose I-I'm bisexual, or gay, Christ, I don't know. I've spent years trying not to think about what it all meant. Whatever I am, I'm not the man in love with Alex I've been pretending to be."

Riley turned to face his friend, his heart sinking at Carter's shocked disbelief. He knew Carter wasn't going to say what Riley wanted him to, but he pressed on, needing to get the words out anyway. "I can't live a lie anymore. I can't let myself become my parents. I don't want to have a complete sham of a marriage in order to make everyone else happy. I'm going to divorce Alex and I'm coming out."

"Why?" Carter sputtered, his voice rising. "You'll come out to, what, fuck guys now?"

"No...look, I don't know, maybe. I want to be with you, but even if I can't be, at least I won't be lying anymore. I want to be myself. To not hide who I am anymore. "

"Do you know what this is going to do to your reputation? To mine? People have been gossiping about our friendship and who we are to each other since we were at college. Fuck, Ri, if you come out everyone's going to assume the rumors are true—that we've been screwing for years!" Carter shouted.

"I wish we had been," Riley responded, taken aback by Carter's anger. "At least it would have been more honest than what we've been doing. We've been lying to ourselves and our wives, Carter, and for what?"

Carter didn't answer the question. "You're going to throw away everything you have? Your career, your wife, your family?"

"I have no idea what will happen with my career," Riley admitted. "Or with my family. My father might hate me so much he'll toss me out of the company and I have no idea how my mother will react. If I lose all of that, yeah, it'll be hard."

"And Alex?" Carter asked sharply.

Riley shrugged. "You know we've never really gotten along well. I married her because it was easier to be married to someone I didn't love, if I couldn't have you." He stepped closer, cupping his friend's cheek. "It's always been you, Carter. I've lied to myself since we met, but I am in love with you. I have been for over fifteen years."

Carter's stunned expression wasn't reassuring. "*What the fuck,*" he breathed.

Riley continued before he lost his nerve. "I can't imagine doing this without you, but I will if I have to. I want to be with you more than anything, but I know you have to make your own decisions."

For a long moment, the two men stared at each other, neither speaking nor moving. Barely breathing. Carter's pulse fluttered rapidly against the side of his hand. He gently traced his thumb across Carter's cheek. "Please. Just think about it. You feel this, I know you do."

He pressed his lips to Carter's, pouring every bit of his feelings into the kiss. Carter responded immediately and hope leapt in Riley's chest. Maybe Carter was willing to risk everything to be with Riley. He deepened the kiss and it was so good, so right. It was everything Riley had dreamed about. Carter's heart hammered as Riley smoothed a shaky palm over Carter's crisp white shirt. He moaned Carter's name and gripped the lapel of his tux.

Carter pulled away, covering the distance across the room in several long strides before turning to face Riley, his expression pleading, his eyes anguished. "I can't." He shook his head, his voice hushed. "Don't ask me to do this, Ri. Please."

"I'm sorry," Riley said, hope shattering at the expression on Carter's face. "I am. But I'm miserable, Car. Every day I feel a little worse. I'm not sleeping, my anxiety is through the roof… I can't take it anymore."

"My family…" Carter's voice rose with anger. "Christ, how can you ask me to do this? You know my father will disown me. And Kate…and the kids? How can I break up our family? You're asking me to give up everything," he shouted. "Whether I do this or not, if you come out, it'll come back on me, too. I can't believe you're doing this."

"I know," Riley said hoarsely, bracing himself for the rejection he knew was coming. "I'm asking too much. But I need you. I dream about what it would be like to touch you. No pretending it's just in the heat of the moment when we're fucking Natalie."

Carter sank onto the nearby couch and closed his eyes, tilting his head back. Riley knew that move—Carter was trying to calm himself. Riley bit his lip as he watched Carter, tracing his jaw and throat. Carter hadn't shaved after work and he had a bit of stubble. It contrasted sharply with the crisp elegance of his tuxedo. Riley wanted to bury his head against Carter's throat, lick and nip the skin along his Adam's apple, feel the roughness against his lips and tongue.

Instead, he sat and waited.

With a low sound of frustration, Carter lifted his head, his gaze meeting Riley's. He swallowed hard, then leaned forward, resting his elbows on his knees. "Why now? Things were good between us and Natalie. It worked for us."

"It's not working for me anymore," Riley admitted. "I need more."

"And more is what, exactly?"

Riley blew out a breath of frustration and leaned against the dining room table. Rather than answer, he asked a question. "Are you attracted to me, Carter?"

Carter gave him a look of mingled disbelief and irritation that was clear from across the room. "Christ, Ri. What does that have to do with anything?"

"I have to know. If the two of us could be together, without having to hurt our families or disrupt our entire lives, would you want to be?"

"I don't even know how to answer that question!"

"Do you remember the discussion we had before graduation, about running away together?" Riley asked.

"Yeah, I do," Carter replied hoarsely.

Riley ran a hand through his hair and shook his head slowly, remembering their conversation by the river. "I think about it often. I wish we'd done it."

Carter nodded, hands hanging limp between his knees, his shoulders slumped. "Sometimes I wish we'd done it, too."

"You can't say it, can you?" Riley asked numbly. "You can't say the words. You can't admit you want me. You can't admit you have feelings for me that go beyond friendship."

"It's… It's difficult, Riley. Maybe you've been thinking about this—wanting more—but we're not those guys anymore, fresh out of school and talking about running away from responsibilities. You might not love Alex, but I do love Kate. For the most part, I'm content with what we have. Yeah, I care about you. As way more than just a friend. But going to bed with Natalie and having you there with me was enough." Carter stood, his movements tense and jerky.

It stung, hearing Carter's words, but a small part of Riley felt relieved to know the truth. It hurt, and he'd probably fall to pieces after, but at least now he knew. Riley crossed the room and touched Carter's arm.

"It's not enough for me," he said softly. "I want a life with you. I want to come home to you at the end of the day, fall asleep beside you and wake up the next morning in our bed. I want to make love to you, with no one else between us. Make love to you because you're the only person I've ever loved like this. No more lies, no more pretending. Just you and me."

He caught a glimpse of a yearning in Carter's eyes, but it was gone almost immediately. Carter stood and walked toward the door, turning to face Riley for a moment, his expression regretful.

"I can't. I need some time, Ri. To process everything." His voice sounded hoarse and gutted.

"Carter, don't do this."

"I'm sorry. I can't. I can't do it. Please don't ask me to."

Without another word, he left.

Alone, Riley felt heartsick that he'd lost his best friend and the man he loved. He honestly didn't know which was worse.

Chapter One

August, 1996
Cambridge, Massachusetts

"These rooms always look so much bigger online."

Carter Hamilton flinched in surprise at the smooth voice behind him. Blinking slowly, he drew a breath to quiet his heart, then turned to meet a pair of lively blue eyes.

"Sorry." A guy Carter's age stepped inside the door, his expression sheepish. A smile lit his handsome face and an intriguing flush colored his cheeks. "I didn't mean to startle you."

Carter shrugged before standing up from the couch where he'd been reading. "I'll live."

"I knocked, but no one answered. The door wasn't bolted, so I assumed no one was here."

"Ah, that's my bad." Heat crept up Carter's neck. "I got caught up in my book and didn't hear you. I'm Carter and I'm guessing you're one of my suitemates—are you Riley or Daniel?"

"Riley Porter-Wright."

Riley walked forward with a grin. Riley was lean and tall, though still an inch or two shorter than Carter, who stood six foot three. His stylish black shirt and trousers were immaculate compared to Carter's T-shirt and jeans and his dark hair fell forward onto his forehead as he shook Carter's hand.

A small smile crossed Carter's face. He'd been exchanging messages with his suitemates for weeks. Daniel, who had yet to show himself, hailed from Philadelphia, while Riley, like Carter, lived in Manhattan, though the two had never met. They'd coordinated basic furnishings for their Harvard University rooms and agreed to fill in gaps later.

"I'm Carter Hamilton," Carter told him with a laugh, "which you know. And since I was the first here, I guess it's okay for me to say it—welcome to Wigg."

Riley rolled his eyes, making Carter smile wider. He'd been amused by the freshman dorm's nickname, too, but Wigglesworth was highly desired, with large suites and convenient placement for the university libraries. Carter watched Riley approach the window and frowned upon noticing he carried only an overnight bag and nothing more.

"You planning on staying?" Carter eyed Riley's bag when he turned and cocked his head in question. "I know from your email messages that you're not big on decorating, but one bag seems like taking traveling light to new extremes. You said you'd bring a fridge, too, in case you forgot."

Riley glanced down at himself and laughed, the clear boyish sound echoing through the sparsely furnished common room.

"I didn't forget. I did bring a fridge and more boxes and bags, too—they're in a moving van stuck in traffic on Storrow Drive. One of the movers called me twenty minutes ago," he added, drawing closer to set his bag against the side of the couch. "I'm not sure I buy their story, though. They probably got here hours ago and found someplace to have lunch and a couple of beers before they drop my shit off.

"Nice couch, by the way." Riley nodded at the charcoal-colored couch Carter and his father had carried in earlier. "You picked out a bedroom already?" he asked, taking a seat.

"Not really. I got here late this morning, so we moved everything in and pushed it out of the way." Carter sat down too, waving at the boxes and suitcases lining the wall to their left. "The way I see it, once Dan shows, we can figure out who's going to share and who's got the single."

"Someone had a productive day," Riley teased, raising his brows and making Carter laugh.

"Yeah, well, my parents wanted to stay and meet you guys, but I didn't want them hitting rush hour on their way home. You'll meet them soon, anyway—they're already talking about their next trip up.

"I bought them lunch before they left," Carter added, unsure why he was sharing so much information with a guy he'd just met. "I figured that was the least I could do after they helped me drag my stuff up three flights."

Riley blinked several times, appearing vaguely surprised. "Your parents helped you move in?"

"Sure," Carter replied with a shrug. "My dad's an alumnus and my mom graduated from Wellesley—they enjoy visiting Cambridge." He chuckled. "They were definitely excited to help me settle in, even if it meant manual labor."

Riley's expression became thoughtful. Looking down, he traced a spot on the right knee of his jeans with his finger. In a flash, Carter understood Riley was on his own.

Riley glanced up at Carter again. "My parents couldn't make the trip," he said, his voice light. "They're having dinner with friends tonight and didn't want to be late. I took the car up from the city."

Carter nodded. The idea of his parents choosing to socialize over seeing him off to school seemed utterly alien. Did it bother Riley that his parents were uninterested in what had to be an exciting day for him?

An impulse struck Carter to make Riley comfortable. "You know, you never told me where you live in the city."

Riley smiled, though a trace of melancholy flickered in his eyes. "West 86th Street. That's where my parents live, and I suppose I'll be there for a while longer. What about you?"

"East 63rd Street." Carter grinned. "That's funny."

"Funny?"

"We live in the same city separated by twenty-three blocks and the Park. Doesn't seem like much when you consider we had to come to Cambridge, Massachusetts, to meet."

Riley's eyes brightened. They chatted easily about their trips from New York until the door banged open, then watched a figure shoulder its way in with a stack of boxes. The boxes landed on the floor with a thump, revealing a cheerful-looking guy with a wiry build, golden-brown skin and inquisitive gray eyes.

"Dan Conley," he said, flashing a smile. "My dad's parking the car. You guys want to arm wrestle now or later to settle the whole double vs. single room thing?"

After a quick discussion, it became clear Dan and Riley preferred the single room, while Carter was willing to share the double. He sat on the couch with Dan's parents, watching his new friends flip a coin. Dan won the toss and celebrated with an exaggerated touchdown dance, complete with slo-mo action that made Riley roll his eyes.

Riley's movers arrived then and made short work of bringing his load of boxes and bags upstairs. The trio started arranging furniture and unpacking, with Dan's parents providing useful—if unsolicited—feedback.

After the rooms were in some order, the Conleys insisted on taking all three suitemates to Grendel's Den for dinner. They got to know each other better over sandwiches, while Dan's parents asked Carter and Riley about their families. They had a pleasant evening, though Riley shared little about himself and even less about his parents. He talked easily about New York and the traveling he'd done during school vacations but shut down personal questions. He wasn't rude—if anything he seemed the opposite, with his open expression and bright gaze, but spent more time listening to the others than talking about himself.

It was late when Carter finally dropped onto his bed with a grunt. Dan had already been asleep for an hour and Riley had headed for the shower while Carter closed his eyes and took mental inventory of his sore muscles.

The sound of the bathroom door opening roused Carter from his dozy thoughts. He peeled an eyelid open to peer up at his roommate, who was moving around the bedroom and taking pains to be quiet. Like Carter, Riley wore a pair of dark sleep pants, though he had forgone a T-shirt. Droplets of water fell from his still wet hair, shining in the low light as they rolled over his bare shoulders and back. Carter was still trying to understand why he'd even think such a thing when Riley turned, looking pensive. Carter rolled onto his side and propped his head on one hand.

Riley jumped, startled by the sudden movement. "Jesus, Carter!"

"Um, just Carter will do—no need to get formal." Carter bit his lip against a smile.

"You scared the shit out of me. I thought you were asleep, you sneaky bastard."

Riley's words were sharp, but the glint in his eyes told Carter his irritation was mostly for show.

"Sorry. Consider it payback for scaring me earlier today."

Carter pushed himself up to pull back the bedding and slip underneath the duvet and sheet. He watched Riley puttering about, getting ready for bed and his amusement faded. Despite his roommate's smile, Carter sensed Riley had something on his mind. He lay quietly, worrying his lower lip with his teeth until Riley sat on the edge of his own bed.

"Is this bothering you?" Carter asked, waving one hand in a vague circle. Riley eyed him blankly. "The room-sharing thing, I mean. I know you've never had a roommate before, so I can sort of see where you'd be feeling weirded out."

"No, I'm—" Riley began before pausing, his lips pressed into a thin line. He blew out a slow breath before he spoke again, his voice low and calm. "I'm okay. It is a little weird sharing a room. I mean, my room at home is bigger than the whole suite." He grimaced a bit at Carter's laugh, and shrugged. "But you probably guessed that already. You come from the same world."

Carter reached up to fold his hands behind his head. "It does seem like culture shock in a lot of ways. I have almost a full floor at my parents' and now I'm sharing three rooms with strangers. In the middle of freaking Red Sox country, no less." Both guys laughed. "I like it, though. Yeah, it's small and all bricks and ivy but it feels…I don't know, right. At least to me."

"I get it." Riley ran his hands over his damp hair with a sigh. He was quiet for so long Carter wondered if he would speak again. "My parents aren't the warmest people in the world. You probably gathered that when I told you they couldn't be bothered to even meet me here."

Carter nodded, Riley's words settling over him.

"I'm used to it," Riley added, rubbing his forehead. "I've never known any different. Oh, my parents have always taken care of me and they'll give me almost anything I ask for. Except for their attention. They leave that to the nannies and minders and secretaries, who give me attention because they're paid to."

The air grew heavy, charged with emotion Carter understood Riley didn't want to acknowledge.

"My parents aren't interested in me." Riley held up a hand when Carter opened his mouth to protest, though he didn't meet Carter's eyes. "They're not, trust me. I've known it for a long time and I can't remember when I last felt sorry for myself about it. My parents aren't interested in each other, to be honest—they can't even drum up enough feeling to fucking fight with each other."

Riley's words came more slowly as he continued, dropping his fingers to trace a spot on the right knee of his sleep pants. Carter had watched him do the same thing a few times already, always when he seemed to be masking some emotion.

"Watching the Conleys today," Riley said, "listening to you talk about your parents and to them after they called… I started thinking, Carter. I'm so used to the way my parents behave I'm almost at a loss to understand how normal families function."

"I'm not sure my family is what you'd call normal,

Riley." Carter's voice was quiet. "They're certainly not average compared to Dan's parents. The Conleys are pretty well off, but we both know Dan's here on a partial music scholarship."

Riley made a dismissive noise. "Over half of the students here are on some kind of scholarship. It's not like that's particularly unusual. Sure, your family has a lot more money than the Conleys. I'm talking about the connections, though, between people. Between you and your parents, between Dan and his. Hell, between your mom and your dad, and Dan's mom and—"

"I get it."

Something in Carter's gentle interruption caught Riley's attention. Suddenly, he met Carter's gaze and held it.

"I don't know why I'm telling you this. No, that's a lie—I do know. I don't want to be like that. Like my parents, I mean. Frozen with this hard shell wrapped around me." Riley's eyes flashed with something raw. "I don't want to be one of the Porter-Wrights and make my life about the job and the parties and how many cars and houses and boats I can buy."

Carter pursed his lips, struck by Riley's choice of words. "Your focus doesn't have to be about the material things, man. But unless you plan to cut ties with your family, parties and cars and houses and boats are going to be part of your life."

"You're right. Possessions shouldn't be anyone's focus, or at least not all the time." Riley closed his eyes for a moment, fatigue written across his face. "I'm glad I'm here. Away from them and that life."

"At least until Thanksgiving, anyway," Carter teased. He didn't know why Riley was suddenly opening up, but he wanted to offer his roommate some cheer. "You can come to my house for dinner. We'll show you how the Hamiltons party like the Founding Fathers."

Riley grunted, then stretched out, pulling the bedding over himself before he spoke again. "I'm down. My parents usually go away for Thanksgiving. They're partial to Grenada. My mother works on her tan and my father works on his golf swing. I used to go with them, but last year I decided to hang out in New York."

"Was it weird?" Carter couldn't imagine Riley's parents leaving him to rattle around a huge apartment alone while they went on vacation.

"No—it was fantastic."

Riley turned his head and the genuine warmth in his expression made Carter feel lighter.

"Some of my friends from school came over. We bought a ton of Thai food for dinner and smoked some weed and just sat around on the balcony for a while. The party went on for a couple of days."

Carter raised an eyebrow. "Sounds pretty debauched."

"Oh, you know it. I still hear stories about what happened in my own house. Fucking animals." Riley rolled onto his side. "The best day, though, was Sunday. I took the car uptown to this church in Harlem that one of my father's secretaries attends. They put on a Thanksgiving Gospel Concert every year, so I hung out and listened to music. Amazing."

Carter smiled at the awe on his roommate's face. "It sounds it."

"Come with me this year," Riley urged suddenly, propping himself up on one elbow.

"Sure. If you come to dinner at my house," Carter bargained, "assuming your parents will be out of town."

"Fuck it." Riley grinned. "I don't care where my parents are, Car—I'll be at your door for dinner whenever you want me."

"I've never been to a Thanksgiving concert before," Carter mused. "No one's ever called me Car before, either."

Riley's eyebrows shot up. "Really? Not even your parents or friends?"

"Nope."

"I can stop, if you want."

"Doesn't bother me." Carter smiled lazily. "Anyone call you Ri for short?"

"Sure. The nannies and the minders and the secretaries call me Ri. Kids at school. My teachers. Anyone who's known me for more than a couple of hours." Riley's laugh was rueful. "Basically, anyone but my parents."

"Sounds like I'm in good company then." Carter rolled over with a yawn and closed his eyes. "Night, Ri."

* * * *

Carter, Riley and Dan fell into their lives at Harvard with ease. Dan was a music major minoring in French, while Carter and Riley were both business majors. The time the friends spent together each day increased after all three gained membership to the same club, Phoenix-SK.

The final clubs were Harvard's version of Greek fraternities. They promised networking opportunities after graduation but also provided social outlets away from the dorms. Carter's and Riley's fathers had also belonged to Phoenix-SK but had missed knowing one another by a few years.

Carter was pleasantly surprised to find himself comfortable with Riley's almost constant presence. They shared many of the same interests, including cyberpunk novels and Quentin Tarantino movies, and even had similar tastes in food and music. The more they talked and spent time together, the more firmly their friendship cemented.

The one activity Riley refused to consider was heavyweight crew. Carter had rowed with a junior club during high school and was eager to use his height and powerful build as part of the Harvard Crimson. Riley thought Carter was out of his mind.

"I don't understand you." He cocked an eyebrow after Carter explained rowing was a Hamilton family tradition. "What kind of person voluntarily sits in a boat with a bunch of other meaty guys while someone screams at them through a bullhorn?"

Carter rolled his eyes as Dan joined in chuckling with Riley.

"A me kind of person, I guess. You should at least try it before making a decision, guys."

"You know, it sounds fun," Dan said. He held up a placating hand while Riley made an outraged noise. "But I'm an inch under six feet and we both know that's too short for heavyweight crew."

"True. You could try out for lightweight, instead," Carter offered, narrowing his eyes at Riley's snort. "Shut it, you."

Dan gave Riley the finger. "I could, but I need to spend time in the music rooms downstairs, anyway. If you and I were on the same team, that'd be one thing, but…"

"I get it, man," Carter replied and he did. Dan's academic schedule was busy enough before club activities — add time at the piano composing and he needed every spare minute he could find.

Carter aimed a beady eye at Riley. "What about you, funny guy — you up for a free workout with a view? The river's awfully pretty, especially first thing in the morning."

Riley laughed. "Yeah, you lost me at 'first thing in the morning.' Look, you say rowing crew is Hamilton family tradition. Fine, that's your business. The Porter-Wrights have traditions, too. They include not getting up at the crack of ass every morning to risk drowning in a muddy river. Thanks, but no thanks."

Despite the teasing, Riley and Dan seemed genuinely pleased when Carter came home with soggy shoes and a place on the team. Carter suspected they were just being polite, but he appreciated their efforts nonetheless.

Carter enjoyed rowing for the Crimson and losing himself in the simple physicality of the task and feeling part of a team. He looked forward to the quiet hush of the river, the lap of the waves against the side of the boat and the collective breaths and grunts of the team as they worked together.

There were negatives, of course, starting with practice at dawn and the feeling he just didn't have enough hours in the day. Carter focused on being grateful when Riley helped him bandage his blisters and smiled at the protein bars Dan stuffed into his coat pockets. Riley and Dan attended races when they could, sharing thermoses of Irish coffee and cheering while the Crimson's boats slipped by on the river.

As the weeks passed, Riley lost the shell he'd confessed to hating. Carter doubted anyone outside himself and Dan saw the subtle difference in their friend. Riley's dress grew more casual, as did his speech. He talked more about himself, which gave people a chance to get to know him better. He still didn't say much about his parents and when he did, he often dropped his right hand to his knee to draw circles on his pant leg with his fingers. Riley didn't glance away anymore, though, and he met the gaze of whoever he was speaking to unwaveringly.

It was during a Halloween party in one of the dorms that Carter became aware of how others perceived his friendship with Riley. He'd been chatting with Susannah, a pretty girl from his calculus class, and had been about to ask her out for coffee when she put a hand on his forearm and sighed.

"What's that about?" Carter peered under the brim of Susannah's midnight-blue witch's hat and gave her a smile.

Susannah grimaced slightly. "Don't take this the wrong way, Carter — you know I like you. If you were straight, I'd be really, really interested in you."

Carter frowned, the word straight still sinking into his brain while Susannah continued.

"I don't understand why the only guys who ever talk to me at parties are gay. You know?" Susannah twisted strands of her long, dark hair around one finger. "Honestly, I've basically despaired of finding a man of my own. I'll have to hang out with you and your boyfriend and pray people think we have some kind of polyamorous arrangement going on."

Carter shook his head slowly, Susannah's words

beginning to make a kind of strange sense. She wrinkled her brow as Carter stood silent and she stepped closer, to squeeze his arm gently.

"Dude, I'm sorry. Did I…? Was the poly thing too much? I was just joking, I swear."

"Susannah, are you under the impression I'm gay? That Riley and I are together?"

Susannah cocked her head. "Well, yes. Aren't you? Gay, I mean. And Riley's boyfriend?"

"No, I am not. Gay or Riley's boyfriend." Carter fought conflicting urges to be angry and amused. "Riley's not gay, either. Where the hell did you get that idea?"

"Oh, my God, I'm so sorry." Susannah's face flushed deep red and she put her fingers over her mouth. She looked so stricken that Carter gave in to the impulse to laugh. "Jesus, I'm so embarrassed!"

"You should be," Carter scolded, though he laughed harder at the expression of horror on her face. "Why would you think that, woman?"

"You're always together!" she exclaimed. "I've never seen either of you with a girl and you told me Riley is your roommate. I assumed it all added up to the two of you being, you know, together."

Carter laughed hard enough he had to put down his drink. "What about Dan? He lives with us and we hang out all the time. Is he one of the boyfriends, too?"

"Dan goes on dates, Carter. He dates women. Okay, one woman," Susannah clarified, turning to search the crowd, and pointing when she found the right faces. Carter craned his neck to follow her gesture. He nodded at Dan with his arms around Melanie Howard, another music major who often came by their suite. They'd coordinated their costumes, with Dan dressed as a devil and Mel an angel, and come to the party with a group of friends.

"Everyone knows Dan and Mel are dating," Susannah said. "They've been together practically since the first day of classes."

Dan and Mel really were inseparable. She was double majoring in music and psychology and planned to go into music therapy. Mel was a petite beauty, with dark hair, creamy golden skin and greenish-gray eyes. Carter appreciated her bright and sarcastic brand of humor and knew Dan really liked her.

"Okay, I see your point." Carter glanced back to Susannah with a steely expression. "Making assumptions about Riley and me, though, is not cool."

Susannah gulped, and dropped her gaze to the drink in her hands. "You're right. You should know I'm not the only one who thinks you're together, by the way."

Carter frowned, trying to understand how to feel about what Susannah had told him. He'd grown up with a diverse group of friends and he didn't much care whom a person spent their time with. As far as Carter was concerned, whatever and whomever made a person happy was fine by him, provided everyone involved consented. The idea people thought he was someone's boyfriend, however... That didn't fit into Carter's world. It certainly did not fit into his family's, either.

"People really think Riley and I are together?"

"Well, girls, mostly," Susannah replied, "and that's because they're trying to figure out what's going on with you and Riley."

"Nothing is going on, Susannah."

"I know." Her voice dropped low as she tried to smooth Carter's ruffled feathers. "I'm sorry we gossiped. Two good-looking guys, in each other's company more than anyone else's...a girl's gonna try to put the pieces together."

"Uh-huh. Put the pieces together incorrectly, you mean," he replied. Carter imagined his parents' reaction to the rumor and his stomach knotted.

The dejection on Susannah's face softened his annoyance, however. He'd really wanted to take her out for coffee before she'd let her 'secret' slip. And his heart beat a little faster as he understood taking Susannah out would nip the

33

'boyfriends' rumor in the bud, too.

"Are you very angry?" she asked quietly, concern visible in her green eyes.

Carter smiled. "No. You surprised me, that's all. I might have been a little offended, too, but only because you could have asked me instead of gossiping. That shit's not okay, Susannah. Especially because I planned on asking you out."

Susannah's mouth dropped open. "You did?" she squeaked, then cleared her throat, obviously working to recover her composure. "You could still ask me, you know. Or, maybe you should let me take you out. So I can apologize for being a gossipy shrew."

Her words warmed Carter and his grin slowly widened. "Sure. I think I can handle that."

* * * *

A chill fell over New England as the Thanksgiving holiday approached, one that seemed to match Riley's overall mood. He continued to attend classes with Carter but began studying away from the suite. He was rarely available for activities at Wigg or Phoenix-SK and getting him to agree even to share a meal became impossible. Tension crept into the suite when Dan or Carter brought their girlfriends back and both friends became accustomed to Riley leaving the rooms instead of subjecting them to his stiff silences.

Carter tried to talk to Riley about his behavior on several occasions but found himself shut out. He was surprised by how much that stung. Riley and Dan were more than just Carter's suitemates and he'd grown particularly close to Riley. After his family, Riley was the first person Carter thought of to share good news with and the first person he went to with a problem. Riley had become Carter's sounding board and confidant and Carter hoped Riley felt the same about him.

A few days before school let out for the holiday, a thump woke Carter out of a sound sleep. He squinted at the clock through the darkened bedroom and smothered a groan on realizing it was after two o'clock in the morning. A second, louder thump followed a pained grunt and Carter leaned to turn on the bedside lamp, shocked to see Riley lying sprawled on the floor.

Carter sat up and tossed off the covers. "Ri? What the fuck are you doing?"

"Carpet inspection," Riley replied in a strained voice.

"Are you okay?" Carter swung his legs over the edge of the bed to crouch beside his roommate, who still hadn't stirred from his prone position.

Riley grunted again. "Not really. I face planted pretty hard. That's gonna leave a mark." He paused for a moment before rolling onto his side, his voice lower and more somber. "Help me?"

Carter leaned forward immediately, sliding an arm under his friend's shoulder to guide Riley up to sit. The smell of beer and stale cigarette smoke filled Carter's nose, but he said nothing, waiting until his friend nodded before helping him to his feet.

"Too many beers?" Carter kept his voice light and helped Riley to his bed.

"No, not exactly. I had a couple at Grendel's with some guys from the club," he said with a chuckle, "but honestly, I'm just tired. And your goddamned sneakers are inside the door again." He sighed while Carter sat down beside him.

"Shit, I'm sorry." With a grimace, Carter leaned forward to catch Riley's eye. "I meant to move them, but—"

"You forgot, I know. It's fine. I should know by now than to come in here without checking the floor first." Riley lifted one hand, prodding gingerly at his cheek and grumbled in discomfort. "Ow."

Carter stood. "I'll get some ice. Stop," he commanded when Riley moved to join him. "Sit still, and try not to trip over anything else. I'll be right back."

Riley had removed his coat by the time Carter returned with ice cubes and a washcloth. A red welt was already visible on Riley's cheekbone when he glanced up, but to Carter's surprise, he didn't appear to be angry. If anything, he seemed amused.

"Is it bad?" Riley asked.

"It's not good."

Riley sighed and held out a hand for the ice pack, looking puzzled as Carter knelt in front of him. "What are you doing?"

Carter dropped his hands to unlace Riley's shoes. "How bad does it hurt?" He ducked his head after Riley pressed the ice to his face and swore.

"Enough to make me want to kick your ass," Riley replied, an undertone of humor in his voice. He lifted one foot, then the other for Carter to remove his shoes. "Too bad my parents will be out of town over Thanksgiving. A black eye would have given them something interesting to talk about over turkey."

A hollow feeling settled over Carter at the mention of the holiday. He and Riley had spoken several times about spending Thanksgiving dinner together, but now, Carter had no idea where they stood. Slowly, he eased himself up to sit beside Riley on the bed. Leaning forward, he propped his elbows on his knees, turning to hold Riley's gaze for a few moments. Riley's eyebrows pulled together, uncertainty filtering over his face at Carter's silence.

Finally, Carter dropped his gaze to the floor. He felt almost pitifully grateful Riley was there beside him and talking, rather than pushing him away, so he drew a breath and ignored his nerves.

"You know, the invitation for dinner is still open."

A melancholy smile touched Riley's lips and made his blue eyes darken. "Thanks. But you don't need to do that, Car."

"Do what?" Carter stared blankly at him. "Invite you to dinner when we'll be in the same city and your parents are going out of town?"

Riley began to trace circles on his knee with the fingers of his right hand. "I wasn't sure you'd still want to hang out after…"

"After you froze me out?" Carter nodded at Riley's wince. "Yeah, well. I don't know why you did it but that was pretty lame, Ri. For Dan, too. What the fuck?"

Riley grumbled under his breath. "I wanted to give you guys some space. You know, with the girlfriends and all."

Carter cocked his head. "What for?"

Gesturing with the hand holding the ice pack, Riley waved at the two single beds and the desks crammed into the other corner. "This isn't exactly romance central, Car. The least I could do was try to clear out so you had a little privacy with Susannah and Dan with Mel."

Carter pressed his lips together and tried not to punch his friend. "You're an asshole, you know."

"What? Why?"

"Because you didn't even try talking to us. You just cut us off. Dan and I haven't known what the hell is up with you for weeks. I worried something was going on with your family. Dan asked me if you were planning to transfer."

Riley's cheeks flooded with color. "Shit, I'm sorry. None of that is happening. I'm fine! I just didn't want to be a fifth wheel, you know?"

Carter's irritation faded as he understood his friend was actually fine. "Talk to us. Talk to me. We could have worked something out about the rooms and Susannah. We'll have to when you bring girls back here, anyway."

A cocky grin flashed over Riley's face. "Who says I haven't?"

Carter's brows shot up before he grimaced playfully. "Really, dude? What, in between classes?"

"Maybe. I don't kiss and tell, Hamilton. I'm a gentleman."

"No, you are a jackass."

Riley burst out laughing and that clear, boyish sound made Carter's whole being feel lighter. He nudged Riley's knee with his own.

"Come to the East Side for dinner. You can tell my parents

you tried to fight my sneakers and lost."

Riley laughed again, softly, and something tight in Carter's chest unfurled. Standing, he motioned with his hand for his friend to lie down. He talked about his mother's amazing apple crisp recipe while Riley stripped off his sweater and crawled under the duvet. His eyes were already closed, the ice pack balanced on his cheek as Carter switched off the lamp.

"I'm sorry about your face," Carter told him before turning back to his own bed.

"I know, Car. S'okay."

"You coming to dinner?" he asked, holding his breath for the few moments that passed before Riley replied.

"Yeah." Riley's words were slightly slurred with sleep. "Someone's gotta look after you."

Chapter Two

As soon as freshman year was over, Riley headed to the Hamptons. His family owned a beach house in Southampton and he'd always spent a good portion of his summers there. His parents hadn't stayed at the house in years. His father couldn't leave his business and his mother was always complaining it was too small and rustic, which made him roll his eyes. By any normal standards, it was large and luxurious. After the cramped quarters of dormitory housing, it seemed massive to Riley.

The minute he arrived, he dropped his bags on the floor and headed straight to the beach. Already dressed in shorts and a polo, he kicked off his sandals and crossed the warm white sand. Just shy of the waterline, he sank to the ground and let out a sigh. He closed his eyes, breathing in the fresh, salty air and letting the tension seep from his shoulders.

It felt good to be in Southampton again, although he had to admit he already missed Carter. He'd never expected to make a friend like Carter—one he could trust without reservation. Riley knew how to be charming and he'd never been without an entire crowd of people who called him a friend. But they'd been the shallow types, the social hangers-on who were never there for him when push came to shove.

Carter, though? He was someone genuine. From the first day in Wigglesworth, Riley had known he wasn't like his former acquaintances. Dan was a great guy, too, but there was something more to his friendship with Carter. Something Riley couldn't quite put his finger on.

Riley spent the rest of the first afternoon swimming

and relaxing on the beach, then grilled a steak and some vegetables for dinner. He didn't cook much, but grilling he could handle. He ate on the sprawling deck, then nursed a beer, staring out at the ocean while the sun set behind him. The first few days were quiet as he slept in, swam and relaxed. By the end of the third day, he was a little stir-crazy, though, and headed out to his favorite bar. He drank a little, flirted a lot and ending up going home with a pretty redhead.

All in all, it made for a nice way to start his vacation, but he missed Carter. His friend was spending a few weeks back in Manhattan with his parents and sister, Audrey. Riley felt a pang of disappointment that other than a brief phone conversation the week prior, he'd barely had any contact with his own parents. He was used to it by now, or he should have been, but sometimes it still stung.

His friendship with Carter reminded him that not everyone's parents were so uninvolved. Some parents wanted to spend time with their children. Some took the time to praise them for a successful first year at Harvard, he thought bitterly. In fact, Carter's mom had been more enthusiastic about Riley's success than his own ever had. His parents only got involved when he didn't live up to their expectations. It shouldn't have mattered, not after all these years, but sometimes it crept up on him and made him resentful.

At least Riley had Carter in his life now. Dan, too, and a decent number of other people he genuinely liked. Jonathon and Geneva Porter-Wright might not have been the kind of parents he wanted, but he had friends now—good friends—and that went a long way.

Riley managed to kill the time for the next week and a half until Carter arrived, but the minute he opened the door to see his friend's grinning face, something in him relaxed. Carter's hazel eyes, striking features and broad smile were so familiar, so disarming. In the past year, Riley had opened up to Carter more than he'd intended to. He'd never been so honest with anyone in his life. And yet it never seemed awkward or out of place with Carter. It felt right.

"Miss me?" Carter asked, draping an arm around Riley's shoulder before Riley began a tour of the house.

"You wish," Riley muttered, wondering why the weight of Carter's arm felt so good. It anchored him. The uneasy restlessness he'd been fighting in the last two weeks vanished and the weird, tight feeling in his chest receded. Once he'd helped Carter carry his bags up to the room he'd be staying in, they immediately headed outside. He paused on the deck, sun beating down on both of them, and looked into Carter's eyes. "I am actually really glad you're here, Car."

Carter gave him a crooked grin. "Yeah, I am, too."

Carter spent most of the summer there with Riley, although he went home to visit his family every so often, leaving Riley adrift when he was gone. They spent half their days in the water, the sun bronzing their skins and streaking Carter's soft brown hair with gold. The few freckles Riley had on his nose and the tops of his shoulders popped out and Carter teased Riley endlessly about it. It was an easy, relaxing time. They swam, played Frisbee and beach volleyball, partied and slept. There were always pretty girls to flirt with and take home.

Riley's favorite moments were around dinner time, though, when they either ate the simple meals Riley made — because Carter couldn't cook to save his life — or they ate what the housekeeper had made for them. She was in and out like a ghost, making sure the place was kept tidy and that the refrigerator was stocked, but it still felt like they were alone.

They relaxed on the deck with a few beers. Feeling mellow from a long day in the sun and good food, the few barriers remaining between Riley and Carter dropped and they talked about everything.

"I just don't want to be like them, you know," Riley said one night. "I couldn't live with myself if I was." An earlier phone call from his mother, the first in a month, had made him melancholy. The more he drank, the more depressed he got. "Swear to me you'll kick my ass if I ever fucking turn into them."

Carter chuckled and sipped his beer. "I don't think you could be like them if you tried, Ri."

"I'm serious."

Carter shifted to face Riley. They were lying on two lounge chairs a few feet apart and Riley could see Carter's worried face, even in the dim light. "So am I. Why are you so hard on yourself? I've never seen you act anything like the way you describe them."

Riley swallowed a lump in his throat. "That's only because of you."

"Me?" Carter asked, a puzzled frown creasing his brow.

"Yeah." Riley picked and peeled at the label on the beer bottle he held. "I needed someone to remind me I didn't have to be like them. Without you, I could have become some horrible Upper East Side robot. I could have turned into Jim Montgomery." He tried to keep the mood light, jokingly referring to one of the assholes in their dorm neither of them could stand. Jim was the kind of guy who lived for social advancement, every decision made with thought to what kind of advantage it could give him. In short, he was exactly the kind of person Jonathon Porter-Wright wanted Riley to be.

Carter snorted. "Trust me when I say that with or without me, you could never be that guy."

"I'm just really fucking grateful we got placed together, you know?"

"Yeah, I know." Carter held his beer bottle out for Riley to clink. "Me, too."

Their gazes locked and long after Riley looked away, he could still feel the heat in Carter's eyes.

Something seemed to shift that summer, although Riley could never put his finger on exactly when or where it happened.

Was it the first time they'd gone skinny-dipping? It had seemed so natural. They'd gone swimming after a late dinner one evening. Too lazy to go upstairs to put on swim trunks and buzzed enough to think it was a great idea, they'd plunged into the water, naked and laughing. They'd teased each other, Riley playfully shoving Carter under the waves so he came up out of them sputtering and tossing his dripping wet hair out of his eyes. Was it that moment, watching the water stream down Carter's sculpted torso, that his heart had started racing? As Riley had stared, Carter's expression had grown more serious, staring into each other's eyes for a long moment. Riley had wet his lips, heart stuttering, then Carter had shoved him and everything had gone back to normal for a while.

Was it later, in the outdoor shower at the Porter-Wright's beach house when they'd stripped and stood under the water, their bodies shielded from the outside world by the glossy white wood divider, but never from each other? Had Riley stared at Carter's toned body a little too long? Had his eyes lingered on Carter's cock? Had Carter looked back? An anxious, anticipatory feeling had lingered in Riley's mind when he'd finally gone to bed.

As the summer progressed, they did things like that more often, skinny dipping, showering together outside, wandering around in nothing but boxers. Carter occasionally got weird about it, like he felt suddenly shy, but Riley didn't worry about it. The moments were few and far between and although Riley wasn't an exhibitionist by any means, something about casual nudity when it was only him and Carter always seemed natural.

There were plenty of opportunities to bring home girls and throw parties, and during one of those parties the lines began to blur. Carter sprawled on the couch with a giggling brunette on his lap and Riley sat next to him with a strawberry blonde on his. They were all plenty buzzed, the lights were low and a lot of people had paired off. The party wasn't out of control, but it was headed in that direction and Riley didn't really care.

While the girl on his lap nibbled on his neck, Riley watched the couples across the room from them. He realized with some surprise that one of the paired-off couples was actually two guys. What they were doing was tame, but Riley watched anyway. He was kind of fascinated by it—the sight of two guys kissing—and he shifted, wondering what it felt like. What would it be like to have someone of equal size and strength pin him to the wall and kiss him like that? Would it be odd to feel stubble against his jaw instead of soft, smooth skin? What would it be like to experience the hard length of a cock against his own? Riley's chest constricted all of a sudden and he flushed, his hand tightening on the girl's hip. The weird part was, it wasn't just any guy Riley was picturing doing those things. It was Carter. That somehow made it both more weird and less. It was only because he was sitting next to his friend and could smell his cologne that he pictured Carter, right?

He blinked and shook his head, tearing his gaze away from the guys across the room, and tried to focus on the girl on top of him. He closed his eyes and tilted his head back so she could have better access. She kissed and licked her way down his neck to the top of his shirt, sending a shudder through his body.

Riley and the strawberry blonde went upstairs to his room a short while later. He probably should have stayed downstairs to make sure the whole house didn't get trashed, but he couldn't quite muster up the enthusiasm to care.

With his shorts around his ankles and the pretty girl—whose name he couldn't quite remember—sucking his cock, he shouldn't have been thinking about anything but the way it would feel when he came. And yet, it was Carter his thoughts kept drifting to and when he climaxed with a breathless groan, it was Carter's face he pictured.

After, the girl lifted her head and gave him a smile. "That was good, yeah?"

With his chest heaving and his thoughts scattered and

muddled, Riley didn't tell her she wasn't necessarily the reason it was so good. He smiled reassuringly at her and reached up to brush his thumb across her cheek, suddenly feeling guilty. "Yeah, it was great. The best I've had in a long time. Let me return the favor."

He rolled them both over and kissed her but didn't know why he felt relieved when she passed out before they could fool around much more. He chalked the sudden attraction to Carter up to too much sun and alcohol, along with seeing those two guys making out.

He knew Carter had been bothered by the gossip last fall that the two of them were gay. They did spend a lot of time together and hadn't dated a whole lot in those first few months, so it wasn't entirely surprising. Riley didn't know why anyone would care if there was something going on between him and Carter — didn't they have more important things to worry about?

But Carter had really freaked out, worried about possible rumors getting back to his parents and had gone on a bunch of dates with a girl named Susannah. Riley had gone on a few dates, too, although he couldn't be bothered to worry about the off-chance his parents might hear something. He could not imagine going home to his parents and telling them he was gay. That would get their attention but not in a good way. But being gay wasn't an issue, so it wasn't like Riley had anything to worry about, right?

* * * *

Their easy, idyllic summer eventually wound down and Riley felt a little wistful when he packed up his things and he and Carter returned to Manhattan for a week before the fall semester started.

They roomed together again in Lowell House. Harvard Houses were essentially dormitories where the majority of students lived for the final three years of school. Like Wigglesworth, where Riley and Carter had lived their freshman year, Lowell House was set up as suites with a common room, a bathroom and two bedrooms. The suites were much smaller, though, and rumor had it Lowell had the least square footage of any Harvard House. They were rooming with Dan again and Riley and Carter agreed to take the double. What did it matter? They were busy with classes and slept like bricks, so if one of them stayed up late studying, the other slumbered through it anyway. Besides, if they weren't sick of the other after a whole summer in each other's company, there was no reason they couldn't live together again. Crammed into the bedroom, Riley and Carter's beds were so close they could practically touch each other if they reached out, but rather than bothering Riley, it almost seemed comforting.

One night, mid-semester, Riley woke to the sounds of ragged breathing and skin on skin. He forced himself to hold still, not wanting Carter to know he'd woken. Any guy would recognize the sound — Carter was masturbating. But as Riley's cock began to fill, twitching in the soft cotton of his boxers, he had to wonder — would any guy get hard hearing his roommate jerk off? It was because he was horny, he nearly convinced himself. It had nothing to do with his best friend. Riley wasn't picturing what it would feel like to have Carter's long, strong fingers wrapped around his cock. Was he?

Riley tightened his hands into fists and he willed himself to stay still and quiet. He didn't want Carter to stop. By now his cock was fully hard, leaking against his belly. He'd been sleeping on his stomach, one arm thrown up over his head, the other draped over the edge of the mattress. He couldn't move to adjust himself, or relieve the tension. Thankful the beds didn't squeak, he rocked his hips, which made the sensitive head of his cock rub against the fine hairs of his belly, trapped between his body and the mattress. It wasn't the friction he wanted, but it felt too good to stop.

Carter grunted and it sent a jolt of arousal through Riley's body. Riley pressed a little harder to the mattress, trying to time the subtle rocking motion to the rhythm of Carter's stroking. Carter must be jerking off with lotion. The sound was too wet and too fluid not to be. Riley pictured Carter moving his thumb over the head of his own cock. Riley sank his teeth into his lower lip to stay quiet. Carter stifled a low moan and Riley's cock hardened further, his balls drawing up tighter.

Fuck, was he about to shoot? Riley could hardly believe it. He wasn't even touching himself. But when Carter's rhythm grew uneven and a low, hoarse sound left his lips, Riley's cock spasmed, his cum spilling out onto the sheets. He gritted his teeth, pressing his mouth against the pillow to keep from crying out. He thought of the last girl he'd fucked, the pretty blonde from Cornell. God, it had felt good, the tight grip of her body, the way she'd clenched around him.

But this—coming with no help from his hand or another body, coming to the sounds of Carter's orgasm—was the hardest he'd climaxed in a long time.

What Riley scarcely admitted to himself, lying there sticky and spent, was that he'd pictured Carter coming on him. In his mind, Carter had stood over him, jacking off, and his cum had covered Riley's body.

In the morning, Riley was uncomfortable and ashamed, his cock a little raw where the sheets had chafed.

Riley managed to sneak into the shower and he was fully dressed and tossing his books into his bag for class when Carter awoke.

"Hey, man," Carter said roughly. "You're up early."

"Yeah, I slept really well and woke up early so I could get some studying done," Riley lied.

Carter stretched, the blankets shifting lower until his bare chest was revealed. Riley tried to convince himself he wasn't staring at the soft tuft of light brown hair on Carter's chest, between his pecs. Instead, Riley tried to keep his cheeks from flushing at the thought of what had happened the night before.

"Oh, good," Carter said, his tone casual, "I was afraid I woke you up. I hope you don't mind, but I got crazy-horny last night and rubbed one out. Dan was in the shower and I didn't feel like waiting."

"No, slept through it," Riley lied again, the words feeling funny on his tongue. He didn't like lying to Carter.

"Cool," Carter said, but Riley wondered if it was his imagination, or if Carter actually seemed a little disappointed.

Riley was nearly out of the bedroom door before Carter stopped him dead in his tracks. "If you want to do it sometime, I'm fine with it."

"Do what?" Riley asked hoarsely.

"Jerk off in the room. I mean come on, we both do it, and we're buddies. It's no big deal, right?"

"Right, no big deal," Riley said numbly. "Sure, I'll... I'll keep that in mind."

For the first time Carter seemed to notice something was off with Riley. "You okay?"

"I'm fine," Riley lied for the third time that morning. "Worried about my calc class, that's all."

He was out of the door before Carter could reply. Despite his confusion, the thought was thrilling. A few weeks after Carter had first masturbated with Riley in their room, Riley felt brave enough to do it himself. He'd been tempted, every night, but it took him a while to work up the courage. Riley came hard and fast, knowing Carter was a few feet away. Riley thought his friend was asleep, but when Carter did the same thing a few moments later, Riley's heart stuttered.

They continued slowly, until they were masturbating at the same time with the covers off, watching each other in the dim room. It became an unspoken ritual that didn't happen every night, but often.

Nothing else changed between them. They still hung out. They still went to parties. They still studied their asses off. A lot of the classes overlapped, so they were able to study together, spending endless hours quizzing each other before exams and correcting term papers. Riley still showed up at Carter's crew meets to cheer him on when he rowed.

Lowell House had an opera company that had been established in the late 1930s. It was the longest continually performing opera company in New England, featuring students and professionals from both Harvard and the Cambridge-Boston area. Dozens of professional and student artists volunteered their time to stage the company's annual production each spring in the Lowell House Dining Hall, which boasted a full orchestra, costumes, sets and lighting.

Riley's parents had often dragged him to the opera during his childhood. Neither his mother nor his father enjoyed the music – it was all about seeing and being seen. But as Riley matured and his interest in music grew, he'd begun to enjoy going. Despite Riley's irritation with his parents for constantly showing him off during intermission, like nothing more than a yacht or real estate investment, he'd never stopped going to the opera.

Half the reason he'd hoped to be placed in Lowell House was because of the operas, so when the spring performance their sophomore year came around, he was eager to go. Dan had volunteered to play in the orchestra and, despite his grumbling protests, Carter finally agreed.

"I've gotten my ass up out of bed more times than I can count to see your ass row, dude," Riley reminded him. "And you know how I feel about getting up early in the mornings."

"But opera? Really?" Carter made a face.

"You love music, I know you do. I swear you have every CD that's ever been produced and we go listen to bands play all the time."

Carter gave him a skeptical look. "Rock bands are a far cry from opera, man."

"You liked the gospel performance at the church in Harlem I took you to last year," he pointed out. "And this isn't your ordinary opera."

"What is it again?"

"It's called *Yossele Solovey: A Work of Genius*. It was written by Noam Elkies—Harvard's youngest tenured professor of mathematics. It's about a Jewish cantor who—"

Carter cut him off. "Right, right. You've told me three times."

Riley shook his head. "Then quit asking me, asshole." Although his words were harsh, his tone was teasing.

"Fine. Whatever. I'll go."

Carter made a big production of acting put-out, but Riley knew he'd cave. He always did.

So, they went to the opera. It was fantastic—Riley enjoyed every minute of it—but found Carter a distraction. Carter's height made him sprawl and his knee constantly bumped Riley's, his thigh pressing warmly against his friend's. A slow crawl of warmth suffused Riley's body and he couldn't stop shifting in his seat. It didn't matter how incredible the music was, it was hard to think clearly when he was half-hard from a simple touch.

That night, Dan invited them to a party thrown by some of the students who'd worked on the opera, but Riley declined. Carter begged him to go, but Riley's head was muddled and the thought of having the suite to himself for a little while was appealing. Back at the dorm, he pulled up porn on his laptop and jerked off, trying to pretend it wasn't Carter he was thinking of. He wasn't sure he liked how much harder that had become.

He and Carter both continued to date and bring home the occasional girl. Harvard was full of beautiful, intelligent woman, but Riley spent less and less time checking them out. For a while, the idea that maybe he was attracted to guys too crossed his mind and, sure, maybe there were some equally handsome and intelligent guys around, but the only one who made him so hard he ached was Carter. That thought hovered in his mind every time they watched each other jerk off. They continued to do so until the end of the semester, when Carter and Riley stumbled drunkenly into their room after a party.

Riley could barely hold Carter up and it took forever to drag him through the suite and into their bedroom. He dumped Carter on the bed, but Carter's arm didn't unlock from around his neck. Losing his balance and falling awkwardly, Riley landed on the bed, half on top of his best friend.

"You're awesome," Carter slurred. "I don't know what I'd do without you."

Riley was drunk enough to find that funny and he didn't even try to move away when Carter tightened his arm, keeping it around him, pushing Riley's face against Carter's neck. They both froze suddenly, bodies pressed together, the tension in the air thickening. The scent of Carter's cologne lingered in the air and his heart thrummed through the thin shirt he wore. Carter's face was flushed, his skin damp and warm, and Riley wanted to know what it would taste like. He had his tongue out, licking the skin along Carter's neck before he made a conscious decision to do it. *Salty*, Riley thought before Carter gave a low moan and all coherent thought evaporated.

Suddenly they were kissing roughly, gripping each other's hips to grind their bodies together. *We're both hard*, Riley realized, his heart lurching at the unfamiliar feeling. He'd never done anything like this, hardly even let himself consider that it could happen, but it didn't seem strange at all. It felt amazing. There was no question that Riley was turned on, either. The proof was digging into Carter's hip and Riley threaded his hands through Carter's hair, sliding his tongue between Carter's lips, not wanting to ever stop.

Their fumbling hands were awkward and desperate. They didn't touch each other's cocks, but it didn't matter. In no time at all, both of them were coming, jerking their hips erratically, Riley panting against Carter's neck.

Riley intended to get out of Carter's bed and clean up, but, drunk and sated, he fell asleep almost immediately, his body still tangled with his friend's. In the morning, he woke up before Carter did and hastily got up. He stood for a long moment, staring down at his friend as if he'd never seen him before. Carter sprawled on his back, snoring a little. Riley wanted to regret what had happened the night before and forget all about it, but he couldn't. He knew, trudging to the shower—wincing in disgust at his boxers glued to his skin where the cum had dried—that if Carter had woken and asked Riley to come back to bed, he would have done it in a heartbeat. Riley didn't like thinking about the implications of what that meant.

Once again, he and Carter didn't talk about what had happened. At first, Riley suspected Carter had been too drunk to remember it, but he knew Carter had spotted the faint whisker burn Riley's stubble had left on his neck. In fact, Carter fingered the abrasion absently while he and Riley ate breakfast.

Riley wolfed down his eggs and toast, shifting in his seat. He liked the sight of Carter's fingers touching the mark he'd left on him. He wasn't sure what the implications of that were, either.

Riley was never particularly talkative in the mornings and even Carter was subdued, although he was usually annoyingly alert at breakfast, thanks to his rowing schedule. Dan and Jim joined them, Jim bragging about the parties he'd gone to and the girls he'd hooked up with.

"What about you two losers?" Jim asked. "Did you manage to find something that halfway resembles a woman, or did you jerk each other off like usual?"

Carter started, nearly knocking his fork off his plate, and Riley was too busy watching Carter's reaction and trying not to blush to form a reply. Dan saved them. His voice was dry when he spoke. "Trust me, Jim, those two get plenty of tail from women. In fact, I'm jealous of this fucker"—he hit Carter in the arm—"the chick he brought home from the party last weekend was smokin'."

Jim was being an insensitive prick as always, but he wasn't really aiming it at them, or even at gay people. If there was one thing they could count on Jim Montgomery for, it was finding a way to be an asshole to everyone. The comment had rattled Carter, though—Riley could see it. And Carter was weirdly distant for a few days after.

Riley wanted to talk to him, try to figure out what they'd done and sort through how they both felt about it, but he was afraid of spooking Carter further.

Above all else, Riley was afraid of losing the one person he could most be himself with.

Chapter Three

Carter took pains to set boundaries between Riley and himself as the semester drew to a close. Jim Montgomery's stupid mouth had served to remind him how easily misconceptions formed and how quickly gossip traveled. At his core, Carter knew it was time to make some changes to keep his and Riley's reputations safe.

He hooked up with girls any time the opportunity arose, particularly in public places where he could count on an audience. Riley didn't comment on Carter's behavior—if anything, he seemed understanding. It wasn't easy for Carter to brush off his friend, though. More than once, he caught the hurt in Riley's gaze before Riley covered it with a careless grin or joke. Carter felt like shit every time.

He was packing his belongings a few days before the semester's end when Riley strolled in. Without a word, Riley toppled face first onto his own bed and let out a soft "oof" when his body hit the mattress.

Carter chuckled. "Bad day?"

"I'm so fucking tired," Riley replied, his words muffled by his pillow. "Just kill me now."

"What's the matter?" Carter frowned and watched his roommate roll himself over. Riley was unshaven and appeared exhausted. Dark circles had bloomed under his eyes and his Oxford shirt and jeans were rumpled. "What the hell happened to you?"

"The fire alarm went off last night. Twice."

"Oh, shit."

"Yeah, oh, shit. You'd know this if you'd been here instead of screwing some co-ed from another dorm into her mattress. The first one went off at three a.m. and the second at four a.m. I was up studying anyway, but I have no idea if I ever really slept." Riley yawned suddenly and when his eyes opened again, they were bleary and watering.

"Dude, get some sleep," Carter urged. "You don't have to be anywhere else today, right? I'll finish packing tomorrow and get out of your hair—"

"You don't have to go," Riley protested, pushing himself up onto his elbows. "Stay and pack, Car, it doesn't bother me."

Carter bit the inside of his cheek and tried to gauge his friend's mood.

Riley gave him a tired smile. "Seriously, it's fine. At this point, you could set a bomb under my bed and I'd sleep through it. Just…I don't know, wake me up before you go." He flopped back on the bed and threw one arm over his eyes.

"I'll wake you for dinner," Carter offered.

Riley yawned again. "You're actually gonna stick around and eat with me?"

"Is that okay?" Carter cocked his head.

Riley grunted. "Sure, it's okay. Been a while, though. Figured maybe you didn't want to break your streak of avoidance before you went home for the summer."

Carter stayed quiet for a long moment, processing Riley's words and rough tone of voice. He'd opened his mouth to respond when a soft snore told him Riley had fallen asleep mid-conversation.

The next few hours passed quietly. Carter packed and Riley slept on, curled up on his side and hardly stirring, even after Dan let himself into the suite and began his own packing. It was after five p.m. when Carter changed his sweaty T-shirt for a soft plaid flannel shirt and gave Riley's shoulder a shake.

"Ri. Wake up, man."

Riley came back to the surface reluctantly, blinking and stirring under Carter's hand. His sleepy expression changed after he focused on Carter's face, growing pensive, and he dropped his gaze after sitting up.

"You okay?" Carter asked, unaware he was squeezing Riley's shoulder until his friend's hand came up to cover his.

"Yeah, I'm fine. Thanks for waking me."

"Ready to go grab something to eat?"

"Definitely. I could eat a bear. Or something bear-sized." Riley snorted at the absurdity of his own joke. "Like a bear-sized burrito. Or a bear-stuffed burrito."

Carter whistled at Riley's cackling laugh. "Oh, God. You're delirious. Come on, let's go get some food before you get weird."

"Too late," Riley muttered. He rolled out of bed, though, and leaned on Carter's arm to steady himself. He looked around the room for a moment, his eyebrows drawn together when he turned to Carter again. "You packed my stuff."

"I was on a roll."

Carter shrugged and Riley let go of his arm to disappear into the bathroom.

"Speaking of burritos, we can get some Mexican food if you want. Dan and Mel want to come, too."

Riley groaned over the sound of running water. "Aw, fuck. Which lucky girl are you bringing then?"

Carter walked to stand in the door of the bathroom, watching his roommate brush his teeth. "I'm not bringing anyone."

"Wow," Riley mumbled around the brush. He spat and rinsed before shutting off the water and reaching for a towel to dry his hands. "Are you celebrating an occasion, or does your dick need a night off?"

"Maybe a little of both," Carter replied. His chest tightened at his friend's dubious glance. "We'll be gone in a few days—I figured it'd be a good time for us all to hang out before the break starts."

Riley rehung the towel and nodded before he moved

toward the door. Carter stepped back, then held his breath when Riley paused, standing close enough to Carter that their chests brushed. They stood silent, gazes locked, the air between them heavy with unspoken words.

Carter really looked at Riley and his heart began to pound. He took in the bright blue of Riley's eyes, the full lips slightly downturned, the stubble darkening his cheeks and chin. He was so focused on Riley's expression that he started when his roommate finally spoke.

"Are you still planning to come to the Hamptons this summer, Car?"

Carter stared until Riley's cheeks flushed red. "Is the invitation still open?"

Something close to challenge flickered in Riley's eyes. "You know it is."

"Then, yes, I'd planned on making the trip," Carter replied. His posture loosened as the heat in Riley's gaze subsided. "I won't be able to get there until July Fourth, though. I'll be in Ireland and Scotland with my parents and Audrey until the end of June."

Riley nodded and stepped past Carter, out of the bathroom. "I remember. Whenever you can make it, Car. The house is always open to you."

The uncertainty in Riley's face made Carter's chest ache. He'd tried to convince Riley to come to Ireland with him, but Riley had insisted Carter needed time with his family. Knowing Riley would be alone again in his parents' big beach house didn't sit well with Carter. He said nothing, though, and followed his friend into the suite's common room to find Dan and Melanie.

* * * *

Despite Carter's plans, the Hamiltons extended their summer trip by ten days. It was mid-July when he pulled up to the Porter-Wrights' summer house in his Range Rover and he didn't know how he would be received. Riley was in good spirits, though, relaxed and pleased to see Carter, who he immediately teased for a conspicuous lack of tan.

The next several weeks passed quickly, with Carter and Riley playing in the sand and surf by day and hosting parties at night. Though loath to admit it, Carter looked forward to the quiet nights, when it was just Riley and himself and sometimes Dan and Melanie.

Despite their easy energy, though, things were different between Carter and Riley that summer. Carter wasn't ignorant of the fact that he was drawn to Riley in ways he didn't fully understand. He caught himself admiring the golden sheen of Riley's skin and the way the light played on Riley's dark hair as it tossed in the sea breeze. His chest warmed whenever he met Riley's gaze at a party and Riley smiled like Carter was the only other person in the room. He liked that Riley's voice was often the first thing he heard in the morning and the last thing he heard before he fell sleep at night. And when Carter returned to the city at the summer's end, an empty Riley-shaped space followed him, waiting to be filled again.

* * * *

Carter, Riley and Dan immersed themselves in their third year at Harvard. They secured a suite in Lowell House that autumn, where Carter and Riley's beds were still an arm's length away from each other in their tiny bedroom.

Carter quickly found a rhythm in the cycle of classes, studying, Phoenix-SK events and crew practice. He and Riley no longer spent the majority of their time together, because there simply wasn't the opportunity. The awkwardness that had pushed them apart at the end of their second year had faded, however, and their friendship felt settled and familiar again.

Carter knew something was wrong as he let himself into the suite one October morning after crew practice. He couldn't pinpoint the moment it had happened, but Carter knew he'd hurt himself rowing. Moving his head even slightly sent jolts of pain down the right side of his neck and into his shoulder, making him curse when he clumsily dried himself after showering.

After dressing in sweatpants and a flannel shirt, Carter dry swallowed three ibuprofen and made his way to class. Carefully, he kept his head still, but his messenger bag seemed to grow heavier with every step. The instructor was already speaking by the time he slid into his seat beside Riley.

"Where were you?" his roommate murmured. "You were supposed to meet me for breakfast."

"Shit. I'm sorry," Carter pulled his bag onto his lap, then closed his eyes against the throb in his neck. "I left the boathouse late and I just forgot."

"Should have texted me, man—I'd have brought you a coffee."

Carter blew out a quiet breath, his gaze fixed on their instructor at the front of the room. "Sorry."

A beat of silence fell before Riley leaned forward in his seat to put himself into Carter's line of vision. "What's wrong with you?"

"Nothing."

"Bullshit." Riley frowned. "You're too quiet. You didn't even give me shit for not bringing you food or caffeine."

"Nothing's wrong," Carter repeated before he made the mistake of trying to turn his head toward Riley. The sharp pain that shot through Carter's neck and shoulder made him grunt and grip his bag with both hands.

Riley's eyes widened. "Whoa. Okay, let's get out of here."

"I'm fine," Carter muttered, "I pulled something in my neck. I just need to—"

"You need to get the hell out of here and go to health services," Riley finished.

"I'll go see one of the trainers after class."

"Uh-huh." Riley gathered up his things. "You mean one of the trainers who'll send you to health services and yell at you for waiting to get checked out."

Carter sighed. "What about the lecture?"

"We can get the notes from someone else." Riley grabbed Carter's bag and waved at him to stand. "Get your ass up, Carter," he muttered. "I'm not in the mood to carry you. You're all tall and gangly and I'm not awake enough to deal with it."

A couple of hours later, Riley's bossy attitude had ceased to bother Carter. He was floating on a haze of muscle relaxant and sitting on the edge of his bed while his friend clattered around the bathroom.

"How do you feel?" Riley asked when he emerged, holding towels and a bottle of what appeared to be hand lotion.

"I don't feel much," Carter replied, smiling slowly while Riley scoffed. "No, really, I don't feel anything. I'm kind of... I don't know, wobbly."

"Wobbly, huh?" Riley shook his head and grinned. "You're so stoned, dude." Putting everything down on the bed, Riley helped Carter take off his jacket, then knelt to pull off his sneakers.

Carter closed his eyes and the world spun slightly. "Oh. Yep." He hummed and opened one eye to peer at his friend after a touch on the buttons of his shirt. "What's going on?"

"The doc said some light massage would help with the muscle spasms," Riley told him. He unbuttoned Carter's shirt, then waited for him to lift his arms so he could ease it off Carter's shoulders. "I can do that for you."

Carter said nothing and let Riley help him out of his sweatpants. His drug-fuzzed brain was still processing the words 'massage' and 'do that for you' as Riley covered the mattress with a towel.

"Lie down, Car."

Easing himself clumsily onto the bed, Carter lay with his head pillowed on his forearms. Two big, slick hands began moving over his neck and upper back, flooding his body with warmth, rubbing soothing circles into his skin, turning his already loosened muscles to mush.

"Jesus." His voice was a low rumble in his chest and he struggled to open his eyes.

"Hold still, Car—I won't hurt you, I promise."

"I know," Carter murmured. He lay boneless while Riley set his muscles ablaze. His body responded and he groaned, his cock growing hard.

Those capable hands moved steadily lower over Carter's muscles, soothing knots that he hadn't known were there. He grunted when Riley's palms slid underneath the waistband of his boxer briefs. Talented fingers trailed fire across the base of his spine, making him shiver, and he sighed as lips pressed gently over his shoulders and neck. He'd nearly fallen asleep when a weight settled beside him at last, slipping one arm around his waist.

The room was dark when Carter woke up alone in his bed, his cock so hard he ached. He started as Riley strolled out of the bathroom clad only in sweatpants, his hair still damp from the shower.

The sight of all that glorious skin made Carter's entire body twitch. He tried not to cringe when Riley insisted on helping him to the bathroom, and his hands trembled as he stripped out of his underwear. Carter stood under the hot spray, his body buzzing, and when he wrapped his fingers around his cock, it took just a few pulls before he came so hard his knees went weak. He stood panting until Riley banged on the door and forced him to finish cleaning up.

Carter took it easy for a few days, skipping practice and taking the muscle relaxants before bed. Riley babied him shamelessly. He carried Carter's books to class and did his laundry, though neither spoke of the massage. Carter thought about Riley's warm hands on him often, usually as he slipped into sleep, but couldn't bring himself to ask for more.

By the following Sunday afternoon, Carter had recovered enough to take his place with the Crimson for a championship race in the Head of the Charles regatta.

Huge crowds had turned out and the applause from the riverbanks was loud when Carter's shell clinched the championship against the University of Washington. When he could get away, he sought out Riley in the crowd by the Eliot Bridge and swept his friend up in a bear hug that made Riley yelp with surprise.

"Thanks," Carter said, stepping back with a smile.

"You're welcome." Riley looked both confused and pleased. "What did I do?"

Carter nodded toward the river. "You helped get me here. I'd have been in no shape to row today without you."

"Oh, c'mon. You'd have been fine." Riley grinned. "I just bossed you around and made it a little easier."

"You liked bossing me around."

"More than you know, friend. You liked getting a buttload of good drugs from the doc."

Carter laughed sheepishly. "The drugs were a bonus. Either way, you did help me get here, Ri."

Riley muttered another 'you're welcome' while Carter pulled out his phone. He smiled, cheeks rosy, slipping up one hand to rest at the small of Carter's back while Carter snapped a photo.

There were parties all over Harvard Square and the university campus that night. It was late when Carter, Dan and Melanie finally made their way home, still laughing and joking. They'd lost Riley early in the evening, cheering as he'd left a party with a pretty redhead on his arm. Carter only noticed *where* Riley and the girl had gone at two a.m. after finding his blanket and pillow on the couch in the common room. He grumbled and burrowed into the cushions, hoping he'd get a shower next morning without running into a half-naked stranger. He wasn't truly upset at being shut out, or at least that was what he told himself.

The redhead was still there the next morning, curled up against Riley when Carter ducked into the room to gather up some clothes. Carter tried not to stare, dressing quickly and ignoring the odd pressure filling his chest so he could leave the suite in search of breakfast.

A heavy course load and crew practice kept Carter busy for the next few weeks. Riley seemed equally busy, buried under his own workload and still seeing the redhead, Kim, a nursing student at Tufts University. Outside of class, Carter spent less and less time with his friend, particularly when Riley slept over at Kim's apartment in Somerville.

So when Riley showed up at the suite one Saturday afternoon making noise about going out for lunch, Carter quickly suggested a tiny Tex-Mex restaurant not far from Harvard Square. There, he'd just filled their glasses with margaritas when Riley pulled out his phone.

"Let's see what Kim's up to," he said with a grin.

Carter tried his best to smile in return while Riley scrolled through the contacts on his phone. "You've got a thing for the redheads, huh?"

"I've got a thing for Kim, sure," Riley agreed. "She's fun. She has a roommate, too, and I'll tell Kim to bring her along."

Carter eyed his friend and put the pitcher of drinks down on the table. "Roommate? Who is not a mass murderer? And who you've seen with your own eyes?"

"Sara's cool. You'll like her." Riley's dark sweater made his eyes very blue.

"Why haven't you mentioned her before?"

"I'm pretty sure I have, Car—you never listen to me. Sara's your type, too."

"I do too listen to you." Carter pulled at the collar of his denim shirt, frowning. "And since when do I have a type?"

"No, you don't listen to me and never have." Riley waved a hand dismissively. "Of course you have a type. Tall and slim, with dark hair, a pretty face and brains."

"Huh." Carter had to admit his friend had a point. "That's...pretty accurate."

Riley smiled. "I know what I'm doing, Car. Just leave things to me."

Forty minutes later, Kim and Sara arrived to make their

party of two into four. Sara *was* Carter's type—tall and striking, with warm golden skin and almond-shaped eyes. She also happened to be in a relationship with her neighbor, another Tufts student named Emily. Carter's jaw tightened with irritation after he recognized Riley's mistake, but he quickly shrugged it off.

He had no good reason to feel put out. He didn't have class or practice the next day and was enjoying dinner and conversation with a pretty girl. So he poured himself another drink, and almost succeeded at tuning out Kim and Riley, who were wrapped up in each other across the table.

Everyone was feeling the alcohol when it came time to settle the bill. Riley and Kim had bypassed snuggly to handsy and Sara exchanged a wry glance with Carter at Riley's insisting they go back to the girls' place for more cocktails.

"Riley has no idea I'm gay, does he?" she asked, hiding a smile behind her hand.

Carter shook his head. "Nope," he replied as everyone stood and ambled toward the exit. "To be honest, I think he wanted to set you up with me."

"Oh, shit, really? He hasn't mentioned it to Kim, then, because she would have set him straight." Sara shook her head, her dark hair falling across her cheek. "Heh, no pun intended."

Carter's chuckle was dry. "That's on you and Kim. You see Ri a lot more than I do these days, Sara—you could have told him."

"I thought my girlfriend coming and going from the apartment was obvious enough."

Carter snorted with laughter then paused at Sara's touch on his forearm, making him sway slightly.

"You should hail a cab," she said. "Our place is close, so you can go on home if you want."

Carter opened his mouth to agree when Riley caught his eye, and any notion of Carter returning to Harvard disappeared. It didn't really matter where he slept, or that he'd be doing it alone—having fun with Riley after so many weeks of missing out seemed like reason enough to stay.

"I'll call a cab from your place," he lied, then held the door open for Sara as they walked out into the night.

The foursome spent an hour or so sitting in Kim and Sara's living room, working their way through a six-pack of beer. Carter felt dimly surprised when Sara turned back to him and pressed a soft kiss to his cheek.

"I've got to go," she murmured. "I'm staying at Emily's tonight, so if you need a space to crash, take my bed."

"Okay," Carter agreed before they helped each other stand. "I'm gonna take a leak, but do you want me to walk you next door afterward?"

Sara reached up, ruffling Carter's hair with gentle fingers. "You're awfully sweet, but I'm good." She faced her roommate, her face serious. "Later, y'all. You kids behave, okay?" Sara pursed her lips and Kim winked.

When Carter returned, he found Riley alone and looking apologetic. "Dude, Kim told me Sara's got a girlfriend. I'm sorry—"

Carter waved him off, then sat down and reached for his beer. "S'okay. You didn't know."

"I really didn't, I swear. If I had, I wouldn't have invited her along."

"I'm glad you did," Carter insisted, meaning every word. He'd liked Sara and had enjoyed spending time with her. "Sara's a cool girl."

"Yeah, well, I feel like a dick. And an idiot." Riley sighed and ran a hand through his hair. "I'll make it up to you. Kim's gotta have more cute friends who are into guys, right?"

Carter laughed. "I don't know and, honestly, don't really care."

"Why the fuck not?"

"I'm too busy for dating. I don't even see you anymore, and you're my goddamned roommate." Carter swallowed, aware of his sharp tone, then took a long drink from his beer. He was tired and the alcohol had soured his mood. When he looked up, he found Riley watching him with something like regret.

Carter made a show of glancing around the room. "Where's Kim, anyway?"

Riley's smile was sheepish. "Oh, um, changing the sheets, she said."

"Right. Let me call for a cab and I'll be out of your hair in a few minutes."

Riley caught Carter's hand when he reached for his phone. "Don't go." Riley's cheeks, pink from drinking, flushed darker as Carter watched him. "You can crash here."

Carter watched his friend for a moment, seeing an unspoken plea in his gaze. He didn't understand why Riley wanted him to stay, but that didn't stop him from nodding. Riley rarely asked anything of him these days and Carter couldn't bring himself to say no.

He was still wondering why he hadn't after he'd stripped off his clothes in a stranger's room with Riley's and Kim's whispers echoing from across the hall. Carter climbed into Sara's bed and closed his eyes, floating on a cloud of fatigue and booze, and dozed off.

He stirred back to consciousness when the mattress beside him dipped. Blinking in the dim light coming from the hallway, Carter saw Kim lying beside him and his confusion became alarm. She wore only white underpants and a thin tank top and was carding one hand lightly through Carter's hair.

"What… Kim? What's going on?"

"We thought you could use some company." Kim curled her lips up in a smile. "I told Riley you'd be lonely over here all by yourself."

"Riley?" Carter caught sight of his friend in the doorway and his mouth went dry. Riley was wearing black boxer briefs and an expression Carter had never seen before. Riley looked almost hungry.

Carter moved to sit up, his heart pounding with nerves

and surprise.

"I don't understand." His jaw slackened as Riley stepped closer, hands held up in a gesture clearly meant to calm.

"It's okay, Car." Riley walked slowly to the side of the bed, pausing a moment to lay something on the nightstand. Carter blinked and stared at the bottle of lube and foil condom packets. "We didn't mean to scare you," Riley said. "Kim thought...maybe the three of us could have some fun."

"What kind of fun?" Carter glanced from Riley to Kim and back again, very aware of Kim's hand after she dropped it from his hair to rest against the side of his neck.

"The kind of fun two guys and a girl can have, sweetie." Kim moved this time to cup Carter's cheek. "Riley didn't know if you'd go for it, but I've got a feeling about you." She smiled again, running her fingers along his jaw. "You come off all proper and stoic...such a Harvard man. But I think...no, I know you'd be down for having a little fun if it came your way."

Carter stared at Kim, his skin prickling with nerves at the implications of her words. He could only imagine it was a misunderstanding or trick, or even a drunken impulse gone too far, until Riley crawled onto the bed, too. Riley stretched out on Kim's other side, his gaze on Carter. Carter swallowed hard.

"Ri, I don't know..."

Kim lay back, gently pulling Carter down until his cheek rested on her shoulder. He lay wide-eyed and silent, while Riley leaned down and kissed Kim. The wet sounds of their mouths were loud in the night-time silence. Heat spread over Carter's skin as Riley cradled Kim's head in his hands and when he tugged at Kim's hair, her gasp made Carter's cock twitch.

"Oh, God," he breathed without meaning to, making the lovers beside him break apart and turn to face him. Carter shot up off Kim's shoulder, his face blazing with heat. "I-I should— Shit, I'll go, sorry."

Kim's warm fingers on Carter's lips stopped his words. She reached for him with her free hand, pulling Carter toward her with surprising strength, and his breath hitched while he braced his hands on the bed. Every instinct warned him this was a disaster brewing and that he must get out of the bed and away from his best friend's girl.

"Sweetie, relax." Kim's low voice cut through Carter's panic. "No one here has to do anything they don't want to, including you. Okay?"

Carter swallowed hard, and caught Riley's eye. The hungry look was back on his friend's face and it seemed more intense with Riley only inches away in the same bed.

"Okay…?" Carter managed to croak out before Kim rolled toward him, fitting her soft body against his. He stared down at her, holding his breath and going rigid after she brushed her thigh against his half-hard cock.

A slow smile spread over Kim's face. "Mmm, getting to okay, I'd say," she murmured.

Kim licked her lips and Carter's body began to buzz. The panic reared its head again, freezing him in place as he locked eyes with Riley.

Riley slid closer on Kim's other side, his gaze never wavering from Carter's. "I'm right here."

Riley's husky voice sent a thrill through Carter. Riley reached over Kim to grasp his hand, that simple touch utterly piercing Carter's tension. He clutched Riley's fingers, desperate for the contact, and sank back, his breaths shallow and Kim's body pressing against his.

Kim laid her hands on Carter's cheeks, finally drawing his attention away from Riley. He held still while she kissed him, the first brushes of their lips careful and almost chaste. Riley tightened his fingers around Carter's and Carter stiffened at Kim's moan. He opened his eyes to see Riley run his tongue along the shell of Kim's ear while his heated gaze found Carter's.

Things became frenzied after that moment. The few clothes they wore came off in a tangle of arms and legs and hot, wet mouths. Finally convinced Riley was not going to kick his ass for pawing Kim, Carter allowed himself to enjoy the experience. The touch of so many grasping hands and eager lips was incredibly exciting and the contrast of Kim's curves and Riley's hard muscles drove him crazy.

Still, something kept Carter from truly letting go. Despite being almost painfully aroused, he couldn't bring himself to go further than kissing and touching Kim, not even with her grinding against him. As much as Carter wanted to fuck someone, he settled for watching Kim and Riley's bodies wind around each other's and his. More specifically, he settled for watching Riley.

Riley's gorgeous mouth, licking and sucking at Kim's skin as he climbed over her and Carter. His strong hands holding both their bodies close. His lean body flexing, muscles rippling. His cock, oh, God, so fucking hard, pressing for a long moment against Carter's hip. His eyes, burning with blue fire, watching Carter right back.

Finally, Riley fell back with a grunt, reaching for a condom and the bottle of lube on the nightstand. He covered and slicked himself with trembling fingers, then reached for Kim, gasping after Carter twined their fingers together, aligning Kim between them. Riley's gaze locked on Carter's as he slid inside Kim and the desperate noise she made went right through Carter.

Enraptured, Carter watched Riley begin to move. He rocked into Kim with long, slow strokes while she turned her face into Carter's chest, her breath puffing over Carter's skin. Kim slid her arms around Carter's waist and he groaned at the pleasure on Riley's face.

"Jesus," he mumbled. He'd never been so hard in his life, never so aroused and never so desperate to come. Riley's eyes snapped open and Carter licked his lips, letting out another, much shakier noise after Riley reached out to grab his hip. He pulled Carter closer against Kim lying between them. "Oh, fuck, Riley."

Kim lifted her head, her smile knowing. She reached

behind Riley for the lube, and her clever fingers were slippery and cool when she circled them around Carter's cock. His eyes fell shut once Kim began to pump him in time with Riley's thrusts.

Desire rattled down Carter's spine, making his head spin. He reached out, past Kim, grasping for an anchor to keep him grounded while his body throbbed and burned. His fingers dug into the hard muscle of Riley's shoulders as a second, larger hand wrapped around his dick and Riley's low rumble pushed all rational thought out of Carter's head.

How long the three of them moved together, giving and taking pleasure, Carter didn't know. He held Kim when she came and his breaths grew ragged when Riley started to tremble, his thrusts becoming erratic.

Carter drew in a sharp breath—Riley sped his hand over his cock more urgently, knocking Kim's smaller hand aside, twisting over the head until Carter lost it. White noise filled his head while his cock pulsed in Riley's fist, painting all three of them with stripes of cum. Dimly, he heard Riley's broken cry and Carter's last conscious thought was to pull his friend close, pressing their mouths together over the girl lying between them.

Carter tried to open his eyes as Kim stirred, but his lids were simply too heavy. He lay still while she wiped him clean, hissing when something warm and wet trailed over his still sensitive cock. Kim's grumbling about guys falling asleep and wet spots forced him to open his eyes and his gaze fell on Riley, lying fast asleep on the other side of the bed. Carter mumbled an apology to Kim, who crawled over her boyfriend to settle between them again.

"You don't mind, do you?" She drew the sheet up over them all and curled into Carter's chest, her eyes sleepy. "I'd try to get Riley back to my room, but he's down for the count. Besides," she said through a yawn, "you're both all warm and snuggly already. It's nice."

Somnolent and sated, Carter listened to Kim's breath

even out into sleep. He continued watching Riley, however. Riley's long lashes fanned across his cheeks and his kiss-swollen mouth was pursed. *He's beautiful,* Carter thought to himself. A chill swept over him and he swallowed hard, his eyes stinging.

Riley inhaled sharply then and he burrowed against Kim while he slept. His cheek brushed Carter's arm and one hand moved, seeming to search until it found Carter's body through the sheet. Riley snuggled in, his head pillowed on Carter's arm, and that roving hand came to rest on Carter's waist before he fell quiet.

Carter wondered at the turn the evening had taken. He couldn't remember ever being so aroused. How often did Riley and Kim bring others into their bed? Would they ask Carter again? Did he want them to?

Carter's stomach twisted and he admitted to himself that yes, he did want them to, not so much because of Kim but because of Riley. And what the hell did that even mean?

Listening to the quiet breaths of his bedmates, Carter felt no regret. Instead, he watched Riley sleep, his chest tight with feelings of longing that he didn't fully understand.

Chapter Four

May, 2000
Cambridge, Massachusetts

Riley awoke to Carter's snoring. His arm, heavily muscled from rowing, lay across Riley's waist. There had been a girl between them when they'd fallen asleep, or—more accurately—passed out. But now she lay on the far side of the bed, curled into a little ball, sleeping deeply. Riley wasn't sure why he'd woken. The room was quiet and dim, but although he closed his eyes, he couldn't seem to fall asleep again.

It had been a while since they'd done this and, helped along by plenty of alcohol, they'd been up until the early morning celebrating the completion of their senior year finals. Graduation was in a few days and they were making the most of their remaining time on campus, participating in the senior week activities and partying with their friends. Riley groaned quietly when he glanced at the clock. He'd only been asleep for a few hours.

Riley always initiated these encounters and Carter usually had to be drunk to go along. It worried him sometimes that he pushed Carter to do something he didn't want to do. And yet, in the moment, Carter was always into it. He was always eager and ready. Although there was a certain line the friends never crossed. They'd never discussed it, but they'd never moved beyond kissing and the occasional hand job.

Riley remembered one threesome vividly. He couldn't remember the girl's name, but there was a moment imprinted on his memory he couldn't shake. He'd been kneeling behind the girl, fucking her hard, while Carter leaned against the headboard and jerked off. Riley's gaze had kept drifting to Carter's cock as it disappeared into his fist. He'd had a sudden curiosity about what his dick would taste like and what it would feel like on his tongue. In keeping with his height, Carter's dick was long and Riley had wondered if he'd be able to take it all without choking. Flustered, he'd glanced up at Carter and realized Carter was watching him. Their gazes met and Riley had felt a jolt go through him, a flush suffusing his body at the intensity of the look Carter had given him. Riley had reached out, wanting to touch Carter, who'd risen to his knees and crawled over to him. Carter's large, warm hand had landed on Riley's back and he'd leaned in for a kiss. Riley had met Carter's lips in a deep, hungry kiss and for a second, his rhythm had stuttered. Carter had swept his hand down Riley's back and grasped his ass, encouraging Riley to thrust harder. Blindly, he'd reached for Carter's cock, knocking his hand away so he could jerk Carter. Carter had groaned against his mouth and in moments, Riley and Carter had both been coming.

Riley would swear they both came harder when they were touching each other, but something made him hesitate to go any further. He wondered if it was fear that if he did cross that line, it would push Carter to end the threesomes.

In the past year, he and Carter hadn't indulged often. Finding the right girl wasn't easy. They needed someone adventurous enough to go for it, but discreet enough that rumors wouldn't make their way around campus. They preferred girls who went to neighboring schools and who had reputations of their own to protect. It had worked and Riley and Carter had made it through the year unscathed by any hint of the truth. Even though they'd developed a reputation as womanizers and partiers, their grades had been high enough for them to graduate with honors and both had been accepted to Harvard's business school.

They'd somehow managed to find the right balance, although there was always an undercurrent of unease.

Riley's pleasure always mingled with worry that the occasional threesomes would damage his friendship with Carter, but mostly worry that at some point, Carter would tell him to stop. The thought made Riley queasy. Riley questioned some of the things he and Carter did together, but the one thing he knew was that he couldn't live without being able to touch Carter or share himself in the only way they could. It was fucked up — he knew that — but what else could they do?

He must have shifted, or disturbed Carter somehow, because the arm around his waist tightened. "What the fuck are you thinking about so hard at four in the fucking morning?" Carter asked quietly, his voice gritty and hoarse.

Riley flipped onto his back and scrubbed his hands over his face. He pitched his voice low, not wanting to disturb the girl next to them. "Just thinking about how fucked up this is. What we do, I mean. Why we do this."

"Do you want to stop?" Carter asked, a note of apprehension in his voice, or maybe that was Riley's wishful thinking.

"No. No, of course not," he said hastily. "It's just…"

Carter finished the thought for him. "Fucked up. Yeah, I know."

It was the most either of them had acknowledged that they weren't doing this simply because it was a thrill, or a kink. There was more to it, even if neither of them was willing to admit it. Carter sighed and shoved at Riley's shoulder. He took the hint and rolled onto his side, letting Carter wrap around him. He closed his eyes as the heavy arm pinned him in place once more. It scared him how right it felt, how badly he needed Carter. Carter's soft breath on his shoulder, his ankles tangled with Riley's — those were what mattered. They were all he'd ever get, and they'd somehow have to be enough.

* * * *

The next few days were a blur while Riley and Carter packed their belongings and moved into a two-bedroom apartment in the Riverside neighborhood of Cambridge. Riley took one last glance at their room at Lowell House. As seniors, their suite of rooms had been bigger than those of the previous year, but he and Carter had still shared a bedroom. Dan had thought they'd gotten screwed over and the guys had pretended to piss and moan about it, but in the end, Riley had been relieved. He was going to miss sleeping a few feet away from Carter. He was going to miss jerking off while Carter watched and vice versa. He'd never admit it aloud, but the thought of moving into an apartment with separate bedrooms dismayed him.

Riley's melancholy mood lingered while they unpacked and set up their new place. Dan was moving out of state for grad school, along with his girlfriend Mel, and Riley was acutely aware of how fast their lives were changing. Even more, he dreaded his parents' arrival the following evening.

Of course, he was sweaty and disheveled when they arrived — two hours before they'd said they'd be there. He answered the door and his stomach dropped at the sight of them. Geneva Porter-Wright pursed her lips as she scrutinized him. "Well, you look…" She didn't finish her thought, but the sentiment was clear. She did not approve.

"Sorry, we were unpacking," Riley replied defensively. He stepped back, ushering them both into the new place. There were boxes strewn everywhere. Riley had planned to clean up the apartment and shower before they arrived, but of course, they'd caught him at the worst time possible. It was a poor start to what was guaranteed to be a strained few days.

He hastily cleared space on the new sofa and gestured toward it. "Have a seat, please."

Riley resigned himself to the lecture about his appearance

and other failings he was sure was about to come. The way they always treated him stung. He braced himself for the criticism every time, but it didn't necessarily make it any less painful. Their behavior was such a sharp contrast to Carter's parents, who'd arrived the previous morning to help them move out of Lowell House and pick out furniture. They had greeted both Riley and Carter with warm hugs and congratulations on the completion of their undergrad degrees. A part of Riley wanted to tell his parents to go home. So what if they missed his graduation ceremony? Did either of them really care, or were they only showing their faces for appearances' sake?

He observed them perched on the edge of the sofa, looking uncomfortable. His mother was tall and slim, with the same dark hair, fair skin and blue eyes as him. Younger photos of her showed he'd inherited her freckles, but she was meticulous about hiding them, along with any sign of aging. Geneva was polished and sophisticated, and to the right people she came across as warm and open, but it had been years since Riley had personally seen anything but cool indifference or disapproving disappointment from her. He turned his attention to his father. Jonathon Porter-Wright was polished like his wife, but grayer and more tan. Riley had inherited his height and bone structure, but if he didn't resemble his parents so strongly, he would have wondered if he'd been adopted.

Sometimes he wondered that anyway. In a way, he was grateful for the nannies who'd raised him, Sarah in particular. She'd been there for most of Riley's formative years with hugs, kisses and bedtime stories. She was the reason he hadn't become a carbon copy of his parents. She'd been forced to retire because of her health, but he'd kept in contact with Sarah until her death a few years prior. At her funeral, Riley had wondered if he'd feel nearly as torn up when his parents died someday, then felt guilty. But it was true.

"So," he said, clearing his throat and trying to break the

ice, "how was the ride up from the city?"

"Tedious," his mother said with a sigh. "Traffic was terrible. I don't know how you stand dealing with these Massachusetts drivers."

"You get used to them, I suppose," Riley said diplomatically. Even after growing up in Manhattan, he had been somewhat taken aback by the aggressive drivers here, but he knew his parents hadn't driven themselves. They'd probably spent the time coolly ignoring each other in the backseat of their town car while the driver dealt with the traffic. He stood, relieved, when Carter entered the living room.

Riley's anxiety ebbed in Carter's presence and his warm demeanor broke some of the thick tension in the room. He introduced his friend to his parents. They had never once met in the four years he and Carter had been rooming together. He caught Carter's sympathetic gaze when it landed on him several times throughout the conversation. Carter—used to his own family—was clearly taken aback by Riley's, despite the warnings. He was good at making small talk, though, so Riley used that opportunity to grab a quick shower and get ready. He slipped on a suit and nervously knotted his tie. After his rumpled appearance earlier, he didn't want to give his parents a single reason to find fault with him.

When he was finished showering and dressing, he rejoined the three people in the living room and Carter excused himself so he could also clean up and change. Riley gritted his teeth and sat through the lecture his parents delivered about all the things he wasn't doing right. He was absurdly grateful when Carter reappeared and they headed out to dinner. Riley and Carter drove in Riley's Audi S5 and the Porter-Wrights followed in their town car. They crossed the river into Boston and once they reached Maison Robert, they met the Hamiltons, along with Audrey, Carter's sister, and her fiancé, Max.

At the table, Carter's and Riley's fathers struck up

a conversation, quickly realizing their own Harvard connection as alumni and former members of Phoenix S-K. Their mothers discovered common ground in mutual friends and acquaintances. While they sipped drinks and enjoyed their appetizers, Riley and Carter were left to talk to Audrey and Max. Riley was grateful. He liked them both and it took the pressure off him. It wasn't until the main course, when Audrey and her mother were discussing the upcoming wedding, that the conversation grew strained.

Riley's mother turned a speculative glance on Riley and he tried not to visibly cringe. He knew what was coming. "So, Riley," she said. "Any serious girlfriends? Your father and I would love to see you settle down soon."

He swallowed hard, trying to keep the irritation out of his voice. "I've met a few nice girls, but I'm only twenty-two. I want to finish grad school and get established in my field before I worry about a family."

His mother appeared less than thrilled, but for once, his father approved. He clapped a hand on Riley's shoulder and nodded. "Let the boy get his foothold at Porter-Wright Publishing before you marry him off."

His mother pursed her lips, but she was too concerned about making a bad impression on the Hamiltons to say what she really thought. Riley tried not to sigh at the assumption that he'd be following in his father's footsteps at the publishing company. It wasn't the largest in Manhattan, but it was quite successful. Started by his grandfather, it had grown under his father's control and it was expected Riley would take it over. His hand reflexively clenched on the table and he fought to relax it before anyone noticed.

Riley hadn't realized how tense he was until Carter brushed a hand on his thigh and pretended to straighten the napkin on his lap. It was the briefest trace, but his hand scorched through the fine wool of Riley's trousers. The tension drained out of him at the reassuring touch. Carter was there for him and he could handle this, he reminded himself.

He turned his attention to his father and made a sound of agreement to show he'd been listening. No point in agitating his mother by siding too strongly with his father, but he was grateful Jonathon was for once being supportive. Riley wanted to focus on his career before he began to think about settling down—he just wished he didn't have such ambivalent feelings about joining the family company.

A part of him wanted to—it was what his degree was working toward—and yet...sometimes the assumption that he'd do whatever his father wanted irked him. Plus, Jonathon wouldn't listen to his suggestions that the company explore digital publishing. Riley knew there were people creating digital readers and with the invention of electronic paper—technology that allowed a display screen to reflect light like ordinary paper without the need for a backlight—once a solid, marketable device was out there, electronic publishing would take off.

That was what thrilled Riley, the idea of breaking into new territory for the company. His father scoffed at the idea, but Riley was sure of the direction the field was going. He hoped when the time came and the market opened, his father would be willing to go for it. Although he dreaded the thought of returning to Manhattan and working with Jonathon, he did love the publishing industry and he was desperate to begin. The degree from Harvard Business School was critical and he was eager for the next two years, but a part of him itched to begin his career, not just talk about it in class.

The rest of the meal continued fairly smoothly, although there was the ever-present tension between his parents as a couple, and between them and him. Riley hoped he was the only one who noticed it, but he doubted it. The Porter-Wrights and the Hamiltons seemed to get along well, and he was grateful for that, but he caught Carter's mom giving him the occasional sympathetic glance when he was on the end of one of his mother's thinly veiled barbs.

By the time they made it to desserts and coffee, he wasn't

sure how much more he could take. As if sensing his growing discomfort, Carter leaned in, propping an arm on the back of Riley's chair. Carter angled his head so his lips were hidden by Riley's cheek, and he pitched his voice low. "You hanging in there? You look like you're about to lose it."

Riley nodded tightly, but he discreetly dropped his hand to Carter's leg and squeezed it in thanks. He was grateful for his friend's concern. Carter sat back, still searching Riley's face. Riley squeezed again and tried to force his fingers to lift. It was almost painful, pulling his palm away from the muscled thigh. He had a sudden urge to slide his hand higher, cup between Carter's legs and tease him, feel his cock thicken in his hand. It was a wild, insane idea. He'd never do it, afraid it would spook Carter and potentially damage the fragile equilibrium, but a part of him was still tempted.

Riley was grateful when the final course was over and they left the restaurant. He received a cool, clinical hug from his mother and a pat on the shoulder from his father. There was sympathy in Eleanor Hamilton's eyes when she hugged him goodbye, the motherly embrace lingering a little longer than usual. He swallowed hard, pushing away the hot sting of tears. Goddamn it, he didn't like the pity there. Fine, he was a poor little rich boy with parents who ignored him. It wasn't that unusual. He'd gone to school with half a dozen other guys with families like his. Just because he longed for a family like Carter's didn't mean he was unhappy, he reasoned. The lie twisted in Riley's gut and he shook his head, trying to clear it.

When they left the restaurant and the valet pulled his car up, Riley gestured Carter toward the driver's side and stepped up to the passenger-side door.

Carter raised an eyebrow at him. "You sure about this? You never let me drive your car. Unless you're drunk. Are you drunk?" he asked. "You only had a gin and tonic and a glass or two of wine."

"I'm not drunk," he replied, opening the car door, "just exhausted and in no mental condition to drive right now."

Carter frowned as he settled into the driver's seat with a muffled oath about short people before he pushed the button to slide back the seat. Riley's mouth quirked in a smile. It was a long-standing joke between them, since Riley was by no means short. Just shorter than his friend. "It's not my fault you're a fucking giant," he retorted and Carter's worried frown disappeared. He put the car in drive.

"Lilliputian," Carter teased, revving the engine.

"Behemoth," Riley countered as Carter pulled smoothly out onto the street. They continued to banter on the way back to the apartment, and Riley relaxed. This was good. He didn't have to deal with his parents until the following day. It was just him and Carter tonight.

They spent the evening ignoring the half-unpacked boxes scattered around the apartment. They had a couch and the entertainment system had been hooked up. They found the shot glasses and a bottle of tequila so they were set. For the first time in a long while, both guys forgot the tension between them, forgot everything but the warm, mellow glow of liquor and friendship. It wasn't sexually charged when they belatedly realized they'd never unpacked and washed the sheets for their new, much-larger beds. They crashed on the couch, still half-dressed. Riley was wearing his suit pants and a sleeveless white undershirt. Carter stripped down to his boxers and nothing else. The wide sectional allowed them to sprawl out, but when Riley woke up to piss, his body was intimately twined with Carter's. He mumbled groggily when Riley disentangled himself but immediately went back to sleep. When he was done in the bathroom, Riley stumbled to his bedroom and rummaged through boxes until he found blankets for them both.

He carried them into the living room, covering Carter with one and pulling another over himself. He got comfortable on the couch and tentatively wrapped an arm around Carter. It was Carter who pulled him closer, Carter who drowsily muttered, "You always take such good care of me, Ri."

Riley pressed his lips to Carter's soft brown hair, his chest aching. What he wanted more than anything else was to take care of Carter. Whatever that meant, whatever the implications of that were, it was what he wanted. To fall asleep beside Carter and know that he trusted Riley to take care of him.

* * * *

The following day was a chaotic blur as they went through the pomp and display of a Harvard graduation. Beginning at eight a.m. there was a senior class chapel service, senior procession, academic procession, the commencement ceremony, a luncheon and finally, the diploma presentation ceremonies and the alumni parade. It was exhausting, especially for the two hung-over guys. He managed to reconnect with Carter—they'd lost each other in the crush of celebrating graduates and their families— who looked equally shell-shocked. Riley's parents had already left. Once the diploma presentation was over, they'd perfunctorily congratulated him, taken the requisite pictures then excused themselves.

"There's an event tonight, Riley, you understand," his mother had said.

He'd nodded tightly. "Sure. Thanks for coming."

And with that, they had gone.

Riley was welcomed back into Carter's family, though, and he stayed with them for the remainder of the day. They ran into Mel, Dan and his family on campus. Riley realized it was probably the last time all four of them would be together. Dan and Mel, still going strong after four years of dating, were moving halfway across the country for grad school. Riley took a seat on a nearby bench while Carter discussed something with his family and Dan took photos with his parents and younger sister. He didn't want to intrude.

Mel sat next to him and flashed him a wistful smile. "It's going to be strange in Chicago without you two around."

Riley's answering smile was tinged with sadness. "I'll miss you and Dan, as well. Now I'm stuck with him." He gestured toward Carter.

Mel laughed, her green eyes lighting up as she turned to face him. "You two bitch about spending time together, but we all know you're just pretending. You got an apartment together for grad school, for goodness' sake. You can't be that sick of him."

"Better the devil you know…" Riley joked.

Still laughing, she squeezed his upper arm. "The four of us need to stay in touch. I know we promised we would, but we're all going to be busy and I know if we leave it up to Carter and Dan, it'll never happen."

Riley laughed ruefully. "You have a point."

"So it's up to us. Promise you'll email and call?"

"I will. I promise." He leaned in and kissed her cheek. "I don't want to lose contact with you guys, either."

"Hey, quit hitting on my girlfriend, Riley!" Dan called out and Riley sat back, grinning at him. Carter looked over, rolling his eyes at all of them.

"Mom wants pictures with you, too, Mel," Dan said, gesturing for her to come over and she stood and patted his shoulder. She walked toward Dan's family and Riley glanced at the Hamiltons. Bradley Hamilton was on the phone, frowning, and Riley gave his friend a quizzical glance. Carter walked over, plopped onto the bench beside him and explained. "My dad was having trouble adding another person to the dinner reservation for tonight, but I think he got it straightened out."

"Oh," Riley said, swallowing past the lump in his throat, imagining returning to their apartment alone. He hadn't thought about plans for after graduation—he'd been so focused on finals, senior week activities, commencement and dealing with his family it hadn't crossed his mind to make plans for after. "Who are you inviting?"

He gritted his teeth at the thought of Carter bringing one of the girls he'd been seeing casually to dinner with his family. Carter laughed and bumped his shoulder playfully. "You, man, who else would I bring?"

Riley shrugged. "I didn't know."

"My parents just…didn't realize you wouldn't have plans with your own family."

"Yeah, well…" Riley smiled bitterly. "You know how it is. They have their priorities."

The look in Carter's eyes made Riley's throat ache and he wasn't aware he'd been tracing patterns on the silky fabric of the graduation gown like he always did when he was anxious, until Carter's warm hand covered his own. He stilled and his breath caught when he met Carter's gaze again.

"Well, I have mine, too, and you're one of them."

Riley was so absurdly grateful he had to blink back tears and his eyes were still glassy when he thanked Eleanor for including him at dinner and she shook her head in bewilderment.

"You're family, Riley, of course we'd include you."

Dan interrupted, asking the guys if they'd pose for a picture with him, and Riley was grateful for the distraction. When a warm flush moved through his body at the pressure of Carter's hand on the back of his neck while they posed for pictures, a fleeting thought crossed his mind. Would Carter's family be so welcoming of him if they knew what he did with their son? If Brad and Eleanor knew the way Riley felt about Carter, would they welcome him with open arms? The Hamiltons were good people, kind people, but they weren't perfect. Carter had talked about their deep homophobic streak, and it was a chilling reminder that no matter how Riley felt, he and Carter were never going to be anything more than friends who occasionally fooled around. Riley was afraid his strained smile would ruin the photos, but then Carter brushed his thumb against the soft skin behind his ear and Riley relaxed.

He had this. And it had to be enough.

* * * *

May, 2002
Cambridge, Massachusetts

Riley began to panic in his final days at Harvard Business School, as time wound down and the idyllic days with Carter waned. He felt it acutely — they both seemed to — but there was nothing they could do to stop it.

The two years of grad school had passed so quickly and Riley couldn't believe — didn't want to believe — it was almost over. Returning to Manhattan meant giving up the apartment with Carter, giving up the threesomes, giving up pretending that life would always be the two of them, side by side, doing everything together. Every time Riley thought of the future, he got a cold feeling in the pit of his stomach and an ache in his chest which nothing seemed to take away.

Tonight was the final time he and Carter would have a girl in bed with them and Riley struggled to pretend he wanted her there. His hands never left Carter's skin while he buried himself inside her. He didn't want to be an asshole and make the girl feel unwanted, but Riley ached for her to disappear, to have it be only him and Carter for once, with nothing and no one between them. The kisses and caresses he and Carter exchanged were frantic, heated. Their gazes remained on each other and Riley bit his lip so hard he nearly bled to keep from calling out Carter's name as he came.

They were at their apartment, in Riley's bed, and neither of them protested when the girl made excuses to leave after they finished. Neither of them moved and Riley prayed Carter would spend the night beside him. Carter did, muttering something about being too tired to drag himself to his own bed. They both knew it was a lie, but Riley was grateful for it. Riley awoke a few hours later. He was sleeping on his stomach like always, and Carter's arm was thrown across him. It was rare that they slept in the same bed after, just the two of them, their nude bodies tangled. They hadn't started out that way, but after Riley had fallen asleep, lulled by the soft sound of Carter's breathing, they'd shifted together. The rest of the world had disappeared and nothing mattered but those few stolen hours. They would have to last the rest of his life.

He drifted off again and he had no idea if he'd dreamed it, or if it actually happened, but he would swear Carter whispered his name in a choked voice and tenderly kissed his shoulder. For years, Riley had been trying to make sense of his feelings for his best friend. There were words that had swirled through his head, growing more and more insistent, but he hadn't allowed himself to think them, afraid of the implications. Even if those words — those labels — applied to him, they didn't matter. Riley couldn't be with Carter, no matter how much he wanted it. And he did. He ached to be with his best friend.

After sharing a bed all night, they slept late. Actually, Riley was fairly sure neither of them had slept as much as they'd pretended, but he suspected they were both lingering, unwilling to move apart. Reality wouldn't hit until they got out of bed and so they stayed there. Under the heavy down duvet, they were warm, their naked bodies pressed together intimately. Riley screwed his eyes tightly shut, trying to memorize the feel of Carter's hair-roughened thigh against his, knowing this would be the last time he'd ever get to be with his friend in this way. Their friendship would survive, but the threesomes would stop and he'd have to content himself with platonic interactions.

Carter finally sat up and spoke. "The movers are going to be here soon."

Riley nodded. "Yeah, I know." His voice was hoarser than he expected and he swallowed hard and looked at his friend. Carter's hair stuck up wildly and his cheeks were flushed from sleep. Riley ached to smooth his fingers over his friend's hair and tug him in for a kiss. Instead, he turned away, stepped out of bed and tugged on his boxers before trudging to his shower.

After they met with the movers, instructing them on what to pack and which items went to which address in Manhattan, Riley and Carter left the apartment. Riley was enough of a control freak to feel anxious about leaving the movers there unsupervised, but his friend coaxed him into spending a final day visiting their old haunts. By late evening, they ended up on the banks of the Charles River, deepening twilight making the familiar view into something magical.

They took a seat on the grass, knees drawn up to their chests, silent while the sky went from pink-tinged gray to black. Or as dark as it ever got with so much light pollution.

"I can't believe we're graduating tomorrow," Carter finally said with a sigh, lying back.

"Yeah, me neither. I feel like we just moved in for undergrad. It doesn't seem like it's been six years," Riley replied, his foot scuffing at the grass.

"I'm not ready to be an adult," Carter confessed.

Riley laughed softly. "Trust me, you're not the only one. I should be grateful — I've got a place at the family company and a trust fund…Christ, compared to most people, I've got it made. But it feels like I don't have a choice about any of it."

"At least you like publishing," Carter huffed. "I mean, I don't hate advertising and it's what dad's been grooming me for, practically my whole life. I…I don't feel like I'm ready for it."

"We're such poor little rich boys," Riley said snarkily, first feeling sorry for himself, then growing guilty because he knew he was lucky. He was damn fortunate to have the opportunities that were waiting for him and yet he wanted nothing more than to throw them away.

"No shit." Carter chuckled, then was silent for several long moments. "You ever think about running off, starting over somewhere without the family names to rely on, without the expectations and the pressure? Christ, I know my parents expect me to settle down soon."

"Mine, too. They've been parading suitable future wives in front of me and my mother is always talking about so-and-so's daughter who would be perfect for me." Riley groaned and fell back onto the grass, covering his eyes with his forearm, as if that could block out the future unfolding before him. "And, yeah, I do think about it sometimes."

Riley thought about it a lot, actually. Just disappearing, running away from the future his family had planned out for him and creating a new one. In it, Carter was always by his side. Aching desire for that life tore through him. "I couldn't do it alone," he said quietly.

"No, me neither," Carter said.

Riley lifted his arm and turned his head, realizing how close he and Carter were. It was dark, but there was enough ambient light to see Carter lick his lips, and the tension built and built. Riley wanted to open his mouth and tell Carter they should do it, they should run off together and forget what awaited them in Manhattan.

So much remained unspoken. What running away together would mean, what all their drunken fumbling had inched toward. What Riley's mixed-up feelings for his friend implied. Those big, scary words he'd be labeled with would alienate him from his family. Carter would never see his sister, Audrey, again and neither of them would ever get a dime of the family money.

If Riley and Carter took that step, they'd be doing it alone. Starting over nearly from scratch. *At least we'd have each other, though,* he thought wistfully.

Riley didn't think he was ready to make that leap, however, and he knew Carter wasn't. As much as they joked about it, as much they both wanted it on some level, it wasn't going to happen.

He sat up abruptly and Carter blinked, following more slowly.

"I guess we should head back to the apartment," Riley said roughly, the image of a quiet life together dissolving like smoke.

He wanted it, hell, he *ached* for it. *But when push comes to shove, I don't have the guts to do a damn thing about it*, he thought bitterly.

With a suddenness that surprised both of them, he lunged forward, pulling Carter's mouth to his. The kiss was rough at first but quickly gentled as Carter's surprise melted away. They said everything in the kiss, everything that couldn't be said aloud, everything they longed for and were giving up. They were both panting when they broke apart and Riley felt the moment everything shifted. Carter's expression changed, desire melting into worry as he glanced around to be sure no one had seen them.

Riley nodded to himself and stood, holding out his hand to his buddy. He helped hoist Carter to his feet, mourning when his hand slipped away. He had done the right thing, he knew that, but it didn't make it any easier.

They walked side by side in silence during the return to the apartment, stopping to pick up a six-pack and a pizza. From that moment on, they'd just be friends.

Chapter Five

August, 2002
New York, New York

"I have to say, Ri, when you mentioned shopping, I didn't expect to go house-hunting." Carter raised an eyebrow and his friend grinned slyly. "I thought we were going to Barneys, for Christ's sake."

"We can do that afterward, if you want." Riley opened the door to a tiny closet in between two bedroom doors and tilted his head. "I know you said something about needing a new jacket."

Carter nodded absently and Riley walked past him into the master bedroom, followed by a young realtor named Janelle Lewis. Janelle had spent the better part of that Saturday morning showing Riley and Carter condos around the West Village. She dutifully noted Riley's many desired amenities and smiled any time he reminded Carter it wasn't too late for them to share another apartment. Carter was amazed by her seemingly endless energy and patience, even as he wondered why Riley had invited him along on this outing.

The months following Carter's return to New York after six years in Cambridge had been uneventful, almost to the point of feeling anticlimactic. His life had changed, but without much intervention on Carter's part, and he'd simply sat back and ridden the waves.

He'd moved back into his suite of rooms in his parents' home and accepted a position at Hamilton Advertising. He'd thrived in the high-stress environment but had quickly become aware of the disadvantage of being the owner's son. Every employee and client knew him, and many assumed he was only there for show. That had only made Carter work harder to distinguish himself and earn the respect of his peers.

His days had fallen into easy patterns of work and social outings, broken up by regular trips to his athletic club and time spent with his family. He'd made new friends at work, reconnected with old ones and dated a number of pretty, wealthy girls without letting anything get too serious.

The only thing that had kept Carter from truly enjoying rediscovering the city around him had been Riley's absence. And though Carter had been loath to admit it, he'd struggled with feeling abandoned by his friend.

From the start of their friendship, Riley had occupied a unique place in Carter's world. He'd become Carter's friend and brother and something more, too, carving out a space in Carter's life and becoming an essential part of it. Now, Carter and Riley were in their home city, once again separated by twenty-three blocks and the Park, and seeing each other less and less. They spoke on the phone and emailed, but their busy schedules kept them from seeing each other and their circles of friends rarely mixed.

"Why don't we ask Carter?"

Janelle's voice startled Carter. He turned from the window he'd been gazing out of to face her. Janelle crossed the room toward him, tall and slim in her beautifully tailored black dress, the heels of her sandals clacking over the hardwood floor. She returned Carter's smile and as she gazed up and down the length of his body, Carter felt a thrum of attraction.

Riley trailed in behind Janelle, his hands jammed into the pockets of his fitted blue blazer. He'd reverted to more formal and stylish clothing since coming back to New York and Carter thought he looked underdressed in his own dark jeans and black Oxford shirt.

"What do you think, Car?" Riley asked.

"What do I think about what?"

The realtor glanced between them before she spoke. "We were discussing making this our last stop. I'm enjoying spending this afternoon with you gentlemen, but it seems unlikely Riley will make a decision today."

"That's because none of these places are right." Riley's eyebrows rose after Janelle simply nodded.

"I didn't expect you to find something on your first day out," she said. "Each buyer is different and, with your wish list, it will take a bit longer to find something you can live with."

"And live in," Carter murmured and Riley rolled his eyes.

Janelle nodded again. "Exactly. We could go on and see the three remaining units on my list, but I think it makes sense for me to come up with an all-new list." She tapped the notebook she'd been carrying all afternoon. "I have a better idea of what you want now and I know I can find something that will hit closer to the mark."

Riley looked at her askance. "I thought you realtors were the never-give-up types," he said dryly. "Don't you just keep showing me places until I either collapse from exhaustion or agree to live in a refrigerator box under a bridge?"

Janelle blinked at Riley for a moment before meeting Carter's gaze. "Is he always this dramatic?"

"Yes," Carter replied, "especially when he's tired and hungry. He's a lot better than he used to be when we were in school, though."

Riley raised a hand over his head, glaring when Carter and Janelle faced him. "I'm right here, you know—"

"Definitely overdue for something to eat," Carter added.

"I'm not a toddler, Carter," Riley grumbled, though his words lacked heat.

"No, you're not, but Janelle's got a point. You can keep going—even though a lot of these places are starting to look the same—or call it quits and try again another day."

"I can show you some more tomorrow if you're not busy,"

Janelle chimed in without missing a beat. "I can also meet you during the week, if that works for you."

Riley's expression turned doubtful. "Won't some of these places be gone by then?"

"That's a possibility," she admitted. "Sales tend to slow down a bit during the summer months, though, because the city empties out on the weekends. There will still be plenty of properties, I can assure you."

Riley nodded. "I wish I could say I'm free tomorrow, but I have a family obligation outside the city."

"No problem." Janelle smiled. "If something comes up that I am certain you will love, I'll go myself, take photos and text them to you."

Carter grinned as the worried crease in his friend's forehead smoothed out.

"I knew I liked you," Riley told Janelle before his phone chimed and he turned away to answer.

Carter sensed the realtor's attention on him once Riley stepped out of the room.

"What about you, Carter?" she asked, her smooth voice drawing his attention. "You're not in the market for a new home, too, are you? Or are you planning to move in with Riley after all? Once he finds the right place, of course."

Carter's brows drew together. "I spent the better part of the last six years living with Riley—I think it's safe to say neither of us is eager for us to be roommates again."

Carter's easy smile hid the lie beneath his words. He'd gladly share a space with Riley again, if he thought their families would be supportive.

Janelle hummed. "I could take you on as a client, too, if you like."

Carter stood still, considering Janelle's words. His skin warmed under her frank gaze before he nodded once. "That's an interesting proposal."

"I'm extremely good at my job," she told him with a slow step forward. "And something tells me it wouldn't be difficult to find you the right place. I don't think you're a

West Village kind of guy, though."

"No?"

Janelle shook her head, her eyes narrowed. "You strike me as more of an East Side man and a little bit farther uptown. Murray Hill, maybe? No, wait—Gramercy," she said, her voice certain.

Carter laughed softly, stepping forward until only half a foot separated them. "I dated a girl in high school who lived on Irving Place. I've always liked that neighborhood."

"Send me a list of amenities." Janelle handed Carter her card, her gaze lingering on his lips. "I'll see what kind of magic I can work with the databases when I get back to the office. And unless you also have a family obligation, I'd be happy to show you some places tomorrow afternoon."

"As a matter of fact, I'm free." Carter pulled his wallet from his back pocket to tuck Janelle's card into the billfold. He plucked out a card of his own to present to her with a flourish as Riley stepped back into the room, then slid his wallet back into his pocket with a smile. "I'll look forward to hearing from you, then."

Riley said nothing about the exchange after they'd bid the realtor goodbye. He and Carter made their way to a tiny wine bar a few blocks east where they ordered a bottle of white merlot and plates of antipasti, talking about work and how they'd been spending their time. The main course was on the table before they circled back to the condos and Riley finally cracked.

"Are you going to tell me what you've got going on with my realtor, or am I wining and dining the wrong person?" Riley asked, eyeing Carter over the rim of his wineglass.

Carter stilled, his fork frozen halfway between the plate and his mouth. After a long moment, he blinked and ate the bite of shrimp and risotto, chewing while his brain worked to formulate a response. "Is that what you're doing with me tonight, Ri?" he asked once he'd swallowed. "Wooing me? Because the last time I checked, you and I are not dating."

The corner of Riley's mouth quirked up in a smile, but

Carter thought his friend looked uneasy.

Riley put his glass down on the table, running his fingers over the foot for a moment before he spoke. "You're right— we're not. Poor choice of words on my part, I guess. Doesn't mean you can't answer the question, though."

Carter dipped his head in assent and took another bite of his food. Riley fidgeted in the silence and Carter stifled a chuckle after his friend finally sighed in irritation.

"What's up with you and Janelle?"

"Real estate," Carter replied, his tone light, laying down his fork and dabbing his lips with his napkin. "Real estate is what's up with Janelle and me. She's going to show me some condos tomorrow."

Riley's mouth fell open slightly as Carter's words registered. His face lit up with a grin. "Seriously? Why didn't you tell me before today?" he demanded, reaching for the bottle of wine.

"I didn't know myself until Janelle asked me about my plans." Carter murmured his thanks after Riley topped off his glass. "I've got to move out of my folks' place at some point, and Janelle seems to know what she's doing. I'll check out the listings she brings me and we'll see what happens."

"Are we going to be neighbors?" Riley speared a meatball with his fork, pointing it at Carter in his excitement. "Hell, maybe we should just find a bigger place and go back to sharing. It's not as if we don't know we could make it work, Car."

For a moment, Carter allowed himself to imagine living with Riley again, in one of the luxurious spaces they'd seen that day instead of a cramped dorm suite or apartment. Starting and ending their days together, sharing meals and chores and time off. Sharing girls again, perhaps. Sharing a bed. Carter swallowed hard, longing curling in his belly before he could stop it.

In the next breath, a chill broke over him. His parents had seemed…relieved when Carter had told them he'd be moving home for a while. Neither had asked him about Riley's plans, or said anything specific, but something in Carter's gut had told him they wanted Carter living apart from Riley.

Carter met his friend's bright gaze and heaviness settled over him. "I'm not sure that's such a good idea," he said quietly, pressing his lips together when Riley's grin faltered.

"Why the hell not? We were living together six months ago—what's the difference if we move back in together now?"

"It's not that I don't want to," Carter hastened to assure him. "I loved living with you and with Dan, too, before he moved to Chicago."

Riley's brow furrowed and he visibly deflated. "So what's the problem?" he said around his mouthful of meatball.

"No problem, Ri. I just figure we're finally growing up, that's all. We both know we can't live together forever."

"Well, I didn't mean forever."

"Until when then?" Carter's smile was tinged with melancholy. "Until we finally get tired of each other? Or until we find some nice girls to marry and have kids with?"

Riley's mouth opened and closed and his cheeks flushed. "Christ, I'm not ready to get married," he said at last. "I'm not even seeing anyone right now."

"You mean you're not screwing anyone on the regular," Carter scoffed, his tone rougher than he meant it to be, but his eyebrows still rose at Riley's disgruntled appearance. "Oh, come on, man, you can't possibly be offended. You haven't seen any girl for more than a few months since the redhead from Tufts during our junior year."

"Her name was Kim," Riley muttered, shoving his food around on his plate with his fork. "Is that really what you want to do?" he asked, the abrupt topic change taking Carter by surprise.

"What do you mean?"

"I mean meet a nice girl and settle down and have kids, take over the family business. Are those things you want,

Car?"

"Well…sure. Are you saying you don't?" Carter watched the way Riley's lips thinned, and understood his friend was upset. "Ri." He waited several long moments until Riley met his gaze. "What's going on?"

A solid minute passed while Riley stared at him, his face strangely blank. When Riley did speak, a quiet conviction filled his voice. "I know we talked about this before we moved back to New York, but do you ever think our parents' plans aren't right for the people we've become?"

Carter chewed the inside of his lip, his stomach clenching with tension. "No, I don't. Not since moving back to New York."

Riley's eyebrows shot up. "Really? So the conversation we had in Cambridge about wanting something different—none of that matters to you now? Doesn't matter that we work a sick number of hours every week? That I never get to go to the opera anymore, or that you've stopped rowing?"

"Sure, all of those things matter," Carter argued, "and, sure, I'm still surprised by the way things have turned out. But work is surprisingly okay, even with the crazy pace, and I do have a social life. I've been reconnecting with people I used to hang out with and getting to know New York again. It's not like the downtime I had at school, but I never expected it to be. I assumed things were good for you, too?"

"Yeah, yeah, work is great. It was always going to be great, though, right? Because, let's face it, I'm the son and heir to the family fortune, whether I want it or not." Riley waved impatiently as Carter opened his mouth to speak, and tossed his fork down onto his dinner plate. "How well I do at the firm is irrelevant, Carter."

Carter's confusion became apprehension. "So what's going on? Is everything okay?"

"I'm fine," Riley replied hoarsely, looking so miserable that Carter's heart ached. Without thinking, he reached across the little table and laid a hand on Riley's forearm.

His friend's eyes flashed as they met Carter's.

"You're kind of scaring me here, Ri. It's been a while since you showed me your drama-llama face."

Riley choked out a laugh and lifted his hand to cover Carter's. "I'm sorry."

"You don't have to apologize," Carter insisted. He squeezed his friend's arm with gentle pressure and watched the stiff set of Riley's shoulders soften. "I asked you earlier, but you still haven't answered me. What's going on with you?"

"I wish I knew how to answer that question." Riley lips twisted. "Maybe I'm having a quarter-life crisis. Maybe I regret agreeing to work with my father when neither of us can stand to be around the other." He paused, his hand still resting on top of Carter's. "Maybe I miss Cambridge and school... Hell, even you."

"Gee, thanks." Carter sat back in his seat and withdrew his hand to reach for his wineglass. "I miss you, too."

Riley smiled. "You know what I mean. It's been a little weird coming back here and assuming what amounts to a new identity, even though it's really an old identity. It hasn't been all bad, but my life changed overnight. I don't know about you, but I'm still getting used to it."

"I'm definitely still figuring things out." Carter swirled his wine around in the glass, watching the light play on the pink liquid. "I'm sorry you haven't been going to the opera, though. I am still rowing," he admitted, "just not competitively."

"Why?" Riley asked, his brow creasing with confusion. "You love the competition. That's why you kept rowing with that Cambridge club after undergrad. Is it because of work? Or is it your parents?"

Carter dropped his gaze to the table at Riley's scowl. "My parents have no problem with my rowing. It's the job. I don't have time to train like that anymore. I can still work out with a master's team, though, and maybe even compete at a lower level when it fits into my schedule."

"Don't you miss it?"

"Sure, but it's not the worst thing in the world." Carter shrugged. "There are other things I miss more. Like you, you ass. I meant it when I told you that earlier."

"So spend more time with me," Riley encouraged. "Move in to my new place." This time Riley's grin was wry and Carter could see his friend had prepared himself for a refusal.

"I still think it would be best if we had our own places," Carter replied gently. "I don't want to have to explain to my parents why their twenty-four-year-old son can win multi-million-dollar ad campaigns but can't manage to live on his own."

Riley stiffened and Carter imagined he was thinking about his own parents' reaction to the idea.

"I liked what you said earlier about being neighbors, though," he continued. "Janelle wants to show me some places in Gramercy Park." He dipped his head as Riley hummed in appreciation.

"Does she now? And what will you be showing Janelle in return?"

"Nothing at all," Carter assured him with a grin. "Or at least nothing for now. She seems interested and I must say she has a glorious ass, but I'm not doing anything until I've signed a purchase and sale. Not to be crude, but I don't want to fuck up my house hunting by fucking my house hunter, if you get my meaning."

Riley cocked an eyebrow and raised his glass. "And what about me? Janelle is my house hunter, too, you know."

"Then you'd better stop being such a picky pain in the ass and buy something," Carter retorted. He grinned when Riley gave him the finger. "All you need to do is focus on finding a place. Once you do, you'll see me often enough to finally be sick of me."

"Hmm, I doubt that. Living with you for so long left me with an exceptionally high tolerance for Hamilton bullshit." Riley smiled and Carter laughed outright. "Though I'm sure you'll give it your best shot."

Carter nodded and held up his glass for Riley to tap with his own. "Would you really expect anything less of me?"

* * * *

As Janelle predicted, it didn't take Carter long to find a place he desired for himself. Something about the townhouses around Gramercy Park spoke to him and everything he wanted and more was right there in a renovated building on East 19th Street. The duplex was large, with two floors and four bedrooms, and beautiful without feeling sterile. A dining solarium filled most of the lower level and looked out onto a large, terraced garden shaded by old trees and other buildings. Carter kissed Janelle for the first time in that garden and planned to do far more with her in the solarium and other rooms in the house after the closing.

After signing the purchase and sale, Carter messaged Riley to tell his friend of his plans to pursue Janelle. He was in a cab and on his way to his parents' home when Riley called, letting loose a tirade of swearing after Carter had picked up.

"I hate you so much," Riley finally grumbled after he'd run out of steam. "If Janelle ends up dumping me over some lovers' spat with you, I will kick your ass, Carter."

Carter snorted in response. "Hey, it's your fault you're still homeless."

"I'm trying to find the right place!"

"Yeah, but you've already seen every open condo in the West Village. You're going to have to branch outside the neighborhood if you don't stop dragging your ass."

"I am not dragging my ass, thank you very much," Riley insisted. "I'm just…particular."

"Try impossible."

"Try going to hell. Anyway, meet me for drinks. I want to see what kind of money pit you're saddling yourself with, so bring photos."

"Sorry, I can't tonight." Carter sighed with sincere disappointment—dinner and drinks with Riley would have been the perfect ending to the day. "I'm meeting up with my parents so I can tell them about the condo."

"Such a mama's boy."

There was a waspish undertone to Riley's teasing that Carter recognized and ignored. Riley sounded like that nearly every time he spoke about Carter's relationship with his family.

"Meet me tomorrow," Carter urged. "I'll beg the keys off Janelle and show you around the place."

Riley made a doubtful noise. "I'm not sure I can get away tomorrow, Car. That's why I asked you to meet me tonight—"

"It's my turn to buy," Carter cut him off quickly, "and I'm not taking no for an answer. Meet me at the bar in the Gramercy Park Hotel by seven tomorrow night or I'm coming to your office with a six-pack of beer and a bucket of chicken."

Riley burst out laughing. "Fine, fine, I'll see you tomorrow. Give my best to the family."

The quiet warmth that mellowed Riley's voice seemed to filter straight through Carter's phone to fill his chest.

* * * *

"Oh, Carter," Eleanor Hamilton murmured, scrolling on Carter's phone through photos of the townhouse. "It's lovely. Perfect for you, sweetheart. And large enough to live in when you're no longer single, too."

Carter managed not to roll his eyes. "Try not to get ahead of yourself, Mom—I haven't signed the closing papers yet."

Eleanor handed Carter his phone and adjusted the soft green cardigan that lay over her shoulders. "When it comes to you and your sister, it's my job to get ahead of myself. Who else would remind the two of you about all of the important things you're always too busy to attend to?"

"Who indeed?" Audrey put in, winking slyly at her mother. "God forbid your adult children live their own lives, Mother."

"You're more than welcome to live as you please and certainly capable of doing so from what I've seen. However, I want to make sure you don't lose sight of certain things." Eleanor leveled a look at Carter. "Like marriage. And family. I'm not getting any younger you know, sweetheart."

"Oh, God, Mom." Carter dropped his head with a groan. "I promise, when I meet someone who feels…right, I will bring her to dinner. Or lunch. Hell, I'll bring her over for a midnight snack, if it's that time of day." He grinned and his mother laughed, then reached up to loosen his shirt collar. "Really, Mom, don't worry about it. I meet plenty of women."

"You just need to find the right woman," Audrey put in. Carter felt a pulse of dread when his sister's eyes lit up. "Speaking of which—"

"No," he said hastily. "Aud, I am not going to let you set me up with anyone."

"Why on earth not?" Audrey demanded, her slim frame practically vibrating underneath an oversized black tunic. "I know someone, Carter. She's a friend of a friend who I'm almost sure you'd hit it off with." His sister appealed to their mother. "I'm thinking of Kate Easton, Mom."

His mother's face brightened. "What an interesting match. I think you may be on to something, Audrey. Now we need to get them to agree to see each other."

Carter put his chin in his hand and slid a glance to the head of the table, where his father and brother-in-law were sitting, observing everything and eating slices of cheesecake. Brad smiled at his son, the laugh lines around his eyes deepening, while Max's grin was sympathetic.

"The easiest thing to do is submit, son," Brad said, his voice low and amused.

Max nodded, swiping at a smear of cheese on his shirtsleeve. "You know they'll keep at it until they get their way."

Carter scrubbed his face with his hands before pulling a dessert plate toward himself. "Since when are my dating habits a democratic process?"

"Since you're almost twenty-five and not dating," Brad replied.

"I am so dating, Dad, holy Jesus."

"Yes, well, that may be, but no one your mother and I have ever met." He met Carter's gaze across the table. "Honestly, what's the big deal? Go out, meet your sister's friend, have a little dinner, maybe some drinks. That'll make your mother happy."

"And if I don't like this Kate Easton person?"

"Then you thank each other for a nice night and you never see her again," Max offered. "Seems simple enough to me."

Carter groaned and forked up some cheesecake. "Why is this such a big deal?"

"We want to see you happy, sweetheart," his mother chimed in again.

"I am happy," he mumbled around a mouthful.

"And while I believe that, I think you'd be happier with someone to share your life with," she assured. "Someone other than Riley, I mean."

Carter frowned, laying down his fork while the others exchanged glances. "What's that supposed to mean?"

Eleanor sighed. "Nothing. You know how much I like Riley and your father and I are glad he is such a good friend to you."

"We were glad to hear the two of you are finally beginning to settle down, too," Brad continued with a wry smile. "After you told us about Riley's house hunting, your mother and I wondered if you two weren't planning to live together again."

"Riley offered to let me move into his place, as a matter of fact," Carter admitted, then watched his parents exchange another glance. "Honestly, it sounded like a good idea, but I think it makes more sense for each of us to have our places."

"That's a good decision, son," Brad replied, relief plain in his voice. "For appearance's sake, at the very least."

"Appearance's sake?" Carter looked from his father to his mother, then to his sister and Max, both of whom surprised him by glowering at his parents. "Do you know what they're talking about?" he asked Audrey.

"In a roundabout way, they're talking about Jamie Newhouse," she replied, her expression grim. "He was in my year at school, but you may remember him."

Carter nodded slowly, remembering glimpses of the slim young man who had been part of his sister's crowd. Jamie had been a musician and usually wore a bright smile at odds with his Goth clothes and style.

"I do remember him. I don't understand what Jamie Newhouse has to do with me or Riley, though."

"Jamie came out as a gay man a couple of weeks ago," Audrey explained. "Anyone who knows him even slightly is aware Jamie is gay. He never went out of his way to hide that part of himself."

"Is…? Jamie being gay is a problem?" Carter asked, still nonplussed.

"The Newhouses are devastated," Eleanor cut in. She pursed her lips as Audrey shook her head. "Audrey, I realize that to you and your friends being a homosexual isn't something scandalous, but Jamie's decision will have long-lasting implications for the family."

"Why?" Carter asked while Audrey made a disgusted noise. "Some of my friends in high school were gay, Mom, and so were some of my friends at Harvard. No one cares."

"I can assure you people do care, son, and very much at that," Brad replied, his voice neutral. "It's one thing to be gay, but it is another thing entirely to be in Jamie's position and choose that lifestyle."

Audrey rapped her knuckles on the table, her gaze keen. "Dad, are you listening to yourself? Jamie didn't choose a lifestyle — he was born into one."

Brad's jaw tightened, though his voice remained pleasant. "You can choose to believe that, Audrey, but I do not share that opinion. And regardless of how or when Jamie formed his preferences, the fact is he chose to reveal them publicly, against the wishes of his parents. His decision has caused a great deal of gossip to be aimed at the Newhouse family, something his father can ill afford in his position."

Carter stifled a groan as the penny finally dropped. Jamie's father was the headmaster of a prestigious prep school. Established by the family in 1920, Newhouse Day School catered to some of the wealthiest families in the city. The last thing Stanton Newhouse wanted for himself or his family was gossip, particularly if the talk happened to be salacious.

"I know you feel your mother and I are being too judgmental—"

Audrey was quick to interrupt. "It's not just you two, Dad. It's your friends and Jamie's parents. They're not speaking to him, you know. Rumors are going around that he's going to be disinherited, for crying out loud and I'm sorry, but that's all kinds of fucked up."

Brad's gaze hardened. "Jamie has always been well aware of the possible consequences of his actions. Simply painting Stan and Lily as villains in this story is unfair. Like all Newhouses, they are protective of their school and family. Jamie betrayed their trust."

Carter watched his family argue, taking in the conviction in his parents' faces and Audrey's and Max's outrage. He stared at the remains of his dessert and coffee and the sounds of the debate faded. He wasn't terribly surprised by his parents' reaction to Jamie Newhouse's revelation. Brad and Eleanor held many liberal views, but Carter had long known they disapproved of anything smacking of deviant behavior. The conversation left him strangely winded, though, as if he'd been struggling physically against a burden.

Carter's blood ran cold as he thought of Riley and the

moments they'd shared over the years and how the lines of their friendship had blurred and changed. What would Brad and Eleanor think if they knew Carter had shared jerk-off sessions with his best friend? That Carter and Riley liked to pick up a girl and share her and that Carter always came hardest with Riley touching and kissing him? What would they make of that night when Carter and Riley had sat on the riverbank, talking about running away together? Or if they knew that Carter had nearly broken down and cried when the time had come to return to New York?

A lump rose in Carter's throat. Jamie Newhouse had hurt his parents, endangered his father's career and was on the verge of being disowned, all because the poor bastard wanted to be happy and himself. The idea of Carter's own family tearing itself apart over him — things Carter did or said — seemed unbearable.

"What's got you thinking so hard, Carter?" Eleanor asked then, startling him out of his reverie. She was frowning slightly when he met her gaze. "You look like the weight of the world is on your shoulders, sweetheart."

"Nothing much," Carter replied. "Mostly that this Kate Easton you were talking about sounds interesting." He sighed and rubbed the back of his neck with one hand. "Is there a photo? Or can I not ask that because you know her, Aud, and I should trust you?"

The warm light in his mother's eye soothed some of the ache in Carter's chest. He turned to his father while Eleanor and Audrey searched Audrey's phone for a snapshot. When Brad smiled, Carter's smile was nearly genuine.

Chapter Six

October, 2003
New York, New York

"And I can't imagine a woman more perfect for Carter than Kate. So, please, raise your glasses to the happy couple!" Riley lifted his glass of gin and tonic and held it out toward them. He watched Carter slide his hand under Kate's hair and pull her in for a kiss. Carter grinned down at her when he drew back and Riley felt a pang when he recognized the smile. That was the smile Carter had always had for Riley.

Riley forced a happy expression onto his own face and swallowed a large sip of his drink before taking a seat again. He stared down at the ice cubes clinking in his glass for a moment, then drained it. He was desperate for anything to numb him right then. Carter was getting married the following day and Riley had no idea how he was going to make it through the next twenty-four hours.

It had been agony when Carter had met Kate Easton the year before. Riley had seen that his friend loved the intelligent, beautiful blonde. Hell, Riley was fond of her, too. He knew she was good for Carter, but that hadn't made it fun watching their romance blossom, or stopped the sick feeling he'd had when Carter had told him he'd proposed and had asked Riley to be his best man. Of course he'd said yes—how could he not? But that hadn't made it any easier.

The brush of a hand on his shoulder made him look at his date. Alex let out a quiet sigh of frustration. "Are you okay, Riley? I've been trying to get your attention and it's like you're in another world. "

He did his best to smile reassuringly and nodded. "Yeah, just tired for some reason," he fibbed. "Sorry."

Carter smiled across the table at him. "I think he's still recovering from the bachelor party."

Carter's groomsmen laughed uproariously. The bachelor party had taken place the previous weekend and had involved plenty of booze, gambling and scantily clad women.

Carter had thoroughly enjoyed himself, which was what had mattered to Riley. It had taken all of them a few days to recover, though. They weren't nineteen and partying every weekend anymore.

Dan grinned at both Riley and Carter. "I guess we're all out of practice. It has been a few years since I partied with these boys." He turned to Kate. "You don't even want to know what they were like in those days."

Kate laughed and took a sip of her wine. "You're right, I don't. Whatever they did in their past can stay there. You guys had him for years and I shudder to think of what you all got up to. Just remember, after tomorrow, he's mine."

The rest of the table laughed at Kate's comment and Riley tried not to wince. She had been joking, but it was true. After tomorrow, Carter would be hers alone and Riley felt like she'd buried a knife in his chest and twisted.

"Somehow, I don't think that's it," Alex said, her tone shrewd.

Riley reluctantly faced his date again. Alexandra Macomber was someone his parents had set him up with and they'd gone out a handful of times. Her mother was friends with his—or something like that. He could never remember. His mother had set him up with so many women. Riley studied Alex for a moment. She was beautiful. With perfect, pale skin, red hair and huge blue eyes, she was certainly his type. Or the type he'd always gone for in the past, anyway. He was starting to suspect his type was now tall, with brown hair and hazel eyes. He pushed away the thought and focused on her.

Right now, she stared at him, eyes narrowed as if she was trying to see through him to figure out what was going on. A cold shiver ran down his spine at the thought of her knowing exactly how he felt about Carter. That could never happen.

"It's just strange," he said finally. "My friends are all starting to settle down and get married. It's taking me some time to adjust."

That was partially true and he figured a half-truth would be more plausible than a lie. He was suddenly grateful for the waiter who appeared at his elbow with a fresh drink and he forced himself to sip it slowly. He took a deep breath and met Alex's gaze, willing himself to remain calm and detached.

Alex seemed satisfied with his response and leaned in, sliding her fingers through the hair at the nape of his neck, and spoke into his ear. "If you come home with me, I promise I'll take your mind off it."

They'd had sex a few times. It hadn't been bad — certainly nothing like the sex he'd had when Carter was there — but not awful by any means. He could spend a few mindless hours with her. He opened his mouth to answer but was interrupted.

"Hey, Ri," Carter called out. Alex dropped her arm from Riley's shoulder when he sat up straight. "Dan and the guys want to go out after dinner, grab a few drinks. That okay?"

"Ask your wife-to-be, not me," he said, his tone joking, but inside, he felt anything but humorous. "I'm not your keeper anymore." He winced internally. Fuck, he was losing it. He had to find a way to pull himself together or he'd never make it through the rest of the night, much less the wedding tomorrow.

Carter laughed. "I mean, are you coming with us?"

"Sure, I'm in," Riley agreed. "Sorry, Alex." He tried to appear disappointed. Truthfully, a few drinks with Carter was still better than sex with her. In a way, he felt relieved he wasn't going home with Alex. He swallowed hard. If that didn't tell him something about his feelings about his friend, he didn't know what did.

Alex ran manicured fingers along Riley's thigh and leaned in. "Make it up to me tomorrow night after the wedding."

He agreed half-heartedly and the rest of the dinner passed quickly enough while he drank steadily and put on a happy face. Out on the street in front of the restaurant, he said goodbye to Alex with a brief kiss, helping her into the waiting car. She hated cabs with a passion. Alex was like too many of the women in his social circle, self-absorbed, without a real purpose in life. There were exceptions—Carter's mother was one and so was Kate. They both volunteered and did a great deal of fundraising for the causes they believed in. Alex was more the-lady-who-lunches type. It didn't make her a terrible person, but it didn't exactly give them much to talk about.

"Sorry we cock-blocked you," Dan joked, slapping Riley on the shoulder.

"I'll live," he said with a wry smile.

"Still," Dan joked. "I wouldn't pass up a woman like her if I had the chance."

Dan's wife, Mel, tapped him playfully on the shoulder. "You'd better."

He grinned at her, hooking an arm around her shoulder and kissing the top of her head. "You know I'd never go for her when I have you."

"Like you could get her," she teased. "You're not a pretty boy like Riley here."

Dan made a face at his wife, but Riley saw the love he had for her. Riley swallowed hard, desperately wishing he could muster up similar feelings for Alex—for any woman. But every time he tried, he thought of Carter instead. Every thought, every desire always led back to his best friend. And they would get him nowhere.

"Well, guys, let's head out," he said cheerfully, pushing aside his melancholy mood. Time to keep the mask firmly in place and play the part of the happy best man. Carter deserved it.

The friends said goodbye to their wives and girlfriends and Riley tried not to stare when Carter slowly, lingeringly kissed his fiancée goodbye.

They headed out to the Old Town Bar—an old-school tavern the former suitemates loved. Riley tried to focus on the friends around him, the people celebrating this huge step in Carter's life, but it seemed as though there was a glass wall surrounding him. He could see and hear them laughing, but it was all muted and distant. He clinked glasses with Carter's cousin, Ryan, and laughed at one of Dan's jokes, but all he could focus on was Carter's thigh pressed against his and the way he kept slinging an arm on the upholstered booth behind Riley. His forearm continually brushed Riley's shoulder and the back of his neck, driving him crazy.

He drank steadily, hoping it would help him block out Carter's touch, but it only made it worse. Carter was even more drunk than Riley, who winced when he glanced at the gleaming watch on his wrist—a gift from Carter for his birthday the previous year. Shit, he had to get Carter home if he was going to wake up in time for his wedding.

He reached out to get Carter's attention and when his hand landed on Carter's firm thigh, he tried not to notice the way the muscles tensed under his touch. "C'mon, guys. I think it's time I get the groom home or Kate will kill us both tomorrow."

The men groaned in disappointment but didn't protest too much. Carter was more drunk than Riley had realized and he had to hoist him out of the booth and prop him up. Getting him out onto the street was a challenge, but Dan helped deposit Carter in a cab. Riley went to climb in beside Carter, but Dan stopped him.

"You okay, man?"

"Yeah, I've got this. I'll take Carter to my place and keep an eye on him. I'll get him to the church in the morning."

Dan frowned. "That's not what I meant."

Riley raked a hand through his hair and gave Dan a puzzled glance. "What the hell *are* you talking about then?"

"C'mon, I know this is hard on you."

Dan's voice was gentle, but there was something in the tone of his voice that made Riley pause. His head swam from the drinks and he struggled to understand what Dan was implying. His stomach lurched sickeningly when he figured it out. Shit, could Dan tell what was going on? If there was anyone who knew him and Carter well enough to put the pieces together, it was Dan. For a moment, he was tempted to open up, to say something to Dan and let it all come pouring out.

Carter muttered something in the back seat of the car and Riley shook his head. No, Carter would hate Dan knowing and what was telling him going to accomplish anyway?

"I have no idea what you mean," Riley said, his tone clipped and terse.

Dan gave him a long look, then nodded once. "Right. Well, best of luck getting that one to be human in the morning. Let me know if you need any help."

Riley relaxed, glad Dan wasn't going to push. "Thanks. I will."

The cab ride was agonizing. Carter was so drunk he wasn't able to remain upright and slumped against Riley. He finally gave up on pushing Carter against the cab door and let him drape himself on Riley's shoulder. He shuddered at the soft brush of his friend's hair against his cheek and the way Carter's hand landed heavily on his thigh. He reminded himself over and over that Carter was getting married the next day, that whatever this feeling was that he had for his friend, it was impossible, and the best choice for both him and Carter was to ignore it.

As Riley navigated Carter up to his condo, he wondered why Carter had drunk so heavily that night. The bachelor party the previous weekend was supposed to have been the final hurrah to Carter's single days — the heavy drinking was no surprise then. But why tonight?

Riley had to prop Carter against the wall and pin him in place with his own body as he fumbled for the keys. Carter slumped against him, his breath hot on Riley's neck, his long, firm body pressed to Riley's.

"Hang in there," Riley muttered as much to himself as to Carter, his fingers brushing along his own half-hard length when he dug in his pockets for the keys. Jesus, just being near Carter was enough to turn him on. He groaned quietly as he shifted his hips and inadvertently pressed tighter against Carter. Riley hastily shoved the key into the lock and hoisted his friend up to drag him into the apartment. Rather than pour his drunk friend into the guest bed, he took him to his own.

"'m I doin' the right thing?" Carter slurred, while Riley lowered him onto the bed. Riley froze with Carter's arm locked around his neck and their faces inches apart. *God, how many times have we been in this position?* Riley wondered. He reached up, unwound his friend's arm and sat back, but left his hand pressed against the front of Carter's shirt for a moment, enjoying the heat of his body underneath.

"What do you mean?" he asked hoarsely.

He started to pull away, but Carter reached up and covered Riley's hand with his own, his long fingers holding it in place.

"Mar-marrying Kate," Carter said thickly, hazel eyes dazed and glassy. They appeared especially dark right then, more brown than their usual greenish hue. Riley breathed shallowly, the words heavy on his tongue. He wanted so badly to tell him no, make him doubt what he was doing. The sight of Carter sprawled on his bed and the feel of their clasped hands made a spot in Riley's chest ache. All night he'd been fighting his feelings for Carter, struggling to be happy for his friend, trying not to let anyone see his secret.

Here in private, Carter was giving him the chance to speak up. Perhaps Carter was ambivalent on some level about marrying Kate. He knew Carter loved her, but maybe some part of him was as conflicted as Riley. Riley could feel the words on his tongue and knew his friend well enough to suspect that if Riley told him he shouldn't marry Kate, he wouldn't go through with it the following day. But wasn't that delaying the inevitable? Because Carter *would* marry. Eventually he'd give in to the pressure of his family's expectations and marry someone.

Why not Kate? His toast to the couple at the rehearsal dinner earlier had been true. There was no woman in the world better for Carter than Kate. As much as Riley wanted to return to the times when they'd been in college — when they'd been friends who lived together and shared a woman between them — they could never go back. The vague, nebulous want inside Riley never seemed to coalesce into something concrete. He wanted Carter, but what did that mean? And what did he have to offer him?

Riley stared at his friend, watching Carter's unfocused, almost hopeful gaze. Riley felt the beat of Carter's heart through the soft, polished cotton shirt under his palm and he ached, wanting to tell his friend to call off the wedding.

But the answer to his earlier question was *nothing*. Riley had nothing to offer Carter. He couldn't give him the life and family he wanted, couldn't give Carter the chance to make his family proud. Hell, Riley didn't even know what he wanted or if he could ever give Carter what he deserved. With his fucked-up family, maybe he wasn't even capable of caring about Carter like Kate would.

Carter would be happier married to Kate and Riley knew it was the right choice for his friend. For both of them. With Carter married, Riley could make his parents happy by finally settling down with a woman. He could stop wasting his life wishing for something that would never happen.

"Yeah, buddy, it's the right thing," he lied, feeling the weight of the words close over him, like the thud of a door slamming shut. He could never take them back.

Carter nodded once and Riley watched his eyes grow heavy, his blinks becoming slow and lazy. He parted his lips, making his tongue perform an unhurried sweep across them.

"Let me get you some water or you're going to feel like shit at the altar tomorrow," Riley said roughly. That was it then. He knew he'd made the right choice, but why did it feel so wrong?

Carter was asleep by the time Riley came back with a couple of bottles of water and painkillers. Riley woke him long enough to drink some water and take a couple of pills, then helped him out of his shoes and tucked him under the covers. He sat by Carter's side for a long time, watching him sleep, trying to will away the ache in his chest. After a while, he lay down beside him, listening to the sound of Carter's deep, even breaths.

But the ache was still there in the morning while he forced water, pills and enough coffee to caffeinate a herd of elephants into Carter. It was there when he straightened his friend's bow tie, when he held his tongue at the minister asking if anyone objected, and when he handed Carter the wedding band to slip onto Kate's slender finger. It was there when Alex caught the bouquet and Riley obligingly caught the garter. His chest ached when he took her to bed that night, trying not to imagine his best friend making love to his new bride.

He slipped out of Alex's bed afterward, feeling worse than when he'd crawled into it. She didn't protest when he dressed, merely kissed him goodbye and told him to call. He agreed that he would, his mind already returning to thoughts of Carter. He felt numb and had since the previous night, but his thoughts wouldn't stop whirling.

Riley snagged a cab, planning to go home to his apartment, but as it pulled up in front of his building, he mentally switched gears. He leaned forward, a sudden impulsive urge popping into his head. "Wait, I changed my mind. Take me to Chelsea."

"I need an address," the cabbie huffed.

"Uh, give me a moment." He hastily dug his phone out of

his pocket and did a quick search. He rattled off a location and the cabbie pulled away from the curb.

"It's a gay bar," he said inanely.

The cabbie nodded, completely uninterested. What did he care where Riley went? As long as the man got paid, he didn't give a damn where he took his customers. Riley fidgeted on the ride there and realized he'd been tracing patterns on his thigh like he always did when he was anxious. He closed his hand into a fist, trying to push away the nervous discomfort rising in him. He tugged at his bow tie, managing to loosen it, then slip it into the pocket of his tux while unbuttoning the top two buttons of his shirt.

The bar Riley ended up at was upscale and it had gotten good reviews online, although why that mattered to him, he had no idea. *What am I even doing here?* he wondered. Riley wet his lips and pushed the door open, his palms growing sweaty. Apprehension furled in him as he headed directly for the bar. The place didn't seem any different from the bar he'd gone to after the rehearsal dinner, except for the gender of the patrons.

"Gin and tonic, please," he told the bartender hoarsely.

He gave Riley a slow once-over, then winked. "Sure thing," he said, subjecting Riley to one last, long look before he turned away.

Riley stared at the bartender, trying to decide if he was attractive or not. He wasn't unattractive by any means, tall and broad, with sun-streaked blond hair and brown eyes. Riley watched him move to mix the drink, noticing the play of muscles in his arms and shoulders under the black shirt he wore. The bartender winked again when he caught Riley staring at him. Riley flushed and glanced away, leaning his elbows on the bar.

"Sit down, stay a while," he teased. "We don't bite."

Riley took a large gulp of his drink and met the bartender's gaze. "Isn't your line supposed to be, 'I don't bite. Unless you ask nicely'?"

The bartender smirked and leaned against the back

counter, crossing his arms. "Well, I'd love to think you're offering, but it's pretty clear you're too skittish."

Riley laughed hollowly and sat, taking another long swallow of his well-made drink. "I'm that obvious, huh?"

The bartender shrugged. "I've seen enough guys come in here to tell who's comfortable and who isn't. You look like you might jump out of your own skin if someone said something to spook you."

Riley dragged a hand through his hair. "Yeah, well, you're not wrong."

"So, what brought you in here tonight?"

"I don't really know," Riley admitted. "I'm just…"

"Confused? Questioning things?"

Riley nodded and fidgeted with his drink. "Yeah."

The bartender gave him a sympathetic smile and leaned in. "Plenty of us have been there."

"I get so hung up on how people's opinions of me would change depending on what I label myself as."

"You don't have to label yourself as anything," the bartender said with a shrug. "I'm guessing you've always considered yourself straight but there's a guy you're attracted to for the first time?"

Not for the first time, Riley thought, *but certainly the only man I've felt that intensely about.* "More or less."

"When it comes right down to it, you're still the same man you were before the attraction. Some people need a label to define who they are. They need to figure out an identity based off their sexuality, but not everyone does. Some people love who they love and don't worry about the labels."

Riley slumped his shoulders relieved by the easy way the bartender described some people's attitude. That worked for him, but it was also a reminder that Carter wasn't someone he could ever be with. "Yeah, well, I was the best man at his wedding today," Riley said morosely, draining the glass and knowing no amount of liquor would be enough.

"Shit," the bartender commiserated. "That is rough."

"I guess I came here to see if it's just him, or if I feel that way about other men too."

Leaning forward, the bartender grazed his fingers against Riley's. "Well, let's start with me. Do you find me attractive?"

Riley chuckled, not repulsed by his touch, but not turned on by it, either. "I can see the appeal, but no, sorry. You don't do it for me."

The bartender shrugged and gave Riley a crooked grin. "It's fine. I like to flirt, but at the end of the day I am happy to go home to my boyfriend."

He gave Riley a long searching glance and inclined his head toward the rest of the bar. "Anyone out there strike your fancy? Browse for a bit, see if anyone does it for you. Shit, if you show any interest, you'll be beating them off with a stick."

Riley swiveled in his seat and perused the room. Most of the men were paired off, although there were a few sitting alone or in small groups. Looking at them with a different eye took some getting used to, but Riley observed them while he finished his drink. There were some he immediately dismissed and it didn't take him long to figure out the men his gaze lingered on were built like Carter, tall and lean. He preferred brown hair to blond or red, and men who seemed like they'd be comfortable in the boardrooms and office spaces Riley frequented.

Riley made eye contact with a man built like Carter who had light brown hair and was sitting at a table with a small group of people. His features didn't remind Riley of Carter at all, but he was attractive. They continued to make eye contact as Riley surveyed the room and the glances grew more and more heated. Riley shifted on the bar stool, incredibly aware of the fact he was beginning to grow aroused. Flustered, he faced the bar again and ordered another drink. The bartender smirked at him. "Found someone you like?"

He flushed. "Yeah, I guess."

"Well, he's headed your way. Just relax. You'll be fine."

The bartender disappeared and Riley took a huge gulp of his drink. *What the hell am I doing?* he panicked.

"Fuck" — a low, rumbling voice spoke over his left shoulder — "you really know how to wear a tux."

Riley jerked, spilling his gin and tonic on the bar. He mopped it up and forced himself to face the man. His knee brushed the front of the man's trousers and he opened his mouth to apologize but nothing came out.

He settled onto a stool beside Riley and stuck out his hand. "I'm Jared."

"Riley," he croaked. Jesus, this was ridiculous. Fine, he was nervous — terrified actually — but he was acting like a fourteen-year-old boy. He'd never been at a loss for words like this before. He'd cultivated a charming, slightly flirtatious persona years ago, but he couldn't seem to manage it right then.

Jared gave him a long searching look. "You new at this?"

Riley chuckled and shook his head. "I really am obvious, huh? The bartender spotted it right away."

Jared shrugged. "Yeah, well, most of us have either been there before or we've met guys who are in the process of coming out."

Riley flinched at the words. He wasn't coming out. He just wanted answers.

Jared brushed his knees against Riley's. "Let me buy you a drink and you can tell me why you're here in a tux."

Riley drained the remainder of his gin and tonic and accepted another that Jared ordered for him. They spoke for a while about inconsequential topics and the small talk made some of Riley's anxiety fade, helped along by the alcohol. The low thrum of attraction was still there, though, and Riley was surprised to find himself flirting. When Jared dropped his hand on Riley's knee, he flinched in surprise, but he didn't push it off and the warm, heavy weight began to feel good. He didn't protest when Jared moved his hand higher, and arousal made him shift in his seat.

Jared leaned in and spoke directly into Riley's ear. "I don't want to push you too hard, but I think you need someone to get you out of your comfort zone."

Riley swallowed, interest and nerves warring within him. "What did you have in mind?"

Jared's lips grazed Riley's ear as he replied. "My mouth wrapped around your cock. Now. If you want that, walk to the bathroom and wait for me. It's to the left of the bar in the back. I'll follow in a few minutes."

Jared pulled away and Riley stared into his bright blue eyes for a moment. Jesus Christ, he was terrified, but a part of him desperately wanted it. He nodded once and stood jerkily, signaling to the bartender that he wanted to close out his tab. He signed the receipt, hand shaking, and the bartender winked at him before he strode toward the restroom.

Riley paced, his heart slamming inside his chest. He whipped his head up when Jared walked through the door. He grabbed Riley by the hand, tugged him inside the roomy stall and latched the door behind them. He stepped close, crowding Riley against the wall.

"Tell me if you want me to stop and I will," he promised, and Riley relaxed a fraction. Jared slid a hand against Riley's cheek, wrapped his fingers around the back of his neck and pressed a thumb against his jaw. "Is it all right if I kiss you?"

Riley nodded and closed his eyes, jumping when lips touched his. Awkward at first, they soon settled into a rhythm and Riley didn't really mind stubble against his cheek or the large, firm body pressing him against the wall. It wasn't like kissing Carter, but the fact that it was a man certainly didn't turn him off.

It wasn't long before Riley was aroused and Jared reached between their bodies, deftly undoing the fastening on his pants while they kissed hard and messily. Riley groaned when Jared wrapped a hand around his cock and his breath hitched when Jared dropped to his knees.

"Tell me what you want me to do," Jared prompted, slowly jacking Riley's cock with long, firm strokes.

Riley's hand was shaking when he threaded his fingers through Jared's hair, but he managed to force the words out. "Suck my cock."

Jared followed his instruction, taking Riley into his mouth and beginning to move immediately. The hot, wet suction drove him crazy and Riley stopped caring who was sucking him. He thrust into the slick heat, feeling the tingling in his groin and the tension beginning to build in his stomach. The tight pressure, the hand playing with his balls, even the knowledge it was a man on his knees in front of him all combined to make Riley lose control.

Riley closed his eyes, tightening his grip on Jared's head. He came down Jared's throat, panting. It was great, one of the best blow jobs he'd ever had, but there was none of the heart-racing eagerness like when he was in bed with Carter. None of the sense of belonging he had when Carter held him, touched him. Riley leaned his head against the wall and took a deep breath, reality crashing over him again.

The blow job had confirmed exactly what he'd always suspected. He was attracted to men, but the only person he truly wanted was Carter. The man who had promised to love, honor and cherish Kathryn Easton—no, Kathryn Hamilton. His chest tightened when he imagined Kate curled up asleep in Carter's arms, sated from a night of making love with her new husband.

Feeling sick, Riley pushed Jared away when he reached for him. He fumbled to close his tuxedo pants and once they were on, he muttered an apology, knowing he was being an asshole, but he couldn't bear to stay. He fled the bathroom and the bar, his stomach churning.

He jogged down the street, eventually collapsing onto a bench. He dropped his head into his hands. God, what had he done? Possibly risked his reputation to find out what he'd known all along? He would never be happy with anyone else — man or woman — and Carter was out of reach.

Taking a deep breath, he steeled himself and sat up. He'd been stupid tonight, no question about it, but he could fix things. Riley stood and looked around, orienting himself before striking out to search for a cab. In the morning, he'd see Alex at the brunch Carter's family was throwing to say goodbye to the newlyweds before they headed to Greece for two weeks. He couldn't have his best friend — that much was certain. Why did he keep fighting what had always been the plan? He had to settle down — with a woman — and live the life his parents had prepared for him. It was what was expected of him and no matter how much he couldn't stand them, it didn't matter. Keeping them happy ensured his place at Porter-Wright Publishing, which was his priority.

Without Carter, what was the point of fighting for the life he wanted? Without Carter, he would never be truly happy anyway, so he might as well please everyone else in his life.

Tomorrow he'd make sure Alex knew he was serious about pursuing a relationship with her. He might not love her, but he wouldn't hate himself for using her, either. She'd be using him too. For the money, the social connections, the lifestyle. Forcing himself to put Carter from his mind, Riley headed home, resolved to make an effort with Alex.

He had to. Carter was gone and it was time Riley did what was expected of him.

Chapter Seven

July, 2007
Southampton, New York

The beach house was quiet as Carter tiptoed out of the guest bedroom. Dressed in a T-shirt and sleep pants, he made his way downstairs with his Border Collie, Leo, at his heels. He walked through the ground floor to the kitchen with one purpose in mind — brewing coffee. Standing at the island in the center of the kitchen, Carter fixed the dog's breakfast while the coffee maker dripped, and thought about how much the house around him had changed.

While they spent little time in the Southampton house, Riley's parents considered it a haven from their high-end life in New York. They'd filled the house with expensive, understated furniture and art, creating an atmosphere of serenity visitors immediately responded to. As Riley had spent more summers in Southampton, he'd added touches of his own to complement the overall appearance and atmosphere of the house.

Carter had always enjoyed staying at the beach house. Not only did it provide an escape from the blistering city summers, it was also where Riley seemed most relaxed. The place put him at ease and softened his sometimes brittle veneer. Carter missed that softer side of Riley any time they returned to the city and Riley's emotional defenses dropped back into place.

After Riley and Alex had announced their engagement, Jonathon and Geneva had thrown an engagement party for the couple in their townhouse on the Upper West Side.

Jonathan had found Carter and Riley in the library chatting over drinks and without ado had handed Riley a deed transferring ownership of the Southampton house from father to son.

"Dad...does this mean what I think it means?" Riley had looked from the documents in his hand to his father's face, his eyes wide. "You can't really mean to give the house in Southampton to me."

Seeming unfazed by his son's reaction, Jonathon had shrugged. "Your mother and I don't spend much time there as it is and you've always been attached to the place. The house has been more yours than your mother's and mine for years."

Carter had been both surprised and grudgingly impressed by Jonathon's perceptive comment. Typically, Riley's relationship with his parents bordered on estrangement.

"Considering what it cost to buy, someone should be making use of it," Jonathon had added. "I'm sure you and Alex will enjoy making it your own, Riley."

Though pleased for his friend, Carter had winced internally at Jonathon's last sentiment. He'd suspected the house he'd come to know would soon change, particularly after Riley had murmured something about Alex wanting a new project.

Carter had not been wrong.

Alex and Riley had begun redecorating the place almost immediately following the engagement party. The existing exotic wood furniture had been replaced with modern pieces in leather, chrome and glass, and the existing color palette of cool blue and green had given way to red, gunmetal and white. Formerly soft and welcoming rooms had been transformed, becoming gleaming hard and immaculate.

Privately, Carter thought the house's new personality reflected that of its mistress—sleek, beautiful and unforgiving. The only corner that had remained untouched was the first-floor office, once Jonathon's and now Riley's. Outside of updated paint and art, the room had stayed the same, down to the original furniture and spicy smell of cigar smoke in the air. Bookshelves lined the walls, legal pads covered in Riley's notes were strewn across the coffee table and desk and opera often played softly from the iDock.

Carter pushed back the bowl of dog food and considered another area of the house he knew to be the opposite of immaculate. He tried not to chuckle, recalling the horror on Alex's face when she'd opened the door of the guest bedroom the evening before. She'd frozen, her eyes flitting over the collection of half-packed bags, box of Pull-Ups and toys suited to both kids and dogs.

Carter couldn't really blame Alex for her reaction—the functional chaos his family was accustomed to had no place in her life. Glancing at the stainless steel appliances and marble counter tops around him, Carter wondered how hard the housekeeper had been working to keep everything free of sticky little handprints and doggy nose smudges.

A low whine interrupted Carter's musings and he glanced down to meet a pair of eager brown eyes.

"Okay, then, boy." Carter bent, placing the dog's bowl on the floor and chuckling as Leo tore into his food with an appreciative yip.

Straightening, Carter turned to look through the sliding glass door that opened out onto the deck. He watched the sun light up the surf and sand, relishing the near silence. Quiet time had become an increasingly rare thing in Carter's world of late and he loved the early morning hours when everyone was still in bed.

He smiled at the thought of his wife and daughter asleep upstairs. Sadie had started out in the trundle bed the night before but had crept into the big bed sometime before dawn to snuggle down between Carter and Kate. When Carter had woken, the girls had been sharing a pillow, Sadie's dark hair mixing with her mother's gold, her wiry little body tucked against Kate's.

Carter shook his head and poured coffee into one of Riley's old Harvard coffee mugs. Nearly four years after his wedding, Carter still found his life surprising. He felt genuine wonder when he considered who he appeared to be in the eyes of the world—businessman, husband, father. Thinking about that man for too long left Carter vaguely uneasy, though he wasn't sure why.

"You know you can brew single cups in the Miele, right, Car?"

Carter's body jolted in surprise. Hot coffee sloshed over the side of the mug, splattering across the marble countertop, making Carter yelp and wetting the front of his T-shirt. Swearing under his breath, Riley darted from the kitchen door to Carter's side, grabbing a handful of tea towels from a drawer in the island.

"Jesus Christ, don't do that!" Carter complained as Riley thrust a towel at him. "Are you trying to kill me?"

Riley helped mop up the spill, laughed breathlessly and snorting after Carter glowered at him. "I didn't mean to scare you, man—I'm sorry."

"Do you always sneak around the house like a fucking ninja?"

"Are you always this grumpy before you're caffeinated or is being an asshole in the morning a new thing?"

"I've always been an asshole in the morning," Carter groused. "You were always too hungover to notice until now."

They stood quietly for a moment, eyeing one another, each wordlessly daring the other to carry on bitching. The moment broke when the dog by Carter's foot huffed, startling both men and making them laugh.

"I had no idea it was Scare Carter Shitless Day," Carter joked.

"You should have seen yourself," Riley replied, wiping up the last of the coffee spill. "You jumped so high."

Carter made a face and dabbed at his shirt. "Laugh it up, funny guy. Why are you awake, anyway?" he asked, noticing for the first time that Riley appeared to be dressed for a workout.

"Going for a run. I usually go a little later in the morning, but I woke up early today. Wanna come?"

"No, thanks. I'm not even awake yet."

"What the hell happened to the guy who used to get up before dawn to row on the Charles River? You are getting old, Carter Hamilton."

"Dude, I'm tired!" Carter protested. "We'll see how alert you are when it's your turn."

"My turn?" Riley's brow wrinkled. "My turn to do what?"

"To be sleep deprived from having a toddler's foot jammed in your ribs all night while your pregnant wife sleeps." Carter grabbed for the coffee pot to refill his mug, while Riley blinked in surprise.

"Wait, Kate's pregnant again?"

Carter sipped his coffee greedily and nodded. "Yup. She's around twelve weeks or so."

Riley gave him a smile. "Congratulations, Car. That's great."

"Thanks." Carter smiled in return. "It wasn't exactly planned, but the baby is welcome news." He gestured at his friend with his coffee cup. "You and Alex have some catching up to do."

"Oh. Well…that's probably not going to happen anytime soon."

Carter read uncertainty in Riley's expression and frowned. "Why not? Listen, if Alex is worried about the mess in our room, just tell her it's temporary. Kids start picking up after themselves as they get older."

Riley raised an eyebrow. "Yeah? How's it going with Sadie doing chores?"

"Very, very badly," Carter admitted, sipping more coffee while his friend laughed. "To be fair, though, she's not even two years old — she's still working on her fine motor skills and exploring the potty. We've got plenty of time to work on her organizational expertise."

"Better you than me."

"From what you said, apparently so. I…well, I wanted to

ask if you'd be interested in being the new baby's godfather, but—"

"Are you serious?" Riley interrupted, the start of a smile brightening his face.

"Of course." Carter laughed, pleased his friend appeared receptive.

"Well, shit. Yes." Riley's smile widened. "I'd be honored. And scared out of my mind, but mostly honored."

Carter blew out a breath. "Excellent. One of Kate's sorority sisters is already lined up to be the godmother, by the way, so Alex is off the hook."

"She'll be glad to hear that," Riley muttered.

Carter leveled a look at him, silently giving his friend the opening he seemed to need to explain himself.

Riley wet his lips with his tongue. "Alex and I aren't planning to have any children of our own for some time," he admitted, his tone careful. "If ever."

Carter nodded, feeling strangely weighed down by his friend's confession. "So, you and Alex are in agreement on the subject…?"

Riley's lips thinned and Carter swallowed. He liked Alex well enough. She was pleasant and could be engaging when discussing topics that interested her and she had a sly sense of humor Carter appreciated. However, she made no bones about being wholly uninterested in things not directly related to her own comfort and privileged life. Unlike Kate, who sat on a number of boards of organizations dedicated to social causes, Alex appeared content to spend money on herself. She mostly ignored children, including Sadie, who loved everyone with a toddler's immediacy and intensity.

"I'm the one who suggested waiting." Riley's gentle tone surprised Carter. "That said, Alex and I made the decision together—no one is forcing anyone into anything."

"Of course." Carter's face heated. "I'm sorry, that was out of line."

Riley waved a hand reassuringly, though Carter thought he appeared a bit wan. "Don't worry about it. You're not the only one who's been expecting news about a Porter-Wright heir. Imagine the fun conversations we have at those rare dinners with Jon and Geneva, and Alex's parents as an added bonus."

"Shit, that sucks," Carter commiserated with a grimace. "You can't blame me for trying to enlist a partner in crime, though—I need male company for play dates at the park." He knew his attempt at levity had fallen flat once Riley looked at him askance.

"Should I be flattered you want to spend time with me or mock you for whining?"

Carter saluted his friend with his raised coffee cup and Riley's eyes shone with humor.

"Listen, come for a run with me," Riley said, shaking off the topic of children without missing a beat. He stepped away from the island to open the refrigerator and pulled out an insulated water bottle. "It's only thirteen miles from here into East Hampton and back—if we leave now, we can be back by the time everyone else gets up and fix them breakfast."

"You mean you can fix them breakfast—I still can't cook to save my life, Ri. And I already told you, I am not going running."

Riley's grin widened. "Why not? It's not like you can't run that distance. I know you're still working out at the club, even if you've stopped rowing. Come on, we've been out here for over a week already and this might be the first time I've talked to you alone for more than ten minutes."

Carter wavered as Riley's words sunk in, because his friend was right. They'd spent a lot of time together during their vacation but always in the company of others. Dan, Mel and their kids had been there the week before and while the men tried to find quiet spots in the house to talk, the interruptions were constant. Even when Carter and Riley retreated to the library to smoke cigars, Alex intruded, pulling Riley out of the room to help with the menu or wine.

True to form, Sadie's voice echoed down the stairs in the

next moment, followed by Kate's vain attempts to shush her. Leo woke from his doze at Carter's feet and scrambled up, darting out of the kitchen to add his sharp yips to the cacophony.

"Oh, shit." Carter grimaced at Riley. "How pissed is Alex going to be that it sounds like Grand Central Station in your hallway?"

Riley clapped a hand on Carter's shoulder. "Not at all. She started taking sleeping pills after the first night."

Carter gaped at him for a moment. "Because of us?"

"Only partly," Riley replied. "She's been in Japan with her parents and her sleep cycle is still off. She planned to take the pills anyway, to get herself back on track. The Conley and Hamilton families just made it easier to get started."

"I'll talk to Kate—we'll figure out a way to keep Sadie quiet in the morning," Carter offered, speaking over Riley's protests. "I'm up, anyway—it's not like I can't take her out for a ride or something."

Riley shook his head stubbornly. "And I'm telling you that it doesn't matter how loud Sadie is right now. Alex is out until the pills wear off. You could stand next to the bed right now with a chainsaw running and she'd sleep through it."

Carter frowned at the counter, considering Riley's words. He straightened up as Riley dropped a hand onto his shoulder, and was struck by the fondness in Riley's gaze.

Carter opened his mouth to speak, but his words were drowned out by the rising babble his family made on their way toward the kitchen. So he smiled at his friend instead, raising his hands in a gesture of surrender.

Riley turned to the sliding door with a wistful grin, water bottle in his hand. "I'll be back in a couple of hours," he called and, with a wink, ran off.

Busy minding Sadie while Kate made them all breakfast, Carter didn't notice when one hour slid into another. They'd already eaten and loaded their dirty dishes into the washer when Alex breezed into the kitchen and went to the cabinet for a cup.

"That coffee isn't fresh, Alex," Kate told her. "Why don't you let Carter start a new pot?"

"I do know my way around a coffee maker." Carter handed Sadie off to Kate. "This'll only take a minute. I'll make enough for Ri, too."

Alex flapped a hand at him, the light catching her manicured nails. Her white sundress seemed impossibly crisp next to the Hamilton family's comfortable sleepwear.

"Don't trouble yourself, Carter. Riley always takes forever when he's running and I'm more than happy to use the Miele. I'm too impatient to wait for a whole pot to brew," she added as she moved toward the sleek espresso maker built into the wall. "Knowing how much you like coffee, I'm surprised you didn't make use of it yourself."

"Ri said the same thing," Carter replied, still busy measuring grounds into the brew basket. "When I have time to wait out a whole pot, I do. It's sort of a holdover from my days at school, I guess."

"One of the many Harvard leftovers," Kate teased, plaiting Sadie's hair while the little girl watched her father talk to Alex.

"One of many?" Alex looked from Kate to Carter and back again.

Kate rolled her eyes. "Oh, yes. The rowing club, the raggedy Crimson sweatshirts, the fascination with Boston sports teams, the bitching about Manhattan clam chowder—"

"Riley complains about clam chowder, too!" Alex exclaimed, arching her eyebrows high. "What is the big deal? It's soup, for heaven's sake."

Carter played at scowling while the women commiserated. He knew at least one complaint was justified because tomato-based clam chowder was just *wrong*. After the coffee maker began to drip, he let himself out onto the deck through the sliding door, Leo following close behind. The sky was cloudless and the air warm despite the steady breeze blowing in off the water. The day promised to be perfect for beach play provided there were umbrellas and sun shelters providing shade.

Carter leaned against the railing, moving his gaze over the landscape. He was unaware he'd been scanning for something until he found it – Riley, made small by distance, moving steadily along the beach toward the house. Something loosened in Carter's chest. He'd been tense since realizing how long Riley had been gone.

"What the fuck is wrong with you, Hamilton?" he muttered, shifting to look over the water instead of at his friend.

Recalling Riley's earlier teasing words, Carter understood he'd been acting needy. In the last several years, he and Riley had fallen back into a pattern of seeing each other infrequently. It had begun after Carter and Kate had married and increased after Riley and Alex's wedding. Before the Hamptons' vacation, they'd been communicating mainly through email and text messages, and only seeing each other at the opera or other occasions where their social circles crossed.

So much had changed in such a short time that it was no wonder they'd grown apart. *Things don't have to stay that way though,* Carter thought, aware he had to fix the situation. As had happened after he'd returned to New York, Carter had become so immersed in his job and family he'd lost touch with things that kept him grounded, including spending time with Riley.

Clearing his throat, Carter glanced west again. Riley had gotten much closer to the house, and Carter froze, suddenly aware that Riley had removed his shirt during his run. Carter stared at his friend's toned body, at sun-burnished skin gleaming with sweat, and he drew a breath before forcing himself to turn away.

Carter raised his hands to scrub over his face, struggling to make sense of his reactions. Between swimming and playing on the beach, he'd seen Riley in less clothing every day of this vacation and not once thought anything out of the ordinary. This time, he'd caught his friend alone and unawares, and something about the combination felt different to Carter. Voyeuristic, perhaps. Even forbidden. And more than anything, tempting.

Carter bit his lip. He wanted to see more of Riley's bare skin and it was all he could do to keep from spinning around and ogling all over again. Instead, Carter looked around for a distraction and he blinked after catching sight of Sadie on the other side of the sliding door. She pressed her hands against the glass and smiled at her father, her eyes round and bright.

Carter stared at his daughter. "What the fuck is wrong with you?" he asked himself again, his whispered words catching in his throat.

"Da!" she called through the glass, her undisguised pleasure making Carter's heart ache.

"Hey, little baby," he called back softly, pushing away from the railing to reach for the door, Riley's running steps on the sand beside the deck echoing in his ears as he slipped inside the house.

* * * *

A month passed before Carter forced himself to reach out to Riley again. He wasn't sure why he'd responded so intensely to Riley on the beach that morning, but he intended to make sure whatever it was stayed buried. He spent long hours at the office before going home to Kate and Sadie, only to log in to the office network again after dinner and work until his eyes burned.

A simple text from Riley soon cracked the walls Carter had been busy building.

One Saturday night, Carter decided to indulge in a series of minor vices instead of working—bourbon, ice cream and Quentin Tarantino movies. He was settled on the couch with a drink and a bowl of chocolate ice cream when his phone chimed, drawing Carter's gaze. He read a strangely random message from Riley and smiled.

About to ride a mechanical bull. Not optimistic this will end well.

Carter put his bowl on the coffee table and sat up, moving his fingers over the screen to reply when the phone chimed again.

Crisis averted. Faked a college football injury to get out of it.

Laughing softly, Carter thumbed the Call icon, unsurprised when Riley answered after a single ring.

"You didn't play college football," Carter said, speaking over the sound of music and voices in the background.

"Well, you know that," Riley replied loudly, "but these people have no idea. Which is not surprising, considering they are bordering on very, very drunk."

Carter drew his eyebrows together. "You're not? You're the one who was about to ride a mechanical bull."

"Ah, but I didn't ride it," Riley gloated. "I based my decision not to ride on fear rather than booze, though. I quit drinking about an hour ago."

"Not much in the mood to break a limb?"

"I'm not much in the mood to break a sweat right now, 'cause I've already been there, done that tonight."

Carter thought from the way the background noises changed and faded slightly that Riley was on the move.

"This is what happens when publishing geeks get together for a friendly game of softball in the park, though," Riley told him. "There's always someone with a post-game big idea. Last week, they dragged me to a Tiki bar, for God's sake."

Carter snorted at the disgust in his friend's tone and bent to pick up his glass.

"It's not funny! They tried to get me to wear a grass skirt, Carter! I actually considered buying a coconut bra for Alex, too, though I would have had to leave it in a cab on the ride home."

A few moments passed before either man could stop laughing enough to speak.

"As much as you're complaining, it sounds like fun," Carter said at last. "I'm sorry I missed it." His face heated at Riley's silence, but he didn't have time to retract his statement before Riley spoke again.

"Come out with us some time," Riley offered. "I know softball's not your game, but we just play for fun."

Carter nodded, forgetting for a moment that Riley couldn't see him. "Actually, I've been thinking," he began, then faltered, his mind flitting to the morning at the beach house when he'd seen Riley running.

"Always a dangerous prospect," Riley interjected, clearly pleased to take advantage of the two-second pause in conversation.

"Shut up, jackass, I'm trying to be the mature adult at almost one in the morning."

"Okay, then." Riley's voice was indulgent and warm. "Go on and say what's on your mind."

"Let's go out," Carter urged. "We could grab some dinner and drinks next Thursday night, maybe catch some music. You know, the way we used to before the wives and the kids."

"And, what, make it a regular thing again? Is Kate going to be okay with that? I mean, there's Sadie and you guys are having another baby...I don't know how happy your wife's going to be when you start disappearing every Thursday night."

"So, we make it every other Thursday," Carter countered, smiling when Riley laughed softly. "Or every third Thursday of the month. Kate's been after me to lay off working so hard and you know she likes you. She'll be okay with me going out for dinner and drinks every now and again."

"Okay, then." Riley's smile carried in his voice. "You, my friend, have got yourself a date. For next Thursday, as a matter of fact."

Chapter Eight

April, 2012
New York, New York

Two hours into a leisurely dinner at one of their favorite restaurants in Manhattan, Carter leaned forward and rested his elbows on the table, his face suddenly growing serious. "Ri, do you ever think about what we used to do in college?" His voice was quiet, a little husky, and it took a moment before his words sank in.

Riley's heart leapt and he took a sip of his espresso before he responded. Carter could have been talking about anything—drinking, sleeping in late—but Riley had no doubts what he was referring to even now, more than ten years since their sexually adventurous days in Cambridge. He glanced around the restaurant, but they were in a fairly private booth and no one from the wait staff was within earshot at the moment. He pitched his voice low anyway. "The threesomes?"

Carter nodded, his hazel eyes strangely intense as he stared at Riley, waiting for his answer.

"Jesus, of course I do. Why do you ask?"

Carter glanced down at his own coffee, stroking his thumb over the smooth white porcelain. He chewed at his lip for a moment before he answered. "I've been thinking about it a lot lately."

Riley watched his Adam's apple bob in his throat.

"Missing it."

Riley flushed, the ever-present urge to reach out and touch Carter rising to the surface. Mostly he was able to ignore it, push it away, but the reminder of what it had felt like to touch Carter obliterated his self-control. Instead, he hummed noncommittedly and tightened his grip on the small cup, his long-fingered hands dwarfing it.

"Don't you?" Carter pressed.

Riley's laugh sounded hollow to his own ears. "Yeah, I do." He lowered his gaze. *You have no idea how much.*

Carter shoved his empty cup and saucer away before folding his hands on the table and leaning forward. His expression was earnest, hopeful. "What do you think about starting that again?"

Although Riley knew the question was coming, his heart rate still sped up at the images it conjured — Carter's long, smooth back, his warm lips on Riley's, the strength of his hand around Riley's cock. Riley wanted it so much he physically ached, but he couldn't do it again, couldn't let himself. Carter was married, so was he, and they'd both agreed it was too risky to cross that line.

"Isn't Kate satisfying you in bed?" he snapped, regretting the words the moment they left his lips.

Carter clenched his jaw and pursed his lips. "That has nothing to do with it and you know it."

"Shit, I'm sorry," he said, feeling guilty. It wasn't Carter's fault that Riley was so on edge. He had resigned himself to never having a chance to be with his friend that way — the sudden possibility that he could again shook him. The longing for it and the million reasons why it was a terrible idea clashed in his head. He wanted it all so badly and yet... he knew there was no possibility it would end well.

Carter scowled at him. "That was uncalled for."

"Yeah, it was," Riley admitted. "I shouldn't have said that."

Carter sighed heavily. "Look, you know how much I love Kate, but what we had before...it was different."

"That's for sure," Riley agreed. "I just don't know why you're asking me this now, Carter."

He laughed ruefully. "I just had this dream the other

night about the time right before graduation and…"

Riley nodded, remembering. He couldn't remember the name or face of the girl who had been there, just Carter's hoarse groans of pleasure, the taste of the sweat on his neck, the way Carter had gripped Riley's hip, hard. Heat pooled in his belly and he shifted on the leather bench. He drew in a shaky breath, wishing he had the guts to agree. He wanted to so desperately, but he knew it would only complicate their lives further.

"C'mon, say yes." Carter's pleading gaze met Riley's and Riley felt almost dizzy at the earnest expression, at the need there. He wanted nothing more than to give Carter what *he* wanted, but Riley knew he'd regret it if he did.

He shook his head. "I can't."

"Why not? We both want it."

"And we both know why it's a bad idea," Riley said, his tone sharper than he intended. He tried to soften it when he continued. "Look, we talked about this. It's too dangerous. We have too much to lose if anyone finds out."

Carter sat back with a sigh. "Christ, I know you're right, but, Ri…"

"I get it, Carter, I really do. Yes, I miss what we had, but I can't do it. Not when our careers and families are on the line." *Not when I have to pretend like you aren't the one I want*, he continued in his head. That was the crux of it. Allowing himself to be intimate with Carter was only going to make things worse. Lord knew he and Alex had sex rarely enough and he hadn't been with anyone else. He idly wondered if Alex was faithful, but the thought of her with another man didn't bother him nearly as much as it should have.

Since Carter's wedding, since the night of the ill-advised blow job in the bathroom of the bar, Riley had promised himself he'd never put himself in that situation again. Whatever his mixed-up feelings for Carter and his confusion over his attraction to men, it was too much. Too dangerous for him. But he couldn't exactly tell Carter. It was easier to focus on the fact it could ruin the lives they'd so carefully built. "I don't trust some random woman we meet in a bar to be discreet. And unless you know someone you trust who'd be interested…I can't do it. I'm sorry."

Carter sighed and nodded. "Shit, you're right. I know you are. I'm glad one of us is thinking straight."

Riley gave him a sad smile. The last thing he wanted was to tell Carter no. He was desperate for a chance to be close to Carter, to not feel so alone, but he knew it was the right decision. His chest ached at what a sham his marriage was. As much as he'd wanted a better relationship than his parents had, he was beginning to realize it wasn't altogether different. That was never the kind of life he'd wanted, but he couldn't go back now. Besides, his life wasn't terrible, was it? A beautiful wife, a fantastic job and more money than he knew what to do with—most people would envy the way he lived. Except it all felt hollow sometimes. As though he'd taken a wrong turn somewhere and was living his parents' life instead of his own. Instead of the one he'd always imagined for himself.

A warm hand suddenly covered his. "You okay?"

He blinked and shook himself out of the stupor he'd been in. "Yeah, yeah, I'm fine. Just got lost in my thoughts for a second."

"You were thinking about it, weren't you?"

Carter's eyes twinkled suddenly and Riley couldn't resist the smile on his friend's face.

"Yeah, I was," he admitted, returning the smile. Carter hadn't moved his hand and he slowly brushed his thumb against the back of Riley's. The touch was unconscious. Carter probably had no idea he was doing it, but it still made Riley's heart beat faster. He suppressed a shudder at the sensation, stomach-clenching need for Carter tearing through him.

"Think about it," Carter coaxed. "Please?"

"I'll think about it," Riley agreed, knowing he shouldn't be considering it, but unable to say no when Carter looked at him like that. Carter moved his thumb lower, brushing across the soft, sensitive skin on the inside of Riley's wrist, and Riley licked his lips. He struggled to breathe, anticipation building within him, threatening to make him do something stupid and reckless, like tell Carter he did want to find another woman for them to share. Or, worse, lean across the table and kiss him, consequences be damned.

"Gentlemen, can I get anything else for you?"

The waitress's voice broke the spell they were both under and Carter jerked away as if he'd touched something hot. *Or like someone who had been caught doing something he wasn't supposed to be,* Riley thought hollowly. God, he hated it.

Initially flustered, Carter pulled himself together enough to flirt with the waitress and by the time the meal was paid for, Riley was reasonably certain Carter could have talked her into joining the two of them in bed. Carter kept flicking his gaze to Riley while he flirted, as if encouraging him to jump in. Instead, he pulled out his phone and pretended to be engrossed in an email. Carter finally got the hint and they left the restaurant shortly after.

"What the hell?" Carter said, bumping Riley's shoulder with his own. "She was definitely into both of us."

"I told you, I don't think it's a good idea," Riley protested. "She may be the nicest girl in the world, but we have no way of knowing. I can guarantee you she's probably not raking in the big bucks as a waitress, no matter how generous a tip you left. Blackmailing us would be awfully tempting."

Carter scowled and shook his head. "You're too goddamn cynical."

Riley shoved his hands in his pants' pockets and shrugged. "Maybe I am, but I'd rather be cynical than too trusting. We both have a lot to lose, Carter—we can't afford to risk it."

"Yeah," Carter muttered, a frown creasing his forehead. "You're right." But he didn't sound entirely convinced.

* * * *

Riley didn't see Carter again for a few more weeks. He

was immersed in work and although Carter called several times, he didn't have time for anything more than a brief texted response.

Since Jonathon Porter-Wright had given Riley the go-ahead to pursue e-publishing, it had taken off. It had required a hell of a lot of work to catch up to some of the other firms who had jumped on the bandwagon earlier, but through some miracle and an insane number of late nights at the office, Riley had managed to make electronic publishing a success.

Third quarter figures were in and they were damn good. The best they'd seen so far. With them, plus the results from the first two quarters, Riley felt as if he could finally ease up a fraction. This was what he had been busting his ass so hard for. This was why he'd felt like he practically lived in his office these days.

Although he loved the suite of offices he'd made his own, the hours were becoming exhausting. The office was more his taste than the Upper East Side apartment, like the West Village place he still hadn't gotten around to getting rid of.

Riley glanced around his office, the warm wood paneling, the striking marble desk, the framed pictures on the wall. His gaze landed on the photo from graduation. He stood up and walked over to it, shoving his hands into his trouser pockets while he stared at the image. God, they looked so young. Carter's grin was wide and boyish and Riley hardly recognized himself. His hair was lighter and a few freckles dotted his tanned skin. He shivered at the memory of Carter's warm hand on the back of his neck and the length of his body next to Riley's.

Riley's phone beeped on his desk and he picked it up, only half paying attention as he sat back in his chair. It was a text from his wife, reminding him that he needed to head home for the dinner party they were hosting. He winced and swore under his breath. He had completely forgotten about the party. The day had been chaotic and it was later than he'd originally planned to leave. Their marriage might be shit, but there was no doubt Alex knew him well. He took a moment to tidy his desk before texting Alex to let her know he was on his way home. He felt a funny twinge when he recognized he was more excited knowing Carter would be there than about spending time with her.

Guilt lingered while he navigated through the Manhattan traffic and he swung by a florist shop on his way home. *I should take Alex out, maybe a nice dinner and a Broadway show,* he mused. They hadn't been in a while and she asked for so little from him.

When he got home, Alex was in the dining room, directing the staff preparing for the party. She parted her lips in surprise when her eyes met his. "Riley, you're home."

He smiled and stepped forward, greeting her with a kiss on the cheek. "I told you I was on my way."

She shrugged, the ivory silk dress she wore slipping down her arm, exposing one bare shoulder. The dress was draped at the top, loose there, but clung to the rest of her body.

"You look stunning, by the way."

She smiled prettily at him, then mock scowled. "Well, you're always home so late, I never know when to expect you."

"I'm sorry," he murmured, pressing the large bouquet of orchids he'd purchased into her hand. "I'm a terrible husband."

Her frown turned genuine. "Is everything all right, Riley?"

He sighed and shook his head. "Feeling guilty for neglecting you. I want to take you to dinner and a show soon. I'd like to apologize for the long hours at the office."

Her expression of surprise and pleasure was so genuine he felt a pang at the way he'd treated her. "I'd like that."

She leaned in to kiss him, for once not worrying about her carefully applied makeup. Her fingers were cool against his jaw as he returned the kiss, trying to summon up more than the guilt and obligation he usually felt. But there was no heat, no tearing need ripping through him. At most, the flicker of something lukewarm, nearly extinguished. *I'm sorry, Alex.*

Alex softened against him and she slid her hand into the hair at the back of his head. She let out a quiet sigh and he cupped her cheek, grazing his thumb along the skin there. Alex drew away, her eyes bright, her smile beguiling. "If we didn't have guests on their way over, I'd suggest we take this to the bedroom."

Carefully pushing a lock of her curly red hair off her face, Riley struggled to smile back at her, inwardly relieved that they had an excuse not to go further. He'd tried, he really had, to muster up a genuine desire for her, but it was getting more difficult by the day. "After the party," he offered, knowing full well he and Carter would wind up drinking in the library and Alex would be in bed long before they finished.

There was a flicker of something in her eyes, as if she knew he was lying, but she nodded and pressed a gentle kiss to his cheekbone. "Thanks for coming home."

He held her close, savoring the rare moment of tenderness in a relationship that had started off as more of an obligation than a desire and had grown more distant as the years passed. Maybe Alex had known all along that they weren't going to have the fairy-tale marriage some couples had, but Riley still felt guilty he couldn't give her more.

* * * *

The dinner was a success, as always. Alex certainly knew how to host an excellent party. It was a small one, with just their respective sets of parents, Carter, Kate and a few other couples they often socialized with. Riley was immersed in a conversation with Kate about the latest production at the Met over the dessert course when his father cleared his throat.

"Can I have your attention for a moment?"

The table quieted, everyone looking at Jonathon

expectantly.

"I think you all know how reluctant I was to pursue e-publishing. I thought it was a fad that would die out. Riley wouldn't give up on the idea, though, and he finally convinced me to take the firm in that direction. This may be the only time you'll hear me say this, but I was wrong." He paused when everyone at the table chuckled. "Electronic publishing is our future and I owe my son a great deal for being so tenacious about this. Riley, you've proven an old man wrong and that's hard to do. After seeing the third quarter returns, I can honestly say Porter-Wright Publishing's profits are the best they've ever been and I couldn't be prouder. The board is ecstatic and voted unanimously to hand over the e-pub portion of the company to you. I feel confident that leaving it in your hands is the right decision."

Jonathon raised a glass toward his son and Riley simply stared at it for a moment, stunned by his father's praise. He rarely acknowledged any of Riley's successes, at least not unless there was someone else there he was trying to impress. Riley had essentially been doing the work of an executive vice president for a while, but his father had overseen everything and all final decisions went through him. This promotion gave Riley the opportunity to truly be in charge and it was the moment he'd been waiting for since grad school had begun. His heart beating hard, he lifted his glass to acknowledge his father's praise and a wide grin broke out on his face. At the moment, he felt invincible.

Everyone at the table murmured their congratulations, but it was Carter he looked to first. Carter was beaming — perhaps the only one at the table who knew Riley's pleasure was as much about his father's praise as the success of the company and the title — and Riley couldn't seem to turn away. It wasn't until his mother spoke that he snapped out of it.

Geneva's tone was dry. "The only better news would be that Alex and Riley are going to make us grandparents.

When will we be getting that good news?"

Riley gulped, fumbling for an answer, but Alex beat him to it. "Oh, Geneva, you're much too young to be a grandmother. Give us time." She smiled and her tone grew sardonic. "Besides, until Riley cuts back his hours at work, I don't see that happening."

Trying to hide his grimace, he forced a smile onto his face and pretended he found Alex's comment funny. Leave it to his mother and his wife to put a damper on his moment of joy. Having children was a topic he'd been trying to avoid thinking about. Throughout their marriage, he'd attempted to picture Alex as the mother of his children and had always come up blank. He wasn't completely opposed to the idea of children in general. Carter's children, Sadie and Dylan, were sweet and he liked being called Uncle Ri and enjoyed being Dylan's godfather. But children seemed too messy for Alex. Sticky fingers and chaos didn't suit her lifestyle. If they had children, they'd be raised by nannies, just like Riley had been. It wasn't the kind of life Riley wanted for a child, and he knew that although Alex expected that they would have children someday, she wasn't eagerly anticipating it, either.

"Congratulations," Kate murmured. Her smile was warm and genuine, although there was a hint of wariness in her eyes. Had she noticed the way Riley had stared at Carter? Flustered by the idea, he reached for his wineglass and nearly knocked it over, righting it and taking a large gulp before he responded.

"Thanks, Kate."

"You okay, Ri?" she asked, laying a hand on his arm, and the concern in her voice made him think he'd imagined it entirely.

"I'm fine," he said, relaxing a fraction. "You never did finish telling me what you thought about *The Marriage of Figaro*, though."

Her face brightened. "Oh, I loved it. If I'd had the time, I would have gone to see it at least once or twice more.

Didn't you think the use of a piano instead of the traditional harpsichord was a brilliant move?"

Riley agreed and they went on to discuss other fine points of the show. He relaxed, pushing away the worry about what Kate might have noticed. Threesomes aside, he knew his closeness with Carter wasn't typical of most friendships. He'd spent years compartmentalizing his feelings and hiding the emotional closeness between them from the rest of the world. He thought he'd been pretty successful. It had been easier once they'd stopped the threesomes, but he wondered if he could manage it if he caved in to Carter's suggestion about resuming them.

Carter hadn't mentioned it again since the first night he'd brought it up, but Riley had caught Carter staring at him several times with a speculative expression on his face. Riley glanced down the table and saw Carter talking earnestly with Jonathon. Carter had obviously been aware of Riley's attention, though, because he shot Riley a grin that made Riley's chest warm and Riley caught a glimpse of his father's scowl at the look the men gave each other.

A short while later, Alex moved the party into the living room, the night winding down with cocktails and conversation. Riley's parents were the first to leave and his father clapped him on the shoulder and told him once again what a great job he'd done. Even his mother congratulated him on his success.

Riley was still glowing from the praise when the rest of the guests said their goodbyes and Carter offered to walk Kate downstairs to grab a cab home. "I think I'll stay a bit longer with Ri," he said, shooting Riley a questioning glance, and Riley nodded.

"I have a great bourbon I think Carter will like," he said and Kate smiled fondly and rolled her eyes.

"Fine, fine. I'll leave you guys to your fun." She hugged Riley goodbye and he kissed her on the cheek. "Don't keep my husband too long. I do need him back, you know."

"I won't, I promise," he said with a chuckle.

Alex walked the other couple to the door and Riley poured Carter's bourbon and fixed himself a gin and tonic before heading into his study. Carter would know where to find him. Alex peered in through the door a few moments later.

"Goodnight, Riley. I'm headed to bed."

He set his drink down on his desk and joined her at the door. "I'll try to come to bed soon."

She waved him off with a resigned sigh. "I figured you and Carter would want to celebrate."

He winced internally. What did it say about him that he'd received some of the best news of his life and he wanted to celebrate with his best friend, not his spouse? And that she knew? "Sorry."

She shrugged and her lips tightened for a moment before she relaxed. "I didn't expect anything else."

She left the room after giving him a quick kiss on the cheek and he stared after her retreating form for a moment before walking over to the wall of windows. It had been an odd day, full of so many ups and downs, and his head was spinning.

"Ri?"

Riley faced Carter, surprised when he closed the door behind him. Carter stuck his hands into his pockets, sauntering toward Riley with a grin on his face.

"What are you so happy about?" Riley asked suspiciously.

Carter didn't answer until he was standing right in front of Riley, so close Riley could feel the heat from his body. He could have leaned forward and touched his lips to Carter's with almost no effort at all.

Carter's eyes gleamed, crinkling around the corners as his lips turned upward in a broad grin. "I have good news, my friend. I've been waiting to tell you all night."

Riley smirked at him, stepping back so he could cross his arms over his chest. He leveled a disbelieving look at Carter. "And what's that?"

Carter leaned in and Riley tried to suppress the shudder caused by Carter's warm breath on his cheek. "I found the perfect solution to our dilemma."

Riley narrowed his eyes. "What dilemma?"

Despite the fact that they were in Riley's office with the door closed, Carter still lowered his voice. "Finding a woman we can trust."

"Carter…" Riley protested.

"It's a brilliant solution, I swear."

Riley quirked an eyebrow at him and shook his head. "Okay, lay it on me."

"I was talking with my cousin Ryan—remember him?"

"He was in your wedding party. Yeah, I remember him."

"Well, we went out for drinks and to play pool the other night and he was talking about an escort service he uses."

Riley groaned. "You have to be kidding me. How can you possibly think that's a good idea?"

"Hear me out," Carter coaxed. "It's the solution to your concerns. An escort will have every bit as much to lose as we would. She'd know how to be discreet—hell, we'd be paying her to be. She'd be equally invested in keeping it a secret. Not to mention she'd be smoking hot and skilled in bed."

Riley laughed, despite himself. "Carter, you're over-simplifying it."

"Fine, maybe I am, but I honestly think this could work."

"You have some valid points," Riley conceded, leaning back against the window. "But we still run the risk of being blackmailed. If someone decides our bank accounts are too tempting…we're screwed. I don't think it's worth it."

"Ryan knows the owner, Colin. They went to business school together and they've been friends for years. He swears this guy is completely trustworthy and I trust Ryan."

Riley had to admit the information did make him feel a little bit better. Carter must have seen him wavering, because he pressed harder.

"It's high-end, extremely discreet. It isn't some ring of hookers from Craigslist."

Riley snorted. "What the fuck do you know about

Craigslist?"

Carter laughed. "Fine, I don't exactly buy my furniture there, but, come on, you know what I mean."

With a sigh, Riley nodded. "Yeah, I do. So, I'm glad to hear it's well run and we aren't going to have to worry about the escort also being an axe murderer. I still think it's too risky. Besides, what about our wives?"

Carter leveled him with a look. "Are you trying to tell me you're really that concerned about Alex?"

Riley shrugged. "She's my wife. We may not have the perfect marriage, but yeah, I'd feel shitty for hiring an escort to fuck along with my best friend. I'm at work all the goddamn time — isn't that bad enough?"

"I'm struggling with this every bit as much as you are. Kate and my children mean everything to me, but I need this, Ri." Carter's voice trembled a little. He stepped close to Riley, his shoes on either side of Riley's crossed feet.

Riley glanced up at his friend, simply staring at him for a moment. "I don't know…"

Carter rested a hand on his shoulder, pressing heavily for a moment. He brushed his thumb across Riley's collarbone, over the crisp white fabric of his shirt. His eyes were serious, hopeful. Riley let out a heavy sigh of frustration, his resistance beginning to crack.

"This is that big of a deal to you?"

"It is. Please. I need you to do this with me, Ri."

Riley heard the words Carter actually said, but all that registered was, "I need you, Ri."

The words hit him square in the chest and, although he knew just how much he was setting himself up to be hurt, he agreed. "Okay."

Carter squeezed his shoulder and grazed a thumb across Riley's jaw as he pulled away. "You won't regret this, I swear."

With the way Riley's heart raced at the simple touch, he was utterly sure that Carter was wrong.

* * * *

It was surprisingly easy for them to pick an escort, once Ryan put them in contact with Colin. Deciding against either a blonde or a redhead, they chose Natalie, a stunning brunette. Even Riley, ambivalent about the whole thing, was surprised by how appealing he found her. Granted, he was still anxious about the entire situation, but when they met at a hotel for drinks and to discuss the arrangement, Riley relaxed. Natalie had a way of putting him at ease and she answered frankly the questions and concerns he had. There was no question how beautiful she was, and although it had been a damn long time since Riley had felt much of an attraction to any woman, he responded to her.

If Natalie hadn't grown up on the Upper East Side, she faked it flawlessly. Her speech, her demeanor and her dress were all impeccable. Her features were exotic, her large, dark eyes and olive-toned skin hinting at an Italian heritage.

"So, this isn't something new for you two then?" Natalie asked, flicking her gaze from Riley to Carter.

"No, it's something we did in college," Carter answered. "With our careers and other obligations, we thought it best if we didn't continue once we moved back to Manhattan, but lately…it's something we've been missing."

"Both of you?" Natalie asked, assessing them with a shrewd air.

No matter how apprehensive he was, he'd certainly missed the opportunity to be close to Carter. "Yes, and you have done a lot to allay my fears. I have too much at stake to risk losing it over a fantasy, but I think this might be a good way for us to go about this."

Natalie smiled reassuringly and grazed her fingertips across Riley's forearm. "You have my word I would never do anything to jeopardize your personal or professional lives. I'm here to fulfil fantasies, but not at the expense of the rest of your life. You can trust me, Riley."

Strangely enough, he did.

Between her full red lips and Carter's warm thigh against his own, Riley was more than ready to follow them both upstairs to the hotel room after the conversation wrapped up. However, it was a little more complicated to execute. Natalie left the table for the room she'd checked in to earlier and Riley and Carter staggered their arrivals so as not to draw attention.

Once in the hotel room, Riley's nerves returned, but Carter's warm, solid presence reassured him. He hardly took his eyes from Carter while Natalie unbuttoned his shirt with deft fingers and Carter unzipped Natalie's dress. He shuddered at the first brush of Carter's bare skin against his own. While the two men touched and tasted Natalie, most of Riley's focus was on Carter.

Riley shook when Carter's lips touched his for the first time in over ten years. He closed his eyes, the familiar taste of bourbon on Carter's tongue making his head swim. Carter's hand rested on his hip, the heavy weight of Carter's body pinning him to the bed.

Natalie was right beside them and Riley forced himself to focus on her, too. He reluctantly tore his lips away from Carter's and focused his attention to her. She, in turn, seemed to know exactly what to do. She worked as a bridge between the two men, allowing them to regain their previous closeness without crossing the arbitrary and unspoken line they'd drawn years ago. He watched Carter fuck her, his long, lean body flexing while he found a smooth, even rhythm, and Riley's heart sped up.

Natalie had come several times by the time the friends were spent and Riley allowed his head to fall onto Carter's shoulder. Carter traced long, nimble fingers idly up his sweaty back and, without thinking, he briefly pressed his lips to Carter's chest. The low sound of contentment Carter let out made Riley smile.

Carter slid a hand through Riley's hair and looked Riley in the eye, his expression tender. "Thank you. I needed this."

Riley nodded, wondering why his chest and throat felt so

tight. "Of course, Car. Whatever you need."

Natalie stirred on the bed next to them, stretching gently, then sitting up in a graceful, fluid motion. When Carter turned to her, Riley shifted, drawing away from his friend. "We should head out, I suppose," Carter said, sounding reluctant.

Natalie's lips curved up in a smile. "You don't have to leave on my account."

A part of him wanted to stay, wanted to draw out the time with Carter, feel his friend's touch for as long as he possibly could, but he shook his head anyway. "Not this time."

Natalie cocked her head. "There will be future times, then?"

Riley glanced at Carter who indicated his agreement. "Yes. If you're willing."

"More than," she purred, leaning down to brush her lips briefly across each of their mouths. "I thoroughly enjoyed myself tonight, gentlemen. I look forward to seeing you both again. How often did you have in mind?"

The friends glanced at each other and shrugged.

"Once a month, maybe?" Riley offered. "Would you be willing to set aside one evening a month for us?"

Natalie stood and sauntered over to the dresser where her purse was sitting. She pulled out a phone and thumbed through it, seemingly unconcerned with her nakedness.

"What do you think about the third Friday of every month?" she offered.

"Will the third Thursday of the month work?" Riley asked.

Natalie nodded slowly, clearly thinking through the proposal, before she smiled. "Sure, that works for me."

"Me, too," Carter agreed.

Riley chuckled, knowing they didn't need a plausible cover story for why they were busy one Thursday a month but feeling a pang of guilt all the same.

Carter shifted on the bed and Riley tried not to focus on the bare torso just a few inches from him. "What do you think about doing this at your West Village apartment?" Carter suggested.

"Huh?" Riley tore his attention away from the fine trail of hair that disappeared under the smooth white sheet and focused on Carter's face.

"It seems like it's less risky for us to meet Natalie there. We'll have the privacy we need and are less likely to run the risk of someone seeing us."

"Hmm," Riley mused. "Yeah, that's not a bad idea."

"Perfect," Natalie smiled at them. "Why don't you set everything up with Colin? I'm very much looking forward to this."

She gave them each a lingering kiss goodbye and disappeared into the bathroom. Riley tried not to drag his feet while he dressed to go home, but he was reluctant to leave the hotel room. Although he'd been hesitant to start the threesomes again, he was already thinking about the next time with Carter. *And Natalie*, he reminded himself.

Before he left the room, Carter stopped him with a hand on his arm. "I meant what I said earlier, Riley."

He tilted up his head to meet Carter's eyes. "What was that?"

"Thank you for doing this."

"It wasn't like I didn't enjoy myself," he joked.

Carter squeezed Riley's biceps. "I know, but I know you wouldn't have done it if I hadn't pushed. I owe you."

"You don't owe me anything," he protested.

Carter shrugged. "I want you to know how glad I am to have you in my life. You've always been there for me."

"And I always will be," Riley promised.

He was still thinking about those words when he left the hotel and went home to his East 77th Street place. He showered and set his suit out for dry-cleaning, careful to leave no evidence of his tryst with Carter and Natalie. Alex was asleep in their bedroom when he entered and hardly roused at all when he slid in beside her. She turned onto her side, resting her cheek against his chest, and he stroked her hair for a moment, staring at her face in the dim light coming in the window.

"I'm sorry, Alex," he whispered. "I wish I was the man you want me to be."

A sad smile twisted his lips when he thought about earlier that night. Being with Carter had been everything he'd hoped for, but now it all hit him at once. How fucked up this was, how much he missed Carter already and how desperately he wished the person lying in his arms was his best friend, not his wife.

Chapter Nine

Carter let himself in to the lobby of Riley's West Village apartment building, holding his cell phone between his ear and shoulder. Pressing the elevator call button, he nodded to the doorman and shifted his weight from one foot to the other, waiting for the car to arrive. The amount of pleasure he found in his arrangement with Riley and Natalie still surprised him. What surprised him more, though, was his capacity for compartmentalizing the two parts of his life.

"I'm meeting Riley in forty-five minutes," he told Kate, his gaze on the shining tips of his black shoes. "We'll probably be out late tonight, though, so—"

"So I won't wait up," Kate finished for him. "That's nothing new with you two, Car. I don't even feel bad admitting I'm glad that you don't wake me when you finally slink into bed."

"I do not slink." Carter looked up as the elevator chimed. He stepped aside while the doors slid open and a young couple moved past him. "I would never purposely do that," he continued, boarding the car and punching the button for the sixth floor. His gut twisted at the uncomfortable truth in his words.

Carter enjoyed his sex life with Kate. Things had tapered off slightly after they'd had children, but they still put effort into connecting with one another every week. The last thing Carter needed—or wanted—after his get-togethers with Riley, however, was to make love to Kate. Unless…

"I'm getting some mixed messages here, Katie," he offered quietly. "Do you want me to wake you when I get in?"

"It's not that I don't want you to, sweetheart," Kate said

with a sigh. "But I'm not going to pass up a little extra sleep, either. I do feel guilty for sleeping right through you getting into bed, though."

"Don't feel guilty —"

"It's not like I have a good reason to be so exhausted," Kate argued. "You're the one working ten-hour days while I'm at home."

Carter frowned and stepped off the elevator. Pausing to the left of the doors, he gave his full attention to the voice on the other end of the line.

"Where is this coming from? No, you don't have a full-time job outside the house, but we both know you've got a lot going on, too. I love our kids, but I think staying home with them all day is actually harder than dealing with a boardroom full of grown men and women. Or are you forgetting that time you went away and I slept on the floor of Sadie's room because I was too wiped out to make it back to our bed?"

"I knew I married you for a reason," Kate replied with a laugh. Carter heard the sincerity in her voice. "But thank you. I don't agree with you one hundred percent, but I appreciate what you said. Speaking of Sadie, by the way, she noted your absence tonight at dinner."

Carter grimaced as he walked toward Riley's apartment. "Uh-oh. Did our daughter have some unkind words for me?"

"I wouldn't say unkind, but she was pouting pretty hard. Apparently, it is unacceptable for you to be absent from dinner when Miss Sadie has helped make dessert."

"Aw, shit." Carter paused again, this time outside Riley's door. "I'll make it up to her this weekend. You and Dylan, too. I'll take the kids out for the day, give you some time to do your own thing."

"They'll love that." Kate's voice shifted and Carter knew she had gotten to her feet. "I'll let you go, Car. Be safe tonight and call the car service if you don't want to take a cab home, okay?"

"Okay. Thanks, honey," Carter replied softly before ending the call. He stood staring at his phone for a long moment before he shifted gears. Drawing a steady breath, he pushed the homey conversation he'd had with Kate out of his mind and unlocked Riley's door.

As he'd expected, Carter was the first to arrive. He left his briefcase and keys in the entryway, and set about preparing for the evening ahead. He pulled off his suit jacket and tie and dropped them on a chair in the living room, then made his way through the apartment, unbuttoning and rolling up his shirtsleeves while switching on the lamps. Carter went to the kitchen, leaving his vest on and buttoned, aware both his lovers would appreciate the gesture. He smiled, his thoughts turning to Natalie, who insisted on the more formal term 'waistcoat,' and Riley, who loved to slowly peel the garment from Carter's body.

After opening two bottles of wine, Carter poured a glass of red for himself and put the bottle of white on ice. While his cooking skills were still nearly nonexistent, Carter didn't hesitate to arrange a selection of fruits and cheeses from the refrigerator on a platter. He left the real dinner preparation for Riley and Natalie, who enjoyed cooking together.

Carter caught himself humming and felt a prickling of guilt. *What about Kate?* a tiny voice in his head whispered. *What about the kids?*

That Carter didn't know how to answer those questions bothered him more than anything.

"What are you thinking about?" Kate had asked him earlier in the week during a dinner with a gathering of her fellow opera lovers. Her fingers had come up to smooth the lapel of Carter's suit jacket and he'd given her a smile.

"Nothing in particular—why?" he'd asked.

Kate had shaken her head, her voice almost hesitant when she'd spoken again. "You're a million miles away, that's all. Did I catch you daydreaming?"

Carter had cleared his throat. Kate's comments had been truer than she'd known. He'd been daydreaming, all right, of sucking on Riley's tongue. Of feeling Riley's fingers massaging his balls while Natalie rode Carter's cock, her head thrown back in pleasure.

"I'm fine. Just thinking about work," Carter had lied, knowing how Kate would feel about his inability to leave work at the office for more than a few hours at a time.

Kate's sigh had been sharp. "Carter. We're at a dinner party with our friends. Talking about opera, for heaven's sake. What am I going to do with you?"

"Forgive me for having the artistic appreciation of a house cat?" He'd given Kate a slow, crooked grin and her lips had twitched.

"I've met house cats with better taste in the arts than you."

"Ouch. I guess it's lucky for me that you're allergic to cats then, hmm?" he'd teased, leaning closer to make Kate laugh outright. "You knew I was a philistine when you fell in love with me, sweetheart."

"You enjoy reminding me of that far too much," Kate had grumbled, pushing her lips into a pout as Carter had ducked forward for a quick kiss.

"Don't the two of you ever tire of these public displays of affection?"

Carter and Kate had both frozen as a cool, familiar voice had settled over them. They'd pulled back to meet Alex's amused and slightly disdainful gaze, while Riley had stood behind his wife, his face tight.

"Alex, I told you it could wait, for God's sake," he'd chided. "There's no reason we have to talk about this now."

Riley had reached for his wife's wrist, only for Alex to swat at his hands with a sigh, and Carter had nearly laughed.

Kate had ignored their friends' antics. "What's going on? Do you need one of us for something?"

"The Board of Directors is calling a meeting," Alex had replied. "They want to discuss inviting additional performing artists for special events in the spring. I know that Riley has some strong opinions about whom to invite, as do you."

"That's right." Kate had looked from Alex to Riley.

"It's in our best interest to submit our opinions to the Board sooner rather than later," Riley had explained before narrowing his eyes at Alex. "I also told Alex we have at least a month before the meeting will be held."

"To which I say, why not tonight, Riley?" Alex had replied. "The Board members are all here, filled with a five-course meal and half-drunk on some excellent booze. Time to strike while the iron is hot, as your father would say."

Carter had been unable to hold back an appreciative hum, particularly after Riley and Kate had exchanged scandalized glances.

"Alex is right," he'd told them. "High art or not, you need to take the advantage when it presents itself." Holding up his glass, he'd nodded in Alex's direction. "You should have gone into advertising, Alex — clever sharks with a nose for business are always in short supply."

"I'll leave the sharking to you, Carter." Alex's eyes had sparkled with enjoyment and rare humor. "My good looks would put you all at a disadvantage, anyway, and that would hardly be fair."

"All's fair in love and war," Riley had cut in with a roll of his eyes. He'd held out an arm each to Alex and Kate, who'd stood and smiled. "Now if you're done flirting with the heathen, Alex, it's time to approach some of the Board members with our ideas."

That night, Carter's dreams had been filled with erotic images that made desire curl in his gut and rattle down his spine.

He'd watched Natalie and Riley, his heart squeezing as they kissed, their skins flushed and gleaming with sweat. When they'd turned their attentions to Carter, their kisses and caresses had filled a hole inside him he'd never even known existed.

"I've got you," Riley had murmured, gazing at Carter with his pupils blown wide.

Natalie's body had been warm against Carter's as he'd drawn her closer with one arm. "We've got you," she'd amended, wrapping her fingers around Carter's dick, the intensity of his pleasure making him gasp.

Carter had woken with a grunt, his pajama pants wet and stuck to his cock and thighs. He'd pressed his face into his pillow and worked to quiet his breaths, thankful Kate had slept through his first wet dream in twenty years. His legs had still been shaking when he'd climbed out of bed and into a hot shower to wash the cum from his skin.

Now, he laid down the knife he'd been using to slice cheese, his hands trembling slightly. He closed his eyes to draw a calming breath and a sound from the entryway startled him. He grinned as Natalie's voice echoed through the rooms toward the kitchen.

"Hello, boys."

"In the kitchen, beautiful. It's just me for the time being, I'm afraid." Picking up the knife again, Carter then glanced over his shoulder to see Natalie appear, her dark eyes dancing.

"Ah, now this is what I like to see — a handsome man with a big pile of delectable things to eat. What a pleasant way to begin my evening." She crossed the room to run a hand across the width of Carter's shoulders. "I love this gray glen-plaid suit on you," she murmured. "Very nice."

Carter gazed at Natalie's body, appreciating the way her dove-gray dress accentuated every curve. "Thank you."

Natalie plucked a black olive from the platter of appetizers Carter had prepared and popped it into her mouth with a fond smile. "Hello, Carter."

"Hello, Nat." Carter held up a piece of the cheese he'd been cutting, chuckling when she accepted it between her teeth with an appreciative hum. "I opened a bottle of sauvignon blanc."

Natalie sighed happily. "And you left your *waistcoat* on, too." She smiled at Carter's eyeroll. "You're too good to me."

Carter bumped her hip gently with his own as she reached toward the cabinet where the wineglasses were stored.

"Any word from Riley?" she asked, pouring wine for herself.

"Not yet." Carter glanced at the clock in the stove and shrugged. "He had a meeting in Connecticut this afternoon. At this hour, they probably ran into traffic coming back into the city."

Natalie frowned thoughtfully. "I know Riley enjoys cooking when we get together, but I think we should call in delivery if we don't hear from him soon. He'll be too tired to spend time in the kitchen by the time he gets here."

Carter slid the last of the cheese onto the platter before placing the knife and cutting board in the sink. "Good idea. Why don't you take the steaks and other groceries Ri left in the fridge home with you? Seems a shame to waste them."

Natalie nodded and Carter picked up the platter of food and his glass. "Grab the take-out menus and meet me in the living room. Let's see if we can polish this off before Ri gets here."

They spent a pleasant hour sitting together on the sofa, chatting over the wine and snacks. Carter had eased Natalie's high-heeled shoes off and was giving her a foot massage when his phone chimed. He pulled it out of his pocket with a smirk and glanced significantly at Natalie.

"You don't suppose he's canceling, do you?" she asked, cocking one elegant eyebrow while Carter thumbed his phone's lock screen.

"Doubtful," Carter replied. "Riley looks forward to these evenings far too much to let something like a long day get in the way. He'll grab a shower, mainline a Red Bull and be ready to go."

Carter turned his attention to his phone. "Hey, Natalie and I were beginning to wonder where the hell you were. You run out of gas?"

"More like ran out of road," Riley replied, his voice weary.

Carter frowned and sat up straighter in his seat. "What's wrong? Where are you?"

"We, ah, had a little accident with the car coming back

161

from Stamford." Riley sighed, sounding stressed out and unsteady. "I'm in the Mount Sinai emergency room on Madison Avenue."

All of the air in Carter's body seemed to whoosh out with one breath. He set his glass down hard on the table, wine sloshing over the edge as Natalie pulled her feet from his lap. Carter swallowed hard, gripping the phone tightly, his voice strained when he spoke again.

"What happened? Are you all right?"

"I'm fine, just stiff and bruised," Riley replied. "The EMTs thought I might have partially dislocated my right shoulder, but the ER doc thinks it's only a bad strain. He ordered an X-ray to make sure—I'm waiting for them to bring me up to radiology."

"Jesus, Riley." Carter raised his free hand to scrub at his forehead, feeling jittery with worry that Riley might be downplaying the true extent of his injuries.

"What can I do? Is Alex with you?" Carter closed his eyes and Natalie brought her warm hand to rest soothingly on his shoulder.

Riley's tone was dry. "Alex is in Dubai giving her credit cards a serious work-out, so nope, no wife here."

"I'll come get you," Carter told him, his heart leaping at the opportunity to be there for his friend. "I'll grab a taxi right now and meet you there."

"Would you?" Carter's throat ached at Riley's obvious relief. "I wouldn't ask, but the car's obviously out and I just don't feel like taking a cab by myself right now…you sure you don't mind?"

"Don't be ridiculous, of course I don't mind." Carter dropped his hand and glanced to Natalie. "Let me just get Nat an Uber and I'll be on my way."

"Oh, shit, Natalie." Riley groaned. "I almost forgot we were seeing her tonight. Tell her I'm sorry, okay? Obviously, she should still bill us for the hours—"

"I agree," Carter soothed. "I'll take care of everything and see you as soon as I can." Their experiences with the Archer

Agency had been discreet, but it was risky for either Carter or Riley to even mention Natalie's name in public. Riley's lack of discretion sent another pulse of worry through Carter.

"Thanks, Car, I really appreciate it…" Riley's voice grew muffled as he spoke to someone on the other end of the line. "I have to go," he said after a moment, sounding tense but more alert. "They're ready for me in Radiology."

Carter stood, aware that Natalie had gotten to her feet too. "I'll try to be there by the time you're done," he replied, before ending the call.

"There was an accident," he began, then stopped, his throat tight. The reality of the situation really sank in and his hands were trembling. He clenched them into fists. "Riley's in the ER."

Natalie took hold of Carter's hands, her dark gaze on his. "I assumed, from what I heard. Is he okay?"

"Yeah." Carter breathed out, working to calm the tension rolling through him. "He, ah, may have messed up his shoulder – they were taking him up for X-rays just before we hung up." Carter smiled grimly and relief worked its way across Natalie's face. "Alex is out of town so I'm going to go pick him up."

"Good idea." Natalie gave Carter a little push toward the door. "Don't worry about this or my ride home," she said, waving at the glasses and the platter on the table. "I'll clean up before I go."

"I'm sorry about tonight," Carter told her, grabbing his jacket from the chair as they walked toward the entryway. "So's Ri. Please take yourself out for dinner or something and give the receipt to the agency."

Natalie waved Carter off again, a slight smile tugging at her lips. "You know, ordinarily I'd say don't worry about it," she said, reaching for Carter's briefcase and keys on the entryway table. "But I know you two. You feel badly about canceling."

"Of course we do. We expect you to bill us for the night –"

"Of course." Natalie reached up to rub her hand between Carter's shoulders while he opened the door. "Go take care of your man and text me later."

Carter was in the taxi before the weight of Natalie's words struck him fully. He sank back against the seat, heart thrumming as he murmured them aloud. "Go take care of your man."

Nothing about Natalie's words or tone had been teasing. Did she really think that of him and Riley? That they were something other than good friends who indulged a shared kink for a third partner? That they were…more?

Carter closed his eyes and pressed the knuckles of one hand against his lips. The taxi wove through the evening traffic while he struggled to pinpoint anything he or Riley might have done to give Natalie the wrong impression.

Neither of them spoke explicitly to Natalie about their families. A great deal of information about the Hamiltons and Porter-Wrights was a matter of public record, though, and Natalie knew both Alex's and Kate's names.

Kate. Carter sat up abruptly and he pulled his phone from his pocket, hoping to catch his wife before she went to sleep. He didn't how long it would take to wrap things up at the hospital, let alone get his friend home, and he'd never keep Riley's accident secret.

As he strode into Mount Sinai ER twenty minutes later, Carter's anxiety was at its peak. Speaking with Kate had left him feeling more rattled, and he'd spent the entire call willing the cab driver to move faster.

Carter stood at the desk, scanning the waiting room, and jolted as he caught sight of a familiar figure toward the back. He stood frozen for a long moment, a rush of relief leaving him breathless before he lurched forward.

Riley was dozing in a chair, his right arm in a sling, left arm propped on the armrest to support his head against the knuckles of his hand. He was missing his tie and the suit jacket draped over his shoulders was rumpled and smudged with dust, as were his trousers.

Carter sat down in the empty seat beside his friend, the sounds of the ER fading around him. He examined Riley, taking in every feature of his face, reminding himself that nothing serious had happened. Riley's face was pale and a long bruise ran from his right eyebrow to his chin, but despite the sling and the bruises, he was…beautiful. And Carter had never been so relieved in his entire life.

A sharp pain knifed through Carter's chest. His emotions — the ones he knew were written all over his face — were what Natalie saw during their evenings together.

Carter had loved Riley for years — after all, they were best friends. Now, more than a decade and a half after they'd met, Carter recognized that his feelings for Riley were changing. The idea of something happening to him — of Riley being hurt or in pain — stole Carter's breath. His friendship with Riley had become something bigger and stronger than a simple bond between two people. Something closer to what Carter could only define as passion.

Carter felt the blood drain from his face. What did this realization mean to his life? To his wife and children and the family who expected so much from him wrapped up in a neat little package?

Hesitantly, he reached out trembling fingers to brush the dark hair from Riley's forehead. Riley stirred and blinked his eyes open, his confusion clear for a heartbeat before he focused on Carter and the apprehension gave way to recognition.

"Airbags really stink, you know," Riley croaked out. "Like they smell incredibly awful. It's like you're being punished for crashing."

"Adding insult to injury, huh?" Carter asked, almost smiling as Riley squinted at him.

"Punny guy." Riley gave him a tired smile. "Thanks for coming, Car."

"You knew I would," Carter replied. He ran one finger gently over the bruise on Riley's face before letting out a sigh. "C'mon — let's get you home."

Chapter Ten

A quiet rap on his closed office door made Riley jump. He'd planned to spend the early afternoon catching up on emails, but he found his mind drifting. He lifted his head to see his assistant peering inside. She smiled tentatively, her voice apologetic.

"Mr. Porter-Wright? You have a meeting scheduled for three o'clock and it's five to. I know you usually leave by now and—"

"Thanks, Anna. I appreciate it. My mind was wandering and I lost track of the time." He stood, gathering what he needed for the meeting and did his best to focus on work.

By the time the workday ended, though, he was wound tight. He left a large stack of unfinished papers on his desk and too many unanswered emails in his inbox. He'd go into work this weekend if he had to. All he could focus on was what would happen at the apartment that night. Five months into their arrangement with Natalie and he couldn't get enough.

His groin tightened as he left his office imagining touching Carter, feeling their bodies pressed together. The elevator ride to the parking deck and the drive to his apartment were filled with eager anticipation. It wasn't until he was sitting in the living room next to Carter on the couch that the tension finally seeped out of his body, his shoulders relaxing and lowering, the stranglehold his expensive silk tie had held him in all day finally loosening.

He sighed in appreciation when he took a sip of his gin and tonic, smiling at Carter over the rim of his glass.

"How was your day?" Carter asked him.

"Long," he admitted. "I spent all day thinking about tonight."

Carter grinned. "You weren't the only one."

They talked while they sipped their drinks—catching up on their week and venting their frustrations. Riley felt everything slip away from him—the tension with Alex, the stress from work, the pressures from his family all faded while they talked. Although nowhere near drunk by the time he finished his second G&T, he had a mellow buzz. Carter appeared to have a similar buzz—if his relaxed grin after he'd drained his final bourbon was any indication—but he wasn't drunk, either.

"I'm gonna run out and grab another bottle of bourbon," Carter said, standing and walking over to the kitchen to deposit his empty glass in the sink.

"Oh, shit, we're out?" Riley asked, craning his neck to see the bottle where it sat on the kitchen counter.

"Mmhmm," Carter said, lifting the empty bottle to show Riley.

"I'm sorry. I always try to grab some when I notice it's getting low," Riley apologized, standing up. "I guess I've had too much on my mind lately to keep track."

Carter walked over to him, laying a hand on his shoulder. He braced himself, but Carter's touch was gentle and other than an occasional twinge if he moved wrongly, his shoulder had recovered nicely from the car accident. "You're too hard on yourself, Ri," Carter chastised. "You take good care of me—you always have—but you're allowed to forget things occasionally."

"I know," Riley said with a shake of his head. He felt like he'd let Carter down somehow, though. In a weird way, he prided himself on always anticipating Carter's needs.

"Hopefully I'll be back before Natalie gets here, but I'm sure you two have something delicious planned for dinner so you'll probably be up to your elbows in cooking by the time I return, anyway." Carter teased. "Do you need me to pick anything up while I'm out?"

"A bottle of white, if you would?" Riley said. "Pouilly-Fumé, maybe? It's seafood linguine for dinner."

Carter moaned appreciatively. "My favorite. You two spoil me rotten."

"You know we enjoy it." Riley curved his lips in a smile. "You do pretty well spoiling me too." He slid a finger under Carter's charcoal vest, sliding down from his shoulder to where it curved under his arm. Carter always wore three-piece suits on the Thursdays they got together with Natalie. A small reminder of how well Carter knew him. He idly traced a path back up and stared into Carter's eyes, the tension between them suddenly growing thick.

"We try," Carter offered after a moment, brushing his fingertips across Riley's stomach as he walked past, heightening his growing arousal. Carter paused next to Riley, turning his head to speak softly into his ear. "In fact, tonight we have some lost time to make up for. Your shoulder put you out of commission for too long. Now that you're back to full strength…" He cocked an eyebrow at Riley, giving him a crooked grin.

Riley wanted so badly to kiss the smirk off Carter's face that he had to grit his teeth together to keep from doing it. "Hurry back, then," he replied, not bothering to hide the flirtatious tone to his voice. "We'll be waiting."

"Will do." Carter smirked more and winked at Riley. "Don't start without me."

Riley went into the kitchen while Carter shrugged on his coat and left the apartment. Riley rolled up his shirtsleeves, and hummed an aria from *Madame Butterfly* while he prepped the dinner. He'd grown to love these relaxed evenings with Carter and Natalie. Carter was shit in the kitchen, but Natalie had taught Riley a lot and he always felt a small curl of warmth in his belly at the thought of cooking for his friend.

His mind wandered as he deftly deveined the shrimp, then tossed them into the colander in the sink. Relaxed and content, he imagined what it would be like living with

Carter again, no wives, no families, just the two of them. Coming home to each other every night, Riley cooking, Carter picking out the perfect wine. His hands stilled when he pictured crawling into bed beside Carter, their bodies pressed together. He closed his eyes, imagining the wet glide of Carter's tongue, the warm, masculine scent of him, Carter's cock pressing inexorably into Riley's body. He flushed at the image, suddenly flustered by the idea of it. Christ, he'd never pictured that before. He wanted it suddenly, wondering what it would feel like to have his friend inside him, Carter's whispered words of affection coaxing him through the first time.

He chopped garlic and shallots, still aroused when the front door opened, but his fantasies took an immediate nosedive at the sound of Natalie's voice. *Fuck, what had he been thinking?* He cleared his throat and responded to Natalie, letting her know he was in the kitchen. Natalie made the situation possible. Riley couldn't blame her for his disappointment at the reminder that the night ahead wasn't about just him and Carter.

He washed his hands and stepped out of the kitchen with a smile as Natalie approached.

"Sorry I'm running a few minutes late," she said breathlessly, unwinding a vibrant blue scarf from around her throat. "Traffic was terrible tonight."

Riley shook his head. "It's fine."

After he'd hung up her jacket for her, she greeted him with a warm hug and a kiss on the cheek, which he reciprocated. He had no illusions about being anything more romantic than a client to her, nor did he want to be, but he thought Natalie genuinely liked her time with him and Carter. He felt the same way about her. He felt as though they had a friendship with her, despite the fact they were paying her to be there. Certainly, he never wanted to make her feel anything less than appreciated and respected. Truth be told, he liked her far better than most of the women in his social circle. He thought he would have been happier married to a woman like Natalie rather than Alex, but when it came down to it, Natalie still wasn't Carter.

They made small talk for a few minutes while they finished prepping dinner, but he felt distracted. Although eager to hop into bed with Natalie and Carter, his earlier thoughts had turned his mood melancholy, and he'd already begun to anticipate the crash after, when he had to walk away from Carter. When he was reminded that the life he wanted didn't resemble the one he led. These Thursday nights were a tease, a beautiful dream always a little bit out of reach. He was grateful they'd arranged to have the entire night together tonight. Alex wasn't expecting him home until the next day.

Natalie dried her hands on a towel and frowned at him. "Are you okay? You seem a little jittery tonight." Her tone sounded warmly concerned.

He rested against the counter and smiled wryly at her. "It's been a long week."

She hesitated before she spoke, glancing at the door first. "Are you sure that's all?"

"What else would it be?"

"Riley…" she said softly. "Look, I've never said anything because it isn't any of my business, but I can see things are… complicated between you and Carter. I don't want to pry, and you don't have to tell me anything if you don't want to, but I'm happy to listen if you do. He seemed frantic when he found out you'd been in the car accident. And I can see there's…more than friendship there."

He closed his eyes, unsure of how to respond. He'd suspected for a while that Natalie had figured out at least some of what existed between him and Carter, but they'd never spoken of it. "I can't," he finally managed to choke out.

"I won't say anything else, then," she reassured him. "Just know I'm glad to do this for you. For you both."

"Thanks," he said roughly, opening his eyes. She walked over to him, tracing her fingertips across his cheek as soon as she was near enough, her touch soothing. They were still in the same pose when the door opened and Carter stepped into the apartment.

Natalie dropped her fingers, but her warm brown eyes still stayed locked on Riley's for a long moment, her gaze sympathetic and worried. He smiled reassuringly at her as Carter came up behind Natalie to wrap his fingers around her hips.

"I thought I told you not to start without me, Ri," he said teasingly, seemingly unaware of the heavy tension in the room.

She laughed, spinning around to face him. "Of course we weren't starting without you," she said. "You know it wouldn't be half as much fun without you here."

Carter laughed and dipped his head, capturing her lips with his. Riley stood up fully and leaned forward, pressing his body against Natalie's. When his fingertips grazed Carter's hands, he felt the familiar jolt of arousal he always got simply from touching him. His cock began to harden against Natalie's ass as he leaned in, his lips brushing the shell of her ear. The light, subtle perfume she always wore mingled with the woodsy scent of Carter's and he grew harder at the sound of Carter's quiet pleasure.

Familiar wandering hands stroked and teased and clothes were discarded. The three of them moved to the bedroom and fell onto the bed, dinner temporarily forgotten. After so many times together, there was a rhythm to their encounters as if it had all been choreographed. The positions and variations changed, but the ease with which they touched each other did not.

Riley skimmed his hands across Carter's back, exploring the taut muscles under smooth skin, his palms tingling at the contact. He lived for these casual touches, for the chance to be close to his friend.

"Do you want me to suck your cock?" Natalie asked, her voice low and throaty. She settled onto her knees and he knelt on the bed in front of her. He groaned when she wrapped her hand and closed her lips around him, but he couldn't take his eyes off Carter's cock. They worked flawlessly together as always, slipping into the familiar rhythm, knowing when to hold back, when to thrust harder and faster to make Natalie come, when he had to have his lips on Carter's to make the two men come so hard they nearly blacked out.

This time was no exception. Riley came when Natalie stroked the sensitive spot directly behind his balls and Carter plunged his tongue into his mouth. His vision swam as he collapsed on the soft gray sheets, Natalie and Carter joining him a moment later.

They showered together after and Riley couldn't focus on anything but the sight of Carter. His hands seemed so large wrapped around Natalie's small waist and he seemed to tower over her. Carter gave him a slightly surprised glance when he stepped behind him, rather than sandwiching Natalie between them, but Riley suddenly needed to touch Carter, run his hands along his smooth skin. Riley felt hypnotized by the rivulets of water dripping over the muscles of Carter's broad back, over the curve of his ass and down his strong thighs, choking on a sudden desperate need to touch and taste. His hands shook while he soaped his own body instead, his heart thudding too fast.

"You good, Ri?" Carter asked, twisting around to face him.

"Huh?" he asked blankly.

"Natalie and I are finished with the shower. You?"

He shook his head, barely managing to hoarsely answer, "I'll be out in a few."

Carter frowned in puzzlement and Natalie gave him a long, searching look, but he could only reply with a shrug. They closed the glass shower door behind them and left Riley alone. He felt suddenly weak and it had nothing to do with the hot water pouring over his body or the thick steam filling the shower. He braced himself against the tile wall, shaking. How many times had he seen his friend naked?

Hundreds? How had he never noticed the two divots in Carter's lower back? Why was Riley picturing his thumbs resting right there as he slowly pushed inside him?

Riley's racing heart and achingly erect cock shocked him. His thoughts about Carter had always been mostly abstract, more focused on the idea of them together than any specific acts. But now the floodgates had been opened and he was unable to stop thinking of everything he wanted to do to Carter, everything he wanted Carter to do to him.

By the time he finally stepped out of the shower, he had pulled himself together again and his laugh was genuine when he followed the sound of voices into the kitchen and caught Natalie brandishing a spoon at Carter.

"Sit your ass down," she said, pretending to scowl. "You're going to ruin dinner."

Carter wore nothing but a pair of boxers and Natalie had on a silky black robe. Riley smiled at the sight of them, at the easy camaraderie and warm affection. "Yeah, sit down, Carter," he drawled. "A real man is here to help."

Carter searched the room. "Where? I don't see one."

Riley swatted at his ass playfully in retaliation. Warmth rushed through his body when Carter eyed him with a heated gaze, even as he yelped and feigned discomfort.

Together, Riley and Natalie finished cooking dinner, while Carter did his best to make a pest of himself. Riley could only stay so mad when Carter came up behind him, resting his head on Riley's shoulder and begged for a bite. Riley should have known better than to feed Carter a piece of shrimp from his hand, but he was unprepared for the way it felt to have the buttery sauce licked slowly from his fingers, Carter wrapping his tongue around the middle one to suck off the last drop.

Riley flushed, his cheeks and chest suddenly hot, and he had no way to hide his reaction since he wore nothing but a thin pair of sleep pants. Natalie distracted Carter by asking him to open the bottle of wine he'd picked up. Serving the pasta distracted them all long enough for him to pull himself together again and they ate in the kitchen, Natalie perched on the edge of the counter and Carter and Riley leaning against the cabinets on opposite sides of the small galley kitchen. He followed Carter's twirling fork with his gaze and, watching Carter draw the implement from between his lips, humming appreciatively at the taste of his favorite dish, he couldn't stop remembering the way his mouth had felt on Riley's finger.

After dinner, they tumbled onto the expansive bed, coming together until they were all exhausted and spent. Desperation thrummed through Riley, clawing frantically under his skin. There seemed to be a certain heated intensity to their couplings lately and he wondered if the other two felt it as well. He passed out almost immediately after, too physically sated and content to let the nagging voice in his head disturb his rest.

Sometime in the middle of the night, Riley awoke suddenly, disoriented and confused. He lay on his side, a tall warm body pressed tight behind him. He blinked sleepily for a moment before realizing it was Carter. Natalie stared out of the window. Unlike her usual relaxed grace, her shoulders were slumped, her arms wrapped around herself. He wondered then about her personal life, if she had someone she was in love with. Maybe her situation was equally impossible. Her earlier sympathy led him to believe she understood on some level and he couldn't imagine how difficult it must be to maintain a relationship as an escort.

He wanted to go to her, comfort her, but he wasn't sure she'd welcome it. And selfishly, he couldn't bear to spend even a minute away from Carter. This rare chance to be with Carter was something he couldn't waste. He closed his eyes again, threading his fingers through Carter's. It was more intimate than usual and they so rarely spent a whole night together. Tonight, though, he needed this, needed hours of skin against skin to last him the four weeks until they were together again.

Carter muttered in his sleep, burying his head against

the back of Riley's neck. The soft exhalation of his breath sent a shiver down Riley's spine, hardening his cock. Involuntarily, he pressed back against his friend, wanting, just for a minute, to pretend this was his life. Wanting to imagine he could spend every night in bed with Carter with no one else to act as a go-between.

Carter shifted restlessly and sleepily grumbled before grazing his lips across the sensitive skin below Riley's hairline.

Carter prodded his thickening cock against the curve of Riley's ass. His dick wasn't hard enough to lie flat against his belly like it did when he was fully aroused, but aimed straight forward instead. Carter's actions brushed the tip of his cock against Riley's balls and pressed the shaft snugly against the cleft of his ass. Riley caught his breath, imagining the way it would feel if his friend pressed up inside him, filling him. They'd certainly never done it, and he'd barely let himself contemplate what it would be like, but something in him ached for it now that the thought had entered his mind.

Riley couldn't stifle the groan that left him when Carter sleepily pushed forward again. Natalie turned away from the window. Her posture changed immediately, her usual grace returning as she walked toward him.

"What are you guys doing in that bed?" she murmured.

Riley's tongue felt heavy with the words he couldn't say, so he merely held out a hand, beckoning her to join then. Carter settled on his back on the bed and Riley reached for the condoms and lube. Natalie straddled Carter's waist and Riley watched them kiss as he got her ready and rolled a condom onto his cock. He lingered over putting one on Carter, until Carter growled at him to get going. Riley gripped Natalie's hip and took a deep breath before he aligned himself. Her ass was slick and open from his preparations, and he pressed into her, trying to convince himself he wasn't imagining sliding into Carter's ass. He held his breath and guided Natalie onto Carter. They'd done this so many times before, but the feel of his cock separated from Carter's by only the thin wall of Natalie's flesh and two condoms made his head spin. It drove him crazy, made him ache with want.

At first, they moved slowly, the two men barely rocking while they gave Natalie's body time to adjust, time to relax around them. No matter how many times they did this, it was always the same. First, the slow, rocking, then the deep, even thrusts, and finally the frantic, sometimes disjointed desperation as they all chased their orgasms.

Riley felt out of control, his need for Carter eclipsing his usual caution and subtlety. He gripped Carter's hair hard, pulling Carter's mouth to his in a rough, desperate kiss. His teeth nicked Carter's lip, drawing a drop of blood, and Carter cried out, their tongues sharing the taste between them for a moment. It wasn't the blood itself but the idea of having some part of Carter inside him that made Riley lose control.

The idea seemed so shockingly intimate that he came, almost without warning, with a couple of belly-clenching, soul-shattering spurts into the condom that made him cry out, his whole body shaking as he fought back the urge to blurt out the words he'd never allowed himself to say inside his head, much less aloud. He continued to thrust when Natalie's orgasm hit and Carter's followed a moment later. Riley couldn't stop staring at Carter's face when he threw his head back, throat corded and tense.

He buried his head in Natalie's soft curls and he felt her soothing touch against his thigh as if she was reassuring him she understood. Carter tightened his grip on Riley and leaned in for another kiss, this one sweet and deep. They shifted onto their sides, bodies still tangled together. Their slow, gliding touches of their tongues mimicked the lazy way they slid in and out of Natalie, prolonging the pleasure while Riley hovered between ecstasy and agony, sharing a piece of himself with the man he wanted more than anything to be with and could never have.

* * * *

"No, I have no idea what time I'll be home, Alex," Riley snarled into his phone. "I have a pile of work on my desk that has to be finished. Tonight. I might get it done faster if you weren't calling me every half hour to see if I'm still here."

"You've hardly been home all week," she said sharply.

Maybe I'd be home more if you were less irritating, he thought, then winced immediately. It wasn't fair of him to take out his frustration with his life on her. He tried to soften his voice when he replied aloud. "Look, I'll be home as soon as I can, Alex. Give me another hour."

"Never mind," she huffed in irritation. "I'm going out with some of the girls. I refuse to sit here waiting for you to come home while you hole up in your office for the millionth night in a row!"

"I'll see you later then," Riley said shortly, ending the call before she could reply. He sat back with a weary sigh, rubbing his hands over his face. He let the chair spin and stared out the vast expanse of windows in his office on the twenty-third floor of the building where Porter-Wright Publishing was located. The lights of Manhattan glittered brightly. It was dark, nearly nine p.m. on a Saturday night and he felt exhausted. He hadn't slept well since the car accident.

The phone buzzed on Riley's desk and he swung his chair around with a violent jerk, scooping up the phone and briefly contemplated throwing the damn device at the window, but when he glanced down, he saw that Carter, not Alex, was calling.

He swiped his thumb across the screen to unlock it, answering immediately. "Hey, Car."

"Hey, buddy. How are you?"

Riley leaned his head back and closed his eyes, letting his friend's low voice wash over him. It calmed him immediately and the tension slipped from Riley's shoulders, allowing him to relax for the first time all day.

Missing you, he thought. "Tired," he replied.

"Let me guess, you're at the office?"

"Yeah. There's always something to catch up on."

Carter's laugh sounded incredulous. "You mean you're avoiding your wife."

"That, too." Riley sat up and cracked his neck, once more staring out of the window. "Where are you?"

"Home."

"In your office there?"

Carter chuckled. "You know me well."

Riley liked thinking about Carter sitting behind the antique desk in his penthouse. Riley could picture Carter sitting with his feet propped on the desk, drinking his favorite brand of bourbon. Riley liked thinking about Carter's tall, fit body, the way his brown hair curled a little at the ends if he went too long without a haircut, the fullness of his lips.

Riley pressed the heel of his hand to his eye as if he could literally force the image of his closest friend from his mind. As if that had ever worked before.

"Ri?" his friend's voice broke through his thoughts. "Still there, buddy?"

"Yeah, sorry," he said, dropping his hand and leaning his head back against the chair.

"You sure you're okay?" The concern in Carter's voice shone through.

"It's been a long week. I'll be all right," he lied, his voice too tight to be believable.

"Fuck, I wish we were seeing Natalie again," Carter mused.

"We saw her last week," Riley pointed out.

"I know," Carter admitted. "It's difficult not to want it more often, though."

Riley hummed noncommittally. Sure, a part of him wanted that, but each encounter took more and more of a toll on him. Living this double life, wanting more than he could have, drained him and made him feel stretched thin and brittle.

"I don't know. I can't help feeling like we're pushing our luck as is," he said. "Things have been great, but we've been lucky. We can't keep this up forever. At some point, the threesomes will have to stop."

Carter sighed heavily. "Can't you let me have my blissful fantasy?"

"Sorry. I'll stop letting reality intrude on your imaginary world."

Carter snorted and Riley continued more seriously.

"I understand this is your escape and, believe me, I love the Thursday nights we have with Natalie, too, but it's not always easy for me after."

"I get it," Carter murmured, but Riley realized Carter really didn't understand how much Riley struggled with this. It wasn't his fault. Riley hadn't been honest. Riley stood, restless all of a sudden. He wondered how Carter would react if he ever pushed for something deeper. What would Carter do if Riley confessed he wanted to explore more physically between them? Most importantly, what would he do if Riley admitted his feelings for Carter?

"Where the hell is your head tonight?" Carter asked, drawing his attention back to their phone conversation.

"Nowhere," he said, the words thick in his throat.

"I'm worried about you," Carter said.

Riley pressed his palm against the window for a moment, mesmerized by the shimmering lights of the city. He closed his eyes, wishing so desperately that he'd made a different choice all those years before while they lay beside the Charles River, talking about their future. What would his life be like if he'd pushed Carter then? Would they have a place together in the West Village they called home rather than a pied-à-terre that they used for the stolen moments they had together with Natalie? If he'd made that choice then, Riley certainly wouldn't be Executive Vice President of Porter-Wright Publishing, but he might have been happier.

Or, he might have lost all of it, he acknowledged. He might have lost Carter's friendship and the job he loved so much. He'd gambled and wound up with a hand that disappointed him, but it could have been much worse.

"I've had a lot on my mind lately," Riley admitted, then cleared his throat, forcing himself to sound more cheerful. "But I'll be fine. You know me, Carter, by the next time we have an appointment with Natalie, I'll be ready for our next threesome."

The distant sound of a door closing with a muted thud startled him and he jerked in surprise, spinning around and striding through the door of his office. "Look, Carter, I have to go, okay?" he said abruptly. "I'll catch you later."

He ended the call before Carter could reply and slid his phone into his pants pocket as he walked through the dim and deserted halls of the office. He'd been looser with his tongue than usual, but the office had been empty when he'd arrived and, late on a Saturday night, he hadn't expected there to be anyone around. Had someone overheard what he'd said to Carter? Who had been in the office? What if someone put the pieces together and figured out their secret? Had Riley been right that he and Carter couldn't keep this hidden forever? Would the carefully built web of lies come crashing down around them both? The thought made him queasy.

Knowing he'd never be able to focus on work now, Riley tidied his desk and logged out of his computer, trying to quell the uneasy feeling racing through him. As he rode the elevator downstairs to the lobby, he wondered if he should tell Carter that he suspected someone had eavesdropped on his end of their conversation. He hated the thought of blindsiding him when whoever had walked by possibly hadn't heard a thing, so he decided to wait. If there was a problem, he'd let Carter know immediately, but for now, he'd keep him out of it. Whatever it took, he'd make sure the eavesdropper kept their secret, even if it meant emptying his bank accounts. He couldn't bear the thought of his carelessness destroying the life Carter had worked so hard for.

He was lost in his thoughts as he passed by the security desk and he nodded absently to the two guards sitting there. "Evening, Mr. Porter-Wright," one said.

"Evening."

"Hope I didn't startle you earlier," the other said.

"What?" Riley asked, suddenly focused. Had it been the *security guard* on the twenty-third floor?

"In the office a little bit ago. I saw the light on in your office while I made my rounds. Hope I didn't startle you."

Riley tensed. Was that a thinly veiled threat to let him know he'd been overheard? "It's fine," he said shortly. "You did startle me, but you were just doing your job, right?"

The guard grinned sheepishly. "Well, I got distracted, listening to the game on my phone. I didn't even think about letting you know I was up there until I'd headed back downstairs. I hope I didn't disturb you and, uh, hopefully I'm not in too much trouble about the game…"

Riley let out a sigh of relief. He could see the guard had a set of headphones wrapped around his neck, with one of the earbuds in. Even if he had been able to overhear Riley's conversation, he'd probably been so focused on the game he hadn't been paying attention to what Riley had said.

"Your secret's safe with me," Riley said, grinning. He waved goodbye to the guards and headed out into the parking deck. His whole body shook as he slid into his car and he had to take several deep breaths before he could start the engine.

He rested his head on the steering wheel for a minute. That had been too close. This time, he'd been lucky enough that no one had overheard him, but that wouldn't always be the case. He had to be more careful.

He'd begun to wonder if maybe it wouldn't be better if they stopped the threesomes entirely. He knew Carter would be disappointed, but Riley wasn't sure how much longer he could continue them. To be honest, he didn't know how much longer he could continue any of it—the lying, the cheating, the hiding were all wearing on him.

* * * *

Something seemed off with Natalie the next time they met at the apartment. She seemed distracted, a little less focused than usual. Although concerned, Riley didn't want to pry. He gently teased her while they cooked dinner together, promising to treat her with some of the candy he and Carter been amassing to hand out on Halloween night the following week to coax a smile out of her, but there was a distance in her eyes that didn't go away.

Dinner seemed quieter than usual and, although pleasurable, even their time in bed seemed tinged by the strange mood lingering over all three of them. After they showered, Natalie dressed in her street clothes and cleared her throat. "I need to talk to both of you."

Riley and Carter exchanged worried glances and Carter momentarily paused in the middle of pulling on his boxers. Riley was already dressed in sleep pants and he hesitantly took a seat on the bed, concerned about what she had to say. Carter finished putting on his boxers and pants and remained standing, while Natalie paced. "I've been thinking about this for a long time and I feel like it's time I moved on. I am going to miss you guys, but I've put in my resignation with Colin and I'm quitting the agency."

Both men gaped at her for a moment, but Riley recovered first. "May I ask why?"

"It's nothing bad," she assured them. "It's simply time for me to do something else. Truthfully, I loved doing this, especially with clients like the two of you. But although I love it, there's something else I love more. I'm going to be opening a dance studio. I was a ballet dancer, years ago, and it's time I got back to that. I can't perform anymore, but I am incredibly excited about the idea of teaching."

"I won't lie," Carter said with a disappointed smile. "As

happy as I am for you, I'm sorry you're leaving."

"A part of me is going to miss this," she admitted, stopping in front of him and gently patting his chest, smiling up at him. "You two are always the highlight of my month."

Riley stood up and went over to join them. "Carter's right. We are going to miss you. This has been…a lot more than I ever expected. More than the sex," he admitted. "But I am happy for you."

Natalie brushed her fingers across his cheek and jaw and stretched up to kiss him. "I've had a good time with you both," she said when she finally pulled away.

Riley nodded. This stolen time with Carter wouldn't have been possible without Natalie and he'd miss her a lot. She'd become more than a go-between for her clients—she'd become a friend. "Good luck. I think it's great that you're going after what you love."

She leaned forward and whispered in his ear. "It's time you do the same. It's not going to be easy, but the two of you should be together."

The pointed look she gave Riley when she pulled back wasn't lost on him, but he only managed a small shrug and a tremulous smile. Natalie dropped the apartment key he'd given her into his hand and turned to Carter. She kissed him goodbye and whispered something in his ear that made Riley incredibly curious.

"How are we ever going to replace you?" Carter joked, but she didn't respond. Instead, she shot a glance at Riley that seemed as clear as if she'd spoken. He'd never get to be with Carter the way he wanted if they kept hiring an escort.

Riley knew he couldn't continue. The situation had to stop and Natalie leaving was the perfect opportunity for him to make some changes. Carter wouldn't be happy, but Riley needed to start thinking about what was best for himself. He needed either to man up and tell Carter the truth, or end this arrangement. This limbo was killing him.

Natalie left a few minutes later and a melancholy quiet settled over them. Carter paused, partially dressed in navy slacks, a soft white undershirt and an unbuttoned crisp white dress shirt. "Are you headed out?" he asked. "I'll walk down with you."

Riley tossed the spare key onto his dresser, shrugged on a well-worn Harvard sweatshirt and zipped it up before he shook his head. "I think I'm going to crash here tonight. Alex is gone, anyway." Depressingly, he couldn't even remember where she'd said she'd be. The sadder part was that he didn't care.

"Oh," Carter said, a flash of concern crossing his face. "Are you okay, Ri? You've seemed kind of off lately. I started noticing it around when you had your accident."

"Yeah," Riley said. "I guess that's part of it though. They aren't kidding when they say your life flashes before your eyes. It made me realize I'm not sure I'm headed in the direction I want to go. And" — he hesitated — "I realized that even if Alex had been home, you were the one I thought to call first."

"I'm glad you called me. It scared me, though. What if you'd been hurt worse?" Carter looked down for a moment. "I can't stand the thought of losing you, Ri."

"I'm not going anywhere," Riley assured him. "But I came to the realization that I need to reassess some things. I'm not — I'm not happy with my life right now, Car. I think I need to make some changes."

Carter frowned at him, sticking his hands into his pockets. "You want to talk about it?"

Riley hesitated for a moment, then shook his head. God, he felt tempted to blurt it all out and confess his feelings to Carter, but, to be honest, he didn't know exactly what he wanted and it wasn't fair to dump it all on Carter without being sure first. "Not right now, but thanks."

"Of course," Carter reassured him, stepping closer. "I'm always here for you, no matter what."

Oh, please let that be true, Riley thought. *Let it be true after I work up the courage to tell you how I feel.*

Impulsively, he leaned forward and gave in to the

urge to press his lips to Carter's. If he was going to end the threesomes, it might be the last time he had the opportunity. Carter went still against him for a moment, then reciprocated, sliding his hand into Riley's hair, parting Riley's lips with his tongue. Riley responded with a groan, the built-up longing he felt pushing him to deepen the kiss further. It turned needier than he'd planned, but Riley was grateful that Carter responded. He roamed his hands across Carter's chest for a moment, but when he stepped forward, wanting more, Carter pulled back.

Riley swallowed the pang of disappointment he felt.

"What was that for?" Carter asked, brushing his thumb against lips slightly swollen from Riley's kiss.

"I-I don't know," Riley said, truthfully. His head swam from the rare chance to kiss Carter without a woman in the middle and he could hardly make sense of what he'd done, or what he should do from here on out.

"Okay," Carter said, his voice a little rough as he buttoned his shirt. "I…I guess I'll head home now."

Riley nodded and hardly even registered the hand Carter placed on his shoulder, or when he left. He was too busy trying to figure out how the fuck to tell his best friend he loved him. How to ask Carter to risk it all and give up the safe life he'd built with his wife and children in order to be together.

Chapter Eleven

Kate held Carter's hand tightly as a roar of applause swept through the opera house. Carter glanced at her with a smile before he let go so they could join in clapping. Kate had been anticipating this performance in particular and it showed in the way her eyes sparkled as she gazed down at the stage.

She turned to look at Carter after he nudged her, the sound of her laughter audible over the noise of the crowd. Carter raised a teasing eyebrow.

"Not bad," he mouthed. He nodded at the stage and bit back another grin as she stared at him.

"It's brilliant and you know it," Kate scolded, leaning in close so Carter could hear her. "I swear to God, I will divorce you if you can't say you at least like this."

"Such a drama queen," he scoffed, nudging her again. "I'm clapping, aren't I? Should I be standing? I could do interpretive dance to express my appreciation if you think that's appropriate—"

"Stop." Kate's voice trembled with suppressed laughter. "Don't say another word—you're embarrassing yourself." Kate shook her head in defeat, but Carter could see the humor in her eyes as the house lights came up. Her midnight-blue gown set off her fair skin and blond hair beautifully.

"Come on," she urged. "Let's go find Riley so I can talk to someone who actually appreciates what's going on here tonight."

At the mention of Riley's name, Carter's smile faltered. His thoughts turned again to something that had been dogging him since Natalie had quit three weeks before, and he checked the Porter-Wrights' box. He spotted Riley and Alex immediately. He watched them, noting Alex's frown and Riley's strangely blank expression.

"You okay, Car?"

Carter met Kate's questioning gaze.

"You've been a little distracted tonight," she continued. "Is there something wrong?"

"I'm not sure." They stood and Carter took his wife's hand in his and tucked it into the crook of his elbow as they made their way out of the box. "Something's going on with Riley," he added.

"Is he okay? He seems to have recovered from the car accident, at least according to Alex."

Carter frowned. "Physically, he seems fine. Otherwise, I don't know. He's blowing off my phone calls and emails, hasn't had time to get together…he just doesn't seem like himself."

Kate raised her brows. "You're right — that doesn't sound like Riley."

"When we were at school together, he'd sometimes close himself off," Carter admitted. He and Kate followed the crowd. "That was especially true when something bothered him. Riley wouldn't talk to anyone, wouldn't tell anyone why he was upset…he just withdrew." Carter pursed his lips. "It used to drive me and Dan crazy."

"It certainly seems to be driving you crazy now, sweetheart."

Carter glanced at Kate, his curiosity piqued. Before he could ask her what she'd meant, a group of friends approached, eager to get to the bar to talk about the performance.

With a drink in hand, he leaned against the bar, absorbing the conversations around him while saying little himself. He'd come to enjoy attending the opera over the years. He was not — and would never be — a true aficionado, but Carter didn't care as long as Kate and Riley enjoyed themselves.

He gazed over the throngs of people moving around him while he sipped his drink. Concern prickled through Carter's chest after he caught sight of Riley and Alex at the far end of the bar and he stood straighter, watching them closely.

Alex stood slightly apart from Riley, her face and movements animated while she spoke with a group of people. As always, she was flawlessly attired and made up. She'd swept her fiery hair back and away from her face and her black gown set off the fair skin of her shoulders and neck. Riley, on the other hand, appeared pale and listless, despite his beautiful tuxedo.

Pushing away from the bar, Carter then stepped to Kate's side. He brushed her left hip with his knuckles to get her attention and nodded in Riley's direction when she glanced Carter's way. Understanding crossed Kate's face and she gave Carter a slight smile, encouraging him to talk to his friend.

Carter weaved carefully through the crowds gathered around the bar, exchanging greetings with friends and acquaintances. He stopped a short distance away from his friend and felt sick as Riley's posture stiffened, tension visibly rolling across his shoulders when he met Carter's stare.

Despite Riley's stern expression, Carter closed the distance between them and was surprised to catch something like apprehension in his friend's gaze.

Carter forced a smile. "Having a good time tonight?"

Riley sipped his cocktail before he answered. "Very much. I like *Turandot*."

Carter knew his friend's words were sincere. He'd listened to Riley and Kate discuss *Turandot* on several occasions. Riley considered the icy princess for whom the opera had been named unfairly maligned.

"Are you okay?" Carter asked him now, reaching to grasp Riley's biceps with one hand.

"Yeah, I'm fine." Riley's reply was smooth and his gaze

distant almost immediately. "Are you enjoying yourself?"

"Kate's enjoying herself—that's enough for me." Riley's smile twisted and Carter hid his dismay, dropping his hand after a beat.

He nursed his drink while they chatted. They talked about work, Carter's kids and other uncomplicated topics, and Carter's chest burned. He listened to himself make small talk as if Riley was a stranger instead of his best friend.

He started when Riley drew in a sharp breath, his face flushing as though he were in pain.

"Jesus, Ri, are you sure you're okay?" Carter brought up a hand to grip Riley's elbow and when he jerked away from his touch, something in Carter's chest twisted.

"I'm fine." Riley blurted, his eyes never meeting Carter's. "It's just been a long week. I'll be all right, Car."

Carter sighed. He wanted to understand what his friend was going through, but knew this was not the place to ask. The last thing either of them should do was argue in the middle of intermission at the goddamned Metropolitan Opera.

Carter stared hard at Riley before gesturing toward a secluded corner and turning away. He felt almost light-headed with relief as he looked back to find Riley following, his face stony.

They ducked into the alcove and a dozen thoughts flew through Carter's head—so many things he wanted to say and ask. Every word escaped him as he met his friend's unrelenting blue gaze. Carter knew he needed to start talking or Riley was going to bolt, so he swallowed hard, opened his mouth and said the first thing that popped into his head. Much later, he realized he had chosen exactly the wrong thing to say.

"You do know what a week from now is, right?"

A long moment passed before Riley nodded, his voice low when he spoke. "It's the third Thursday of the month."

"Our first Thursday without Natalie." Carter's heart pounded as he considered again what Natalie's absence meant to his life and Riley's.

He'd been supportive of Natalie's decision to return to dance. However, the end of her days playing escort to wealthy men and women also meant the end of the triangle she'd formed with Carter and Riley. Without Natalie, Carter's desire for Riley had no outlet and the means of bridging his unspoken yearning for his friend had disappeared. Now, as what would have been their next appointment approached, his need was peaking.

"I'm going to miss her like hell, but I think we should find a replacement. I don't know about you, but I'd miss those nights," he murmured, swallowing back the things he really wanted to say.

I miss you, Ri.

Riley's throat worked as he set his nearly empty drink on a table and shoved his hands into his pockets. "I'd miss them, too," he said, his voice husky.

Carter's chest ached while he continued to stand and watch his friend, memories of tumbling into bed with Riley and Natalie filling his thoughts. Finding someone to take Natalie's place had proven difficult because Riley was being difficult. Carter had pushed hard after Natalie had quit, in hopes they could find someone before the third Thursday of the new month. Riley had made excuses not to follow through on appointments with Colin Archer's agency, though. He'd started dodging phone calls and leaving email messages unanswered, forcing Carter to back off.

"Look, I...I enjoy those nights," Riley said now in a gentle tone. "You know I do. I'm not sure about finding someone new."

Carter pressed his lips tightly together. "I don't want to give up those appointments," he confessed, his heart pounding in his ears. He hated sounding needy. He didn't care, though, if it got him what he wanted. To get what Carter thought Riley wanted every bit as badly. "I always feel so damned good afterward."

Riley made a sound of agreement, but his skeptical

expression sent a chill through Carter. The idea of no longer being intimate with Riley in any way pained him. He missed touching Riley, missed the rasp of Riley's whiskers against his lips and the sensation of Riley wrapping his long fingers around his cock.

"What's going on with you?" Carter asked at last, his voice strained. "You seem off tonight. Have for a while now, starting with whatever was bothering you during our last time with Natalie."

Riley closed his eyes for a moment before nodding. "Yeah, I…I need to talk to you about something."

"Of course. You know you can tell me anything."

Riley's sad smile made Carter's eyes burn. "Intermission is nearly up and we can't discuss it here anyway. I need you to meet me somewhere private tonight. Tell Kate we're going to go out for drinks or something. I don't care, but I have to talk to you."

Carter gave him a long, searching look, hands clasped together hard to stop them from trembling. "Of course. Where do you want to meet?" he asked just before the chimes signaled the end of intermission rang out.

"Meet me at the apartment on West 10th."

* * * *

Carter sat through the final acts of the opera, silently fighting against a growing sense of dread. He felt chilled by the final curtain call.

"What's wrong?" Kate asked after he took their coats from the attendant, her gaze fixed on his face. "You've looked really stressed since you came back to the box, Carter. Is it Riley?"

Carter shook his head, unsure of what to say. "I don't know how to answer that." He helped Kate into her coat and tucked her hand in his, moving with the crowd toward the exits. "Something's definitely going on with Riley, but he didn't want to talk about it here."

"Do you think it's something with Alex?" Kate shook her head when Carter could only shrug in reply.

"He wants to talk to me—asked me to meet him after I take you home. Normally I'd try to get him to reschedule, maybe for lunch, but he seemed so disheartened, I couldn't say no."

"I understand." Kate steered Carter toward the main entrance. "Go on, find out what he wants. I'll take the car home so you don't have to make the extra trip."

Carter met his wife's earnest gaze and licked his lips, equal parts guilt and gratitude swirling through him. If only she knew what he and Riley got up to when they were alone.

"He's your best friend, honey—I know how much he means to you." She grinned and jerked her head toward the door. "Now be good and walk me to the car—it's the least you can do since this date is turning into boys' night."

Carter couldn't help smiling back, even as a pang ran through him at Kate's unintentional irony. After seeing her to the car, he watched its taillights blend into the traffic on 65th Street then jogged back the way he had come. Following a hunch, he headed for the Revson Fountain, knowing Riley liked to pause there when time—and Alex—allowed.

He caught sight of Riley walking across the plaza, hands clasped behind his back and his head bowed. Carter paused, waiting for his friend to notice him, his heartbeat quickening as Riley's earlier words echoed in his ears.

'I'm just not sure about finding someone new…I need to talk to you about something.'

A sudden thought struck Carter, making his mouth go dry. Could Riley have developed feelings for Natalie? Was that the reason he'd been reluctant to find a new escort to take her place?

"Jesus," Carter muttered to himself, swallowing hard while his brain scrambled to fit together the pieces of his suspicion. The sound of Riley calling his name pulled him back to the present.

He zoned out during the cab ride to the West Village, aided by the ringing silence between them. It had been three weeks since Carter had spent time with Riley. Since Natalie had told them she was quitting and Riley had kissed Carter with a passion that had sent him reeling. Carter rubbed his fingers over his lips and wondered if, after tonight, he'd ever have a chance to kiss his friend again.

The silence grew heavier after they got out of the cab, becoming so thick Carter thought he'd choke on it. They went upstairs to the apartment and for a long moment after Riley took his coat, Carter considered simply walking out. He drew an unsteady breath instead and made a beeline for the kitchen and the cupboard that held the booze.

"You want a glass?" Carter called out, pursing his lips at Riley's continued silence. The first shot of bourbon burned on its way down. The heat that spread in his belly was comforting, though, and made it easier to go back into the living room to face his friend.

He found Riley standing at the wide expanse of windows overlooking the balcony, his gaze fixed on the lights of the city around them. Carter put a hand on Riley's shoulder and immediately sensed tension in the muscles beneath his palm. He nearly jumped when Riley spoke.

"I'm sorry to do this, Carter, but there's something I need to tell you."

Steeling himself, Carter used the hand on Riley's shoulder to turn him so they were facing each other. His breath caught at the raw pain in his friend's face.

"What is going on?"

"I don't think I can keep doing what we've been doing. I…I've been struggling with this for a while, trying to figure out how to tell you—if I should tell you. I still don't know if this is the right choice, but I don't think we should find a replacement for Natalie."

"Why? I don't understand," Carter replied, his voice pleading. "You loved what we did with her. I know you did."

"A part of me did, yes." Riley wet his lips, but his next words didn't make sense. "But they hurt, too. Because they made me want things I can't have."

Carter blinked. "What are you saying, Riley?"

"I'm…I'm saying I can't go on like this. I can't keep pretending anymore."

"Pretending what?" Carter's heartbeat spiked as Riley closed his eyes.

"I can't keep pretending I don't want you. Just you… without the girls in between us."

Carter froze, unable to react for a moment. "I don't understand," he said finally.

"I want to be with you, Carter." Riley's voice broke. "Not once a month, sharing you with a woman we pay to be with. Every night, every day. I can't… I can't live like this anymore."

A tremor began deep inside Carter, working its way slowly outward, making his hands fist and his voice waver. "What are you saying?"

"I'm saying I want to end our monthly appointments. I know this seems like it's out of the blue, but I've been thinking about it for a while. I—we—have been living a lie." Riley's expression was broken, pleading with Carter, though Carter couldn't understand for what.

"What lie? What…what are you talking about?"

Riley faced the window once more. When he spoke again, his voice was soft and sure, though every word sent shockwaves through Carter's soul. Through his world.

"I'm in love with you, Carter. Not with my wife, not with anyone else. With you. I have been for years. I suppose I-I'm bisexual, or gay, Christ, I don't know. I've spent years trying not to think about what it all meant. Whatever I am, I'm not the man in love with Alex I've been pretending to be."

Riley faced him and Carter inhaled sharply. He'd been worried about all kinds of things since Riley had shut him out. That Riley might be sick or going broke, that his marriage had finally crumbled, even that he'd fallen in love with the woman they'd hired to fuck them. But this—that Riley had fallen in love with him—was the last thing Carter could ever have imagined.

"I can't live a lie anymore," Riley repeated, seeming shattered. "I can't let myself turn into my parents. I don't want to have a complete sham of a marriage in order to make everyone else happy. I'm going to divorce Alex and I'm coming out."

Carter's head spun. "Why?" he exclaimed, his voice loud with shock and utter disbelief. "You'll come out to what, fuck guys now?"

"No...look, I don't know, maybe. I want to be with you, but even if I can't be, at least I won't be lying anymore." Riley shook his head, seeming both angry and despondent. "I want to be myself. To not hide who I am anymore."

Anger swept over Carter in an unexpected rush. "Do you know what this is going to do to your reputation? To mine?" he asked, his voice low and dangerous. "People have been gossiping about our friendship and who we are to each other since we were at college. Fuck, Ri, if you come out everyone's going to assume the rumors are true—that we've been screwing for years!"

"I wish we had been." Riley retorted. "At least it would have been more honest than what we've been doing. We've been lying to ourselves and our wives, Carter, and for what?"

Carter didn't reply, unable to answer that question without looking more closely at himself than he felt comfortable doing.

"You're just going to throw away everything you have?" he asked instead. "Your career, your wife, your family?"

"I have no idea what will happen with my career," Riley admitted, "or with my family. My father might hate me so much he'll toss me out of the company and I have no idea how my mother will react. If I lose all of that, yeah, it'll be hard."

"And Alex?" Carter's tone was sharp.

Riley shrugged. "You know we've never really gotten along well. I married her because it was easier to be married to someone I didn't love, if I couldn't have you." He stepped closer, cupping Carter's cheek. "It's always been you, Carter. I've lied to myself since we met, but I am in love with you. I have been for over fifteen years."

The earth dropped out from under Carter's feet for the second time that night. He stared at Riley as if seeing him for the first time, and couldn't help wondering if he'd ever truly known the man he called his best friend.

"What the fuck?" he breathed, his lips barely moving while the pain coursed through him.

"I can't imagine doing this without you, but I will if I have to." Riley said. Every inch of him was taut and trembling. "I want to be with you more than anything, but I know you have to make your own decisions."

Carter stood silent, utterly frozen, his breath burning in his lungs and Riley's hand fever-hot against his face. He couldn't speak, not even as Riley moved his thumb over Carter's cheek.

"Please. Just think about it. You feel this, I know you do."

Carter inhaled sharply as Riley pressed his lips against his. Their mouths moved together and heat flooded his body, the sweet, hot slide of their tongues making Carter's heart pound.

Fuck.

Nothing in his life felt this good or right. Nothing compared to kissing Riley, to the feel of Riley's body against his. Carter's skin tingled, his heart hammered and all he wanted was to sink down, down, down with this man in his arms and never move again.

He shuddered as Riley grasped the lapel of his tux, pulling Carter impossibly closer. Riley moaned and murmured Carter's name, his voice seductive and terribly familiar. Too much like another voice, also intimate and adored, that called out to Carter in the dark of an East Side condo.

Kate.

Carter's whole being jerked into reverse.

He crossed the room, pain twisting through his chest so sharply he nearly cried out.

"I can't," he managed, aware he was begging, though he wasn't sure for what. "Don't ask me to do this, Ri. Please."

"I'm sorry." The life seemed to drain from Riley's face again. "I am. But I'm miserable, Car. Every day I feel a little worse. I'm not sleeping, my anxiety is through the roof…I can't take it anymore."

"My family…" Carter shook his head. Kate's face flashed through his mind, followed by Sadie's and Dylan's. There were people in Carter's life counting on him to be a strong husband and a good father. He considered how selfish Riley was being and how very careless, not only of Carter and his family, but of his own, and anger coursed through him.

"Christ, how can you ask me to do this? You know my father will disown me. And Kate…and the kids? How can I break up my family? You're asking me to give up everything," he ranted, aware he was shouting but unable to stop. "Whether I do this or not, if you come out, it'll come back on me, too. I can't believe you're doing this!"

Anguish flashed over Riley's face. "I know. I'm asking too much. But I need you. I dream about what it would be like to touch you. No pretending it's just in the heat of the moment when we're fucking Natalie."

Carter sank into the nearest seat and closed his eyes, tilting his head to rest against the seatback. As angry as he'd been the moment before, now he felt empty. It was clear Riley didn't understand why he couldn't walk away from his life, and worse, Carter began to suspect Riley didn't care.

With a low sound of frustration, he lifted his head and looked across the room at Riley, leaning forward to rest his elbows on his knees.

"Why now, Riley? Things were good between us and Natalie. It worked for us."

"It's not working for me anymore." Riley's voice was

quiet. "I need more."

"And more is what, exactly?"

Riley blew out a long breath.

"Are you attracted to me, Carter?"

Carter stared at his friend in disbelief. "Christ, Ri. What does that have to do with anything?"

"I have to know. If the two of us could be together, without having to hurt our families or disrupt our entire lives, would you want to be?"

"I don't even know how to answer that question!"

"Do you remember the conversation we had before graduation, about running away together?" Riley asked.

"Yeah, I do." Carter swallowed against the burn of tears in his eyes.

Riley ran a hand through his hair and shook his head, seeming lost in his memories. "I think about it often. I wish we'd done it."

Carter nodded, dropping his gaze back to the floor, his hands hanging limply between his knees. "Sometimes I wish we'd done it, too."

"You can't say it, can you?" Riley asked, the hurt in his voice heartbreakingly clear. "You can't say the words. You can't admit you want me. You can't admit you have feelings for me that go beyond friendship."

"It's...it's difficult, Riley. Maybe you've been thinking about this — wanting more — but we're not those guys anymore, fresh out of school and talking about running away from responsibilities. You may not love Alex, but I do love Kate. For the most part, I'm content with what we have. Yeah, I care about you. As way more than just a friend. But going to bed with Natalie and having you there with me was enough."

Carter stood stiffly, his heart aching. He knew that the most important friendship in his life was dying tonight, with every demand Riley made and every refusal Carter returned. His grief only worsened as Riley crossed the room and touched his arm.

"It's not enough for me, Car." Sorrow and regret twisted Riley's handsome features. "I want a life with you. I want to come home to you at the end of the day, fall asleep beside you and wake up the next morning in our bed. I want to make love to you, with no one else between us. Make love to you because you're the only person I've ever loved like this. No more lies, no more pretending. Just you and me."

For one shining moment, Carter could see it, the life Riley described, filled with passion and laughter and the best kind of affection. An honest life, both true and whole. A life Carter was not free to have.

Slowly, he walked toward the door, his steps loud in the silent room. He imagined he could hear his heart beating in time with Riley's, who stood unmoving, silent even after Carter turned back.

"I can't." He tried not to meet his friend's gaze but saw Riley's anguish nonetheless. "I need some time, Ri. To process everything."

"Carter, don't do this."

"I'm sorry. I can't," he whispered. "I can't do it. Please don't ask me to."

* * * *

Carter's hands trembled as he let himself into his apartment. His breaths were coming fast and loud, and he swallowed hard, trying to get back some semblance of control.

Ignoring the late hour, he headed for his office to pour himself a drink, cursing when the neck of the bottle knocked against the rim of his glass. He inhaled deeply and closed his eyes, dropping his hands back to rest on the bar, while still holding the glass and bottle. A solid minute passed before he opened his eyes again, but his hands were steadier when he raised them a second time.

Chest tight even after the drink, Carter walked through the darkened apartment. He made his way upstairs to slip into Dylan's room, navigating around the toys scattered across the floor. Dylan was curled against the headboard, surrounded by an army of stuffed animals. Carter cleared a space, after easing the little body back under the bedding, and shushed him quietly after Dylan murmured in his sleep.

He stopped by Sadie's room next, where the chaos was more controlled and infinitely pinker, even in the low light from the hallway. Carter pulled a glittery tiara from his daughter's hair and caught sight of a tube of lip gloss on her nightstand. He frowned before deciding to talk to Kate instead of simply pocketing the tube.

He prowled down the long hall to the room he and Kate shared next, gazing at the framed photos that decorated the wall. Smiling faces filled each, telling the stories of his family's life. There were scenes from weddings, birthdays, graduations, vacations and holidays. Many of the photos were of Dylan and Sadie, tracing their growth from tiny babies to precocious preschoolers, and of Carter and Kate with the children. They were a beautiful family, Carter knew, and his eyes stung again as he moved on.

Scattered among Hamilton photos were images from the life Carter had lived before it had been eclipsed by work and family. A much younger version of himself smiled out from those images, often at the side of a similarly young and heartbreakingly handsome Riley.

Carter stopped to look at his favorite shot and his smile died. It had been taken during the Head of the Charles in Carter's third year of undergrad and he stared at the photo for a long time, admiring the good humor and health shining in his face and Riley's, their arms slung around each other's shoulders with an ease Carter missed. His face was wet when he made himself turn away.

Carter had a good life, made full by his family. His parents loved him and so did his sister and Max, his wife and children. If no one knew him as well as Riley, his family appreciated the man he showed them. Playing that role would only be easier with Riley making their friendship impossible to sustain.

Bracing one hand against the wall, Carter drew a deep breath. He had no idea what was left of his friendship with Riley or whether his friend would go through with the claims he'd made. He couldn't even begin to wrap his head around what Riley's life would become if he threw off his marriage like so much unwanted garbage.

After a moment, Carter stood a little straighter, the breath he drew hitching just a little. He wiped the moisture from his cheeks with one hand, then quietly pushed open the door of the room he shared with Kate.

Chapter Twelve

Long after the door closed behind Carter, Riley sat on the sofa, shaking. With his elbows on his knees and his head hanging low, he stared at his trembling hands, trying to stem the rising panic. His chest felt tight and achy, his throat thick with unshed tears. A part of him wanted to run after Carter, although he wasn't sure if he wanted to beg him to reconsider or tell him he'd changed his mind. The two desires warred within him, but he could do nothing except sit there and imagine his life crumbling around him. He dropped his head farther, pressing the heels of his hands against his eyelids.

Unable to handle the thought of climbing into bed with his wife, he sent a quick text to Alex, stripped out of his clothes and crawled into bed. It felt too wide without Carter and Natalie in it and Riley wished the sheets still smelled like his best friend. They were freshly laundered, though, and no matter how many times he pulled the pillow close, he was never able to catch a whiff of Carter's scent. Tight, choking fear rolled over him as he wondered if that was what his entire life would be like now without Carter in it — as sterile and lonely as Riley's life had been before they'd met.

He spent the night tossing and turning and woke up bleary-eyed and barely able to put one foot in front of the other.

For the week following his ultimatum to Carter, Riley waited for him to come around. But there were no calls or texts, not even an email with a single word. Riley wanted to give Carter time to come to him, but as the days passed, he grew more anxious. He needed to tell Alex and his parents the truth or he'd lose his nerve. He hated the thought of the problems his coming out would cause for Carter, but he needed to do what was best for himself. Even for Carter, he couldn't keep denying who he was and what he wanted any longer.

Perhaps more out of habit than anything else, he took Alex out for dinner on Saturday night before he told her. He felt vaguely queasy all night and hardly ate, despite the excellent food. Making conversation felt like a struggle as he tried to decide how to tell her. Even Alex, self-absorbed as she was, noticed.

Back inside their apartment after dinner, she handed him her coat and he stared at it blankly for a long moment before hanging it up in the closet. She frowned doubtfully at him. "Are you all right, Riley?"

"I…no, not really," he finally managed. "I need to talk to you."

"About what?" she asked, wandering off toward the bedroom. He followed and watched as she unpinned her hair, letting the mass of red curls fall down her neck before she removed her jewelry. She turned and looked at him expectantly when he didn't answer.

"I have something I need to tell you," he finally said, feeling the too-rapid beat of his heart. "You might want to sit down."

Alex raised an eyebrow at him but perched at the edge of the bed, waiting for him to continue. He swallowed hard and forced himself to speak.

"I…I want to get a divorce."

She stared at him for a long moment, her eyes wide and her lips slightly parted. Then she shook her head abruptly and stood. "You're being ridiculous."

"Excuse me?" he asked, a little stunned by her response.

"There's absolutely no reason for us to get divorced."

He let out a short bark of laughter and shook his head. "There is for me."

"What are you talking about?"

"I'm not happy, Alex," he said, growing serious again. "I'm not blaming you, but I know I need to change some parts of my life. I shouldn't have married you in the first place. I…I—" He shifted uncomfortably, struggling to force the words to come out of his mouth. He hated the labels, hated having to pick a word to define who he was and how he felt. "I'm bisexual. I've been lying to myself about it my whole life, but when it comes right down to it, I'm primarily attracted to men, and I can't keep living like this."

Alex folded her hands in her lap and leveled a disbelieving gaze at him.

"Why on earth don't you find a lover and be discreet about it? There's no reason to get divorced. The scandal would be out of control and I have no desire to deal with it. Do whatever you need to do as long as you're careful about it."

Her voice sounded cool and controlled, but he could see the flicker of hurt in her eyes and the way she clenched her hands too tightly.

He shook his head. "That won't work for me."

Alex gave him a long, calculating stare, her jaw suddenly tense. "What if I made you a deal?"

A wave of exhaustion hit him suddenly and he let out a heavy sigh. "What could you possibly offer me that would be worth spending the rest of my life lying about who I am?"

"A child."

Riley gaped at his wife for a long moment. "You can't be serious."

"I know you've considered having children. I'll be honest—it's not something I particularly want, but both our sets of parents expect it and I'll do it if it means you'll give up this ridiculous idea."

"Children aren't a goddamn bargaining chip, Alex," Riley fumed. "Yes, I've thought about having kids, but do you know why I haven't? Because you'd treat them exactly the way my parents treated me."

"I'd be more involved," Alex protested.

"Really?" Riley asked tightly. "So when our child wanted to go to the park, would you be the one chasing after him, bandaging his bloody knees and letting him rub his snotty nose on your shirt while he cries?"

Alex flinched, unable to hide her discomfort with the idea, and he knew he'd proven his point.

"That's what I thought. I refuse to bring a child into this world, then dump him with nannies! Can you honestly say you love me?" he continued. "Not my money, or my position, or the life we live? Do you love me?"

Alex remained silent, her jaw tight and her body tense.

"I went into this marriage knowing what your priorities were, so I'm not blaming you. But I won't bring children into a loveless marriage because it's expected of me and I certainly won't do it because you're trying to bribe me into not divorcing you. I truly can't think of a worse reason to have children."

He stepped forward and reached for her, but she wouldn't meet his gaze and he lowered his hand to his side. "I thought I could handle the kind of relationship my parents have, but I can't. I've been lying to you, and to myself, for a lot of years and it's time it stopped. While the last thing I want to do is cause a scandal, I'm not willing to continue to live like this. I'm sorry I'm not the man you wanted me to be, Alex. I really am."

She scowled at him, the earlier moment of vulnerability completely gone. "Your family will never stand for this."

"I know."

"Are you really prepared to lose your inheritance over this? I don't see why you can't discreetly see someone on the side," she said, her voice shaking slightly. "We can continue on like we have been and everyone will be happy."

"But I'm not happy, Alex, can't you see? Living like this is killing me. I don't want to wake up eighty years old, miserable. I don't want to go my whole damn life without ever having a happy relationship. I don't want to be an old man and realize I wasted my whole life never really loving someone."

This time, even she couldn't disguise the expression of hurt on her face, but it quickly became one of frustration. "And you're willing to do that at my expense? And the expense of your reputation, your family and your inheritance? You're a fool, Riley," she said. "There is absolutely no reason you need to go public with this."

"I'm not going to hide who I love," he said with a scowl. "I have no desire to make this a topic of gossip any more than you do, but I'm not going to pretend I'm ashamed of loving him."

He recognized his mistake the moment the word left his mouth. "So, there is someone you're in love with. You're leaving me for another man. God, this is rich. Who is it?"

"I'm not leaving you for anyone specific," he said stiffly. It was only partially a lie. He was doing this as much as for himself as for anyone else. He hoped someday he could be with Carter, but he was rapidly losing hope Carter would come around. And even if being with Carter never happened, he had to be truthful to himself.

Alex crossed her arms and stared at him for a long moment with narrowed eyes before shaking her head at him. "Let me guess? You're leaving me for your best friend. I always knew there was something odd about your relationship with Carter. Have you been fucking him this whole time?"

Riley struggled to keep his face blank. He'd be lying on a technicality. His voice was cold. "I've never fucked Carter and he's never fucked me. It isn't about Carter—it's about me."

"Well, you're being selfish."

"Maybe I am," he agreed. "But this is what I need to do."

They argued for a while longer, but she could say little else and none of it swayed him. Exhausted, he finally put an end to it. "We're getting nowhere, Alex," he said in a firm tone. "My mind's made up."

"And what are you going to do when everyone knows your dirty little secret?" she asked tightly.

He shook his head sadly. "You know, I spent a lot of time wondering about that, but eventually I realized it isn't a dirty secret at all. Being attracted to men isn't something I should have to hide. I'm not ashamed of who I am anymore."

"I don't want all of Manhattan's Upper East Side gossiping about my husband leaving me for a man! I refuse to let you humiliate me like this!"

"Then I suggest you give them another reason. I'm not going to take out an ad in the *New York Times* about my sexual orientation, Alex," he snapped. "I don't plan to shout the truth from the rooftops. Tell people whatever you want about why our marriage ended. There's no reason this has to become a huge scandal."

"And what about the money and assets? You've nullified the pre-nup."

"I'm more than willing to be reasonable when it comes to a divorce settlement."

She scowled at him. "Oh, you'll be more than reasonable. I want every penny I can get out of you."

Riley had no doubt he'd have to pay through the nose to appease Alex, but under the circumstances, he wasn't sure he really cared. And maybe she deserved it. Besides, the sooner the relationship ended, the happier he'd be. "Look, Alex, this can go one of two ways. If we act like civilized adults, we can keep the gossip to a minimum. The less you fight me in court, the easier this will be and the quieter we can keep it. I am sure our lawyers can come up with something that will work for both of us. My goal isn't to humiliate you."

She turned away from him, wrapping her arms tightly around herself.

"I just want to be happy," he said softly, wishing he could make her understand.

She didn't respond to his statement, merely stared at him

with a blank expression. "Leave. If you're going to do this to me, the least you can do is leave. I don't want to see you again. And I'm keeping this place. You can tell your lawyer that right away."

Riley nodded. "I'll pack a few belongings for now, then I'll be back sometime this week for the rest. I'll let you know when I'll be here."

"Fine," she said flatly.

"I'm sorry, Alex, I really am. I wish I'd been able to be honest with myself before you got dragged into it," he said sincerely.

But she seemed to ignore him completely and disappeared through the door of their bedroom without another word.

He packed the essentials — enough to last him for a week or so — and left. He went straight to the West Village apartment, unpacked just enough to hang his suits in the closet and collapsed into bed. He felt drained and exhausted, the nerves and adrenaline that had bolstered him through the confrontation with Alex completely gone. He knew more than anything he'd hurt her pride, but he also knew that, on some level, it had hurt her personally. It had never been his goal, although the guilt was somewhat assuaged by her using children as a bargaining tool. The idea horrified him. Although he'd never decided if he wanted children or not, he'd always known he didn't want them with Alex. With the right partner, it might be a different story.

His mind drifted to the way Carter doted on Sadie and Dylan and he felt an ache in his chest. He rubbed at it absently, then reached for his phone on the nightstand. His fingers automatically brought up Carter's name and he typed in the words, *Alex knows*, but he hesitated. He didn't know if he should contact Carter at all. His stomach churned while he debated if he should send the message. He finally did, hitting Send before he could second-guess himself again. At the very least, Carter would want the heads-up. He slipped the phone into the dock on his nightstand and rolled over, punching the pillow to make it more comfortable. He lay awake for a long time, waiting anxiously to see if Carter would respond. But his phone remained silent. He checked it three times to be sure the volume was turned up and that he hadn't missed a response, his hope sinking a little more every time. Eventually, he fell into a restless sleep, but there was still no message in the morning.

On Monday, he spoke with a lawyer so he could begin divorce proceedings. He also called his mother and told her he needed a few minutes of both his parents' time that evening. He wasn't optimistic about how the conversation would go, but when she tried to tell him they were too busy to meet, he pushed until she agreed. He wanted it over with as quickly as possible.

He spent the day vaguely ill and struggling to focus on his work. He couldn't eat and by the time he walked through the door of his parents' home, he wasn't sure how he'd make it through a conversation with them. As the housekeeper let him inside and greeted him warmly, he tried to smile politely at her. With a sick, sinking sensation, he wondered if he'd ever set foot in the house again. The conversation with Alex had been stressful, but this felt so much worse.

Jonathon and Geneva's plans for him had been quite simple. They'd expected him to marry well, have at least one child and uphold the Porter-Wright name. Riley being gay fit nowhere into those plans. There was a high probability that once they knew the truth, he'd be disowned. Growing up, he'd had few illusions about how his parents felt about him. They'd had a child because it was expected of them, not because they wanted one or had any real affection for each other. They hadn't wanted a family. They'd wanted an asset.

Riley had resigned himself to the truth a long time ago, but it didn't mean it had stopped hurting. For years, he'd tried to pretend it didn't, but at moments like this, knowing he was about to reveal the truth about himself and risk losing his family and his job, their indifference hurt the most.

It also made him melancholy to realize that in some ways, he felt more concerned about losing the position at Porter-Wright Publishing than about losing his family. Over the years, he'd found more joy in his career than anywhere else. Except with Carter, of course. Now, with no guarantee of having Carter in his life anymore, his career was all he had.

He took a deep breath before he stepped into the sitting room where his parents were waiting. His father stood to one side of the room, sipping a drink, and his mother perched on a sofa.

"What is this about?" Geneva asked thinly when she spotted him. "I don't understand why you felt it was so urgent to meet with us."

It took all his willpower to keep his voice from shaking. "I need to speak to you both about something."

"Well, please be brief, Riley. We have other plans this evening. This is a busy time of year."

She glanced at the clock above the mantel and Riley gritted his teeth at his mother's impatience.

"Don't worry. I doubt this will take long." Riley laughed humorlessly. "I just wanted you to know I am divorcing Alex."

His mother arched her eyebrows at him. "Why on earth would you divorce your wife?"

He could have eased into the conversation, told them about how unhappy he felt, but he didn't think it would make a difference. He'd waffled about what to tell them for a while and had ultimately come to the conclusion that he might as well be blunt. Plus, they wouldn't understand the difference between being bi and gay and he didn't want there to be any confusion. He hated that he even needed to label himself. "I'm gay."

The room remained silent for a long moment, none of them moving a muscle until Jonathon scowled and Geneva pressed her lips tightly together. "If you think you're being funny," his father said, "you're sorely mistaken."

"I understand this is a shock," Riley replied tersely, "but, no, I am not making a joke. I've tried to deny it for a long time, but it is the truth."

"Then you can continue to deny it," his mother said. "There is absolutely no reason for you to drag our good name through the mud simply because you have some ridiculous notion that you need to divorce your wife. We expect you to have a child with Alex and give us an heir. Anything else is out of the question."

Riley clenched his teeth. He'd known this wasn't going to go well, but he struggled to keep his cool. "I'm not asking your permission. I am telling you what my plans are. I'll do my best to keep the reason behind it discreet, but I am filing for divorce. And I have no intention of hiding who I am anymore."

His father frowned at him and stood, pacing around the living room for a moment before stopping a few feet from Riley. "You do realize if you go through with this, it will be the end of your inheritance?"

Riley's tone went flat. "I suspected as much."

His father's voice grew cold and hard. "There's nothing I can do about the trust from your grandmother since you have access to it already, but you won't get a single dime beyond that. If I thought I could get the board on my side, I'd fire you. Unfortunately, too many of the members are soft and I won't be able to get a majority vote. The e-publishing division will stay in your hands, but you'll never take over Porter-Wright Publishing while I'm still alive, and I'll do my damndest to keep you from inheriting it after my death." His father's gaze turned flinty. "From now on, no longer consider yourself my son."

Although he'd braced himself for it, Riley still reeled at the words. He swallowed hard, fighting down the hurt and the tears that stung his eyes. The only sliver of good news was that he hadn't lost his job. He loathed the thought of working with his father after this, but he refused to give up the career he'd grown to love. "Understood," he said hoarsely.

He glanced over at his mother, but her expression appeared equally distant and icy. No matter how much he'd tried to prepare for the inevitable outcome, he hadn't been able to brace himself for how much it hurt to be rejected by the people who'd given him life.

"Does this have anything to do with the Hamilton boy?" his mother asked.

"No."

Her lips twisted in a scowl. "I always felt your closeness to him was unnatural."

"I told you, this isn't about him," Riley snapped.

"If you walk out of this door and go through with it, there's no turning back," his father warned. "You'll no longer be welcome here."

He stared at his father for a long moment, then glanced over at his mother. Neither of them appeared upset. They were distant as always, as if disowning their son—their only child—was no more than an irritating inconvenience.

"Sometimes I think I never was," he said softly. Without another word, he stood and walked out of the door. Leaving his family behind and knowing he'd never see them again outside of work felt nearly as painful as when Carter had walked out on him.

And unlike Carter, he had no hope they'd ever come around.

* * * *

Looking around his apartment, Riley felt amazed by how few personal belongings he actually owned. He had clothes, of course, his laptop and several other electronic items, books, some mementos from college and his younger days and a handful of boxes of miscellaneous items and paperwork, but that was all. He didn't care to keep any of the furnishings from the apartment he'd shared with Alex. The West Village place had everything he'd need to get by and he could always buy the rest when he needed it. He'd lost his inheritance but by any normal standards, he remained well off.

He'd officially moved out of the Upper East Side apartment. Alex had gone to her parents' home upstate, so he hadn't seen her when he'd gone to pick up his things. Her lawyer had supervised him moving out. Although he felt guilty for hurting her, he didn't miss her at all. And when he left the place they'd lived in together, he wouldn't miss that, either.

He schlepped the boxes up to his fourth-floor apartment himself, grateful for the physical exertion. Hopefully, if he exhausted his body, his mind would quiet down. Rather than unpack his belongings, he headed straight for the shower, then collapsed into bed. He felt exhausted, but it was more mental than physical.

The chaos of the past few days had kept him from thinking too much, but alone, he couldn't seem to shut his brain off. He tossed and turned for a while before burying his face in the pillow. Once again, he wished it smelled of Carter's cologne.

He flipped onto his back again and rested his forearm over his eyes. As the doubts crept in, he began to wonder if all of this had been pointless. He felt glad his relationship with Alex was over, but had it been worth it? He'd lost Carter completely, and was anything more important than that?

He spent the weekend unpacking and trying to get settled in to his apartment. He felt comfortable there, but the nights were rough as he struggled to sleep, his mind too unsettled to allow his body to rest. Memories of Carter in the bed haunted him like ghosts. Riley was exhausted on Monday morning when he went into work, grateful for the coffee his assistant Anna had waiting for him when he arrived.

On his way to a meeting, he saw his father in the hall. It was unsurprising—their offices were just down from each other—but it was the first time Riley had seen him since he'd been disowned. He glanced up from his phone at the sound of his father's voice. He had his back to Riley while he spoke to his assistant, Gail. Riley paused for a moment, then continued forward. Just as Riley approached his father, the man turned and they were face to face. Riley held his breath, unsure of what his father's reaction would be, but Jonathon didn't have any reaction. He looked past Riley as though he didn't register Riley's presence at all.

Gail gave them both a startled glance and she opened her mouth as if to speak. Riley gave her a subtle shake of the head. She responded with a puzzled frown but didn't pursue it. She'd been his father's assistant for years and he liked her. He didn't want her to get chewed out by his father for asking a question about what was going on. She didn't need to get dragged into the situation. He continued to his meeting, wondering how long it would take before the truth came out and spread through the office.

He felt constantly on edge throughout the week, waiting for the other shoe to fall. But life at the office continued as usual, and he grew accustomed to the chilly aloofness his father displayed toward him at the meetings they were both required to attend. Outwardly, his father seemed completely indifferent to Riley, treating him like a colleague he tolerated and nothing more. He wondered if, deep down, it bothered his father that he'd lost his only child. Or if his parents felt nothing but disappointment that he hadn't lived up to the image they'd created for him. Maybe he was simply a failed investment.

People at work noticed, of course. It was hard not to notice when the CEO and a vice president were at odds with each other, especially when they were father and son. All Riley could do was plow through his day as if nothing was happening, as if his entire world wasn't in flux right now, and hope that somehow it would all work out.

He felt grateful when Friday finally rolled around, but once he returned home, he had nothing to do. He reached for a hanger to put his suit jacket on when it occurred to him just how alone he was now. Without a wife or family, and with Carter not speaking to him, who did Riley have in his life?

It hit him hard, all of a sudden. He left the hanger on the clothes rod and dropped into the nearby chair, still clutching the jacket. He had few close friends apart from Dan. Everyone else he knew socially he considered more of an acquaintance than a confidant. For the most part, they were as shallow and insincere as Alex. He'd socialized with them but never gotten to know them deeper than the surface.

He occasionally went out after work with some of the editors on his team and they were a fun bunch, but he didn't consider himself close to them either. It horrified him to realize how isolated he was. Still lost in his thoughts, he changed into more casual clothes and grabbed his phone. His first instinct was always to call Carter, but with that no longer an option, he dialed Dan.

"Ri!" Dan answered cheerfully. "Hey, how are ya?"

Riley could hear giggling and the chaotic noise of Dan's three girls while they chattered in the background. "I need to talk to you. Do you have some time right now? If not, you can call me later."

"For you? Of course I have time. Let me go into the other room." Riley heard the muffled sounds of Dan telling Melanie who had called before the noise in the background faded. "I'm here. I should have peace and quiet for a little while. What do you need to talk about?" He sounded worried.

Riley let out a heavy breath. "I'm having a midlife crisis."

Dan chuckled. "Riley, you're only thirty-four. I think you're a little early, buddy."

"I've always been precocious," he joked, then grew more serious. "I left Alex."

"Good," Dan replied flatly.

Riley let out a surprised laugh. "I know you've never been a big fan of hers, but did you actually hate her that much?"

Dan hesitated. "I've never thought she was the right

215

person for you. Over the years, I've gotten to know you pretty well, and the guy I knew in college is nothing like the man you are around her. She brings out the worst in you."

"And why didn't you tell me this before we got married?"

"Because you're a stubborn son of a bitch and I knew no matter what I said, you'd do what you wanted."

Riley's laugh sounded hollow. "You're probably right there."

"So, what prompted it?"

"Fuck…uh. Well, I'm in love with Carter."

Dan snorted. "No shit. I've known that for years."

"Again with the information you could have mentioned before," Riley pointed out.

"I tried, you asshole," Dan pointed out. "Do you not remember the night before Carter's wedding? I know you were drunk, but you were pretty adamant about not wanting to talk about it."

Riley did vaguely remember Dan's comment as they struggled to get Carter into a taxi. "Fuck, you're right," he admitted.

"Well, it's about damn time you admitted the truth."

"I've been in denial for so many years."

"Why?"

Riley sighed heavily. "A lot of reasons. Mostly fear."

"Fear of what?" Dan asked softly.

"Of losing him, of being disowned, of having to start my life totally over."

"Fair enough," Dan said. "What made you change your mind?"

"A combination of things, I guess. But it got to the point where I just couldn't do it anymore. It was harder to not say something to Carter than to keep it a secret."

"So, you told him?"

Haltingly at first, Riley opened up to Dan, telling him about the arrangement with Natalie, and about his ultimatum to Carter and the fallout after. It grew easier the more he spoke and it felt good to get it all off his chest.

Dan sounded truly horrified when Riley told him about his parents' reaction. "Jesus, no wonder you waited so long. That's a lot of pressure. I knew you had a shitty relationship with them, but, wow."

"Yeah," Riley agreed. "I have a lot of regrets I waited so long, though. And Carter isn't even speaking to me."

"I'm sorry, Riley," Dan said sincerely. "If it's any consolation, I do think Carter loves you."

"Maybe, but the question is, will he admit it?" Riley said with a sigh. "I wouldn't even blame him if he didn't. I'm asking a lot of him. Maybe too much."

"It is a lot," Dan admitted. "But I think you did the right thing."

Riley relaxed. He'd needed to hear that. With so many doubts, he needed someone to reassure him he hadn't made the wrong choice. "I hope so."

"I think you just need to give him some time."

"I'm trying. It's hard, though. I realized I have very few friends. It's pretty sad, actually."

"Have you thought about going out and meeting people?"

"Like, dating?"

"Sure, or just making some new friends."

"I-I don't think I can contemplate dating at this point. Number one, because I just filed for divorce a little over a week ago, and number two, because I'm not ready to admit I might never have a chance for a relationship with Carter."

"Then what about friends? It sounds like you're isolated right now."

"I am," he admitted. "And I know it's not good."

"Just think about it," Dan said. "And think about coming to Chicago for the holidays. We'd love to have you here."

"I'll think about it," Riley agreed. "Thanks for listening, Dan."

"I'm your friend, Riley. You can call me, any time of the day or night, and I'm happy to listen," he said simply.

"Thanks," Riley said, his voice rough. He felt so grateful for Dan's support.

After he hung up with Dan, he called Natalie. She didn't answer, so he left her a message, asking her to return his call. He wasn't sure if it was appropriate for him to call her now, but she had given him her personal number at one point, and he thought she cared enough about him and Carter to want to know.

Thankfully, she called a short while later and sounded pleased to hear from him. They talked for several hours and once again, opening up helped ease a little bit of the loneliness and hurt in him. He felt grateful to Natalie for her friendship. She gave him essentially the same advice Dan had — to give Carter time. Although difficult to hear, he knew they were both right.

"What are you doing for Thanksgiving?" she asked, when they wrapped up their conversation about Carter.

"Honestly? Sitting in my apartment drinking alone like a miserable, sad fuck," Riley admitted.

Natalie let out a short, surprised laugh, but her voice sounded sympathetic. "Well, we can't have that. I don't have any family around here, either. Why don't we spend it together? We can cook dinner and drink some wine and keep each other company."

"I'd really like that," Riley admitted. "If it's not too much to ask."

Natalie sounded amused. "Spending the day cooking with a handsome man I think I could become good friends with? No, it's not too much to ask."

He smiled at her response. "I'll take care of the shopping then. You bring the wine and come over around noon."

"I'll be there." Natalie fell silent for a moment. "I'm glad you called."

"I'm glad I did, too."

Chapter Thirteen

In the week following his argument with Riley, work proved the only foolproof method Carter had for distracting himself from what he instinctively knew was an estrangement from his friend.

Riley's ultimatum had shocked and frightened Carter. His disappointment had been heartbreaking, but Carter had seen determination in Riley's gaze. He knew nothing would change Riley's mind, even if his actions meant hurting the people around him.

While Carter was desperate to reach out to Riley, he didn't dare. Riley had asked him to take a leap of faith, something Carter simply could not do. He dreaded Riley making his case again, asking Carter to abandon a life he'd constructed with care and love. Even more dreadful was the thought Riley wouldn't ask, because he'd given up on Carter. That possibility, more than anything else, kept Carter silent.

Every day that passed without word between them wore on Carter. He jumped when his phone rang, sure Alex or Riley's parents were calling with the news that Riley had come out. The questions would begin then, from family and friends who wanted to know what role Carter had played in the fiasco.

An entire week passed before the usually smooth surface of Carter's life began to ripple.

He'd taken the kids to the aquarium on Saturday and despite the anxiety at the back of his mind, they'd had a good day. The autumn weather had been mild and the kids' questions about the marine animals a pleasant distraction.

They met Kate at home for homemade pizza and baked

spaghetti and as Carter sipped his glass of wine, he relaxed for the first time in days.

He went to his office after the kids had gone to bed and read through proposals until his phone chimed. Carter noted the time and his stomach sank. Very few people would message him after eleven p.m. and Carter didn't need to run through the list in his head to guess who had now.

He pulled the phone from his pocket and his breath hitched as he read the short message.

Alex knows.

Carter was still staring at his phone when the sound of his name pulled him from his daze.

"Car? Are you all right?"

He glanced up to see Kate standing in the doorway of his office, already dressed for bed. Struck dumb, he watched her cross the room, wondering why she looked so concerned.

"What's happened?" She bent to cup his cheek. "You look like you've seen a ghost."

"I'm... It's okay," Carter managed, his voice low and rough. He had no idea how much time had passed since he'd read Riley's text. He blinked when Kate took the phone from his hand and slid it into the dock on his desk.

"Are you sure? You're so pale," she fretted. "I didn't know what to think when I stopped at the door. Did you get some bad news?"

"I'm—no." Carter glanced away, chest tight and his emotions clawing at him. "I'm sure it's nothing. Just unexpected, that's all."

"Is it Riley?" Kate's gaze was knowing when Carter snapped his head up. "You've been out of sorts all week," she explained. "I didn't want to pry, but I figured something must be wrong. Did the two of you argue after the opera?"

Carter shook his head and hated himself for lying. God, he'd been lying to his wife for far too long.

"No. We had…a misunderstanding," he replied, taking Kate's hands in his own. "I'm sure it'll work out somehow."

"All right." Kate eyed him for a moment longer before tugging at his hands. "Time for bed, my love—you look wrecked. I've held my tongue about the late hours you've been working this week, but I refuse to let you run yourself into the ground tonight."

Carter managed a smile as his wife manhandled him to his feet with a wiry strength that belied her petite frame. He grumbled a little bit for show, but his heart wasn't in it, and he was too exhausted emotionally to do more than follow along. Still, he tensed after Kate paused and glanced back toward the phone on his desk.

"You wanna go back and grab that? Or are you ready to give the old ball and chain a break for the night?" She glanced back at Carter with a cheeky grin. "And by that I mean work, not me."

Carter shook his head and they began moving toward the study door again. "The only ball and chain I want to talk to tonight is you, honey. Everyone else can wait a little longer."

* * * *

The ripple on the surface of Carter's life became a wave the following Monday. Carter looked up over his glasses as Malcolm stuck his head round Carter's office door and the managers Carter had been meeting with fell quiet.

"I apologize for interrupting, Mr. Hamilton."

"Can it wait, Malcolm?" Carter gave a little nod to the others around him. "We're about half-done at this point— shouldn't be more than another hour or so."

Malcolm smiled thinly. His cheeks appeared especially pink against his gray suit and Carter read the apology in his green eyes. "Alexandra Porter-Wright is in reception asking to see you. She doesn't have an appointment and I know you're busy but—"

"That's fine, Malcolm." Carter put down the ad copy he'd been reading and pulled off his glasses. "Wait two minutes, please, then show Mrs. Porter-Wright in."

"Yes, sir."

"Please coordinate additional time with Mitchell and Liz for this afternoon, as well." He glanced back to the project managers, who were gathering their things. "I'd like to pick this back up before close of business today," he told them. "I'll trust Malcolm to find a time that works for everyone."

Carter faced the windows after his office emptied, laying a hand on the edge of the desk, his heartbeat thrumming in his ears. He counted silently, ten seconds, then thirty, and drew quiet breaths until he reached sixty. Then he pulled his suit jacket from the back of his chair and put it on, steeling himself as his office door opened again.

"Mrs. Porter-Wright, sir." Malcolm's even tone of voice made it easier for Carter to turn around.

"Thank you, Malcolm. Please bring coffee service for two and hold my calls."

A heavy silence filled Carter's office after the door closed. Carter and Alex watched each other across the space for a long moment before Carter gestured to the seating area on the other side of the room. He took Alex's coat as they drew closer together and laid it over the back of one of the sleek leather chairs while Alex seated herself on the sofa.

Alex was flawlessly put together. She'd dressed for the cool weather in tall leather boots and luxurious gray and green tweeds that complemented her coloring. Her jaw was tight, however, and Carter knew she was working hard to control her demeanor.

"This is unexpected, Alex—to what do I owe the pleasure?" Carter sat down, keeping his face neutral.

"Life is difficult enough right now, Carter." Alex's voice was soft, but her gaze steely. "I'd appreciate it if you didn't play dumb with me. You know why I'm here."

Carter nodded. "You're here about Riley."

Alex didn't reply immediately and turned her lips down

at the corners. "How long have you known?" she finally asked.

"A week. We had a drink after the *Turandot* performance. He told me what he planned to do then." Carter swallowed as Alex's face twisted. "I told him it was a mistake, and urged him to reconsider. That this"—Carter paused, stumbling over the words as pain streaked through his chest—"impulse of his wasn't worth ruining his life or hurting you."

"I suppose I should thank you, then." Alex's expression shifted, flashing with anger and disdain. "I wasn't asking about Riley's sudden need to upend my life, though. What I want to know is how long you've known Riley is gay. Bisexual." Alex grimaced. "You know what I'm talking about."

Carter stiffened in his seat, a chill sweeping over him at her words. A tap at his door saved him from answering and he called for Malcolm to enter, though his voice sounded hoarse to his own ears. He stood to help his assistant with the tray bearing the coffee service, all the while aware of Alex's gaze. She said nothing after Malcolm slipped out again and the silence between them grew oppressive while he filled their cups.

"How do you take your coffee?" he asked, fussing over cream and sugar, knowing he was stalling but unable to stop himself.

"Carter."

Carter set the creamer down on the tray and sat back in his seat. Whatever ambivalence he felt toward Alex or her place in Riley's life, Carter knew her world truly had been turned upside down. Riley's coming out had stunned and hurt Alex and she deserved an answer.

"How long have you known?" she asked again, her voice quieter but no less firm.

"I was every bit as surprised as you were. I've known Riley for over fifteen years and he never gave any indication he wanted to pursue relationships with men." Carter's heart twisted at the subtle lie, but he kept a straight face, aware of the truth in his words. He'd never considered Riley to be truly gay or even bisexual, because Riley had never shown interest in men other than Carter.

Alex looked dubious. "You don't really expect me to believe that, do you?"

"Of course I do—"

"Because for as long as I've known Riley, you two have been as thick as thieves," she continued, rolling right over Carter. "Riley doesn't tell me much, you know—he never has when it comes to himself. He tells you, though, doesn't he? Not his wife, no. Just you. Riley tells you everything, all his little secrets and lies, things he doesn't trust anyone else to know. So you'll have to excuse me if I can't accept the fact that he didn't tell you something so serious."

"He never told me, Alex." Carter shook his head, stomach churning at the scorn in her gaze. He had the distinct impression he'd been judged and weighed and found lacking. He could easily guess Alex's next question.

"The two of you aren't in a relationship?"

"No." Carter swallowed hard. "Riley and I are friends, best friends, but that's all we are."

"I don't believe that, either," Alex scoffed. "I always wondered about you, Carter, and what made you tick. I could never put my finger on it until now, but I suspect you're as gay as Riley." Her smile was bitter. "It certainly explains that boy toy of an assistant you've got sitting out there. Is he another of your playmates?"

The hairs on Carter's forearms rose. "Malcolm is my employee, and a damned good one at that. Don't be sexist on top of being homophobic."

Alex's eyes flashed with anger. "How dare you. I never thought I'd say this, but my in-laws are right. There's always been something between you and Riley, something unnatural—"

"Whatever you're thinking, you're wrong," Carter cut in. "I don't know what Jonathon and Geneva have been telling you, but it's not true."

"Bullshit."

After another piercing glare, Alex finally glanced away. Rather than relief, though, Carter felt only empty.

"I'm being straight with you, Alex," he murmured, once more reaching for threads of truth in his words. "Riley and I are close, and yes, maybe we're closer than best friends usually are. But he never told me that he was gay or bi. That night after the opera is the first I heard of it. And even if I had known, Riley's decision would still have been exactly that—Riley's, not mine. I'm not gay," Carter gritted out past the slight break in his voice and Alex's eyes flashed up to meet his. "I'm not leaving Kate, for Riley or for anyone."

"Well then." Alex's voice was more fraught with emotion than Carter had ever heard, though her eyes were dry. "Between the two of you, you are the better man, Carter Hamilton. You're certainly the better husband."

"I'm sorry." Haltingly, Carter reached out to lay a hand over Alex's, trying not to wince after she pulled away. "I know Riley doesn't want to hurt you. He has so many regrets—"

Alex gave a harsh laugh. "He'll have more regrets before this is all done." Her expression turned cold, sending another chill through Carter.

"What do you mean?"

"You don't really think Riley's father is going to let this slide, do you?"

Carter could almost feel the blood drain from his face.

"This…lifestyle Riley has suddenly decided he can't live without is one his parents despise. You know it, I know it, Riley knows it. Jonathon is going to take him apart."

"Jesus," Carter murmured, an ache beginning to pound at the back of his head.

"Riley wants me to make this easy for him, too. To just lie down and take it." Alex twisted her lips as spots of color appeared high on her cheeks. "Apparently, I have no business feeling humiliated when my husband announces to the whole world that our marriage is a fraud."

"But is he right, Alex? You know there have always been rumors you and Riley got married out of convenience." Carter wanted to kick himself as Alex's face flushed an ugly red.

"They're not true!" she exclaimed, raising one hand to run over her hair for several moments. "Riley and I did not have an epic romance," she continued calmly, "neither of us would deny that. And there is a level of comfort in our marriage that outpaces passion. But I was faithful to my vows.

"I supported Riley's business plans and played the good wife whenever he asked. I never cheated on my husband, though I had ample opportunity to do so over the years. Whatever Riley's claims, I'm certain he can't say the same about himself."

"Then wouldn't it be easier for you to let him go?" Carter stifled a sigh after Alex shook her head and looked away. "If you take Riley to court—"

"Then everything becomes public knowledge, I know," Alex finished for him, her face still averted.

"That's not all I mean," he persisted, leaning forward to catch her eye. "You must know that if you drag this out, the gossip rags are going to take notice. Porter-Wright isn't the largest publisher in the city, but they have some notable authors. News like the company heir's messy divorce will grab media attention. This is the kind of society gossip that makes headlines, Alex, and I know you don't want that."

"Carter, Riley isn't just leaving me—he's coming out as a bisexual man," Alex bit out. She faced Carter again, her gaze pained. "He's seeing his attorneys today, as a matter of fact. They'll be talking about a plan to go public, to stop 'living the lie,' as Riley put it, so he can live his life with other men instead of with his wife. Because I am the lie."

Carter could only stare while Alex pressed the knuckles of one hand to her lips. She dropped her hand again, her face pale.

"People are going to find out—there's no getting around it," she said. "Our friends, Riley's colleagues, our families... they'll know Riley would rather be with men than with me. So what does it matter if I fight for what's rightfully mine?"

"Riley would never shut you out financially."

"I know. He said as much when we spoke the other night. He may be a selfish asshole, but he would never do that to me."

"Then what do you gain by turning it into a court battle?" Carter persisted. "Is dragging his name—and yours—really going to make you feel better?"

Alex's eyes grew bright before her chin rose and the cool and distant persona Carter knew so well slipped into place. "If Riley feels as shitty as I do right now, then, yes, it'll be worth it."

* * * *

Unlocking the front door later that evening, Carter couldn't remember ever feeling so drained. Placing his coat and briefcase on the table in the entryway, head bowed, he pulled himself together for dinner with his family.

His meeting with Alex had lasted two hours, most of it spent arguing. Carter understood Alex's impulse to lash out and even to blame Carter in the process. As the meeting had worn on, she'd finally admitted what Carter had already known to be true—no matter what Alex did next, Riley was gone. Like it or not, she was on her own and spending a fortune on divorce lawyers and court fees wasn't going to change that.

After Alex had left, Carter had wanted to draw the blinds and hide. His throat had tightened as he'd considered he had no idea of Riley's state of mind. Was Riley hurting or frightened by the cascade of events he'd set into motion? Had he come out to his parents already? Carter had known the chances of that conversation having gone well were slim to nonexistent.

He thought of calling Riley but forced himself to stop. Now, more than ever, Carter's behavior would be scrutinized. And if he wanted to keep the relationship he and Riley had had with Natalie a secret, he needed to keep attention off his friendship with Riley.

Carter caught sight of his reflection in the mirror over the foyer table and winced. He hadn't slept well in days and he looked pale, with dark smudges underneath his eyes. Running his hands through his hair, Carter turned to walk into the apartment, making his way through the warm and familiar rooms to the kitchen.

"Daddy!"

Sadie's shriek sent a pain lancing through Carter's head and he nearly groaned as Dylan let loose a playful roar, too. Carter smiled, though, and knelt to hug his children while Kate watched from her place by the oven.

"Oh, my God, you land-lubbers are in so much trouble," he growled out in the pirate's voice that made the children shiver with delight. He squinted one eye shut and bared his teeth, making them screech with laughter.

"We made a deal with yer mother to keep the breakfast nook clean of yer kiddie crap." Sadie and Dylan looked at Kate, who pursed her lips in mock distress. "But I see a huge pile of those horrible coloring books and crayons on the table this very minute. If they're not gone by the time I count to twenty, I'm eatin' all of yer ice cream tonight after dinner…before I feed ya both to the sharks!"

"This is New York, Daddy, there are no sharks!" Sadie protested, while Dylan laughed helplessly.

"Oh, and how do you know that for sure, missy?" Carter asked, pitching his voice a little lower. "Yer old Dad has a few tricks up his sleeve still. Besides, sharks or no, I *will* eat yer ice cream for dessert if that mess doesn't disappear. Are ya really willin' to risk it?"

Carter held onto the children, gently restraining them while they wiggled to free themselves and clean up their clutter. Kate was by Carter's side after he let them go, holding out one slim hand to help him to his feet. Her touch, like the children's, was a balm against the day Carter had endured and for a moment he felt steady.

That calming warmth drained away as he met Kate's gaze and he knew without asking that she'd heard about Riley.

"Alex stopped by this afternoon," she told him quietly, a crease appearing between her eyes. "Are you okay? You look like hell."

He managed a croaky chuckle. "Thanks, dear."

Kate rolled her eyes, though she was still frowning. "Come on," she told him and pushed up the sleeves of her sweater. "You're my husband, I'm allowed to worry about you."

"I know. I was just…reacting, I guess. My internal barometer's kind of out of whack at the moment. I don't know what the hell to feel right now."

"I can only imagine, especially when you had no idea it was coming." Carter said nothing, squeezing Kate's fingers gently while her eyes grew wide. "Oh…of course. You did know."

Carter nodded as a sad understanding touched Kate's gaze.

"Last week, after the opera, when you met for drinks," she murmured, "that's when he told you. Or maybe you've known all along." Kate sighed. "That's why you've been so jumpy and out of sorts, because he told you he planned to leave Alex. Why didn't you say something? Why didn't you tell her? Or me, for that matter?"

"I honestly hoped that Riley would change his mind." Carter nudged Kate with his shoulder to catch her eye. When that failed, he reached up and took her chin gently between his fingers, guiding her back to meet his gaze. "Yes, Riley told me what he planned to do when we had drinks after the opera. I honest to God didn't know how to react."

"So you didn't know he was gay, then?"

"No. I didn't know that Riley was gay or bi, not that he

planned to leave Alex, not that he wanted to come out—nothing. He took me completely by surprise."

Doubt surfaced in Kate's eyes and Carter braced himself for questions he knew were coming. Unlike Carter's parents and even his sister, Kate had never insinuated that his friendship with Riley had ever been anything but platonic. She'd always gotten on well with Riley, becoming as much his friend as Alex's, and maybe even more so.

Kate was an observant person, though. More than once over the years, Carter had caught her watching him with Riley, a sharp awareness in her eyes before she blinked and it disappeared. If Kate had ever wondered just how close the two friends were, surely she'd pursue those trains of thought now.

Before either Kate or Carter could speak, Sadie and Dylan used the exquisite sense of timing possessed by all children to interrupt parents in the middle of a serious talk. Dylan attached himself to Kate's leg and Sadie wrapped her arms around Carter's waist.

"Table's clean! All your ice creams are belong to us!" Sadie crowed. She squeaked loudly as Carter leaned down and scooped her over his shoulder into a fireman's carry. Kate and Dylan looked on, laughing while Sadie hung upside down, her dark hair streaming down her father's back.

"Only if you eat all of the enchiladas I made for dinner, wee lass," Kate declared, her own attempt at the pirate voice making Dylan snort.

Carter paused, craning his head to catch his wife's eye around their daughter's legs. "Let's talk after bedtime," he suggested, and waited for Kate's nod before he grabbed Dylan's hand and led him into the family room to play until dinner.

When the children were in bed, Carter dragged himself down the hall to the master bedroom while Kate locked up the apartment. He wanted to be comfortable when they talked and hoped to grab a hot shower before she came upstairs.

His phone chimed as he made his way to the bathroom, and though his gut told him to wait, Carter pulled his phone from his pocket. A cold weight settled in his chest and he stared at his father's name on the screen for a long moment before thumbing through to the message.

Received disturbing news from Jon Porter-Wright. Breakfast — my office, 7:30 a.m.

Carter was sitting on the edge of their bed when Kate walked into the bedroom, his head in his hands, the headache that had been building all day pulsing behind his eyes.

"Ri told his parents," he murmured after Kate ran a hand over his hair. "And you know the old saying — bad news travels fast. My dad wants to see me for breakfast tomorrow morning."

Kate sighed and sat beside him. "I'm sorry. I know you and Riley are close, but I'm not sure what anyone expects you to do about what's happened."

"I know," Carter groaned. He fell back against the mattress and threw one arm over his eyes. "I suppose they're looking for a way to spread the blame around or something. Or maybe they think I have some answers. Alex certainly seemed to think I did."

"Riley is a grown man. He's capable of making his own decisions." Kate rested her cool fingers against the side of Carter's neck. "His decisions may not make everyone happy, but they're his to make and his alone."

Carter picked up the arm over his eyes to up at his wife. "Wanna take the breakfast meeting with my dad tomorrow in my place?" Kate wrinkled her nose and he smiled crookedly.

"No, thanks. Your dad always serves those low-sugar scones for breakfast." Kate made another face. "I end up feeling like I have a belly full of sawdust."

Carter laughed, then settled his arm over his eyes again.

"Selfish," he teased.

"Self-preserving," Kate corrected before she squeezed Carter's shoulder. "If I could make it easier for you, though, I would."

"Thank you." Carter blew out a long breath and let his body relax farther into the mattress. Now that he was finally lying still, he felt exhausted.

"I wish they'd leave this thing with Riley alone," he said sadly. "It's not as if he's ever listened to me before. I've known him since we were teenagers and once he makes up his mind, it's basically impossible to get him to change it."

Kate shifted on the bed beside him. "Have you tried to change his mind before?"

"A few times, yes," Carter admitted. He moved to tucked his arm behind his head so he could meet Kate's gaze. "Very seldom successfully."

"Did you try to talk him out of coming out?" Carter knew she wouldn't hold it against him if he didn't answer.

"Yeah, I did," he whispered. "I understand that he's trying to find himself...to figure out who he is. But he's risking so much. His parents...his father," Carter gritted out past his teeth. "They'll ruin him, if not in business then by disowning him. For years, Riley's been waiting for his parents to finally do it, Kate. Now he's handing them that opportunity on a silver platter." Carter's eyes stung. "Riley's life as he knows it is over. And I think he's ready to drag other people down with him."

"Like you?"

"Like Alex." Carter crossed his free arm over his chest to cover Kate's hand on his shoulder with his own. "I'm... yes, some gossip may filter back on me. It wouldn't be the first time, unfortunately. You know people have been making assumptions about Riley and me since we were undergrads."

Kate nodded, her head bowed. Carter gave her hand another squeeze, waiting until she raised her gaze to meet his. Hers was troubled.

"I'm really sorry we're stuck in the middle. You don't deserve to be on the other end of people's bullshit."

Carefully, Kate pushed Carter's hair off his forehead. "Neither do you, sweetheart." She gave him a small smile before sitting back up so they could get ready for bed.

Chapter Fourteen

December, 2012
Southampton, New York

"Christ," Riley muttered to himself. "This seemed like a much better idea yesterday."

The small car slid sideways and he clutched the wheel of the Audi tighter when it was buffeted by the heavy winds and blowing snow.

Yesterday, the weather had been cold and dry and not nearly as windy or snowy. He peered forward, squinting out of the window at the growing storm. The sky was a steely gray and although it was only mid-morning, it grew even darker as he headed toward the ocean.

Riley had spent the last month doing his best to hold it together, but things had grown progressively more tense as the weeks went by. He'd spent much of his time negotiating with Alex through their lawyers. True to her word, she'd attempted to get as much money as she could from him. Riley's lawyer was less than thrilled with his capitulation, but Riley really didn't care. If Alex wanted the Upper East Side place and an enormous settlement, fine. If she thought his money would make her happier, she could have it. The only thing he fought for was the beach house. She'd never really liked it, anyway, and had gone after it purely out of spite.

The apartment on West Tenth still felt lonely, but at least it was beginning to feel like home. He didn't miss the place where he'd lived with Alex at all and, sadly, he didn't miss her, either. Carter's absence hurt acutely, though, and the lack of response wore on him. He wanted to give Carter time, allow him to sort through his emotions and make a decision, but it was impossible not to assume the worst.

To Riley's dismay, a blurb in the gossip columns had hinted at the reasons behind his divorce from Alex. It had only increased tensions at work and he knew office gossip ran rampant. He'd discussed it with his assistant, Anna, only because he trusted her implicitly and needed her to manage some of the calls coming in from reporters.

His father acted colder than ever and with no word from Carter, Riley's attempts to remain positive grew shaky. With the approaching holidays, his mood continued to dim and it grew more and more difficult to remain in the city. The bright lights and cheery Christmas music only made his depression and loneliness worse. It felt easier to wallow in his grief than to force a smile onto his face. The office grew relatively quiet just before Christmas anyway and he rarely took time off so no one seemed too upset when he pushed back a few meetings to January.

Riley had spent Thanksgiving with Natalie, who really was a godsend. She'd been the sole bright spot in the weeks prior and he felt more grateful to her than he could possibly articulate. Without the complications of sex and money, they had become true friends. Thanksgiving had actually been rather enjoyable. They'd made dinner together, then attended a gospel performance in Harlem. They had both enjoyed the music, but mostly Riley had appreciated the company.

It seemed impossible for him to shake the feeling of something missing from his life, though. Spending time with Natalie reminded Riley that the trio had become a duo, but even without Carter there he'd enjoyed himself. Unfortunately for him, Natalie had gone to Italy to visit her grandmother for the Christmas holiday and Riley had declined Dan's offer to go to Chicago to spend the time with him, Mel and their kids.

He'd decided to go to Southampton rather than rattle around his East Village place by himself, wondering how Carter would spend his Christmas with his family. He'd begun to regret it.

He slowed to a crawl when he entered Southampton. The town appeared deserted. He'd never spent the holidays at the beach house before and although he knew that without the summer tourists it would be quite empty, it was even less inhabited than he'd imagined. Of course, most people had families to go to and two days before Christmas, most were probably already there or on their way.

By the time he pulled his Audi into the garage, he felt shaky. He'd nearly slid off the road twice and at that point, all he wanted was to be in his warm apartment in Manhattan. But the beach house felt toasty warm, thanks to the caretaker who'd prepared it for his arrival. He hadn't called his housekeeper. She had family she spent the holidays with and he didn't want to bother her. But the caretaker was an old man who lived nearby without much of a family to speak of and Riley intended to tip him generously. He dumped his bags on the kitchen floor and went to start a pot of coffee. First some caffeine, then unpacking, then he'd figure out what to do with himself for the next few days.

* * * *

Riley cradled the warm mug in his hands while he stared out at the water. He'd done nothing since he arrived but drink coffee and mope.

The house was even larger than the apartment in Manhattan and still decorated in Alex's style, so it didn't feel particularly homey. She'd come to retrieve some of her things, but she'd left a surprisingly large amount of furniture behind, none of which suited him at all. He was half-tempted to pitch it all out into the ocean, just to get rid of it, but he decided to donate it to charity.

He'd only been there for a day, but he wandered the half-empty place restlessly, growing more and more depressed. The weather had worsened and right now, although it was mid-afternoon, the sky was filled with heavy, snow-laden clouds and the wind whipped the waves into a froth. A far cry from the bright blue skies and crystal clear water he'd been used to seeing in the summer months he'd spent there with Carter.

Everything reminded him of Carter. Layered over top of one another were years and years of accumulated memories. There, on the deck—now bare of the usual chairs, table and grill—where he'd spilled his heart out to Carter about his fears of turning into his parents. On the other side of the living room was the spot Riley had first begun to notice his attraction to his best friend during one of the out-of-control parties they'd had. Outside, just around the corner of the deck, they'd showered together, bodies bare to the scorching summer sun, and Riley had realized just how beautiful Carter looked.

Given the chance to go back, Riley would have done things so differently. The question of how much it could have changed both their lives would always haunt him. A part of him thought that maybe—just maybe—if he'd admitted his own feelings sooner and pushed Carter a little, they'd be together now. Riley closed his eyes against the stinging hot press of tears.

Every day that passed chipped away at what little hope he held onto. Particularly, hope that Carter would come to him, ready to admit his feelings for Riley. Or at least reach out as a friend. As much as Riley desperately wanted a relationship with Carter, at this point his friendship was equally important, if not more so. Until now, he hadn't believed he could lose Carter's friendship forever, but he'd begun to have doubts. Perhaps Carter honestly felt so terrified of someone thinking he might be gay that he was willing to lose over fifteen years of friendship.

Riley drained the rest of his coffee before turning away

from the dreary view out of the floor-to-ceiling windows. He refilled his mug and briefly contemplated adding a splash of something stronger before deciding not to. He didn't really think it would help and he wanted to believe he hadn't quite hit a point where he felt like he needed to drink at one in the afternoon. Yet.

He made a face and wandered over to the windows again. He didn't have much of an appetite and he felt as though he was actually living on coffee these days. He wasn't sleeping well and although he'd tried a sleeping pill a couple of times, he didn't like the lethargy it caused. Of course, being half-dead from lack of sleep wasn't doing him any favors, either.

Annoyed by his mood, he drained the mug and decided to go for a run. Although too cold and stormy to run on the beach like he preferred, the treadmill would do. Alex had converted one of the guest rooms into a workout room, and for whatever reason, she'd left it untouched. At that moment, he felt grateful.

He ran to the point of exhaustion, until he could barely put one foot in front of the other, even at a slow pace. He gasped for breath and sweat trickled down his temples and dampened his shirt as he staggered to the bathroom to shower.

Once he was clean and dry, Riley dressed in boxers and jeans and a T-shirt without thinking, but when he opened the drawer containing sweatshirts, he paused. He rifled through the stack and lingered on a crimson and white sweatshirt. It appeared faded and threadbare and Alex had always nagged at him to throw it out. She didn't know that it belonged to Carter. Between the two of them they had plenty of Harvard gear, but Riley recognized this particular sweatshirt because of the hole in the cuff. Carter had burned it in an ill-fated attempt to light a bonfire on the beach and taken it off immediately after, leaving it on one of the deck chairs. It had ended up in the wash, mixed in with Riley's clothing, and he'd kept it ever since.

Riley slipped the shirt on and, for a moment, swore he could smell Carter's cologne, even though the idea was ridiculous. It felt warm, though, and somehow comforting.

Once downstairs, he heated up soup he'd brought with him and ate, even though he wasn't hungry. He let the spoon clatter to the bottom of the bowl, barely noticing when the broth splashed up onto his hand, and wiped it away absently, pushing the dish across the table.

He felt lost, floundering without the anchor of his friendship with Carter. He could hardly remember a time before Carter had been a part of his life. In high school, he'd been popular, although most of the friendships had been shallow and without much substance. He'd felt the loneliness even then, although he hadn't really understood it at the time. It hadn't occurred to him until now that he'd spent a good portion of his teenage years fucking his way through the female half of the school because he'd been lonely.

Now, he could look back and see why he'd done it. *But sex never really replaces distant and absent parents, does it?* he thought grimly. The only person he'd ever really let in was Carter. He'd begun to let Dan and Natalie in, but no one had ever known him the way Carter did. Carter knew every flaw of Riley's and he'd never once pushed Riley away. Not until now anyway. Of course, Riley had hidden his feelings for Carter, so even the one person he'd been closest to, he'd kept at a distance.

He hated that no matter how much he'd tried not to turn into his parents, he'd done so anyway. Maybe not as badly — at least he'd acknowledged it wasn't healthy for him to be emotionally distant from everyone in his life — but he still had a long way to go. Carter had rejected him and it seemed like he'd ended their friendship permanently over this. He was alone except for Dan and Natalie. If the one person he'd trusted with nearly everything had rejected him, would he ever trust anyone again?

He didn't want to spend the rest of his life alone. He

couldn't imagine moving on from Carter easily, but he knew that eventually the hurt would fade and he'd have to get out there again. He couldn't fathom wanting to right now, but intellectually he knew he'd have to try. Could he, though? Was he capable of letting someone in and making himself vulnerable?

He jumped when a particularly strong gust of wind rattled something outside. The storm had come up even harder and the waves were frothy from the wind. The sky had darkened to an ominous gunmetal gray and sleety snow came down. He shivered, more from the imagined cold than any real chill.

For a long time, he watched the waves and snow, allowing his mind to go blank. The house was fully dark by the time he finally stirred, his overused muscles cramped and aching. He got up long enough to turn on a single lamp and grab a bottle of gin and a glass before sinking down onto the couch, sprawling out in an attempt to get comfortable while he worked his way through the bottle.

Riley knew it was a mistake and would only make him feel worse, but he couldn't help imagining what might have happened if Carter had said yes to him. Would they have spent Christmas together here at the house?

What if right now, rather than drinking alone to forget his pain, the two of them were sharing a bottle of wine to celebrate the holiday? He could almost feel Carter's arm around him, the two of them stretched out in front of the fire quietly talking. Riley wanted it so badly he physically ached.

At this point, he could really only blame himself, though. He'd been the one to initiate the threesomes in the first place. Maybe if he hadn't, his feelings for Carter would never have grown to this unbearable level. Or, maybe if he'd been honest from the beginning that he'd wanted more than just friendship and some fooling around, they wouldn't be in this place, either. Without a doubt, telling Carter to go ahead and marry Kate had been a mistake, although if they hadn't married, Carter would never have had Sadie and Dylan, which would have been a shame.

His heart clenched at the thought. He didn't blame Carter for being conflicted about leaving his family. His wife and kids meant so much to him, and Riley hated the thought of asking him to tear apart their home. He felt like a selfish bastard for even asking and the last thing he wanted to do was break Kate's heart and hurt Carter's kids, but what else could he do? At least now they both knew where they stood with each other.

Riley didn't blame Carter for not choosing him, although it hurt worse than anything in his life ever had before.

* * * *

He awoke a second time after noon, head still throbbing but no longer quite so hazy. The expanse of windows across the bedroom showed a world dusted in white, although still gloomy and overcast, the heavy clouds promising more snow. With a jolt, he remembered it was Christmas Day. His heart sank when he considered how pathetic his situation was. All alone with no one to celebrate with. He really should have taken Dan up on his invitation and gone to Chicago for the holidays. It would have been better than what he was currently doing, nursing a hangover and pitying himself.

Holidays in the Porter-Wright household had always been filled with endless parties, his parents trotting him out to show him off but never really making an effort to spend any time with him. The majority of the warm, happy Christmas memories he had had been spent with nannies, especially Sarah.

Riley had a distinct memory of his seventh Christmas, happily rolling out sugar cookies with Sarah in the kitchen. His father had passed by — dressed in a tux for some event or other — and scowled at the sight. Jonathon had pulled Sarah away to lecture her.

"I don't want my son in the kitchen." Riley glanced up from the star cutter he'd been carefully pressing into the dough, watching his father and wondering what he'd done wrong.

Sarah protested, "What harm is it causing? He's having a good time."

His father scowled and adjusted a cufflink. "What are you trying to do, make him queer?"

Riley hadn't even known what the word meant at the time, but he could tell it was something bad. Something his father didn't like. Sarah dutifully agreed that there would be no more cookie baking in the future, but once Jonathon and Geneva left, she offered to let him finish. He shook his head. "It's dumb. I don't want to do it anymore."

Looking back, Riley could see the way all of the comments his father had made over the years had combined to make him wary of admitting the truth about himself.

His father was an asshole, no question about it, and his mother was no better. Still, on Christmas Day, it was impossible not to miss them on some level. He had good memories of opening gifts with his parents, lavish Christmas dinners and trips to Vail to go skiing. No matter how angry or how hurt he was at being disowned, it didn't stop him from wishing—just for a moment or two—that he still had a family to celebrate with.

He closed his eyes against the prick of tears, struggling to keep them at bay. He wondered what Carter was doing right then. Had Sadie and Dylan woken their parents early and climbed into their bed, begging to open gifts? He could picture the happy family celebrating the holiday together and it made his heart ache. A part of him was simply jealous—jealous of the children who would always have happy memories of Christmas with their parents that Riley would never have, jealous of Kate for being the one who spent the day with Carter and jealous of anyone who had a family to share the day with.

The other part felt guilty for wishing that Carter would

leave Kate for him.

Another thought fleetingly crossed his mind. An image of spending Christmas with Carter and his children. What if he was more than just Uncle Ri?

Fatherhood had always been such a vague idea to him, especially once he'd married Alex. Could he help raise Carter's children? Did he want to? He loved the two kids already, but was he really emotionally able to be a good parent? Riley certainly had no examples in his own life to look to for guidance, but he could learn, couldn't he? For a moment, he felt doubtful, but then he remembered a weekend at the beach house years prior.

Alex and Kate had been on beach chairs, Alex sunning herself while Kate—pregnant with Dylan and exhausted—had taken an opportunity to nap. Riley had offered to mind Sadie so Carter could relax with a book. They'd made sandcastles on the beach, Sadie squealing in delight when Riley had carefully upended another bucket and created another tower.

Sadie had cried when the encroaching waves had lapped at their hard work, beginning to wash it away. When Carter had moved to get out of the chair to go to his daughter, Riley had waved him off and taken Sadie for a walk down the beach. She'd squirmed, at first, as he carried her, but Riley had sung softly under his breath until she'd quieted. Riley could barely carry a tune, but she'd seemed to like it anyway and eventually fallen asleep in his arms.

Riley remembered the warm sun and small arms gripping his neck surprisingly tightly, Sadie's dark curls tucked up under his chin. Sadie had smelled of sunscreen and grape juice and Riley thought of the way Carter had stared at him when they'd approached the house. His gaze had been a mixture of pride, pleasure and something tender. If Carter chose him, Riley would do everything he could to create a good family. For Carter, Riley would do anything.

Riley wiped at his eyes and eventually dragged himself out of bed, unwilling to wallow in misery any longer. He bundled up and went for a run, despite the weather. The snow had held off, although the sky remained ominous. It had been a while since he'd run on the beach and between that and the icy wind, it made for slower going than usual. But he was grateful when the physical exertion took his mind off the rest of his life for a little while.

Back home after his run, he showered and lit a fire in the living room fireplace, trying to distract himself with a book. He flicked idly through the pages on his iPad, barely seeing the words in front of him. He jumped when his phone rang, desperately hoping it was Carter, and answered with a slightly breathless, "Hello?"

"Merry Christmas, Ri."

Riley's heart sank but he forced himself to be cheerful. "Merry Christmas, Dan."

"How are you doing?"

"Fine. I'm relaxing in front of a fire with a book. How is your Christmas going?"

"The kids are hopped up on too many gifts and too much sugar and Mel and I are about to collapse from exhaustion. So…the usual."

Riley managed a laugh, although his tone came out a little more wistful than he'd intended. "Sounds great."

"Are you by yourself today?"

"Yeah, I came to the beach house a couple of days ago. It's nice and quiet here."

"Lonely, too, I'll bet."

"Damn it, Dan, you're always just a little too blunt."

"You can't bullshit me, not after all this time," Dan said.

"Yeah, I'm fucking lonely," Riley admitted. "I drank half a bottle of gin and passed out last night. I feel like half of me is…missing without Carter around and I've spent the day wallowing in misery. Is that what you wanted to hear?"

"No. But I'm glad you told me the truth," Dan replied. "I wish you'd come to Chicago. Mel and I really would have loved having you here."

"I didn't want to bring the kids down with my mood,"

Riley admitted. "I didn't want to ruin their Christmas."

Dan snorted. "Nothing could ruin Christmas for them. Not even your mopey face."

Riley chuckled and asked him more about his plans for the holidays. Before they were about to hang up, Riley asked the question he'd been wondering. "Have you talked to Carter at all?"

"No. Sorry. I actually tried calling him a couple of times, but he hasn't called back," Dan apologized.

"I was afraid of that. I don't want what's happening with Carter and me to affect your friendship with him."

"I don't, either, but there's nothing either of us can do about it right now."

"I know. I'm just…struggling," Riley admitted.

"Give him some time. Carter has a lot at stake. I don't want you to give up hope—he might come around yet—but don't drive yourself crazy over this, either."

"Easier said than done," Riley retorted.

"Sure, of course it is, but you can at least try. And I think you have to do what you can to live your life in the meantime. You'll go nuts if you spend every day focusing on nothing but Carter. This is your chance to be who you want to be, Riley. Figure out what makes you happy—besides Carter—and if he comes around, you'll be in a really good place to start a relationship with him. If not, you'll at least be able to move forward. Wallowing isn't going to get you anywhere."

Riley sighed. It wasn't what he wanted to hear, but Dan was right. "I'll give it a shot."

The friends talked for a while longer and Riley was in a considerably better mood by the time he hung up. He discovered a text from Natalie from earlier that morning he'd somehow managed to miss. She wished him a Merry Christmas and he sent a reply even though it was the middle of the night in Italy.

He convinced himself to make the dinner he'd originally planned and ate it at the dining room table, watching the snow begin to fall. There was nothing cozy or Christmassy about the storm—the gray skies and biting wind were anything but cheerful—but as Riley finished his dinner, he felt a little less melancholy than he had the day before.

He spent a few more hours reading in front of the fire. Several times he thought about sending Carter a simple Christmas greeting but ultimately decided against it. As desperate as he was for contact, he had to give Carter a chance to come to him. He shut off his tablet, put out the fire and went upstairs to his bedroom.

"Merry Christmas, Carter," he whispered into the darkness just before he went to sleep.

* * * *

The day following Christmas was far more productive. Riley awoke with the urge to do something other than wallow, and ran on the treadmill. After he showered, he decided he couldn't stand the half-decorated home filled with Alex's cast-offs anymore so he drove into Southampton. He wandered around a paint store with no idea what to do. Thankfully, a store clerk took pity on him.

"Can I help you, sir?" she asked politely.

"Ahh, yes." Riley shoved his hands in his jeans' pockets, incredibly out of his element. "I have a house I'd like to re-paint."

"Are you doing the work yourself, sir, or hiring a contractor to do it?"

"I'd like to do it myself, actually," Riley said. In the past, he'd always hired someone because he didn't have the time or the inclination to do it. But he had almost a week off work and nothing to do unless someone from the office called in with a crisis. He'd go nuts if he sat around and stared at the walls. He laughed self-consciously. "Of course, I have no idea what I'm doing."

"We can help with that." The middle-aged clerk gave him a reassuring smile and he relaxed. "Now, tell me how many rooms you plan on painting and what colors you're interested in using."

Surprisingly, Riley enjoyed picking out the colors, going back to a softer palette of watery blues and greens, although this time he went with slightly darker, warmer browns than his parents had used. He left the store with enough paint and supplies for several rooms and a list of e-books on painting to download to his iPad. He figured if he was really terrible at it, he could always hire someone, but he wanted to give it a try. Although many stores were closed, Riley discovered a furniture shop that was open and wandered in. He spent a while browsing, frustrating the clerk when he refused the offer of their in-home design consultant. He wanted the place to be completely his.

It was hard not to think of Carter while he shopped, though, wondering if the sofa he was considering was long enough for Carter's tall frame and if he'd like the bed Riley picked out. He didn't come close to buying everything for the place, but it was a start. A few of the larger pieces would be delivered the following day and the rest in six weeks. He ended up ordering a custom sofa — large enough for Carter — and a bed in a different finish from the one in the showroom. He stopped at a few more stores, picking up a few smaller items for the house, and returned in a better mood than when he'd left.

"Damn Dan for being right," he muttered under his breath.

The remainder of the week was spent painting. He made an unholy mess the first day, but gradually he got the hang of it and decided he rather liked painting. There was something meditative about the rhythm and the sound system filled the rooms with the chords of his favorite operas. Though he thought about Carter often while he worked, he did his best to not dwell on it. Instead, he did what Dan suggested and thought about what he wanted for his future. It was a strange feeling to no longer be living his life based on other people's expectations. For the first time, he could do whatever he wanted, be whoever he wanted to be. Revamping the beach house was a good first start in that direction, but he had a hell of a long way to go.

He'd never been particularly fond of a lot of the socializing Alex preferred. At heart, he was more of a homebody than she was and he knew he'd probably never see again a good portion of the people he'd called friends and acquaintances before. Much like he'd done at Harvard, he wanted to focus on the people who really mattered. He also decided he'd take Natalie up on her suggestion to try a yoga class, although he smiled to himself at the thought of her comment about bendy men.

He wasn't sure how ready he was for that. Dan was right that Riley needed to live his life, but he wasn't sure about the idea of dating. He couldn't imagine anyone living up to Carter and even if the man did, it seemed too soon. There was still a chance Carter could come around.

Maybe I should keep an open mind, though, he thought. Even if the idea of being without Carter made his chest ache painfully.

One morning, as he was putting the finishing touches on the final wall of the living room, his phone rang. He used a rag to wipe his hands clean and carefully navigated the plastic-covered floor to grab it. "Hello?"

"Riley!" Natalie greeted him.

"Are you home? How was your trip?"

"Fantastic. I had a wonderful time." Natalie paused, her light tone turning serious. "How are you?"

"I'm doing better," he said honestly. "Christmas was rough, but I talked to my friend Dan and that helped. I'm trying to focus on figuring out who I am and what I want out of my life."

"I'm thrilled to hear that," Natalie said warmly. "Maybe you'll say yes then. One of the reasons I called was to invite you to a New Year's Eve party I'm throwing. It's fairly small, maybe fifteen, twenty people. Nothing too formal, just drinks and appetizers, and hopefully a good time."

Riley paused for a moment. "That sounds nice, actually. There's an event at the Met scheduled, but I was dreading it so this gives me an excuse to not go."

She laughed lightly. "Wonderful. I'll text you with the details, or maybe we can get together for lunch before then. I can tell you about Italy."

"I'm actually in the Hamptons right now," Riley said. "I'm in the middle of painting."

"Painting? Did you take up the fine arts in the week I've been gone?"

Riley chuckled. "No, painting the walls. I was sick of staring at my soon-to-be-ex-wife's decorating. I thought I'd make the beach house my own."

"I love that," Natalie said with a laugh. "You sound good. Happier than I've heard you in a long time."

"I'm trying," he admitted. "Some days are easier than others, but I'm trying."

Chapter Fifteen

December, 2012
New York, New York

"Daddy, Dylan's gonna have a meltdown."

Carter frowned, puzzled by his daughter's declaration. He'd brought the kids to their favorite bookstore and both had been happily exploring. Or so Carter thought. Crouching down beside Sadie, he watched her fiddle with the hem of her yellow Hello Kitty sweatshirt.

"What makes you say that, sweetie?"

Sadie heaved a sigh and regarded her father with big, hazel eyes Carter knew were remarkably like his own. "I can hear him whining," she said, turning to point to a corner where a play area had been set up. Several young children were crawling over a kitchen set and table and chairs as they played. Dylan was not among them, however. He'd seated himself on the carpet in the middle of the play area, arms crossed over the front of his red plaid shirt and his face set in a deep pout.

"Dylan always whines when he's gonna have a meltdown," Sadie told Carter, "and right now he's whining a *lot*."

Carter nodded briskly. He knew the signs of an over-stimulated child all too well and reached to tug one of Sadie's curls. "Right. I think it's a good time to buy the books you guys set aside, then go grab some lunch. How's that sound?"

She squinted at him. "Well…I dunno if I found everything I wanted."

"Oh, I don't know, Sadie—I think you guys did pretty well." Carter chuckled and waved at the books and toys he'd stacked on the counter. "If your brother starts in with the waterworks, we might not make it to the checkout anyway."

"Are you still gonna take us ice skating today?"

"Definitely, if you guys want to. We'll go to the rink right after lunch."

"Okay. Can we eat at the Serendipity place?" Sadie bargained while Carter straightened and stood.

"I made a reservation this morning, because I am the most awesome Dad ever," Carter gloated. "Let's hope your brother can hold it together in the cab, though."

Sadie gave her father a smug smile. "Mommy packed some fruit snacks in your bag, in case anyone got hungry."

Carter hefted the stack from the counter with a groan. "Now she tells me."

Several snacks and a quick cab ride to the restaurant worked wonders on Dylan's mood. The hostess seated them in a quieter corner on the main floor so the kids could spread out on the tabletop with paper and crayons. Unfortunately, that left Carter alone with his thoughts while they waited for their food, something he'd been trying to avoid.

More and more, he struggled to control his emotions, while feeling less and less satisfied with his life. Activities that had always brought Carter pleasure and fulfillment now left him empty. He worked, spent time with his children, took his wife out and treated her well—but too much of it seemed strangely hollow.

Carter knew something was wrong. But for the first time in his adult life, he had no idea what to do.

Desperate to hang on to normalcy, he'd put on a happy face at work and home. He'd felt sure he'd fooled his coworkers and even his kids, but his wife was a whole other story. Kate's measuring looks had told Carter she hadn't bought what he was selling, and he didn't blame her. Some days, Carter didn't buy it himself.

As the days had passed and Carter had grown more disconnected from his life, his spirits had gone into a tailspin. He'd been plagued by low-grade anxiety and his appetite and sleep had suffered, leaving him exhausted and snappish. By the time he'd decided to take a week off between Christmas and New Year's, he'd been finding it difficult to get out of bed every morning. That he'd been unable to gather energy to even try to fix things was another sign of the problem.

Sadie and Dylan dove into their food after they were served, sharing cheese ravioli and French toast while their father picked at an omelet. Carter was so busy supervising their chaos he didn't notice the shadow falling across their table until it lingered long enough to catch his eye.

Glancing up, Carter froze as a familiar pair of eyes locked with his own. He stared at Riley Porter-Wright, standing two feet away, tall and handsome and holding a small gift bag in one hand.

Carter's mouth went dry. He had time to notice Riley appeared just as shell-shocked before the Hamilton children broke the spell.

"Uncle Ri!" they squealed in unison.

Dylan pulled his sticky hand free of Carter's grasp to wave, while Sadie climbed down from her chair. She threw her arms around Riley and the sight of her powdered sugar handprints on Riley's dark cashmere coat made Carter groan.

"Oh, God, Sadie, your hands."

"It's no big deal," Riley reassured them, his face hectic with color. "This coat needs to go to the cleaners, anyway." He squatted down to hug Sadie while Dylan ran around the table to join in the hugging.

"We went to the bookstore!" Dylan exclaimed.

"And I had raviolis for lunch!" Sadie chimed in.

"Sounds like fun!" Riley replied brightly, his eyes flashing from their happy faces to Carter's.

"I didn't mean to interrupt your lunch, guys." He offered

Carter an apologetic smile and stood to begin coaxing the children back to their seats. "Especially before you've even had a chance to have dessert! You'd better sit down so your dad doesn't think you're all done and ready to go home!"

Sadie's eyes grew wide. She scurried for her chair with Dylan close behind, both children eyeing their father as they climbed back up to the table.

"Can we still get Frozen Hot Chocolate, Daddy?" Sadie motioned to the mostly clean plates with one hand. "We ate a whole lot and you said we could have dessert if we ate a whole lot."

"I said you could have dessert if you both cleaned your plates," Carter corrected. He bit back a smile as Sadie's face fell and Dylan looked mutinous. "I suppose it's a good idea to leave a little extra room for dessert, though," he continued gently. "Why don't you each eat two more bites, and we'll see what we can do about getting some Frozen Hot Chocolate."

A resounding silence greeted Carter's words, broken only by the sounds of forks scraping on plates and hasty chewing. He was surprised by the sudden warmth spreading through his chest at realizing Riley was laughing.

"Never underestimate the power of sugar, I guess," Riley murmured. He met Carter's gaze again and his grin dimmed.

Still unmoored by his friend's sudden appearance, Carter blinked, at a loss for how to reply. Riley glanced toward the door and Carter's heart jumped—he had to swallow hard against the fear his friend would disappear again.

"Don't judge me for bribing them, okay?" he blurted while his cheeks burned.

Riley shook his head, his expression relaxed again. "You could do worse, I'm sure. Like bribing them with barbecue pork rinds and Mountain Dew instead of actual nutritious food."

"Jesus." Carter grimaced. "I've got heartburn just thinking about that combo. You don't still eat that crap, do you?"

"No-o-o…" Riley had the good grace to look abashed after Carter raised a skeptical brow. "I don't eat that crap at the same time," he admitted. "Of course, I could now that no one's around to bug me about my junk food intake."

A pregnant pause fell over the table and Carter found himself completely tongue-tied. The children, however, were unaware of any awkwardness.

"Have dessert with us, Uncle Ri," Sadie suggested, waving to the empty seat across from Carter. "You can share something with Daddy."

Carter blinked, his anxiety flaring, while Riley offered Sadie a game smile.

"Oh, I don't know, sweetie." Riley's ears were red. "I don't want to butt in on your day out with your dad."

Dylan dissolved in peals of laughter. "You said butt!" he managed to get out while Riley disguised his laugh with a cough.

Sadie, always focused, got out of her chair again and grabbed Riley's hand. Wordlessly, she led him to the unoccupied chair just as a server approached. Carter sat with his old friend, his brain buzzing, and ordered dessert and coffee.

Riley waited until the server had moved on before leaning across the table toward Carter. "She really takes after Kate, huh?" he asked, inclining his head in Sadie's direction.

"You have no idea," Carter replied. "Dylan's no slouch in the bossy department, either. The two of them can be terrifying when they get an idea in their heads."

Riley nodded before shifting to watch the kids again, an odd expression on his face. Riley had always liked Sadie and Dylan and been proud to be Dylan's godfather. He'd never expressed any interest in having his own children, though—if anything, he'd scorned the idea of having an heir. Still, if Carter hadn't known better, he might have called his friend's expression wistful.

"You okay?" he asked.

Riley shrugged. "Sure. I'm surprised to run into you,

though," he added, meeting Carter's gaze and seeming uncertain. "It's been a while."

Carter said nothing for a moment, his throat tightening at the very obvious understatement. All the things he'd wanted to say to his friend for weeks died on his tongue, their weight pressing him flat while he tried to breathe. With so much uncertainty and so many bruised and broken feelings between them, Carter didn't know how to talk to Riley now.

"What are you doing here?" he heard himself ask. "This place seems kind of off the beaten path for you."

"Well, I could say the same of you."

Carter shrugged. "The kids like it here. It's an easy trip from the bookstore we visited this morning, too."

They broke off talking after the server approached the table again and there was a shift in activity while Carter helped Sadie and Dylan with straws and spoons. Turning back, Carter nudged his plate of pecan pie toward Riley without thinking, wordlessly inviting Riley to share as he'd done many times over the years. Looking up, he found Riley watching him, his expression unreadable.

"What was I saying?"

"That you took the kids to a bookstore earlier," Riley prompted. "I'm still stuck at seeing you here in the middle the day, though. It's Monday, Carter, and you're wearing jeans and a Crimson sweatshirt. You just told me you've been at a bookstore with your kids. Are you on vacation or something?"

"Sort of." Carter licked his lips. "I've been putting in a lot of extra hours at the office recently. I decided to take some time off between Christmas and New Year's and chill out."

Riley said nothing for a long moment. "Since when do the words 'extra hours' mean something negative to Carter Hamilton?"

Carter dropped his gaze to his plate. His father had been similarly skeptical when Carter had told him he needed some days off. Carter rarely took significant vacation time outside of a few weeks during the summer and Brad's obvious reluctance to let his son go rankled.

"You sound like my father," he muttered, his voice tight.

"Car," Riley began, breaking off as Carter spoke over him.

"Guess I'm getting old. Or maybe I wanted to make sure my kids haven't forgotten who I am." Neither excuse was entirely true, but Carter didn't care. Putting down his cup, he ran his fork through the piece of untouched pie. "Maybe I just needed a break for once."

He fell silent, aware Riley had gone very still in his seat. Carter cleared his throat and met his friend's gaze, his skin prickling at the almost palpable tension between them.

"You, uh, haven't said what you're doing here."

"My assistant's daughter is turning ten. She likes this place—has a thing for the desserts, like your kids, especially the ice cream sundaes. I came in to buy her a gift certificate and a couple of T-shirts." Riley gestured to the gift bag by his cup before glancing at his watch.

Carter's stomach twisted at the thought of Riley leaving. His old friend looked good—great, in fact—and appeared surprisingly even-keeled. Carter could hardly believe this was the same devastated man he'd last seen in the West Village apartment. When Carter took a moment to check, though, he caught faint circles under Riley's eyes and worry lines across his brow.

"How are you really?" Carter watched Riley's face fall, an ache in his chest. "Are you…are things okay?"

"I'm managing." Riley's demeanor cooled as he ran a hand through his hair. "Alex is staying in our place uptown, so I've been splitting time between the Village and the Hamptons. Work's…weird. People know we split and that my father's not speaking to me, but nothing about the work itself is different. The e-pub division is a separate entity of the business, so I'm left to my own devices there for the most part." He grimaced. "It's a relief to still have that, frankly."

"And…Alex and your folks?" Carter asked. He sighed at

Riley's bitter smile.

"About what you'd expect," Riley replied, sipping his coffee before he spoke again. "You know them pretty well—I'm sure you can imagine how things are among the Porter-Wrights at the moment. They've made it clear they have no use for me anymore." He gave a short, harsh laugh. "Hell, I'm surprised you haven't heard their side from the horse's mouth—"

"I have, actually." Carter cleared his throat, watching surprise flit across Riley's face. "Alex came to see me a couple of days after you left. She spoke to Kate, too. Jonathon and Geneva had words with my parents before your father approached me directly."

Riley winced. "Damn. I didn't know, Car—I'm sorry."

Carter blew a long breath out through his nose. His meeting with Jonathon had been particularly painful, filled with pointed questions and veiled insinuations. Talking about Riley with his own parents had been similarly dismaying for Carter, though. They'd stared at him as they would a stranger, searching for cracks in Carter's demeanor. Their silent attention—and unspoken doubts— had been exhausting.

"It was to be expected," he told Riley. "Our folks have known each other a long time—there's no way they were not going to talk about this."

"They didn't need to involve you, though, or your family." Riley's sharp tone caught the children's attention and he looked embarrassed.

"Sorry."

Carter gave him a sidelong glance and swallowed the words he wanted to say. He'd known their families would react poorly to Riley's revelation and even that they'd find ways to blame Carter. Hurtful as their reactions had been, he hadn't been surprised. The real surprise had been Riley. His best friend's years of secret keeping had hurt Carter more than anything else.

"Don't worry about it," he murmured finally. "It's my

fault for bringing it up." He glanced at his children, ignoring Riley's questioning gaze, and smiled at the whipped cream on the tip of Dylan's nose. "Probably not the right time or place for this conversation."

Riley got to his feet, looking rueful. "That's the problem, Carter — it's never the right time or place. Sort of the story of my life."

* * * *

The days leading up to the New Year passed in a blur. Carter spent time with his family and steered clear of the office in his apartment. He tried not to dwell on the stilted conversation he'd shared with Riley, and every day, he felt less connected to the world around him.

Carter's gathering anxiety also gave him insomnia. He read books and watched classic movies after his family went to sleep, only crawling into bed for a couple of hours before the next day began. By midweek, he was running on fumes. He managed to hide the extent of his exhaustion, until the inevitable crash occurred and Kate called him out.

On the Friday before his return to work, Carter woke to a ringing silence, something unknown in a dwelling that housed two small children. He rolled over in bed, aware that his body was stiff and the light in the bedroom seemed oddly low. Frowning, he reached for his phone to check the time, and jerked upright in surprise when he saw that it was nearly 6:00 p.m. He stared through the window at the purpling sky and glow of the city lights in the gloaming and felt a surge of fear to know he'd slept away an entire day.

He turned at a soft sound to see Kate pushing open the bedroom door, holding a steaming cup and a plate with a sandwich.

"You're up!" she exclaimed, walking quickly to Carter's side. She put the cup and plate on the nightstand and laid the back of her hand on his forehead as if to check for fever.

"And thank God for that, because I'd started to worry. Are you feeling any better?"

Carter frowned, his cheeks heating after he recognized relief in his wife's expression. "I feel fine. Why didn't you wake me?" he rasped, gratefully accepting the mug Kate handed to him. "Where are the kids?"

"It's warm tea with lemon," she told him. "The kids are having dinner with your parents. I let you sleep because you are exhausted and needed the rest. I thought for sure you were getting sick."

"I'm fine—"

"You are not fine," Kate countered. The fierceness in her face snapped Carter's mouth closed so sharply his teeth clicked. "Even if you're not actually ill, you're far from okay. I…I think you're depressed, sweetheart." Kate sighed out, then drew her cream cardigan closed.

Carter shook his head vehemently. "That is ridiculous," he scoffed.

"You are, Carter, and there's not a whole lot you can say to convince me otherwise." Kate sat beside him and ran a hand over his hair, clearly thinking about what she wanted to say.

"You're not a perky guy and you never have been. One of the things I've always liked about you is your mellow attitude. Lately, though, your mood has been in the toilet. You haven't been sleeping, you're hardly eating…you're practically a zombie. I've never seen you like this before."

"I've been working too hard," Carter replied, trying not to sound sullen. "I took this week off for that very reason."

"Yes, and do you know your father's called to check up on you?"

Carter blinked, stunned into silence for a moment. "He… my father called you?"

Kate looked tired. "Twice in the last several days. Asking if you're feeling any better and ready to get back to work."

"Jesus." Carter shoved his cup roughly onto the nightstand. "I don't understand why the fuck he's so hung up on this. I'm not a machine. Can't I take time off like a normal human being?"

"Of course you can," Kate soothed, "but you have to admit it's not something you do a whole lot of." She gave him a small smile. "Working is part of who you are—I knew that before we ever got serious. I like that you're so driven. You're always there when the kids or I need you to be, and you're here in our bed with me every night. Usually, you balance work and life really, really well. Recently though… you're not yourself. I like to think I know you better than anyone," Kate told him, unaware her words were like little knives under Carter's skin. "And right now I know you're not happy."

Carter swallowed hard after Kate took his hand between hers, running a thumb over his knuckles.

"I wish you'd let me in," she coaxed, her voice tight. Kate's eyes were achingly blue and so much like Riley's that Carter's breath caught. "I'd put this all down to overwork and maybe even a touch of holiday burnout, but I can't. I get the feeling there's more going on with you than just being tired."

Kate raised an eyebrow at Carter's weary sigh, her next words stealing his breath entirely.

"Is it about this thing with Riley?"

Carter didn't respond. Pain radiated in waves from the center of his chest and the tea he'd drunk left a sour aftertaste on his tongue.

"You told me you ran into Riley when you had lunch with the kids," Kate reminded him. "Sadie said Riley seemed upset about something. She thought the two of you were arguing."

Carter closed his eyes at Kate's careful tone, then scrubbed his face with both hands. "I told Riley about Alex and his parents dragging us into their drama. He wasn't happy about it."

When Carter glanced up again, Kate's eyebrows were drawn together. "Riley didn't know until you told him?"

"Jonathon's not speaking to him, which can only mean that Geneva is following suit. As far as Alex goes, I got the impression from her that she's done talking to Riley. That could change…I don't think they want to be enemies, at least not forever." Carter licked his lips and shrugged. "I'm sure the lawyers are handling everything for the time being, though."

Kate drew a breath as if to reply before she nodded. Her troubled expression didn't waver, however, prompting Carter to nudge her with his elbow.

"What?" he murmured.

"Honestly, I'm just… I'm confused." Kate ran her hands over her hair, pushing the long waves behind her ears. "I know you and Riley argued when he told you he planned to come out. You were concerned about the families and the gossip and that all made sense at the time.

"But it's been weeks now, and you and Riley still haven't patched things up. I'd hoped the two of you would be back to normal by this point." Kate gave a helpless little shrug. "I thought you were emailing or talking on the phone, even if you weren't spending time together. But if you're still not talking to each other…well, then things between you are not back to normal and I don't understand why that is."

Carter's eyes burned. "It's complicated," he told her, his voice rough.

"How complicated can it be?" Kate pressed. "Riley's been your best friend since before I even met you. You've gone to bat for him every time he's asked you over the years, sometimes without his asking at all, and he's done the same for you. You've certainly backed him up for smaller things than coming out of the closet."

Carter blinked, his face heating at the implication in Kate's words. "What does that mean?"

"I mean I don't understand why you're not supporting your friend right now, Carter." Kate shot him a level gaze. "Do you have a problem with Riley being bi?"

The hairs on Carter's arms rose. "Of course not. How can

you ask me that?"

"What else am I supposed to think?"

"For starters, you're not supposed to think that your husband is a bigot and a homophobe!"

"I'm not sure I don't think exactly that!" Kate exclaimed, throwing her hands up. "Riley's in the middle of this huge, life-altering change and you're hanging back and letting it happen without even talking to him? That doesn't sound like the man I married."

Carter's breath hitched. Without warning, his emotions went into overdrive, storming through him with a force that made him shake. He was horrified to realize that he was only moments from weeping. Quickly, he tossed back the bedding still covering his legs and swung himself the long way over the mattress and away from Kate.

"I'm gonna take a shower," he ground out as he stood. Striding to the dresser to gather some clothes, he was aware Kate had gotten up, too, and come around the bed to stand nearby. "I'll, uh, go downstairs afterward and wait for the kids to come back from my—"

"I'm sorry!" Worry and regret were clear in Kate's tone. "I didn't mean to—"

"Yes, you did," Carter spoke over her and made his way to the bathroom. "But you're wrong about my having a problem with Riley being bi. Yeah, I was surprised when he told me and I hate that he hid it, but I don't...I don't hate him for it."

He jerked to a stop outside the bathroom after Kate closed her hand around his upper arm. He stood, body stiff and head bowed, as she came around him to block the door. Carter couldn't meet her gaze, though. He couldn't bear the thought of seeing scorn in his wife's eyes, or worse, pity.

The need to finally come clean choked Carter. It would be so easy to be rid of the burden, to finally tell Kate about the threesomes. He wanted to say he loved sharing his bed with Riley, that he felt so fucking good every time he touched his friend, kissed him, made him groan and come.

That Riley had fallen in love with him and wanted Carter to share his life.

Carter shuddered, his eyes welling with tears that he tried to hide by scrunching his lids shut.

"Please tell me what's wrong," Kate begged. "It's obvious you're unhappy about something and have been for a while now. I know some of it has to be with what's happened with Riley, but I...I don't understand what's going on."

"I told you already that it's complicated." Carter cleared his throat roughly after his voice cracked. "If I could explain it to you, I would, but that's just not... I can't, that's all."

Kate brought a warm hand to rest on Carter's cheek and sighed after he pulled away. "Oh, Carter. Don't shut me out. All I want is to help you make it better."

Carter shook his head, gently pushing past his wife and into the bathroom. He paused inside the door before answering, his voice low when he spoke. "There's no making it better. You're right — I haven't been a good friend to Riley."

"Honey," she murmured.

Carter shook his head. "It's true. He trusted me and I...I let him down." He blew out an unsteady breath as the tears began to roll over his cheeks. "I'm not sure there's anything I can do to make it up to him, either."

Kate continued to assure Carter that he was mistaken, but he couldn't bear to listen. Instead, he carefully shut the door against her words. Once alone, Carter finally, finally, let himself fall apart, if only for a little while.

Chapter Sixteen

On New Year's Eve, Natalie greeted Riley at the door of her apartment with a kiss on the cheek. He kissed her back, smiling down at her. "Thanks for inviting me."

"I'm glad you came." She returned the smile and held out her hand when he took off his coat. "You look great."

He smoothed his hands over the jacket of his gray suit and straightened his silver and blue tie. "Thanks."

She hung the coat in the entry closet and tucked her arm through his, taking the bottle of wine he'd brought. "Let me introduce you to my friends."

Natalie's apartment was on the small side but nicely decorated and he saw her personality reflected in the space. Everything seemed warm, cozy and welcoming. He commented on how much he liked the apartment and Natalie chatted about it for a moment while they walked into the living area.

There were at least a dozen or so people there and he felt a sudden surge of anxiety. Give him a roomful of board members to schmooze and he could handle it, but meeting new people and trying to make a genuine connection intimidated him. He stopped Natalie when a thought occurred to him. "Wait, if someone asks, what's the story about how we met?"

"Oh," she said with a startled laugh. "I hadn't even thought of that. Let's just say we were introduced by some mutual friends. It's close enough to the truth."

"That sounds good," Riley agreed.

The next half an hour or so was spent mingling with Natalie's guests. By and large they were artists, dancers and musicians and the odd accountant and lawyer. Riley was unsurprised to find he liked her friends. They were all intelligent, well-spoken and eager to discuss a wide variety of topics. Drawn into a debate on e-books versus print copies, he thoroughly enjoyed the good-natured argument.

"I understand the appeal of paper copies," Riley said, disagreeing with a dancer named Meredith. "You can't beat the texture or the smell, but practically speaking, e-readers have the advantage in nearly every other way."

She opened her mouth, but a voice behind Riley spoke up. "And I sell a hell of a lot more digital books than I do print copies these days."

Riley turned to face the man and, for a moment, was stunned. He was incredibly attractive, with artfully tousled brown hair, blue-gray eyes and fine, sculpted features. Wearing a sleek, tailored black suit and crisp white shirt—open at the collar—with a neat white pocket square, he looked like he could have stepped off a runway. He grinned suddenly, his full lips parting to reveal a dazzling smile, and Riley temporarily forgot what they'd been talking about.

The man spoke again. "Why were we debating book formats?"

Riley shook his head to clear it and managed a reply, staggered by his reaction to the man. "To be honest, I can't remember. I was arguing in favor of e-books, but not everyone is convinced." He paused for a moment and held out a hand. "I'm Riley Porter-Wright, by the way."

"Will Martin."

His palm felt warm against Riley's and Riley had a hard time tearing his gaze away. "Nice to meet you, Will."

"The feeling is mutual." Will gave Riley a long, appraising glance. "Am I correct in assuming you're with Porter-Wright Publishing?"

Riley nodded. "Vice president of the e-pub division. You're an author?"

Will grinned and stepped forward, slipping both hands into his pockets. "Mostly a law professor, but, yes, I am a writer as well. I'm afraid my writing probably isn't something you're familiar with, though."

Riley raised an eyebrow. "I don't know. I'm pretty well read."

"With your job, I'd assume so, but I write extraordinarily boring non-fiction—legal history."

"Ahh, well, you're right, then. I doubt I've read your work," Riley admitted.

Will gave him a dimpled smile and touched his forearm. "No hard feelings."

Riley became aware that they'd completely drifted off from the small group that had been discussing e-books and when he glanced over, everyone else had moved on to other topics. He was surprised to realize he liked Will's casual touch and flirting. He flirted back. "Glad to hear it."

"Porter-Wright got into e-pub late," Will commented, changing the subject slightly.

Riley attempted to hide a grimace and his words came out more bitter than he intended. "My father is president and CEO of the company. Let's just say we don't see eye to eye on a great many things."

Will gave him a concerned, puzzled glance. "Why does that sound more personal than I think you intended?"

Riley gave him a weak smile. "Because I'm not a very good poker player, I suppose. You're not wrong, but it's... complicated."

Will changed the subject completely. "So, how do you know Natalie? I don't think I've ever seen you at any of her parties before."

"This is the first one she's invited me to," Riley acknowledged. "And we met through some mutual friends. You?"

"I've known Natalie for years. She used to date my roommate."

"She's become a good friend recently," Riley said honestly. "I had another event I could have gone to tonight, but I'm glad I took up Natalie on her invitation to come here instead."

Will gave him an appraising glance and Riley's skin prickled. "I can't believe you're hurting for company."

Riley glanced down for a moment before glancing up at Will. "You might be surprised. I'm in the midst of a divorce right now and…re-evaluating my life, I guess you'd say. At any rate, I've reached a point where I realized I want more substantial relationships than what I currently have."

Will nodded thoughtfully. "It can be a challenge."

Riley let out a rueful laugh. "You know, this is a rather heavy discussion for a New Year's Eve party."

"I thought you were searching for more substance," Will countered.

"Fair point. I might need another drink, though." Riley held up his empty glass with a self-deprecating smile. "And I've monopolized you so much you haven't even had a chance to get a drink. I'm sorry."

"I'm not."

Riley rather liked Will's bold gaze and attention. He had no doubt that Will was interested in him and, well, it was mutual. Thinking about Carter still made his chest ache, but he couldn't live his life waiting for his friend to come around. After the conversation with Carter at Serendipity 3, Riley couldn't keep pretending he was going to suddenly change his mind about wanting a relationship. One day, perhaps he and Carter could repair their friendship, but he knew Carter wasn't going to leave Kate for him. He also knew that even if they could be friends again, their friendship would never be the same. He had to move forward and be open to the idea of dating. Flirting with another man at a New Year's Eve party was a good start, right?

"Can I at least get you a drink while we talk some more?" Riley offered, pushing away thoughts of Carter and focusing on the man in front of him.

"Yes, please."

Riley caught Natalie's knowing glance when he and Will walked over to the bar she'd set up. Natalie's smirk made him wonder if she had been playing matchmaker. Or at least had a good idea that he would hit it off with Will well enough to have an interesting conversation. When his gaze lingered on Will's body, he thought maybe it would be a little more than just conversation. Perhaps Natalie had guessed that, too.

Riley offered to mix a drink for Will, but he declined. "I'll take a glass of red wine, the Grenache there," he said, gesturing toward an open bottle. "I can only stay at the party a short while before I head to another one, and I'm driving."

"Of course." Riley poured him a glass, handed it over and was rewarded with a brilliant smile.

They took a seat on an unoccupied couch and sipped their drinks while they talked, one conversation flowing seamlessly into the next. He was surprised to find himself opening up to Will. He seemed so genuine and Riley's attraction to him made his tongue looser than usual.

Will was charming and Riley welcomed the attention, his skin tingling at every casual touch. He liked watching Will speak, seeing the bob of the Adam's apple in his throat and the way he wet his lips every so often. Something deep within him relaxed. He'd always wanted to respond to a man this way but had been forced to suppress those feelings. Riley shifted on the couch, trying to hide his response to Will, but he wasn't sure he was fooling anyone and, in truth, he wasn't sure he cared. As the night progressed, the volume of conversation in the apartment rose, along with the music, and Riley had to lean in to hear Will better. He didn't mind being close to Will—far from it—and he liked the heat of Will's hand on his thigh, but the volume had begun to make conversation difficult.

Will said something to him and he shook his head. "Can't hear you," he mouthed. Will leaned in, his breath warm against Riley's ear, sending shivers skittering down his spine. "Natalie has a little balcony—do you want to go out there so we don't have to scream to have a conversation?"

Riley nodded and let Will escort him outside, liking his hand against the small of his back. They closed the narrow balcony door behind them and Riley relaxed at the sudden quiet. It had stopped snowing and the air outside was cold enough that he could see their breaths. They'd both abandoned their empty glasses and Riley suddenly remembered Will had said he had another party to go to. "Not that I'm trying to get rid of you, but didn't you have another place to be tonight?"

Will smiled and leaned in, close enough that Riley could faintly smell red wine on his breath, and he idly wondered what it would taste like on Will's tongue. Despite the cold, he felt flushed all of a sudden, wanting to make a move but too hesitant.

"I decided that I'd rather be here with you than at a party with people I should be networking with. I prefer substance over superficiality, too."

"I'm glad," Riley said huskily. "I feel slightly guilty for monopolizing you all evening, but not enough to let you go."

"You're very intriguing," Will said, smiling at Riley. "I know you said things are complicated for you now, and you mentioned a divorce, but I'm curious to know where you stand."

That could mean a lot of things. He wasn't quite sure if Will was referring to his marital status or sexual orientation— maybe both. "I'm in the process of getting a divorce from my wife and attempting to be open about my attraction to men for the first time," he finally said, heart hammering at his admission and Will's proximity.

Will reached out and cupped Riley's cheek, sliding a thumb across Riley's lower lip. "And are you attracted to me?" Will asked.

Riley was sure Will already knew the answer. "Very much so," he replied as his heart sped up and his lips parted automatically, anticipating the kiss. The sound of the door opening and someone asking them if they wanted champagne for a toast broke the mood. Riley had to force himself not to jump and move back from Will. It was going to take some getting used to. Being open about his sexuality and not flinching every time someone saw him with a man felt foreign to him, but he supposed he'd adjust to it eventually. Will took the champagne flutes and the woman disappeared through the door.

Will grinned, handing a flute to Riley. "Terrible timing."

"I agree."

Will took a sip of the champagne and glanced at his watch. "I suppose it is nearly midnight."

"I hadn't even noticed." Riley discarded the champagne on the railing of the balcony without taking a sip and stepped closer to Will. Despite the cold air, Will's body felt warm against his as he leaned in. Eyes never leaving Riley's, Will set down his glass too. Riley closed his eyes and he met Will halfway. The touch of his chilled lips on Riley's only heightened the sensation of being kissed by another man. It felt different from kissing Carter, different from the kiss with the man he'd met at the bar the night of Carter's wedding, whose name he had long since forgotten. Hours of conversation and slow-simmering attraction had led to this moment and Riley was every bit as eager as Will.

Will parted his lips slightly, beginning to deepen the kiss, and Riley's head swam at the sensation. Will was a very good kisser. He brushed chilled fingers against the bare skin at the back of Riley's neck and he pressed closer to Will. Dimly, through the crack in the door, Riley could hear the crowd inside counting down to midnight. "I think we're a little early," Will murmured against his lips.

"I don't have any complaints," Riley countered, threading slightly trembling fingers through the soft hair at the back of Will's head. He brushed his lips across Will's teasingly, and Will pulled back, grinning at him.

"Is this how you saw yourself ringing in the New Year?"

"No," Riley said honestly. "But that doesn't mean I'm unhappy with the way things turned out."

270

Will drew him in for another kiss as the crowd inside yelled, "Happy New Year!"

Happy New Year, indeed, Riley thought, parting his lips before Will's warm tongue softly but thoroughly tasted his.

It was too cold for Will and Riley to linger on the balcony much after midnight and the party broke up shortly after. As they left Natalie's apartment, Will suggested they go back to his place. He must have seen the hesitation in Riley's expression, because he hastily added, "Even if it's just for drinks and more conversation. I understand this is all fairly new to you, but I want to be honest here. I like you a lot—you're one of the most interesting and attractive men I've met in a long time. I won't lie—I'm attracted to you. If you wanted to continue what we started on the balcony, I would be more than happy to do that. But I'm perfectly content to just talk, too. Or something in between."

Being intimate with any man aside from Carter felt strange, but there was no denying his attraction to Will. On some level, he knew fear of the unknown made him panicky, but remembering Will's body against his and the way he'd kissed pulled Riley in the complete opposite direction and he wasn't sure which instinct to follow.

Ultimately, Riley declined Will's offer, but not because he wasn't interested in continuing what they'd started. His body was most definitely on board, but his brain wasn't quite there yet. "I'm sorry, but I can't," he said honestly. "Not tonight, but I would like to see you again."

They exchanged phone numbers and Riley promised to call Will sometime in the coming week so they could go out. Will kissed Riley goodbye before he left, and the sensation of Will's mouth lingered on Riley's lips when he left the building.

Riley was too busy watching drunk New Year's Eve revelers from the back seat of the car to think much on the ride home and it wasn't until he stood in the shower in his apartment that the events of the night caught up to him. He braced his hand against the wall as he hung his head and let the water rush over the back of his neck and down his shoulders.

Alone, with time to think, he let himself consider what had happened with Will. He didn't have any regrets, but it was a lot to process. For once in his life, he didn't feel uncomfortable about pursuing a relationship with another man, but he did felt a stab of guilt that it wasn't Carter. Although totally unrealistic, he felt as though he'd been disloyal to his best friend, a difficult emotion to swallow. Should he be able to enjoy kissing Will so much when he was still in love with Carter? He sighed and straightened, scrubbing at his face with his hands for a moment before turning off the water. Then again, he considered, he'd married a woman while in love with Carter, what was kissing a guy?

Chapter Seventeen

The first weeks of 2013 slid by and Carter hardly noticed. His days melted one into another, punctuated only by Sadie and Dylan's sharp, noisy joy.

After falling apart in front of Kate, Carter had made an effort to pull himself together. Neither addressed Carter's depressed state of mind, but he could hardly articulate the word in his own head, let alone say it out loud. Their argument over Riley also went unmentioned, but Carter knew Kate regretted the things she'd said. No matter how much Kate disapproved of the way Carter had treated Riley, she didn't like to see her husband hurting.

Instead of talking, he stood at Kate's side to welcome friends and family into their home for cocktails and dinners. While Carter struggled to put on a cheerful front, he read gratitude and encouragement in his wife's eyes when their gazes met.

Returning to the opera for the opening night of *Die Fledermaus* was excruciating, however. Not even Strauss' vibrant arrangements could distract Carter from the whispers swirling around the Porter-Wrights' empty box and the glances of people he'd known for years.

The party on the theater's promenade following the performance was equally stressful. Conversation danced around topics that made Carter squirm and speculation ran wild. He heard guesses as to what had caused the Porter-Wright split, to whose side the families had taken and even about the terms of the divorce.

Carter stayed mostly silent through cocktails and dinner before he reached the limit of his patience. After dessert and a few words with Kate, he retreated to a darkened alcove off the promenade. Sitting on an empty sofa, he closed his eyes against a building headache and forced himself to ignore the empty feeling in his gut. Midnight was approaching when Kate startled him out of a light doze, but Carter accepted the champagne flute she held out and toasted the evening's success with a smile.

Carter found it easier to cope at the office when he buried himself in meetings and copy. Work was familiar and comforting, even safe, and Carter clung to the routine. He worked later and later, not always making it home for dinner or the kids' bedtimes, pushing himself through his exhaustion.

He swallowed back a sigh when he came home one night and found Kate in his study, a Tom Collins in one hand and determination written all on her face.

"We need to talk."

"I know we do," he agreed, tugging at his collar and tie to loosen them. "If it could wait until tomorrow morning, though, I'd really, really appreciate it. I'm so fucking tired, Kate, and I just want to go to bed and sleep for the next six hours or however long I have until I have to get up again."

"I'm done waiting."

A scowl twisted Kate's features. There were dark circles under her eyes and her skin was pale against her black sweater. She appeared just as worn out as Carter felt.

"If you really wanted to go to bed, you wouldn't be here in your study. You'd be upstairs, looking in on the kids—who miss you, by the way—and maybe, I don't know, talking to your wife for the first time in four days."

"We're talking right now, aren't we?" he replied dryly and sighed after Kate's frown deepened.

"This isn't a joke, Carter—this is your life."

"I'm well aware of that."

"I'm not sure you are," she countered, her cheeks coloring. "You know, I thought things were bad a couple of weeks ago, when you were physically present but emotionally on another planet." Kate stared at the glass in her hands before she spoke again, her voice raspy. "Now you're not even bothering to show up in body anymore."

"Kate—"

"How long before you start sleeping in your office?" she pressed, her gaze over-bright as it met Carter's. "Or are you planning to just move out entirely? Is that how you're going to play this? Just one long fade until you're out of our lives?"

Carter shook his head, exhaling sharply through his nose. "What are you talking about? I spend some extra time in the office to catch up from being on an unplanned vacation and now we're splitting up? How many cocktails have you had?"

He flinched as Kate threw her drink at the office door, sending pieces of glass flying and liquid splattering. Before Carter could draw breath, she was on her feet and moving toward him, her face contorted with anger. Carter managed to catch her before she could strike out at him, curling his fingers around her wrists as she made to smack him with her open palms.

"Stop it," he ground out, pushing Kate forward and forced to take a step back before he could twist her around. Despite Carter's superior height and bulk, it was a challenge to contain Kate's struggling. "Kate! For Christ's sake, stop it!"

Winding his arms around Kate, Carter pulled her in against his body to contain her flailing movements. The restraint seemed to anger Kate more, though, and Carter let out a grunt as she jabbed his stomach with her elbow, forcing him to loosen his grip. Twisting free, Kate whirled around to face him, the pain on her face stealing the breath he had left.

"Don't you dare mock me," she bit out, the tremor in her voice making Carter's chest ache.

"I'm not!" he began and snapped his mouth shut when Kate clasped her own head in frustration.

"Just…God, shut up." Kate closed her eyes, visibly trying to rein in her emotions. "I've tried to be patient. Tried so hard to be understanding, to listen to you, to help you get through…whatever the fuck this is," she said with a wave of one unsteady hand. "But nothing's working. Every day, no matter what either of us do, we end up farther apart than the day before. You just keep pulling away."

"I know."

Kate covered her mouth with one hand.

Carter's voice faltered. "I…I'm sorry, Katie, I really am. I'm trying, I swear to you, I don't want this—"

"Do you even know what this is?" Kate dropped her hand to her side. Her voice was raw as she stared at Carter. "Because I don't. I really don't. I have no idea what the hell is going on or…or what happened from one day to the next. Because things between us seemed pretty good, you know? All this time, I thought we were pretty happy until suddenly you just weren't."

Kate crossed her arms over her chest, seeming to hug herself. "You're here, with us, but your heart's not in it. I've watched you try these last few weeks but you're miserable—"

"I'm not miserable!"

"Jesus, do you hear yourself?" Kate almost shouted. "How can you stand there and just lie to me?"

"I'm not lying." Carter nearly choked on his words.

"And I'm not blind. You're just so unhappy with everything, including our life together." Abruptly, Kate laughed, the hard, humorless sound at odds with the tears in her eyes. "Shit, maybe it's especially our life together that you're unhappy with."

"No," Carter began again, stepping forward and freezing after Kate laughed again, tears sliding down her cheeks.

"Are you going to stand there and keep lying, after everything we've been through together?"

Carter kept quiet for a long moment. "I'm not lying."

"You are. I know you are—I just don't understand why."

Kate shook her head sadly. "You know, it took me a little while to catch on that something was wrong. To see that you were just, I don't know, along for the ride with us... like you didn't care all that much about what happened in the end. Once I figured it out, it took even longer for me to accept that you were actively lying. Because you've never lied to me. Except...maybe you have."

Carter's body went cold. His stomach burned as his lies—years of omissions and untruths—flashed through his mind.

"I started wondering if you had lied to me—and I couldn't stop." Kate's voice was ragged but determined. "I thought...that maybe you didn't realize you were lying. Or that maybe you've been lying to yourself, too." She nodded, her gaze moving over Carter's face with certainty.

"What the hell is that supposed to mean?" Carter whispered, unable to stop himself from stepping forward. Kate fell back a step in return and his chest constricted. "Kate, please, talk to me."

Kate scrubbed at her face, wiping at the tearstained skin. "Yeah, now you want to talk. Kind of ironic, don't you think, after you tried to blow me off ten minutes ago? After months of walking around your own goddamned house like you don't even live here?"

"I know." Carter's voice broke. He took another careful step forward, his heart thundering, and held his breath as Kate stood her ground, slowly closing the distance between them until he was at her side. He stayed silent, not daring to touch her, his heart aching at the unhappiness that radiated off her in waves.

"I could be such an asshole to you right now," she murmured. "I could kick you out. Take you for half of everything you've got, keep you from seeing the—" she stopped abruptly, and shook her head. "I probably should be an asshole."

Carter drew in a shaky breath before he laid his hands on her stiff shoulders. "I know. I deserve it. I hope you won't.

I don't want to lose my family, Katie."

"I know you don't. I don't want that, either." Kate sighed, bowing her head slightly though she still held herself rigid. "We can't go on like this, though. Whatever's broken in this family has got to be fixed somehow."

"We'll fix it," Carter replied automatically. Kate lifted her head to meet his eyes again, and her penetrating gaze sent another chill through him.

"I don't want promises right now. I want you to work on this with me. For me, and for the kids, even if we end up splitting up." Kate looked at Carter, no doubt taking in the dark circles under his eyes, and her face softened. "If you can work on it for yourself…maybe we'll get somewhere."

Carter's heart lurched as she turned to go. "Wait," he almost cried, his voice ringing through the quiet room and startling them both.

"Hey, I was just going to get some things to clean up the broken glass," she told him, concern written on her face.

"Sorry, I—you just sound like, I don't know," Carter stammered, blinking rapidly and trying to organize his scrambled thoughts.

"Calm down," Kate urged, bringing up a hand to lay on his right shoulder. "Your face is flushed, Car. You're kind of freaking me out here. Do what you're always telling the kids to do, and take a breath."

Breathing in deeply, Carter nodded, forcing himself to exhale before he spoke again. "Sorry. It's just…you make it sound like we're done. Like we're over already and we haven't even started working on putting things right."

Kate gave him a sad smile. "I've had to get used to the idea that you might not be around."

"But why?" Carter asked, his eyes stinging at both his wife's words and the resignation in her voice.

"You've had one foot out of the door for a long time. You just didn't realize it." Kate gave his shoulder a little squeeze before she stepped back and walked away.

It took Carter a long moment before he could force himself

to follow Kate out of his office.

Chapter Eighteen

"Happy belated birthday," Natalie said, kissing Riley on the cheek as she greeted him at the entrance to a crowded restaurant for brunch.

"Thanks. I'm glad we could finally find a time to get together." It had been nearly three weeks since the New Year's Eve party and he wanted to talk to her about what had happened with Will.

They followed the waitress to a small table and once they were settled, Natalie gave him a searching look. "How are you? Did you hear from Carter on your birthday?"

Riley smiled tightly and shook his head. "No." It had been nearly a week and a half since he'd turned thirty-five and he hadn't had a single word from Carter in that time.

"And how are things with Will?" Natalie asked lightly.

"It's…going well," Riley said. Will had taken him out to dinner and they'd had a good time, but he'd been disappointed that neither Carter nor his parents had reached out to him. "I think. I don't know."

"You seemed to hit it off well at the New Year's Eve party."

Riley flushed when he told her about the kiss. Natalie grinned at him and patted his cheek. "You're cute."

"You're making this worse," he muttered.

"I think it's adorable that you're so shy about it," she said, cutting a bite of her mushroom and Gruyère omelet. "Especially considering what we've done together."

"I'm not…shy, I'm just not…used to it yet," he protested.

"Oh, fine," Natalie said, growing serious. "So, what happened after you left my place?"

"Nothing that evening. Although we did exchange phone numbers and, like I said, he took me out to dinner for my birthday."

"Did you have a nice time?"

"I did," he admitted.

"I think it's great that you hit it off so well."

"But what about Carter?" he said, pushing aside his plate of half-eaten eggs Benedict. "One minute I think there's no chance he'll ever come around and the next…I think maybe he just needs more time. That's probably just wishful thinking, but it's hard to let go of."

Natalie paused for a moment, then spoke. "I think that you both need to do what's best for you individually. Go out with Will, see what else is out there now that you have the opportunity to make the choices you want, not the ones that are expected of you. I think it'll be the best thing for both you and Carter in the long run."

"Were you trying to set me up with Will?" Riley asked.

Natalie shrugged and gave a little hum. "Not really. I planned the party before I left on my trip, but I didn't think about inviting you until I got home. I invited you because I thought a night out would be good for you. After, it did occur to me that you two might hit it off and I planned to introduce you to him, but you did that all on your own." Natalie beamed at him.

"And you think I should continue to see him?"

"If you're interested? Yeah, absolutely. He's a great guy, always has been. I've known him for years. You two have more in common than you'd think."

"He hinted at that," Riley replied, taking a sip of his coffee. "It made me curious."

"Well, ask him out then. It can't hurt. At the bare minimum, I think he'd be a good friend. No harm in seeing if there's more to it than that."

"Yeah, okay," Riley agreed, a nervous flutter of anticipation growing in his chest. "I'll do that."

* * * *

Going back to the office the following day and dealing with his father's coldness felt like a slap in the face. They had meetings all day that forced them to interact and by the time they wrapped up, Riley felt tense and irritable. The following day was no better and by the time he got out of work on Friday, his shoulders were tight and his head throbbed.

He picked up dinner on the way home and texted Natalie to ask her about a yoga class. If he didn't learn to deal with his stress better, he would wind up a wreck. She invited him to come with her the following day to the class she'd been attending regularly and he apprehensively agreed.

After dinner, he pulled out his iPad and decided he'd read for a while, but his mind wandered to Will instead. After a few moments of indecision, Riley texted him.

Will responded a short while later and they sent messages back and forth. Riley caught himself smiling down at his phone at some of Will's responses. When their texted conversation became more in depth, Will called him. "I hope I'm not interrupting your evening," he said and Riley snorted.

"Ahh, no. I'm almost ashamed to admit how boring I really am. I am sitting at home alone on a Friday night. You?"

"I was out with some friends, actually," Will said. "I ducked out to talk to you."

"You didn't have to," Riley protested.

"And if I wanted to?"

Riley momentarily felt taken aback. "Then…then I'd guess I'd say I'm flattered."

"Good." Will paused for a moment. "Are you still interested in going out again sometime?"

Riley swallowed hard. "Yes."

"Do you have plans tomorrow?"

"I'm going to a yoga class with Natalie tomorrow, but I'm

free after that."

Will chuckled. "That conjures up intriguing mental images."

Riley flushed. "We'll see how it goes. I'm prepared to humiliate myself awfully."

"I don't know," Will replied. "You seem like the kind of guy who would be good at anything you put your mind to."

"You've never heard me sing," Riley said drily. "I love music, but I can't carry a tune."

"What type of music?"

Riley answered him, encouraged when he realized Will was interested in some of the music he liked. Riley stopped abruptly in the middle of discussing the merits of traditional versus new staging of various operas and groaned. "I'm sorry, I'm probably boring you to tears."

"You're not," Will said warmly. "I like your enthusiasm."

Despite Will's assurances, Riley wrapped up the conversation and changed topics to their plans for the following day. They transitioned to talking about books, a subject they both had strong opinions about, and it made for an animated and lively discussion. Riley relaxed on his sofa, his stress melting away. "That reminds me," Riley said. "What name do you write under? I'd like to read some of your work."

Will laughed softly. "I'm flattered. I write under my own name, William Martin. Promise me you'll still go out with me, even if my books put you to sleep?"

"I promise," Riley agreed with a chuckle.

"I should get back," Will said, sounding reluctant. "I like thinking about you reading my work, though. Or maybe I just like thinking about you."

Riley felt a little thrill run through him at the words. "I'm looking forward to seeing you tomorrow," he admitted.

"Me, too."

Riley could hear the smile in the man's voice.

They said goodbye and Riley hung up the phone with a

smile on his face. He was pursuing a relationship. With a man.

His heart sped up at the thought, nerves mingling with the anticipation. He was really doing this, moving forward and trying to live the life he'd always wanted. No second-guessing himself because his father might not approve or wondering if someone would get the wrong impression about him. No wondering how it would affect his standing in society. Finally allowing himself to decide who he really was and what his future could be like.

He looked around the apartment, seeing it as his new home, and felt a sense of contentment for the first time.

* * * *

Yoga wound up being sweaty, painful and surprisingly enjoyable. He felt calmer and more relaxed after and he agreed to join Natalie for the Saturday class as often as he could manage it. He read a bit of one of Will's books that afternoon and while it wasn't necessarily what he'd consider light reading, it was interesting and Riley liked his style of writing.

That evening, he met Will at a wine bar. He felt grateful it was a place he'd never gone to with Carter. Although Will intrigued him, he wasn't sure he could handle an onslaught of memories of his best friend. The entrance was crowded and when he saw Will, he skirted around a small group of people waiting for tables to reach him. Will leaned in, then hesitated, as if unsure how comfortable Riley would be with a public display of affection. Swallowing his initial discomfort, Riley closed the distance and greeted him with a hug and a kiss on the cheek. Will smiled, his hand on Riley's back. They were seated at a small, relatively private booth and though packed, the place was quiet enough that they could talk. Over wine and appetizers, Riley told Will about the yoga class that morning.

"I was surprised by how much I enjoyed it," he admitted.

"I'll be lucky if I'm not hobbling tomorrow—I worked muscles I didn't know I had, but I think it'll be good for me. Natalie was right about the stress relief."

"Racquetball is my stress relief," Will said with a grin.

Riley laughed, picturing Will sweaty and tousled after a good game. He shifted in his seat and changed the subject, asking Will about his day. Conversation flowed while they enjoyed the food and drink and continued long after they'd finished their meal. The dinner to celebrate Riley's birthday had been relatively brief, since Riley had had a meeting the following day, so it had felt more platonic than this evening did.

Riley soon forgot that there was anything out of the ordinary about being on a date with another man, and the urge to look over his shoulder and wonder who might be watching them faded. Will was witty, charming and just the right amount of flirtatious. Enough that Riley kept thinking about what would happen after dinner, though he never felt uncomfortable.

Long after dessert plates had been cleared and they'd finished their drinks, they continued to talk and flirt. Riley felt bold as they left the restaurant and when they were out in the cold wind, Riley knew they couldn't linger long. He rested a hand on Will's upper arm, his body thrumming with eager anticipation. "I'm not quite ready for the evening to be over. If the offer's still open, I wouldn't mind going to your place for…conversation and maybe something more," he said, echoing the words Will had spoken to him on New Year's Eve.

"Let's call it a standing offer." Will grinned. "And, yes, I'd like that, too."

Will gave Riley his address in Tribeca and they went their separate ways to find their vehicles. Riley's palms were sweaty on the wheel and his heart hammered as he followed the GPS directions to get there. When Riley arrived at the building Will lived in, he sat in his car for a few moments, trying to calm his racing heart and push away the panic that was beginning to rise in him. Will had waited in the lobby, his cheeks flushed from the cold and hair disheveled. Will had run a hand through it occasionally as they'd talked earlier in the evening and he wondered if Will felt as nervous as he did.

"I wasn't sure you were coming," Will said, escorting him toward the elevator.

"I'll admit, it crossed my mind to head home instead."

"I'm glad you didn't."

Riley felt the brush of Will's hand on his shoulder when Will held the elevator door open for him and he turned and looked at him. "I am, too."

Still, Will's reassurance didn't soothe the tension in him, which only grew when they entered Will's apartment. Riley had a vague impression of sleek, contemporary furnishings, but he felt too anxious to really study the space.

"Would you like a drink?" Will asked after hanging up their coats.

Riley shook his head. He'd had a few drinks with dinner and wanted to keep a clear head. "But thank you," he added.

"Coffee? Tea?"

"Coffee would be perfect," Riley said with a grateful smile. Some of his anxiety finally eased as he and Will stood in the kitchen talking while the coffee brewed. By the time they took their mugs into the living room to sit on the leather sofa, Riley had grown increasingly aware of Will on a physical level again. Will shrugged casually out of his jacket while he spoke and Riley couldn't tear his eyes away from the sliver of skin at Will's throat, which was exposed by his open collar. Will stood only an inch or two taller than Riley, but leaner, with a narrow, fit body. Riley followed his lead, discarding his jacket and loosening his tie while they talked. They were in the middle of a fairly mundane conversation about Manhattan real estate when Will paused, mid-sentence. They'd both finished their coffees and had abandoned the cups on the glass coffee table.

"I'd really like to kiss you again," he said bluntly.

Riley nodded before he could think twice.

Will didn't hesitate, as if half-afraid that Riley would change his mind. He didn't. Not even when Will's long, lean body pressed him down onto the couch and his kisses became more demanding. Riley moaned instead, feeling Will's weight over him. Although Will's jaw was still smooth from what Riley assumed was an earlier shave, Riley had no trouble remembering he was kissing a man and that knowledge only turned him on more. With one elbow planted on the couch beside Riley's head, Will threaded long fingers through Riley's hair as the kiss deepened further. Riley clutched at Will's shoulder and gasped when Will moved his mouth to his neck, pressing wet, eager kisses along his throat. Will's cock pushed hard against his thigh and a jolt went through him.

It was a mixture of anticipation and nerves and Riley panted as Will unknotted his tie, slipped it from his collar and tossed it onto the floor. "Is this okay?" Will asked roughly as he unbuttoned Riley's shirt, trailing his lips along the path he'd newly created.

"Oh, God, yes," Riley said. He shuddered at the sensation of bare lips on his sensitive skin and warmth flooded his body. He raked his hands through Will's hair and moaned low and long when Will reached the waistband of his pants. It was so arousing, but it also made him slightly anxious, wondering what Will would do next. Will must have felt the sudden tension in his body, because he slid up again, capturing Riley's mouth in a heated kiss. Riley moved his hands under Will's now-untucked shirt and splayed them on his back, feeling the strength of the muscles there and liking the contrast with the smooth, soft skin.

They tangled their legs while they kissed. A slow rhythm built, gentle rocking becoming more forceful, deliberate movements as their desire increased. Riley fumbled to undo Will's shirt and Will hovered over him while he unbuttoned it, continuing to kiss Riley. Will sat back just long enough to pull the piece of clothing off and throw it aside, then returned to kissing. Their bare skin pressed together made Riley sigh and he was surprised by how close he was to coming.

He tore his mouth from Will's and took a few deep breaths, trying to calm himself. Will trailed his fingers down Riley's bare chest, moving between their bodies to cup Riley's erection through the fabric of his suit pants. "More," Riley pleaded, his control slipping away. "Please, Will. More."

Will didn't waste any time, deftly undoing Riley's pants and slipping a hand inside. He shuddered when Will wrapped a warm hand around his cock. He didn't know if it was Will himself, or being with a man and not having to pretend he didn't want him that made it so arousing, but it only took a few strokes of Will's hand to make him come. He threw his head back, everything going white and fuzzy for a moment as he moaned and writhed under Will's firm grip. "Holy shit," he said. Will smirked down at him, clearly pleased by Riley's reaction.

Ignoring the wetness on his stomach, he reached for Will, flipping their positions so Will lay underneath him. Before he could change his mind, he reached for Will's zipper. Will helped him, shoving his pants down over his hips. Will's cock felt hard and hot in Riley's hand and he felt torn between wanting to watch his hand move over Will and watching Will's reaction. Will's cheeks were flushed, his eyes closed and his lips parted with pleasure. Will came quickly, too, crying out Riley's name in a choked voice before reaching up to pull Riley down for a kiss. He stroked Will slowly while they kissed, spreading the wetness along his length and swirling a thumb across the sensitive tip. Will shuddered under him for a few moments before wrapping his hand around Riley's to stop him.

Riley lifted his head after giving Will one final, lingering kiss. "Damn, Riley," Will murmured, threading his hand through Riley's hair. Between his orgasm and Will's clear enjoyment of what Riley had done, Riley felt almost high.

"I'm really glad you came over tonight."

"I am, too," Riley said. He felt surprisingly comfortable with Will and, unlike after the bathroom blow job, he wasn't ready to run.

"You can tell me if I'm out of line for asking, but was that a first for you?"

Riley hummed thoughtfully before answering. "In a way. I've given another man a hand job but never without a woman there, as well."

Will nodded but didn't comment. Instead, he slid a hand down Riley's bare back and changed the subject. "I'd like to see you again."

"I'd like that, too," Riley said without hesitation.

"I know you said you're getting a divorce—do you need to be...discreet about this?"

Riley thought for a moment before replying. "I appreciate the concern, but no. My ex knows, and although I'd rather not parade around the Upper East Side and rub it in her face, I don't have to hide it if I want to date another man. The society pages have already chimed in about my sudden coming out."

Will gave him a wry smile. "Even in a city of this size, there's no privacy, is there?"

Riley shrugged and sat up. The wetness on his stomach and hand had cooled and it felt sticky and uncomfortable. "I managed to keep it a secret for years. Of course, I wasn't really acknowledging it to myself, either," he admitted.

With a thoughtful nod, Will sat up. "I've been where you are, Riley—maybe not exactly the same place, but close enough. If you want to talk, I'd be happy to listen."

"Thanks." Will stood and disappeared through a door just off the living room. He reappeared with two damp cloths and handed one to Riley. They were both quiet while they cleaned up and it wasn't until they were both nearly dressed that Riley spoke again. "Look, Will, I'll be honest, I'm not always good at opening up to people, but I'm trying to get better about it and having someone to talk to would probably be good for me right now."

"Then I'm happy to listen."

Riley finished buttoning his shirt and glanced up at Will. "Would you tell me about your experience? You hinted you'd dealt with something similar."

"Sure," Will said. "Let me just grab some water. Do you want some?"

"Please."

When they were settled back on the couch with bottles of water, Will began. "I grew up on Long Island. My father's a state senator and I went to law school expecting to follow in his footsteps. In law school I explored my growing fascination with men and the history of law. For a long time, I was able to dabble in both without my family finding out. I had a girlfriend—of sorts—to trot out at family events, but I began to realize that women didn't interest me the way men did. Worse, I had absolutely no desire to become a politician like my father. The semester I worked as a teaching assistant, I realized how much I loved teaching. All of a sudden every plan I'd had crumbled around me." By the end, Will's voice grew a little hoarse and he took a long swig of water. Riley reached out to touch his knee, knowing exactly how Will must have felt. Will smiled at him and continued.

"I finished law school, took the Bar exam and got hired at a law firm. My father was less than thrilled. He had lined up an internship at another senator's office for me, but I couldn't do it. I told him I wanted to spend some time practicing law for a while before I went into politics, but I didn't mean it. I just didn't have the courage to tell him I wanted to teach. He eased up a little and for a few years, it was good. I worked at the law office and I dated a guy in secret. Everyone was happy. Well, my boyfriend at the time wasn't so thrilled about staying closeted, but he did his best to be understanding." Will frowned for a moment, then seemed to recover. "Eventually, my father started pushing again and I just kind of snapped. I told him there was no way in hell I was going into politics and that I was going to teach, whether he liked it or not. We had this huge screaming fight and I walked out. He didn't contact me for two weeks and when he finally showed up at my apartment, he caught me with my boyfriend. My father lost it completely."

Riley's heart ached at Will's story. Will had been right— he had been through something very similar to what Riley was dealing with. He reached out, covering Will's hand with his. "I'm sorry."

Will shrugged, his face smoothing out. "In the long run, it was for the best. I'm able to live my life on my own terms and I've never been happier."

"Do you talk to your family at all?" Riley asked.

"Not my father. I haven't seen or heard from him since that day. My mother and sister I still keep in contact with, although I wouldn't say we're close."

Riley swallowed hard. "I was disowned and disinherited by my family. Other than dealing with my father at work, I have no ties to them anymore."

Will winced. "Working with him must be difficult."

"It's awkward, but I'm learning to deal with it." Riley looked down at his hands. "What's worse is I lost a very close friend. He's…he's actually part of the reason I came out as bisexual. I've been in love with him for years. It wasn't until recently that I felt able to admit to myself and to him how I felt. I think on some level he feels the same way, but he's not ready to admit it and he probably will never be."

Will's voice was gentle when he spoke. "I'm sorry."

Riley met his gaze for a moment. "It was worth it. Losing him as a friend is…awful, but divorcing my wife was still the right decision for me. Tonight…was—was exactly what I needed."

"You needed to know for sure that you could feel like that about a man—someone other than your friend."

Riley nodded. "I hope you don't feel like I used you."

Will reached out, sliding his fingers through Riley's hair as he cupped the back of his head and looked him in the eye. "No, I don't. Like I said, I know what the uncertainty is like. I've been where you are. Just be honest with me."

"I will," he promised.

"I'm not looking to meet the love of my life right now, Riley. I think what you need at the moment is someone you can explore this with, but even more than that, I think you need a friend." Riley nodded. "So, let's go out sometime next week, we'll see what happens—no pressure, no expectations."

"Why are you doing this, Will?"

Will shrugged and sat back, giving him a small smile. "Because I've been where you are and that's what I needed and wasn't able to find."

"Okay."

Will's demeanor turned teasing. "Besides, you act like going on a date or screwing around with you is going to be a hardship."

"Well, I hope not."

Will grinned, leaning in to kiss him, and Riley relaxed.

As he drove home a while later, the feel of Will's lips against his lingered. A huge part of him wished those lips had belonged to Carter, but he felt ready to move forward. He didn't want to deny himself any longer. What he'd begun with Will tonight felt like a fresh start. If he lived his life in limbo, waiting for Carter to acknowledge his feelings for Riley, he'd be falling back into the same patterns he always had.

He would never stop loving Carter, but it was time for him to let Carter go. Allowing himself to let Will in was progress, a step in the right direction. For the first time in his life he was being honest with himself. No more lying, no more hiding, and that felt better than anything else in the world.

Chapter Nineteen

With a sigh, Carter pulled off his glasses and dropped them onto his desk. He'd been at the office for ten hours already and had to find some energy before he went home and put on a cheerful face for his family.

Three long weeks after his fight with Kate, Carter couldn't deny the obvious—their marriage was failing. They were working hard with a counselor to rebuild their relationship, but things continued to deteriorate. The only bright spot had been Dylan's birthday on February 5 and both Carter and Kate had thrown themselves into the celebration with gusto.

Tiredly, Carter pressed the heels of his hands against his eyes. He knew why things had not improved and knew that he was at fault. Despite hours of sessions with their counselor and endless discussions he and Kate had on their own, Carter still hadn't come clean. Kate didn't know about the threesomes he and Riley had shared over the years, or about their arrangement with Natalie. Carter kept Riley's secrets, too. He hadn't told Kate about Riley's ultimatum, or that Riley wanted a life with Carter. Or that Carter wondered more and more often what that life might be like.

Kate seemed at the end of her emotional tether. She was painfully patient, but sadness permeated her voice and person. She'd become physically distant, too, rarely touching Carter, despite their shared bed. Kate seemed only truly happy when she was playing with the children. Their boundless energy and enthusiasm made it easy to forget the dark clouds hanging over Kate's and Carter's heads.

Carter knew a split seemed more and more inevitable.

The idea of losing his family — of losing his anchor in what had become a very turbulent time — terrified him. He couldn't be angry with Kate, though. She didn't deserve to be stuck with a man who kept secrets. A man who lacked the courage to truly be himself.

A soft knock sounded at the door and Carter dropped his hands, keeping his eyes closed after the door opened. He'd asked Malcolm to hold his calls and visitors unless the topic was urgent and knew his assistant had entered only reluctantly.

"What is it, Malcolm?" he asked quietly.

"I'm sorry to interrupt you, sir. I'm on my way out for the weekend and wanted to remind you you're meeting your parents for dinner at Eleven Madison Park. They're expecting you for cocktails at seven."

Carter straightened immediately, grabbing his glasses from the desk and sliding them on. "Christ, I'd almost forgotten — thank you, Malcolm, you're a lifesaver."

Malcolm smiled and shook his head when Carter met his gaze. "Don't thank me, sir — thank Mrs. Hamilton."

Carter's brows drew together at the unexpected comment. "Kate called?"

"She told me she'd sent you some texts earlier when you were meeting with Sanchez and Hannity. When she didn't hear back from you, she called to ask that I remind you." Malcolm stepped forward as Carter rose from his chair. "Your mother also called with a reminder."

"Does everyone know my schedule?" Carter wondered while Malcolm snickered.

"Everyone except you, if I had to guess, sir."

"Accurate statement." Carter smiled and Malcolm walked behind his desk to help him into his suit jacket. "I'm glad you're all keeping an eye on me."

"It takes a village," Malcolm began, his tone teasing.

"To manage an idiot like me," Carter finished, straightening his tie.

"Not quite the proverb I had in mind, sir, but it'll do."

Malcolm stepped back with his hands clasped behind him, nodding with approval. "Perfectly respectable."

"It's all an act, you know."

"Well aware of that, sir."

Carter laughed, waving at him to go. "Enjoy your weekend, Malcolm. I'll see you on Monday."

"Good night, sir."

Carter paused after the office door closed, turning his body to lean against the edge of his desk. After pulling his phone from his pocket, he flipped through Kate's reminders. He opened the photo, smiling at the sight of the kids in the bathtub, mugging for the camera from under a mound of bubbles. Quickly, Carter dashed off a message of thanks and a hello to Sadie and Dylan, then straightened up to gather his things.

Carter took care to sound and appear upbeat as he ate dinner with his parents, but they sensed something was off. Carter's mother was especially concerned and peppered Carter with questions. She pressed and hounded until he nearly walked away from the table, despite the incredible food and wine.

"He's a grown man, Ellie," Brad finally interceded, then overfilled Eleanor's glass with wine to distract her.

"What does Carter's age have to do with anything?" she asked, seeming unimpressed by her husband's argument. "He stopped talking to us at the age of twelve. We don't know a damned thing about him that he doesn't want us to."

"I'm right here, you know." Carter sipped his wine. "And you're exaggerating, Mom. I've always told you things that I thought you needed to know."

"Oh, sweetheart, respectfully, I must disagree," Eleanor replied. "You started keeping things from us when you became a teenager. We expected that—most boys clam up around that age." She pushed her fork against the Arctic char on her plate, her voice thoughtful when she spoke again. "It wasn't until you went off to school that you really pulled away. We hardly knew you when you were living in Boston."

"Cambridge, Mom," Carter chided. "I never lived in Boston."

"Same city, different riverbank."

"Only a New Yorker would say such a thing." Carter sipped from his glass again while his mother laughed.

"You're not being sensible, dear," Brad observed. "Carter has excellent communication skills. You wouldn't be saying any of this if you could see him at the office. He's developed a real rapport with the clients. It's quite impressive."

"I'm sure that's true."

Carter ignored the heat creeping up the back of his neck while his mother beamed.

"I have no doubt that our son is both good at his job and good at communicating with clients and his peers," she added. "I'm more concerned about how much he's communicating outside of work."

Carter's groan echoed his father's. "Mom, come on— we've been over this already tonight. Kate and the kids are fine. I'm fine. Can't we just enjoy dinner and not talk about the things I may or may not be saying or doing incorrectly?"

"Of course, dear." Eleanor sighed quietly. "I apologize for nagging. I know you're a private person. Believe it or not, I respect that about you."

Carter went still as she placed one warm hand over his. Her touch was gentle and, after the terrible days Carter had been having, wonderfully soothing.

"All of that said, communication is important in a marriage." Eleanor smiled again, oblivious to the chill working its way under Carter's skin. "Try to keep that in mind, all right?"

By the time he pushed through the restaurant doors to head home, Carter was half-drunk, emotionally spent and felt almost physically sore, as though his parents' intense scrutiny had left bruises.

Pausing at the curb, Carter let his mind wander. He knew

the right thing to do was to go home, even though Kate and the kids were well on their way to dreamland. He couldn't bear the thought of being at home, though, of trying to sleep with a wired mind and restless spirit.

Mindlessly, Carter turned left on Madison instead of right, moving in the opposite direction to home. He went east on 23rd Street then south on Park Avenue, and walked away from Midtown, the city blocks passing almost without his noticing. When he finally took stock of his surroundings, he'd reached the Flatiron District and was standing across the street from the Old Town Bar.

Feeling almost breathless, he crossed the street and approached the tavern's door. Carter and Riley had spent many evenings in the Old Town after moving back to New York. The old-fashioned bar was reminiscent of the college pubs they'd frequented at Harvard and held an allure from their first visit. Even now, Dan made a point of arranging a meal with Carter and Riley at the Old Town whenever he visited New York, if only for a few beers and burgers.

Staring at the bar, Carter felt his solitude keenly, and how much he missed his best friend. He'd started to call Riley many times in the weeks since they'd met at Serendipity and composed email messages more than once. He'd even ended up in Riley's West Village neighborhood on one occasion and lingered in a coffee shop near Riley's block. Carter had walked away that night, though. He'd canceled the calls and deleted the drafted emails, still unable to take that final step they needed to reconnect.

The Old Town's cavernous interior was visible through the windows. Always dimly lit and murky with cigarette smoke, Carter knew it buzzed with the rise and fall of many voices in conversation. After so many weeks of being disconnected from everything else in his life, just glimpsing the bar through the window made Carter's breath catch. He longed to slip inside and wedge himself into a space at the long bar, slowly sipping ale while the patrons around him talked and drank.

Just as he'd made up his mind to reach for the door handle, Carter glimpsed a familiar mop of dark hair and set of broad shoulders through the window. His mouth went dry. A man sat with his back to the windows, turned so that only part of his profile was visible. Carter didn't need help recognizing his square jaw and clear blue eyes, though. Riley. Carter would have known him anywhere.

Hungrily, Carter watched the scene on the other side of the glass, taking in his friend's easy body language. Riley was using his hands to sketch words in the air as he spoke and the light glinted off the class ring Riley wore on his right hand. Carter stopped breathing when Riley reached out that same hand to rest against the neck of a man seated beside Riley at the bar.

Carter stared, light-headed, as a dark-haired stranger covered Riley's hand on his neck with his own. He was handsome, with fair skin and graceful features, and he gazed at Riley with a wide smile. In a slow, easy motion, he ducked his head to press a kiss against Riley's thumb, his eyes never leaving Riley's face. Riley trailed his thumb over the other man's mouth, then pushed it between his lips and Carter gasped.

"Hey, dude, you going in or what?"

Carter jerked back, startled out of his daze by the gruff voice speaking in his ear. A group of four men and a woman were standing on his left, obviously waiting for him to enter the bar. The man who had spoken eyed him, as if assessing whether Carter was in some way threatening or just another sad sack with no place else to go.

"Sorry."

Carter stepped aside, acutely conscious of the curious glances directed his way while the man who had spoken held the door open for his friends. He paused, a troubled expression passing over his face.

"You okay?" the stranger asked, brow furrowed, seeming aware of Carter's distress. "You, uh, want me to call someone for you?"

The sudden kindness, spoken with brusque sincerity, shook Carter to his core. Breathing in deeply, he waved the stranger off, murmuring words of thanks that seemed to reassure him enough to leave Carter alone. Only after the bar's door had closed did Carter realize the exchange had caught the attention of the patrons seated nearest the door and he fled before Riley could look Carter's way.

Some time passed before Carter could think clearly. His sore feet and cold hands told him he'd been walking for a while, and as he pulled out his phone to check the time, his stomach dropped — eleven-forty-five p.m. Glancing around at the deserted streets, Carter placed himself a few blocks from the Stock Exchange and knew he'd been lucky to avoid being mugged.

Dragging himself back the way that he'd come, Carter flagged down a cab outside a hotel near the Federal Reserve. He slumped against the seatback, chilled to the bone, and hardly recognized his own voice giving his address to the driver. Drowsy, he checked his messages, flicking through emails and texts before his throat tightened unexpectedly.

He closed his eyes, the image of Riley caressing the jaw of a handsome, dark-haired man still fresh in his mind, and called himself a fool.

* * * *

Once home, Carter prowled through the apartment, unable to stop moving, though his body and mind were exhausted. He thought obsessively about Riley and the man he'd glimpsed through the bar window. Carter imagined them in Riley's West Village apartment, where Carter himself had once spent so much time.

He pictured them at Riley's kitchen table, eating a meal Riley had cooked. Lounging on Riley's sofa with bottles of beer, Riley's smile wide as he heckled the Red Sox. Spread out on the floor working, surrounded by yellow legal pads covered with Riley's crabbed notes. In Riley's bed, moving together, their limbs tangling and skins shining with sweat. Riley's face was slack with pleasure and so, so beautiful as he groaned and sighed and came.

Pain streaked through Carter's core, twisting his insides until he grunted. Pulling out his phone, he then dialed Dan's number, breathing harshly over the mechanical rings on the other end of the line. He started badly as the call connected and moisture sprang to his eyes at the sound of a familiar voice.

"Car!"

"Dan?"

"Hey, what's going on, man, and why the fuck are you calling me so late?"

Carter winced. "I, uh…shit, did I wake you?"

"Nah, don't worry about it. Mel and I are just cleaning the kitchen—one of us had the bright idea of letting the kids make their own ice cream sundaes for dessert—"

"That was your idea!" Melanie's voice rang out in the background.

"—and there are still rainbow sprinkles all over the goddamned place," Dan concluded. "The kids were all jacked up on the sugar, so it took a while to get them to bed so we could come back here and hoover up the mess."

Melanie chided Dan for swearing, making him laugh, and Carter ached as he listened to the happy banter on the other end of the line. What kind of shitty friend was he to interrupt Dan's comfortable life with his own fuck ups? He stopped pacing, coming to stand by the windows in the family room.

"Fuck," he murmured, "I'm sorry. I didn't even think about how late it is…you know what, I'll call you back tomorrow—"

"Hey, it's fine—"

"No, it's not," Carter protested, stopping after his voice cracked.

Dan swore softly and the background noises changed, becoming more muted. Carter heard the sound of a door closing before Dan spoke again. "Car, are you okay? You don't sound so good, buddy."

Carter mashed his lips together hard, fighting to control the emotions that threatened to unseat him. His tugged his tie and shirt buttons with a trembling hand, loosening them and reminding himself to breathe.

"Carter? You there? Talk to me. No pressure, but, ah, you're kind of scaring me a little here."

Carter squeezed the phone until his finger joints creaked. Shakily, he made his way to the nearest chair and sank down. "I'm... I need to talk to you, Danny. I need to tell you some stuff."

"Okay. I'm here."

Carter brought a hand up to rest over his eyes, swallowing hard. He hardly knew where to start, let alone how to free himself of the web of lies he and Riley had built over the years. He stilled then, his breath catching in his throat.

Riley.

Riley was free of the lies they'd told. He'd come clean, to Alex, to his parents, to Carter. Carter knew his friend had been hurting, maybe even struggled to put his life back together, but Riley's life was finally his. And Carter wanted that for himself.

Drawing one more steadying breath, he opened his mouth and started to talk. Dan stayed quiet for the most part. He asked questions here and there but mostly listened to Carter spill out over a decade and a half's worth of deception and fear. Somewhere in the middle of his story, it became clear to Carter that Dan already knew everything.

"You don't sound very surprised by any of this," he observed, trying hard not to sound bitter.

Dan remained quiet a moment longer. "I'm not," he admitted, his voice soft. "Riley told me a while ago about the thing you had with the escort."

Carter closed his eyes against a surge of anger. "Natalie, yeah. That was considerate of Riley. You think he'd tell Kate for me if I asked?"

"Car—"

"No, it's not… I get why he told you. Fuck, I wish I'd told you before today. I hate lying to everyone, pretending things are okay when they're not."

"Then don't. I can hear in your voice how much of a toll this has taken on you."

Carter nodded before remembering that Dan couldn't see him. "I don't even know why I'm lying anymore," he murmured. "Riley's moved on and Natalie's not in my life anymore…who am I protecting? I feel like there's nothing left to hide, you know? Nothing left at all. Jesus, I don't even know who I am right now."

"You're my friend, you jerk." Dan's voice sounded warm and reassuring. "You're also one of the strongest people I know."

"I'm not, though. I'm a shitty friend. I'm a liar and a cheat." Carter's voice cracked. "And now that it's all over, I'm falling apart."

"That's because you aren't that guy."

"I am exactly that guy."

"Sorry, but I don't buy it!" Dan cursed, the frustration in his voice making Carter's eyes burn. "Yes, you fucked up a lot of stuff, but you didn't do it on your own."

"I know."

"So stop taking all the blame on yourself. Not telling Kate is going to drive you crazy with guilt. And she deserves better than lies and a guy who spends half his time hiding."

Dan's voice sharpened with what Carter knew was hurt rather than anger. "When the hell did you and Ri get so good at hiding, anyway? Because that's what the two of you have been doing—hiding from everyone, including each other.

"Christ, you're still not talking to each other and that's what blows my mind the most. Riley is your best friend. It's hard for me to believe you left him twisting in the wind after he came out. It's even harder to believe you haven't reached out to him now that everything you guys did together is about to blow up in your face. Why are you taking all this on yourself?"

"What am I going to say to him, Dan? Riley doesn't need to be involved in my —"

"What the hell are you even talking about? Riley's the only one who really knows what you're going through right now!"

Carter's head throbbed as he paced around his study. "He's got trouble enough between Alex, the divorce attorneys and his parents."

"I know, I know," Dan soothed. "I still think it would be good for the two of you to talk. I'm not going to pretend that I understand why you two went about things the way you did. To be honest, the things you've told me sound like the actions of two strangers, not my two oldest friends. It's like neither of you is the man I thought I knew."

Carter mashed his lips together over a sob — the bewildered disappointment in Dan's voice made his chest ache.

"I know you're hurting over this thing with Ri," Dan continued, "and you're hurting because you lied to your wife. But I think — no, I know — that you're going to have to make this right before you do anything else. Do you honestly think you can go back to the way things were before you called me tonight?"

"No," Carter whispered. "There's no making this right, though, Danny."

Dan sighed. "Maybe not. Some people are comfortable living a double life, but that's not who you are. So, again, don't be that guy."

Dawn had begun to break by the time Carter ended his call with Dan. He sat staring out of the windows of his study, watching the sky turn purple then gray as sunrise approached. Soon he needed to wake his wife and speak the words that would change their lives forever.

Carter fully expected his marriage to end. He had no idea what gains and losses were to come, and the uncertainty of his future terrified him. For the first time in months, however, a deeply buried part of him felt at peace. For all that he didn't know what to expect next, a bone-deep certainty settled over Carter. He wouldn't be able to move on until he'd come clean to Kate. He thought too that, with enough time and healing, both he and his family would be okay.

More books from Pride Publishing

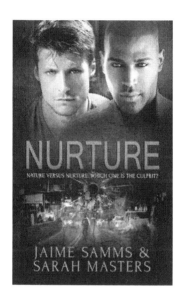

Nature versus nurture. Which one is the culprit?

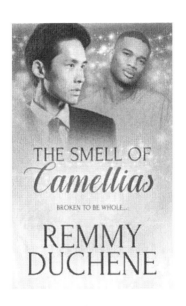

Broken to be whole…

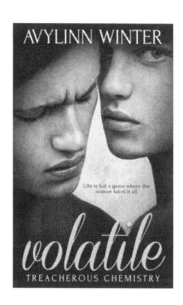

Book one in the Treacherous Chemistry series

Like a depressed moth drawn to a wild flame, Chris hoped that flame would brighten his life, not burn him alive.

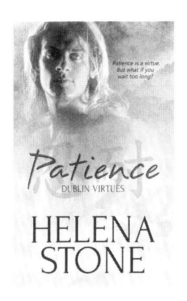

Book one in the Dublin Virtues series

Patience is a virtue. But what if you wait too long?

About the Authors

K. Evan Coles

K. Evan Coles is a mother and tech pirate by day and a writer by night. She is a dreamer who, with a little hard work and a lot of good coffee, coaxes words out of her head and onto paper.

K. lives in the northeast United States, where she complains bitterly about the winters, but truly loves the region and its diverse, tenacious and deceptively compassionate people. You'll usually find K. nerding out over books, movies and television with friends and family. She's especially proud to be raising her son as part of a new generation of unabashed geeks.

Brigham Vaughn

Brigham Vaughn is starting the adventure of a lifetime as a full-time writer. She devours books at an alarming rate and hasn't let her short arms and long torso stop her from doing yoga. She makes a killer key lime pie, hates green peppers and loves wine tasting tours. A collector of vintage Nancy Drew books and green glassware, she enjoys poking around in antique shops and refinishing thrift store furniture. An avid photographer, she dreams of traveling the world and she can't wait to discover everything else life has to offer her.

Our authors love to hear from readers. You can find contact information, website details and an author profile page at https://www.pride-publishing.com/

PUBLISHING

Made in the USA
Middletown, DE
14 June 2017